To Family –

Bobby

Debbie Number Three

All rights reserved. No part of this book shall be reproduced, stored in a retrieval system, or transmitted by any means, electronic, mechanical, photocopying, recording, or otherwise, without permission from the author.

International Standard Book Number
979-8-9863154-1-6

© Bobby Hawthorne | 2020

This is a work of fiction. Seriously. Names, characters, places and incidents are either the product of the author's imagination or are used fictitiously. Any resemblance to actual events, locales, organizations or persons, living or dead, is entirely coincidental. Anything other than that is beyond the intent of either the author or publisher.

Book and Cover design by Bobby Hawthorne
Cover photo created by Photoleap AI

DEBBIE NUMBER THREE

BOBBY HAWTHORNE

Unless otherwise denoted, the story is narrated by the main character, Eddie Dodson.

for Julius "Jack" Getman

"All fiction is largely autobiographical and much autobiography is, of course, fiction."
— P.D. James

PROLOGUE
Three

I was scrunched on a flimsy bath towel at the city pool in Kassel, a dusty, desolate little German-Catholic town in North Texas where my Mom's from, trying to get a little sun on my chest and legs because I hadn't had any in a while, and I was in that mid-afternoon fog between awake and asleep when I heard a voice, a girl's voice — a girl, maybe 9 or 10 — but I said to myself, "It's nothing. You're dreaming. Don't bother," so I stayed there, squirming to keep as much of the towel between me and the chiggers and the Bermuda grass as I could.

I squinted to blot the sun so I could drift off again, but the voice returned, only louder and bossy.

"Hey. You. New guy. I'm talking to you. I know you can hear me."

I slit one eye, and hunched over me, was a girl wearing a one-piece yellow and black bathing suit that made her look like a ripe banana.

"Who are you? What's your name? Where're you from? Why're you here?"

It took a second for this to sink in, and then I replied, "Do what?"

She repeated herself, this time faster while bopping her head back and forth like some ding-dong church bell.

Who. Are. You?
What. Is. Your. Name?
Where. Are. You. From?
Why. Are. You. Here?

So, I shot back, "Why. Do. You. Care?"

"I don't," she said. "My sister does."

"Your sister? Who's your sister?"

She turned and pointed toward a girl on the cool side of the pool and said, "She is."

The sun rippled off the cloudy, chlorinated water, creating a blinding glare, so I had to cup my hands over my eyes to see her. As best as I could tell, the older sister looked exactly like the younger sister, as if they were identical twins, born five years apart.

"That's your sister?" I asked.

"So I'm told," the girl said.

"So, you two are close," I said, sarcastically.

"Close to killing each other," she said.

"What's her name," I asked.

"Her name's Kathy. With a K."

"Why does she want to know my name?"

"I wouldn't know." she said. "We don't share."

"Well, she's pretty," I said, almost under my breath.

"She's mean," the girl said. "Follow me. C'mon. Find out for yourself."

"Is this some kind of a joke?" I asked.

The girl huffed and turned and yelled across the pool to her sister, "Kathleen! He wants to know if this is…some kind of a joke. Is it?"

"Judy," Kathleen yelled back.

Somehow, that was enough said. Judy turned back to me and said, "More questions?"

"Just one," I said. "What's in this for you?"

"A Butterfinger," Judy said. "Besides, what 'dya gotta lose?"

"Nothing I can't do without," I thought, meaning my pride, self-esteem, manhood or what passed for it.

So, I scooped up my shoes and towel and followed Judy — strolling all John Wayne-like — around the kiddie pool toward Kathy with a K, and the closer I got, the more I suspected it was a joke, that one of my cousins had set me up to knock me down, but that's not what happened.

Kathy with a K had no interest in me personally, but she had a friend — her "very best friend in the whole wide world," or so she said — who wanted to know who I was, where I was from, and all that, so Kathy with a K bribed her money-grubbing little sister to fetch me, and that's how I met Debbie Gehring — AKA Debbie Number Three — the first girl I ever fell in love with.

I'd had crushes and puppy-loves and 48-hour infatuations with cousins of cousins, but I'd never experienced the double blindside block of actual "I cannot live without you. I don't want to. Please don't make me" love.

My dad heard about it and decided he needed to chime in.

"Had yourself quite a little summer fling, I hear tell," he said. "This girl gotta name?"

"I assume," I replied.

"You assume?" he repeated. "Here's what you can assume. Smart off again, and I'm going knock you upside the head."

So, I told him her name was Debbie, and he blurted, "You're shittin' me. What are you up to now? Three?"

I didn't answer. I didn't want to think that he was thinking about her.

"So, this girl," he repeated. "She got a real name?"

I shrugged as a way of saying, "You want to keep asking yes or no questions, I'll keep giving you yes or no answers."

Finally, he'd had enough. "You deaf? I'm asking you a goddamn question."

He was driving, and it was early, and he wasn't drinking yet, so he was watching the road and didn't see me make a fist when I answered, "Well, let me see. There's Debbie Number One."

I raised the index finger on my right hand.

"And then, there's Debbie Number Two," and I kept my index finger up and raised my pinkie finger.

"So that would make her..."

I closed my index and pinkie fingers and flipped out my middle finger, and said, "Debbie Number Three."

Then, I pinched my eyes, hunkered down, and expected the tires to squeal, but they didn't because he was fumbling with a cigarette and didn't catch my act of defiance.

The "Debbie Number Three" epithet referred to the fact that my best friend was a Debbie, and the girl I'd had a crush on forever was a Debbie, so my dad felt compelled to prove to me that he could add past two.

If I hadn't been borderline suicidal at that moment, I might have enjoyed the humor in this. I might've even played along. After all, the name "Debbie" back then was as common as pay phones and cigarette machines.

There might have been six Debbies in my grade alone, and no one thought a thing about it so long as they kept track of whether they were talking to or about the Debby with two "b's" and a "Y" or the Debbi with two "b's" and an "I," or the Debbie with two "b's" and an "IE."

As in DebbIE Gehring, the girl I met at the pool that Sunday afternoon and then fell madly in love with.

I didn't notice her right off because I was busy ogling Kathy with a K's tan lines, and because she was hidden in the shadows of a pecan tree, but then, Kathy with a K abruptly announced that she absolutely, positively had to talk to a tall, lanky boy who'd just walked through the pool gate, so — poof — just like that, she was gone.

I stood there, thinking, "Damn. That was weird," and I was about to return to the fool side of the pool when Debbie Gehring emerged, accompanied by a younger girl who was flat and red-headed and rail thin.

I faced them for a moment, then said, "Well, I suppose I'd best be going, too."

And Debbie Gehring replied, "What's your hurry? You're safe. The vampire seeks easier prey."

I couldn't tell if she was kidding or serious, so I flipped out both hands like I was being robbed at gunpoint by a Girl Scout.

Without introducing herself or her freckled friend, Debbie Gehring asked, "Do you like baseball?"

I had no idea how to answer that question. Did I like baseball? Well, compared to what? Bridget Bardot? Butter beans? LBJ?

Besides, what was the penalty for an incorrect answer, if there was such a thing? Given that I had no real options, I did the unthinkable. I told the truth.

"No. Not much."

"Good," she said. "I don't either, so wait here. I'll be right back. I need to grab my things."

I glanced at the skinny girl, hoping she might offer a clue as to what was really going on, but she didn't. She just said, "She'll be right back. She's very — uhmm, you know — punctual."

A minute or so later, she said, "I'll see if she needs help," and she scooted into the shadows to watch Debbie cram her towel and knick-knacks into a flowery knapsack.

"Are you sure about this?" the girl asked, and Debbie whispered, "No, Mom. I'm not, but what's the harm?"

The girl's eyes narrowed, and Debbie tapped her on the nose. "I can handle this," she said.

Then, she reappeared.

"Ready?" she asked, and I stupidly answered, "Like buzz on a bee."

"If you say so," she said, then explained why she wanted to know whether I liked baseball. I don't remember much of what she said because I got a little lost in her raspy voice, her butterscotch eyebrows, her powder-blue eyes, and a quarter-inch scar on her bottom lip that might have been a put-off for someone else but wasn't for me. I wanted to touch Kathy with a K's tan lines, but I wanted to kiss that scar.

Was it love at first sight? Probably not, but it was definitely a game-changer. Something I'd never experienced. A paradigm shift. Haley's Comets on back-to-back weekends. Snow in Dallas on the Fourth of July.

Call it what you like, but it all added up to one thing: I couldn't take my eyes off of her. I had to repeat to myself, "Be cool, for Christ's sake. And wipe that stupid grin off your face."

If she'd realized how rattled I was, she might've bolted, too, and I wouldn't have blamed her. Instead, she seemed genuinely interested in me, and why? Damned if I knew. She was so — I don't know — magnetic.

I figured she had to be the favorite daughter of a local bigwig, an ex-Marine who'd won a Congressional Medal of Honor as well as an NFL rushing title, and was a member of a Fort Worth insurance agency's Million Dollar Roundtable.

He'd look like Rock Hudson's better-looking older brother, and he was both hard and stern and charming, the kind of guy who'd stare a boy down while squeezing his hand until it turned purple, and that was his way of saying, "Lay a finger on my daughter, and I'll squeeze something else until it turns black."

Of course, he'd be married to a former SMU cheerleader from Highland Park, who'd mastered the art of killing with kindness, so if I were to meet the two of them at the same time, she'd say something like, "For goodness sakes, Charlie, let go of that boy's hand. He might need it later."

Then she'd wink and laugh at her slightly racy suggestion, and then she'd slather me with hooty politeness, but as soon as I'd turned my back, she'd roll her eyes and say to her daughter, "Nice boy, but, honestly, dear, we both know you can do better."

So, that's what was bashing around inside the washing machine of my mind while I stared at Debbie Gehring, was waiting on me to answer a simple question: Did I like baseball?

Well, it wasn't that simple. To start off with, I was still convinced one of my cousins was about to prank me in front of all these local Kasselites — or whatever they're called, and they knew it was coming, so they gaped at me with morbid expectation while they got a little sun on our arms and legs because we haven't had any in a while.

Once the blade or the bucket fell, and they'd bust a gut laughing and assure me it wasn't personal.

"What do you take us for?" they'd ask, feigning innocence, and since I hated confrontation, I'd end up apologizing to them and promising to help them drain the pool and scrub out the stains caused by the bucket of whatever they dumped on my head.

So, I was pretty occupied intellectually when Debbie Gehring said, "Here's the plan. Meet me here tomorrow night at 6 at the concession stand. It's right over there. Don't be late. Got it?"

"Got it?" was all I heard.

"Of course," I replied. "But just to make sure, got what?"

"You are going to meet me at the concession stand. Right over there. Tomorrow. Monday. At 6. PM. On the dot. Don't be late."

In an act of desperate self-deprecation, I came up with, "Sunday. Beer stand. With concessions. Bring Dot. Don't relate."

Somehow, it worked. It was a miracle. Thank you, Jesus.

She either ignored or appreciated or forgave my doofus humor. Either way, she smiled ruefully, and her smile sealed the deal — for me — because it revealed a slightly crooked left front tooth, and that tooth seemed to pull it all together.

I've thought a lot about that left front tooth since then. There was a story behind the scar, but the tooth was a gift from God. If she'd come from a well-to-do family, the daughter of a local bigwig, she'd have had it fixed long ago, and that would have been a crime against nature.

That tooth completed the picture. It held back as much as it gave away and remains to this day the most perfectly imperfect thing I have ever seen.

PART ONE | CHAPTER 1

Moron

June 1966 • Marshall, Texas

Debby Bishop wasn't the prettiest girl in my neighborhood, but she was close. Karen Anderson was prettier, but she was a sophomore who hung out with junior girls and snuck out with senior boys, so I'm not including her, which meant Debby won. Again.

Of course, I had a crush on her. All the boys did, not that it mattered. She came from a good family, a solid family. She and her brothers and sisters and parents prayed and ate at the same time at the same table at least twice a day, every day.

They went to church together every Sunday, and their house and yard were clean and neat all the time, and that was because Debby's father wanted it that way, and he generally got what he wanted.

If he wanted a new car, he bought one, and if it needed an oil change or a fan belt replaced or some mysterious rattle unrattled, then he returned it to the dealer, and the shop manager assigned his best mechanic to it while Mr. Bishop sat in the shop manager's office and flipped through the latest Sports Illustrated and sipped coffee the secretary brewed for him, and him alone.

Mr. Bishop never got his hands dirty because he didn't want to, but he wasn't a jerk about it. He made getting what he wanted look easy, and I suppose, for him, and men like him, it was.

Debby was like her dad. She rarely got her hands dirty either. She made being pretty and popular look like a breeze, which was something most girls would've drowned a pillowcase full of kittens for, yet Debby never gave it a second thought.

Better yet, she wasn't a goody-goody teacher's pet or a show-off fashion freak, even though her family could've afforded to send her to the school in emeralds and to church in mink.

They didn't because that's not who they were. They were regular folks. They came from regular folks. They looked and acted like regular folks. Debby wore pretty much the same outfit to school every day — either a black or a Navy-blue skirt with a button-down white cotton shirt or a plaid round-neck jumper dress.

She never wore hoop earrings or curlicue headbands or jangly bracelets or ribbons or bows or sparkles because she didn't need all that clownish crap. Besides, her dad disapproved of frilly ostentation, which means being snooty.

He'd done well as a petroleum engineer, but he saw no reason to parade his success or his good-looking wife or his well-mannered children up one street and down another and act all special, even though they clearly were.

Especially Debby.

She had dimples and dark eyes, and long walnut-brown hair that swished and swayed when she ran, and she ran fast, and not just fast for a girl. Fast, period.

She was athletic without being boyish, and she was girlish without being girly, and she could twirl and hold her own in a game of horse.

Everyone liked her. Even my mom liked her.

"She's not just pretty," Mom told me. "She's pretty to the bone. Poor thing."

Debby was also clueless. She would have died if she'd known guys were constantly trying to look up her dress, or, as we so eloquently put it, "shoot her squirrel." They'd lean way over in their desks, or hang out at the base of the stairwell, or drop a fork in the cafeteria, or sit four rows down from her in the gym. Whatever it took.

Why fathers of teenage girls don't build wind chimes out of rusty butcher knives and place them four feet from their front doors is one of life's mysteries.

As far as Mr. Bishop was concerned, he didn't need a butcher knife to keep me in line. All he needed was a glance because it told me, "If you upset my daughter, you've upset me. If you upset me once, we talk. If you upset me twice, you bleed."

I was sure he loved his daughter more than he did his country, and he killed for his country, so, Debby was safe. When Mr. Bishop decided she was old enough to choose a boyfriend and smart enough to choose the boyfriend he wanted her to choose, she would then choose the boyfriend he wanted her to have.

Why is that? It's because Mr. Bishop ran a tight ship.

That was another one of my mom's keen observations. Debby was pretty to the bone, and her father ran a tight ship.

We, on the other hand, ran a roller rink for retired circus monkeys. I will assure you, no one ever said, "Eddie Dodson comes from a good family. His father runs a tight ship."

That would've been a joke. My father ran his mouth when he wasn't running back and forth to the liquor store.

We lived on a different planet circling a different sun in a different solar system that just happened to be one block over and two houses down from the Bishops. I often wondered what separated us from them, why our yard looked like Omaha Beach two days after D-Day, and their yard looked like the White House lawn at sunrise on Easter morning.

I wondered why Debby's dad drove a new Oldsmobile every year, and my dad drove my mom to the brink every day.

I wondered how it was that Debby's parents threw parties and grilled thick T-bone steaks and sipped wine out of wine glasses, while my parents fried catfish they'd caught on an illegal snood and drank Schlitz out of the can.

I wondered why the Bishops and their friends talked about elections and novels and movies, while my dad and his kinfolk talked about hair lost or weight gained or scars that wouldn't go away.

I wondered why if I'd been forced to choose between my dad

throwing a whiskey bottle at my head and Mr. Bishop tossing me a glance, I'd have taken my chances with the bottle every time.

—

My dad had his favorite expressions, too. One of them went like this: "Did you ever stop to think..."

As in, "Did you ever stop to think before you spilled that glass of tea, or knocked over that vase, or threw that baseball through that window?"

He actually expected an answer, but what was I supposed to say? "Sure, Dad. I thought about it. I assumed it was a bad idea, but then you told me to never assume anything, so I did what you told me. Besides, I knew that if I was wrong, well, heck. We got that money. You said so yourself. I heard you. We'll just hire someone to fix it and pay for it with the dollar bills growing on the two money trees in the backyard."

Of course, I'd never say this to his face. I knew he'd never smack me for smarting off, but it made no sense to give him a good reason to, so I'd mope and mutter and wait for him to get bored of going through the motions of running a tight ship.

The truth is, I didn't throw the baseball at the window. I threw it at the couch. It slipped out of my hand and caught the corner of the window, so his question should have been: Did I ever stop to consider the possibility the baseball might slip out of my hand?"

Either way, the answer to that would've been the same.

No, Dad. I did not stop to think.

And why didn't I stop to think? I didn't stop to think because I was showing off, and showing off wasn't something I needed to stop and think about. It came as natural as blinking. I made it look easy.

I was showing off when I crashed my bicycle into the side of a neighbor's car. I was showing off when I crawled too far out on a pine tree limb, and the damn thing snapped, and I fell eight or nine feet at least and landed on a lawnmower and ended up with seven stitches in my elbow.

I was showing off when I pointed a rusty .22 rifle at the living room wall and pulled the trigger. I thought the gun was empty, but it wasn't. The bullet sailed through a wall and almost hit our piano, nicking high C.

Did I stop each time to ask myself, "Eddie, are you sure about this?"

Of course not. Show-offs never stop to ask questions about strategy or philosophy or psychology or logistics or statistics. They don't have time. If an 18-year-old boy is hot-rodding around with his buddies and sees a railroad crossing coming up, he doesn't ask himself, "Oh, dear. A railroad crossing. A train could be coming. It could be dangerous. What do the number say? What would Freud say? Does this have something to do with my mother?"

No. The 18-year-old boy shouts out, "Hey, guys. Watch this."

That's because he's 99.9 percent positive there's no train coming, and in the one percent of one percent a train is coming, he's 99.9 percent sure he can beat it.

But that doesn't account for the one-tenth of one percent of one percent where a train is coming, and sure enough, he and his buddies get splattered. That is chalked up to either bad luck or God's will.

Cemeteries contain their share of show-offs whose famous last words were, "Watch this."

—

Incidentally, I was the best football player in my neighborhood. I only mention it because it mattered. We played baseball and basketball and some other sports, too, but football was the only sport that mattered. Back then, kids could tell you who the best football player in their neighborhood was, but no one cared who the best baseball or the best basketball or the best ping pong player was.

Russell Bishop — Debby's younger brother — was the best basketball player and the best baseball player in our neighborhood, but no one cared. He might as well have been the strongest reader or the fastest speller.

I mention this because, as the best football player, I was often invited to hang out at Russell's house during the day and watch TV and play pool and so forth for one reason: Football opened doors.

Russell and I weren't best friends. To be honest, we were barely friends, but we were connected by sports. It was if we were partners in an enterprise called "Grace Creek Sports Authority, Inc.," named for the subdivision that was named for the meandering, flood-prone creek that ran through the neighborhood.

I hung out at Russell's because he and I had business to transact and weighty decisions to make about what and when and where and who. Thomas Edison once said — or was rumored to have said — that powerful men enjoy the company of other powerful men even if they don't enjoy the company of the men themselves.

In other words, power attracts power, and that's why I hung out at Russell's. His house wasn't a mess, and we both liked to be near the seat of power.

My best friend, Brian "Jeep" Drobyski, didn't buy it.

"You're not kidding anyone," he said. "You hang out there because you want to shoot his sister's squirrel."

I denied it, but not because I didn't want to shoot Russell's sister's squirrel. I denied it because I couldn't afford to be caught trying to shoot her squirrel. In fact, I had to bend over backwards to make sure I didn't do anything awkward or weird or fresh while she was around. I had to prove that I was 100 percent safe.

Why was that? Well, I was already on a short leash, given that I kind of broke her arm once.

It was an accident. I didn't do it on purpose. We were hanging out in her backyard, and she hopped on a swing, and before long, she had it going about as high as it would go. I was standing off to the side, and then I sort of faked like I was going to grab her leg, and, I don't know, maybe I did it. A little. I'm not sure.

Either way, she flew out of the swing, and I can still picture her sailing up and then dropping and hitting the St. Augustine grass with a thud. She laid there for a moment, then sat up and said, very matter-of-factly, "My arm's broken."

She got to her feet without my help and raced around the corner and into her house. She didn't squeal or wail or anything.

I, on the other hand, did the whole silent scream thing. My mouth went dry, and my eyes bulged, sort of like a squirrel getting run-over by an 18-wheeler. I bolted toward my house, flung open the kitchen door, slammed the hall door, slammed my bedroom door, crawled into my bedroom closet, turned on my transistor radio, and held it to my right ear.

I hunkered down there, trying to convince myself it was no big deal. She just dinged her funny bone. That was all, but just in case, I talked to God. It went like this:

> **Dear God.**
>
> **You saw what happened. You know I didn't do it on purpose. I'd never do it on purpose. You know that, so if you'll take care of this, I promise I will pray twice a day every day for the next five years. I'll go to church every Sunday without complaining. I'll honor my mother. I'll obey my dad if it comes to that. I'll observe the Ten Commandments, even the ones that don't directly apply to me. I promise I'll be nicer to my brothers. I'll stop shooting squirrels (literally and figuratively). I'll go and sin no more. You have my word. In Jesus' name and all that.**
>
> **Sincerely yours.**
> **Your most humble servant...**

Apparently, I wasn't sincere enough.

"Broken left forearm," Debby's doctor told her parents. "She'll be in a cast for six weeks. Maybe seven."

My younger brother heard about it and told Mom, so she and my dad paid the Bishops a visit to inquire as to how Debby was doing and to apologize and/or grovel, if necessary, but the Bishops would have none of it.

"It was an accident," Mr. Bishop told my mom. "There's nothing to apologize for. These things happen. She'll be fine. Can I fix you a drink? Ever had a martini?"

My mom's eyes got all red and misty, and Mr. Bishop placed his right hand on her shoulder and said, "Trust me, it's going to be OK. Now, how about a martini. Vodka or gin?"

"That's very kind of you, but I'd better get home," she said. "If there's anything I can do, anything at all, please let me know."

She didn't say, "Anything we can do."

She didn't say, "Let us know."

She said, "Anything I can do, please let me know."

My dad didn't notice. He stood a few feet behind my mom, fiddling with a Winston and eyeballing Mrs. Bishop when he thought no one was watching, then he said, "Well, I could use a beer. What'cha got? Miller or Schlitz?"

As if those were the only two beers on the market.

My mom's eyes popped wide, then narrowed as she tensed and sucked in her cheeks and fumed. Mr. Bishop pulled a Heineken out of his refrigerator, popped the top and handed it to my dad, who took a swig, smacked his lips, and smiled approvingly. Then he must have felt the carving knife my mom wanted to jab in his heart because he turned to her and played stupid.

"Whut?" he mouthed.

Mom's eyes returned to Mr. Bishop, who shrugged and tried not to grin. He had a talent for seeing the humor in human frailty.

"Anything," Mom said. "Call me."

"Thank you for coming by," Mrs. Bishop said, and they kind of hugged, then Mom headed home, with my dad in tow, chugging the beer whose name he couldn't spell or pronounce.

(By the way, he took the bottle to work with him the next day and showed it off to his pals, none of whom had ever heard of it, but they all had a good time making fun of the name — Hiney Kin.)

Mom marched in the front door and straight out the patio door and stood there, facing the late afternoon sun. She lit a Salem and waited for her nerves to settle, and then she knocked on the patio door window and pointed at me, and I stepped out.

Before I could manufacture a decent enough lie, she said, "Is our life not hard enough? Do you just dream up ways to make it harder? Is that how you spend your free time?"

There was no way to answer, and Mom knew it.

"You'll explain this to me tomorrow morning," she said. "Now, go tell your brothers we're having breakfast for dinner."

And I thought, "That's it?"

"Go," she said.

We had pancakes and bacon for dinner, and we were thrilled.

Mom needed to take a short nap before heading to work, so she left the dirty dishes in the sink. If I'd had half a brain, I would've washed and dried and put them up. It would've been the smart thing to do — the right thing to do — because I thought I might get grounded or possibly even a whipping, even though I hadn't had one in forever.

I figured, "Even though it was an accident, if I'm going to get one last whipping, it might as well be for this."

But it would have been too much trouble. The last time Mom tried to take a belt to me, we both ended up laughing.

Besides, my real punishment, I feared, would come the next day at school. Three or four of Debby's friends would spread a rumor that I had intentionally jerked her out of the swing and then twisted her arm until it snapped.

I had reason enough for suspecting this, and I'll go into it a little deeper in the next chapter.

Anyway, that night, I didn't sleep a wink. I stared at the ceiling and tried to prepare myself for the probability that I'd soon be an object of scorn because I — with malice and forethought — broke poor Debby's arm, thus endangering her dreams of becoming a professional twirler.

—

Mom was right. I had a gift for making things harder, for doing something stupid for little or no reason at exactly the worst moment. For example, I made Lowell Hardwick cry.

If I was the best football player in the neighborhood, then Lowell was the worst. He couldn't run, couldn't throw, couldn't catch, couldn't stay out of his own way. He wasn't the last kid picked because he was never picked. He just ended up on one team or the other.

He lived next door to the Bishops. An only child, he was thin as a pine needle and pale as a clam. As for making him cry, well, that was easy. He was a crier, and I knew that, so the question I wanted to ask his mother was: Did she ever stop to think maybe she shouldn't have let him play football with us because he might get hurt and cry?

Of course, she didn't. She trusted me not to hurt him, which would have been hard to guarantee given that I was a show-off.

Lowell had no business being out there with us, but he posed no threat to anyone except himself. He could've been doing a million other things. He could've been playing his piano. He could've been playing chess. He could've been playing Tic-Tac-Toe with the sheriff down at the courthouse, but he wanted to play football with us, and we had to let him because if we didn't, his bat-shit crazy mother would've chewed us up one side and down the other since she had nothing better to do than make sure her precious little apple dumpling was included in everything, even if we were dueling with flaming machetes.

So, it was just a matter of time before he got himself hurt, and here's how that happened. He grabbed my leg. I still can't imagine how he did it. Pure luck probably. I was just about to break a tackle when Lowell materialized out of thin air and latched onto my leg.

I remember thinking, "Lowell. What are you doing? Let go of my leg. I mean it, Lowell. Dumbass. Let go or I'll be forced to…"

But there wasn't time to explain this to Lowell because two other guys were closing in on me, so I had to do something fast. I pushed Lowell and planted my left foot in his stomach and did a 180, and he yelped and let go of my leg.

I then outran Jeep to the goal line and flipped him the bird right before I crossed it because he'd done the same thing to me not five minutes earlier.

That's how we played football. Those of us who knew what

we were doing didn't allow pasty-faced, oily-haired piano-playing daffodils like Lowell Hardwick to stop us from scoring, and, if by some act of God, Lowell grabbed our legs, then we did what we had to do, even if it meant grinding our cleats into his belly button.

It's a rough sport, and those are the chances you take.

Maybe I didn't explain that to Lowell because he flopped around long enough to draw the attention of Debby Bishop and a couple of her friends, who were standing off to the side, watching us play and pretending like they weren't, but I knew she was watching, so, of course, I was showing off.

When she walked over, I thought she was going to say something like, "Eddie. I couldn't help but watch you score that last touchdown. It was so beautiful. So epic. Take me now."

That's not how it played out. Debbie and her ilk huddled around poor Lowell, and even though it was soon obvious he would survive, Debby turned to me and asked, "Are you happy?"

"Sure," I said. "I scored."

"You didn't need to stomp him."

"I didn't stomp him," I said.

"You most certainly did. We saw you."

One of her friends said, "You did. We all saw you."

"Get some new glasses," I snarled. "He was trying to tackle me! I broke his tackle What was I supposed to do?"

"You didn't need to stomp him," Debby said.

"He wouldn't let go!"

I was just about to get testy with Debby and her prissy posse when Lowell's mother barged in.

"What is going on here?" she demanded to know. "What's wrong with you, Baby?"

She actually called him, "Baby."

I would've murdered my mom in her sleep if she'd called me "Baby" in front of my friends.

"Eddie stomped Lowell in the stomach on purpose," Debby spouted.

"On purpose," Lowell's mother asked. "What do you mean 'on

purpose?'"

"On purpose," Debby repeated, as if to say, "What? You don't speak English now?"

"He," Debby said, pointing a finger at me, "stomped Lowell," pointing to Lowell — same finger — "on purpose in the stomach," pointing to Lowell's stomach.

And I thought, "You little bitch!"

Lowell's mother scowled and leaned into my face and said, "Edward, explain yourself."

And — moron that I was — I replied, "Mrs. Hardwick, my name is not Edward. It's Eddie. E. D. D. I. E. Eddie."

Lowell's mother's face flashed as red as a raspberry.

"You," she snapped, "do not sass me. You do not sass me. You may get away with that in your home, but I will not tolerate it, here or anywhere else. Not for one second. Am I making myself perfectly clear, Edward? I will not tolerate sass from the likes of you."

The "Edward" bit didn't bother me, but the "from the likes of you" stung.

Here's what she was saying: "I will not tolerate sass from the son of the son-of-a-bitch who drinks beer until midnight on a school night and can't find time to rake his pine needles or pick up his cigarette butts or beer cans or wash the fish guts from his driveway."

So, she had me there. I tried to explain through body language and gibberish that I was doing what any football player would do, what our teammates expected us to do, what our coaches at school had coached us to do, what the rules and spirit and history of the game inform us to do.

Need I go on?

I was observing the code, honoring tradition. I was paying the price, going the extra mile, proving that winners never quit, and quitters never win. I was offering Lowell a chance to get knocked to his knees and bounce back, to test his mettle, to claim redemption, to chase perfection, to fulfill his finest moment. I was revealing to him a path to glory.

I mean, I thought that's what his motor-mouth mother wanted us to do, since she forced us to let him play. I should have reminded her that Lowell had no business being out there in the first place, but since he was, the least he could do was to learn from his misfortune.

That sounded reasonable enough, I thought but didn't say. Instead I stood there while Lowell's mother glared at me. She then leaned forward, and I could smell garlic and nicotine on her breath as she said, "Do not abuse my patience or generosity. I know your name is Eddie. I've been trying to help you become an Edward. I may be the only adult around who cares."

I knew I was whipped, so I stared at the ground and kicked around some dirt.

"Stop staring at your feet," she said, so I looked up while still avoiding her stare.

"Don't you ever sass me again, young man," she said. "Ever. And from now on, Lowell's on your team."

She said all of this slowly, deliberately, one syllable at a time, in a flat voice, as if she was scolding a fourth-grade boy who wouldn't stop eating boogers.

Then, she ordered Lowell to wipe his face and follow her home. On his way, he stopped crying and looked back and said, "I'll see you guys tomorrow," like nothing had happened.

Debby seemed satisfied that justice had been rendered, so she and her gang galloped off, too, leaving me there with the guys who had the good sense not to ask what Lowell's mother meant by "abuse my patience or generosity."

Jeep knew. He wasn't crazy about losing the game, but he enjoyed every second of the post-game fireworks. He sidled up to me and grabbed his ball from my hands, and said, "You haf ah-beuwst mein paytshunce und zhenorosity," in a redneck imitation of a German prison camp guard, like those in "The Great Escape" or "Stalag 17."

Everyone giggled except me.

Here's the funny part.

Debby got it right. I was happy. I scored the winning touchdown, and we won. I proved once again I was the best player in the neighborhood. The next day, when we played, I would be the first player picked, and I would quarterback if I wanted to, and I wanted to because I wanted to win, and my team had a better chance of winning when I had the ball in my hands, even if we got stuck with Lowell.

At dinner, I told my dad what had happened, and he laughed until my mom told him to zip it.

"Grow up, Sketch," she said before plopping a slice of meat loaf in front of him. He faked a frown, but when she turned to grab the iced tea, he gave me a little wink, then swiped a slice of white bread across the platter of tomato gravy and shoved the whole thing in his mouth — something he knew would disgust her.

We exchanged glances and snickered silently. I could tell he was drunk. Otherwise, he wasn't that chummy — at least not with me.

Still, there for a second, I thought it just might be possible that my dad liked me. So, all things considered, not a bad day.

CHAPTER 2

Coward

Debby Bishop was pretty and popular, and I had a crush on her, but she wasn't any more of a friend than her brother. She was friendly, but that's all. Debra Lynn Mayfield, on the other hand, was more than a friend. She was my best friend.

When I wasn't prowling around with the guys, I was hanging out with Debra. She was a year older, and five years smarter, and 10 or 20 years wiser. When I first met her at school, she went by her first name. Then, out of nowhere, she started going by her middle name.

I asked her why, and she said the neighborhood didn't need another Debbie, and I couldn't argue with that, although I did point out that there was a Willie and a Billy and a Bill and a Johnny with a "y" and a Johnnie with an "ie" and a John and even a Jonathan who went by Jon.

And she answered, "So?"

So, I didn't press it.

Lynn was super-smart, and that allowed her to look at things big and small from all sides. She even tried to look at school integration from a Black kid's point of view. Most of the white kids couldn't imagine that a Black kid even had a point of view.

But Lynn could think it through, and she could see what it was like for the Black kids who integrated our school, and it nauseated her because she saw with her own eyes the endless and pointless crap they were forced to put up with, and she knew it was wrong, and she knew she couldn't make it right, but she refused to keep her mouth shut. This chapter should be titled, "The Girl Who Refused to Keep Her Mouth Shut."

She once tried to comfort a Black girl who was curled up and crying at the bottom of the main stairwell after one of the school's more accomplished jerks slapped her books out of her hands, and when she screamed at them, another jerk told her to go back to Coon City and, "Take your cooties with you."

I was told that at least two teachers saw the whole incident, start to finish, and didn't lift a finger. One even smirked, as if the Black girl had done something to deserve it. Lynn walked over to him and asked, "You're going to let them get away with this?" and the teacher wrote her up and sent her to the office.

I'm glad now I wasn't there to see it myself. I'm not sure what I'd have done. Would I've intervened? Would I've fetched a wet towel or a glass of water for the Black girl?

In other words, would I have stuck my neck out? I wish I could say I would. I'd have felt sorry for her, but that would have been about it.

Fortunately for the girl, Lynn didn't need my assistance. She helped her to her feet and walked her to her class, then tromped down to the main office and told the principal exactly what had happened and asked him the same question: Are you going to let them get away with this?

An old friend of Lynn's dad, the principal wrote her a note that allowed her take the rest of the day off.

"Collect your books and go home and cool off," he told her.

"That's it?" Lynn said. "What about the girl? Can she go home and cool off, too? She can come over to my house. We'll cool off together."

"That's enough," he said. "I'll look into this, but I don't want another word from you."

Lynn scowled and recited a line from the Gettysburg Address: "Dedicated to the proposition that all men are created equal."

She couldn't help herself. If she thought it, she said it, and it often caused her grief. If she hadn't been such a burr under everyone's saddle, she might have been popular. Her older sister was wildly popular, in part because she was so pretty.

Lynn was not pretty. If she had been, people might've cut her some slack because pretty girls always get the benefit of the doubt.

They can smart off, and people think it's cute.

There was nothing cute about Lynn. She was short, clunky and chunky. Her face was horsey, her eyes too big, her teeth too small, her laugh too loud. She wore drab green dresses that hung straight and clung to all the wrong places. She had one of those Dutch Boy haircuts that made her look like Ringo in 1962.

She would have been a nobody if it hadn't been for the fact that she was so smart. If she'd been merely pretty or cute, she wouldn't have needed to be right all the time. Guys would've been intimidated by her, and girls would've been jealous of her, and no one would've listened to her, and what a waste that would have been.

More than once, she called me a moron to my face, and I never laughed it off. She did for me what I imagined I was doing for Lowell — offering lessons in the art of chasing perfection.

We weren't Lancelot and Guinevere. We were Lancelot and Arthur. She was my best friend because she was fair and kind and honest and brave and smart and plain. If she'd been cute or pretty, it might've been a different story.

—

Lynn had a younger sister, Gina, and an older sister, Karen. Gina was odd in the same way Lynn was plain. If you asked me to describe Gina, I wouldn't have said, "Gina's tall and husky and tomboyish."

I would have said, "Gina's different," but that was just another way of saying, "She's odd." It's OK to be different. It's weird to be odd. So, Lynn was plain, and Gina was odd, but Karen was gorgeous, as in Grace Kelly gorgeous. You couldn't take your eyes off of her even if you tried. Her skin was flawless. No freckles. No moles. No pimples. No bags. No shadows. No renegade hairs.

Her nose was perfect. Not too big. Not too small. Straight from eyebrow to lip. No trace of nostril.

Her pale blue eyes were clear and sharp and perfectly oval and just the right size, not like Debby Bishop's, which were, now that I think about it, kind of lizard-like.

Karen was an alien goddess from Planet Jaw-drop. If you

plopped her on a small island in the middle of the Mediterranean with a megaphone and an extra push-up bra and returned a month later, you'd find wrecked ships and the bloated bodies of love-struck sailors lapping against the rocks. She was that good looking.

Jeep's older brother, Duane, had a massive crush on her. I know for a fact that he had a wad of her underwear shoved under his mattress. Every now and then, he'd sneak into the Mayfield's backyard and snatch a pair off the clothesline.

If he'd been caught — oh my God —rest in peace, Duane. But he figured it was worth the risk.

I, on the other hand, was satisfied to sneak a peek at Karen and wonder what it would be like to brush her cheek or touch her lower lip. I don't mean to go on and on about her because I barely knew her. It's just that she was so out of place. Lynn and Gina heard it constantly: Your sister is so beautiful, which was another way of asking, "What happened with you?"

I pitied every studio photographer who ever attempted to produce a decent portrait of the Mayfield family. Shot after shot after shot of four barren moons and one glorious sun.

Gina and Lynn should've hated her, but they didn't. They loved her and didn't seem to feel the least bit diminished by the fact she made them look like crash test dummies. Lynn didn't choose to be plain. Gina didn't choose to be odd. Karen didn't choose to be gorgeous. They just were, and they didn't fight it.

It was about the only thing Lynn didn't fight.

—

While I wasn't ready to go to war for Lynn every time she refused to keep her mouth shut, I didn't appreciate anyone giving her or Gina shit. On the bus one afternoon, this guy I truly hated — Walt McFarlin — kept calling Gina "dog-face" and woof-woof-woofing at her, and I thought, "Gina. Jab a pencil in his throat."

But she ignored him.

When the bus arrived at our stop, Gina stood, waiting to hop off, and McFarlin started woof-woof-woofing again, but she just stood there, patiently waiting for the door to open.

I was seated about four rows behind McFarlin, and I knew him for what he was — a sorry piece of shit who picked on girls and clammy kids like Lowell, so on my way off the bus, I stopped by McFarlin's row and pretended I had to tie my shoe, and when I leaned over, I blew a wad of snot on his left sneaker. I don't mean to imply I was making a noble gesture, but it was the best I could do under the circumstances.

Like Lynn, Gina could've deflected some of the abuse if she'd wanted to, but she didn't. She invited it. She wore khaki pants, and a wrinkled, white T-shirt or a baggy sweatshirt and a pair of Chuck Taylor All-Stars. When it was cold enough, she wore her dad's varsity track lettermen jacket. Sometimes, she wore red suspenders.

She dressed like a guy and acted like a guy. I think Gina wanted to be a guy. She was about as girly as Lee Marvin. She played football with us, and she could hold her own. At first, we made her play center, for reasons it took her a while to figure out.

Later, we started selecting her second or third because she could throw and catch and tackle. When I had a chance to pick her, I did, and she didn't play center. Lowell did.

We also allowed her to hang out with us. Some nights, we'd put up a tent and build a campfire, and she'd wander out and sit with us and listen and stoke the fire with the sharp end of a stick. And if we decided to toss grasshoppers or cicadas into the fire, she wasn't all yucky about it. She'd just listen to the fizzle.

We liked her because she wasn't in love with the sound of her own voice, but when she said something, she had something to add. Everybody had something to say, but Gina — just like Lynn — usually had something to add.

If we talked about the Dallas Cowboys, she knew who Don Meredith and Bob Hayes were. If we talked about girls, she didn't care, and if she did, she moved out of the light of the fire and played her harmonica.

By the way, she also played the piano. In fact, she was better than Lowell because Lowell gently tapped the keys like a 7-year-old girl playing "Brighton Beach" for her grandmother, while Gina pounded the keys like Jerry Lee Lewis playing "Great Balls of Fire" for Chubby Checker.

Gina was a mystery. I asked Lynn how Gina got to be the way she was, and I wasn't talking about having a dogface. She couldn't help that, but why didn't she try to act a little more normal?

"She is acting normal," Lynn said. "What do you want her to do? Wear a tutu and staple a pink bow to her forehead? Gina has always been who she is. From the day they brought her home, she's been comfortable in her own skin."

For the record, she stole that line — comfortable in her own skin — from her dad. He and I were talking about football players, and Mr. Mayfield told me Jim Brown was his favorite player, and it wasn't just because he was the greatest player of his generation.

"Jim Brown," he told me, "is comfortable in his own skin."

Then, he looked at me like he expected me to add something, but I didn't. Instead, I furrowed my brow like I was looking at it from all sides, but I wasn't. I knew what he was saying, but I wasn't sure what he meant, so Lynn filled in the blanks.

"Because Jim Brown's a Black man, some people believe he's 'uppity,'" Lynn said. "Jim Brown isn't uppity. He's comfortable in his own skin. My dad is saying, 'It's not about the color of his skin. It's about him.' In other words, his skin could be purple, and he wouldn't care because it wouldn't change who he is. That's what makes him special. That's also what scares some people. OK?"

"Sure," I said. "You don't have to spell it out."

"Since when?" she asked, then curled her lip into an Elvis pucker, which was her way of saying, "You're not fooling anyone."

That wasn't true. Maybe I wasn't fooling her, but I fooled people all the time.

—

I met Lynn when I was in seventh grade. I sat in on a Young Historians Club meeting — just to check it out — and she was in charge. She talked about the Battle of Gettysburg and presented maps and old family photographs and even a copy of the Gettysburg Address, which she then delivered from memory. I was so impressed

I got out of there as fast as I could. It was way over my head.

We didn't live in her neighborhood then. We lived about a mile away in a painted brick house about two-thirds the way up a fairly steep hill. I'd always liked it, but we moved because of an incident involving my younger brother and another kid who lived across the street. I don't want to get hip-deep in details because I'm still trying to put it behind me. The only thing that matters is that it wasn't my brother's fault. It wasn't anyone's fault. Some kids were fooling around, and one of them got hurt. These things happen.

Of course, that's not how the parents of the kid who got hurt saw it. They blamed my younger brother and convinced everyone up and down the street that he was solely responsible, so one after another, I and my younger brother and even my youngest brother were told to stay out of their yards.

I wasn't there when any of this happened, so I couldn't figure out at first why we got lumped in with my younger brother, but then I realized I was being a jerk because he wasn't to blame, not that it mattered.

Rumors swirled, and people who didn't have a clue what they were talking about yapped crap like, "It's a miracle that poor little thing wasn't killed."

That was a lie, but once a lie breaks out of its shell, you have a better chance of stopping a wildebeest stampede with a bicycle horn. One day, a guy named Lonnie Dortch said something to me along the lines of, "I heard your brother almost got someone killed."

I should have kneed him in the nuts, but he was twice my size and would have stuffed me in a locker, thrown in an olive and called me a martini, so I weaseled away.

The one time I could've shown some courage, some character, some grit and gumption, I turned as yellow as creamed corn.

Cowards tend not to be comfortable in their own skin.

Now, compare me to Lynn. She heard Marsha Luce say something about my brother and the kid who got hurt, and Lynn interrupted her and told her, "That's not true, Marsha. That's a lie."

Marsha was about to respond, but Lynn cut her off.

"Marsha, do you think Jesus would appreciate your spreading lies? I don't. I think it reflects poorly on your parents to have raised a daughter who peddles lies in a futile attempt to make herself look better."

Lynn actually used the word "peddles." I would have never, in a million years, thought to use that word.

Lynn shamed Marsha into admitting it was just something she'd heard from someone who heard it from someone who probably heard it from Lonnie Dortch.

"Well, Marsha, if that's the standard, I hear you get fingered on the bus every afternoon."

Marsha gasped, but she didn't put up a fight because that was true. Every afternoon. Same seat. Different boys.

My mom adored Lynn. She was welcomed in our house any time, day or night, and Gina was, too. I think Mom saw some of herself in them. Take the very best of each, and you had my mother. Smart. Funny. Brave. Sweet. Odd. Pious. Profane.

Mom was quiet and slightly anti-social, but she was neither timid nor mousy. If you crossed her, she would skin you alive if it was the last thing she did.

One day, during the "stay out of our yard" episode, my little brother, Ricky, came home crying because our next-door neighbor — Mrs. Darlene Gimble — ordered him to stay out of her yard.

When Mom asked Ricky why he was crying, he told her, so she waltzed over, rang the doorbell about a dozen times and ordered Mrs. Gimble to step outside. Mom removed the Salem from her lips and blew the smoke downward, then said, "Darlene — you bitch — if you ever, ever speak to one of my boys like that again, I will slap you so hard, your grandchildren will be born dizzy."

Mom had been waiting forever to call her a bitch because Mrs. Gimble was constantly reminding everyone how much she loved Jesus, and how much Jesus loved her, and right as I thought my mom was through eviscerating Mrs. Gimble, she turned back and took one last drag off her Salem, then flipped the butt right in Mrs. Gimbel's front yard and said, "Jesus wouldn't know you from a dinosaur dick."

Mrs. Gimble literally wobbled.

I watched from the edge of our yard, and I heard almost everything that was said. Back in our yard, Mom ordered us to get inside and take a seat at the kitchen table.

"Stay out that yard," she warned us. "If I see you take one step in that yard, I'll rip you a new one."

Then, she spooned each of us two scoops of vanilla ice cream and drizzled it with Hershey's chocolate syrup, then lit another Salem and put on Bobby Darin's Greatest Hits, and we all sang "Splish Splash" and "Artificial Flowers."

At the end of that school year, we packed up and moved a mile west into this neighborhood. I still attended the same junior high, but everything else changed.

—

My old neighborhood was older, stodgier, full of fuddy-duddies. My new neighborhood was ripping at the seams with kids my age.

You couldn't throw a rock without hitting one, so there was always someone to throw a ball to, listen to records, ride bikes through the woods, dam up the creek, catch crawdads, or just hang out and talk about blisters or birthday parties or girls who wouldn't give us the time of day.

Out of all of the kids in that neighborhood and in that school, Lynn was my best friend.

That was unusual because boys tended to have boys as best friends, and I had plenty of friends who were boys, and I hung out with them because of sports or so forth, but if I felt like talking to someone about something that interested me, I talked to Lynn. I sure wasn't going to call Jeep or Duane and ask them if they'd like to come over and talk about our feelings.

I mention that because that's exactly what Lynn and I talked about one night. Our feelings. I wanted to talk about them because I ran into Mr. Bishop, and he pulled me aside and said, "I have a favor to ask of you. Debby's working hard on her twirling, so if you decide to break one of her arms again, break the left one."

He laughed and put me in a headlock, like he was totally joking, and he then handed me a dollar and told me to go buy myself a milkshake.

But something about it bugged me.

A couple of days later, Lynn and I were sitting out by the curb, watching for shooting stars and mammoth moths, and I asked her if she thought he was joking or making some kind of veiled threat.

She gave me a sad frown, like I was one of those kids on TV with a rare disease.

"You're always surprised whenever someone does something nice for you," Lynn said. "Like it's a gift you never dreamed you'd receive, and you're embarrassed to accept it. You shouldn't be because most people are nice to each other most of the time."

I let it sink in and said, "I'm always surprised you have an opinion about what you think surprises me," but she was right. She always was.

I guess that's why she was the only person I dared to share gossip with. I could tell her anything. Who I liked. Who I thought liked me. Who I disliked. Who I thought disliked me. Who I knew disliked me. Her only rule was, "No lies."

You have no idea how hard that was for me, but I learned the penalty was far worse than giving in to the temptation.

I once said, "I cannot stand Debby Bishop," which was, of course, a lie, and I can't tell you why I said it. I was showing off, I guess, but Lynn pounced immediately.

"You must be kidding," she said. "You love her. You adore her. You worship her."

"No, I don't."

"Eddie. Everybody knows. It's not a big secret."

"Maybe I used to like her," I insisted. "I really don't, now."

"Really don't?" Lynn said. "What does 'really' mean? There's a difference between 'I don't' and 'I really don't.'"

Fortunately, she knew I knew I was caught, so she dropped it. That night, I tried to figure out why I chose to tell her such a bald-faced lie.

The next day, I apologized.

"As much as I hate to admit this, you were right, and I was wrong, so I'm sorry," I said.

"Apology noted and accepted," she said. "I love being right."

She smirked and twisted her arms into a knot, which was something I couldn't do. There was a momentary pause, and then I asked her, "Are girls expected to put up with this kind of crap from guys like me forever?"

She untangled her arms and replied, "It would seem so. Or have you not noticed?"

She was referring to my dad.

"But I don't think it's required by law," she added. "I think we get to make our own rules. And what's our rule? No lying. I won't lie to you. You don't lie to me."

If only she'd been prettier.

—

I once made the mistake of saying something innocent to Diane Ledbetter about Sherry Wilkerson, so Diane Ledbetter blabbed to one of her friends that I had a crush on Sherry Wilkerson, and her friend told someone else, and it got around to Sherry's boyfriend, Charley Allison, who cornered me in the shower after football practice and warned me to wise up and cork it, which meant "stop talking about his girlfriend."

Before I could explain to him that I wasn't talking about his girlfriend and had no interest in her, he punched me in the stomach so hard I couldn't catch my breath for like 30 seconds.

"Fuck you, Charley," I gasped as I tried to pull myself together. "Your girlfriend's a bitch."

"I know. Keep it to yourself," he said, then threw a bar of soap that barely missed my head.

By the way, Charley was my friend. He lived four houses down the street. We went way back. Because he liked me, he punched me in the gut instead of the nose. That was his way of saying, "I still consider you a friend." He was led to believe I was making a move on his girlfriend, so he had no choice. Rules are rules, and I respected that.

I also learned my lesson. Talk to Lynn. No one else. Just Lynn.

Of course, it wasn't hard to keep that promise because no one except Lynn cared about my thoughts or feelings. No one else wanted to sit out and listen to our transistor radios and wait for the DJ to play the latest Beatles hit.

One night, Lynn told me an interesting story. Right about the time "A Hard Day's Night" came out, our music teacher, Mrs. Edith Calhoun, said, "By the end of 1965, you can mention 'the Beatles,' and no one will have a clue who you're talking about."

Well, 1965 came and went, and girls were still screaming, so one day, Lynn raised her hand in music class and asked Mrs. Calhoun if she'd heard the latest Beatles song, "Ticket to Ride."

Mrs. Calhoun said she had not.

So, Lynn said, "But you know who the Beatles are?"

And Mrs. Calhoun said, "Of course, I do."

And Lynn said, "Gotcha'!"

By the end of the class, Mrs. Calhoun had confessed that she was wrong about the Beatles. In fact, she thought another song by the Beatles — "Yesterday" — was one of the most beautiful songs she'd ever heard.

"I clearly misjudged them, and for that, I apologize. You were right. I was wrong."

Students either fainted or freaked out.

Tommy Askew said loud enough for everyone to hear, "I'll be damned."

"She heard him but didn't do a thing about it," Lynn said.

Stranger things had happened, she added, but she couldn't remember when.

"Well, my dad still hates them," I said. "The other night, he was making fun of them at dinner except he kept confusing the Beatles with the Beach Boys, so he sang, 'Help me Rhonda, Yeah, Yeah, Yeah.' Or something like that."

Please remember that my dad was a 10th-grade drop-out whose idea of a modern musical masterpiece was "You Can't Roller-Skate in a Buffalo Herd."

Lynn shrugged, which was her way of saying, "You're shocked?"

Well, not entirely.

I often wondered why my dad hated the Beatles so virulently. I suspected he hated them because they were having fun, and he wasn't. I bet if I'd asked Lynn, she would have said, "Your dad hates them because he doesn't love himself."

She would've nailed that one, too.

I never got around to asking her about that, but I did get around to returning a library book a couple of days later and damned if I didn't turn a corner and catch Debby Bishop and Walt McFarlin together. I froze, then made a sharp U-turn to avoid bumping into them, and then I waited for them to move on, and while I was standing there, watching them, I said to myself, "She's got a crush on him."

She had a crush on my worst enemy. That stung, but I then I thought, "What took her so long?"

Though I needed to go and was getting impatient, I waited for them to leave first. I didn't have the courage to walk up and say something like, "If my eyes don't deceive me. Walt McFarlin and Debby Bishop. What a pleasant surprise. How's the arm, Deb? I hope it's fully healed because you're going to need every ounce of your strength to fight off this cretin."

Instead, I stood and waited and watched her clutch her books tightly to her chest. I watched him lean forward far enough to almost violate her no-fly zone. I knew what he was thinking, and I assumed she knew what he was thinking, too.

It pissed me off that she hadn't already slapped him. Perhaps she'd received permission from her dad to allow Walt McFarlin to get fresh.

Or maybe she'd just started thinking for herself. Maybe I was seeing something that wasn't there. The only thing that mattered was that they didn't see me.

—

And then, maybe I was seeing things.

I ran into Debby the next day. She wanted to chat, and so we did, but she didn't say a word about Walt McFarlin, who, I assumed, was her new crush, soon-to-be her fiancé, her eventual husband, and the father of their six bobblehead kiddos. The whole thing made me sick, especially the thought of Walt lurching over her like a buzzard.

Even after I found out there was nothing between them, just knowing there could be turned my stomach, which wasn't fair. She didn't care for him. She never had. She never would. She was just being nice, and poor Walt had a bigger crush on her than I did.

I never told Lynn any of this because I didn't want to lie. If I'd told her none of this mattered, that I didn't care one way or the other, she'd have laughed in my face. She might've slapped me, so I just hunkered down and waited for it all to blow over.

I stopped insisting that the guys meet at the Bishops' house in the morning, and I stopped going over and watching TV with Russell, and I suppose Mr. Bishop noticed. I bumped into him at a little grocery store where I worked occasionally.

"Hello, stranger," he said. "What 'cha been up to?"

"You're looking at it," I said.

"I admire a man with a plan," he said, then added, "We miss seeing you. Come around some time. We'll shoot some baskets."

Sure, I replied, and he gave me a look that said, "Not really. I'm just being nice. It's a family thing."

Of course, we were neighbors, so I bumped into Mr. Bishop now and then, and it was always weird because he was only being nice, and I could detect in his tone and manners the same voice I once heard him use with his maid. He wanted to sound cordial and respectful, but he came out cold, almost calculated.

His words said one thing. The way he said them said another. They said, "All things being equal, I pity you."

I could understand him pitying his maid. After all, she was paid to empty and clean the cat box, but he didn't need him to pity me. I didn't need his pity, and I never asked for it.

I didn't want him or anyone else being nice to me out of pity because I wasn't that pitiful. Despite everything, I was still the best football player in the neighborhood. And I didn't have to go around, pretending to be nice. In fact, I decided right then and there that I was done with being nice. It was so fake.

"Nice to see you. Nice weather we're having. Nice of you to lick my boots. Sorry about the cigarette ashes I just flicked in your face. Nice of you not to make a fuss about it. Have a nice day"

I wasn't going to be a liar or a fraud. I was going to call a spade a spade, and I was going to start with my dad. He was the biggest fraud of all, and the more I searched for proof of it, the easier it was to find.

Holes in the walls he should have fixed. Empty beer cans and cigarette butts strewn about the yard he should have raked up. Rain gutters choked with pine needles. Weeds in the flower beds. Everywhere I looked, I found signs that proved one thing: My dad didn't give a rat's ass.

He hated his life even more than he hated the Beatles, and he sulked and bitched about every little thing, found comfort in the company of strangers, and took out his empty bitterness on those who wanted to love him by ignoring every birthday, every anniversary, every promise he ever made to Mom, to me and to my brothers.

He drank. He gambled. He fooled around and left us to mop up his muddy footprints and wipe his piss stains off the toilet lid.

One day, a tall guy who looked like Gregory Peck showed up at our front door and handed Mom a piece of paper and said he was sorry to interrupt her, but some bill hadn't been paid in three or four months, and he'd been sent out to reclaim it.

Mom was floored. She'd been giving my dad cash money to pay this bill because that's how he wanted it. In cash. He promised he'd take care of it, and, for one last time, Mom believed him.

She collected herself and didn't take out her anger on the guy who looked like Gregory Peck because he was just doing his job so his wife and kids would never have to watch a stranger haul away their furniture and appliances

"I'm going to leave it on the truck for a couple of days," he told

Mom. "If you can make a payment or two, I'll bring it right back."

Mom nodded and watched the refrigerator roll out the door, up a ramp and into a big truck, right in front of Mrs. Gimble, who stood in her front yard, delighting in Mom's humiliation.

A week later, the refrigerator returned. Somehow, my dad found or stole the money to pay the bill, and he was all proud of himself, but the damage was done, and it was irreparable. They stopped talking. He started sleeping on the couch or in the garage.

Mom retreated into herself. She tried to scrimp by giving up cigarettes, but she couldn't do it. They were all she had.

As for me, I still had football. I told myself, "You might end up one of these days patching tires or pumping gas or hauling off people's refrigerators, but for now, you're still the best football player in this neighborhood. Act like it."

So, I did. There were better players in my grade, but none of them lived in my neighborhood, so I didn't have to be nice, and I didn't have to share the ball if I thought it might cost us a first down in a game that we'd win by 16 touchdowns.

I quarterbacked because I wanted to win. I wanted to win because I wanted the other guys to lose. I wanted them to get used to losing. I wanted to them to start thinking of themselves as losers unless they were on my team.

I wanted every player out there to feel for once what I felt most of the time. I wanted them to feel like no matter how many touchdowns they scored, they weren't and never would be good enough. I wanted to pity them.

CHAPTER 3

Fumes

One night, my dad stayed out late, drinking Schlitz and playing poker at my Uncle Wally's service station in Longview. It was Mom's night off, so he figured he could cat around even though he had to work the next morning. He considered himself a pro because he'd gone to work drunk lots of times and gotten away with it.

So, my dad dragged in around 3 a.m., but this time, Mom was waiting. I couldn't make out what they said at first, but it escalated quickly, so I buried my head under my pillow and turned on my radio to drown them out, and it worked. I fell back asleep, and then, around 3:30, my dad kicked at my door and yelled, "Turn'nat sheeut'toff."

I switched it off as fast as I could because I didn't want him starting in on me, and 10 minutes later, he was snoring on the couch in his clothes, and I was wide awake, listening to his wheezy snorts and knowing my mother was sitting up in bed, smoking a Salem and reading "Gone with the Wind" for the umpteenth time.

I should have gone in and checked on her to make sure she wasn't weepy or in the process of setting the house on fire, but that wasn't how we operated. We bruised and brooded.

As for my dad, I didn't know what to think except the obvious: He didn't want to be here. He didn't want to be married. He didn't want to be a father. He didn't want to coach Little League or attend school band concerts or honor roll assemblies. He didn't want to kowtow to the Bishops and Mayfields or anyone else.

My dad wanted to be left alone so he could drink and play poker with his brothers and brothers-in-law and buddies until 2:30 in the morning and then sleep it off. He didn't understand what was so wrong with that, or why my mom was always mad at him.

He helped pay the bills, most of the time.

Since he didn't think he had anything to apologize for, he'd come home after work and pretend nothing had happened. As hungover as he must have been, he'd still breeze in and announce himself and order us around just to sustain his delusion that he was running the show.

Then, he'd wash up for dinner. Here's how we knew he knew he was still in trouble: He whistled. He whistled in the same way some nuns hum.

He whistled, and Mom bristled. She knew how to punish him: Make him feel small, irrelevant, unnecessary. Play the martyr by taking care of everything. Meals. Laundry. Bathrooms. Us. By the time my dad rolled in, we'd already been ordered around plenty. Put your clothes up. Do your homework. Dry those dishes.

Then, she'd fry chicken or bake a tuna casserole for dinner and ignore my dad's feeble attempts at breaking the ice. When it became obvious to him that she was still livid, he'd retreat to the garage to tinker with his Dodge Polara until he heard dinner plates rattling and Mom calling me and my brothers to the table.

He'd sneak back in right after Mom had led us through the same Catholic prayer we robotically muttered before every meal:

**Bless us, O Lord, and these Thy gifts,
which we are about to receive from Thy bounty,
through Christ our Lord. Amen.**

Then, we'd eat in silence. If we wanted seconds, we'd point. Everyone knew the drill. When we were finished, my dad would say something like, "Honey, you go sit down and put your feet up. Me and these boys will do these dishes," and she'd retreat to her bedroom and her book and her cigarettes, and he'd turn to us and say, "You boys do these dishes."

It was his way of thinking all was forgiven and forgotten, which was insane, especially this time because Mom was royally pissed.

Anyway, I did the dishes by myself because it was faster and easier. My younger brothers could screw up a dinner mint, so I was glad to get them out of my hair.

I was stacking and washing and drying the dishes, and I couldn't help but wonder why it had to be like that. If my dad had some beef with us, why didn't he just spit it out, or scribble a note, or sneak out in the middle of the night? We wouldn't have been any worse off.

As it was, I still had to get up and go out and pretend like everything with my family was fine, like we were normal, and that was getting harder and harder to do. In fact, the next morning, Lynn and I were sitting on her front porch steps, and she whispered, "Your parents are fighting, aren't they?"

It was a statement, not a question, and I could have admitted the obvious, but I acted all huffy and shocked, and I was about to say something when she interrupted me.

"I woke up really late. Your living room lights on, and the curtains were open, and I watched your mom, so don't tell me they were playing dominoes," Lynn said. "I know it's not my business, but if you need to talk to someone, I'm glad to listen."

I muttered something which she correctly translated as "I have no idea what you're talking about."

"I'm trying to be your friend," she said. "Friends help their friends. That's how it's supposed to work. If I show up right after dinner tonight with a busted lip, I'd like to think you might ask me what happened."

"I wouldn't have a chance," I snapped back. "You'd be holding a sign. If I've learned anything, it's that you love to talk about the family problems your family doesn't have."

I regretted it immediately, but instead of apologizing, I hemmed and hawed because I couldn't deal with it right then, so I gazed up at the sky and asked, "What kind of clouds are those?"

"OK. If that's how you want to play it, fine," Lynn said. "You're not hurting my feelings. Go home."

She stood and paced and turned to go indoors and then wheeled back around and said, "You're a moron. You know that? You're a fool. You like being miserable. You think it's noble. Well, it's not. It's pathetic. Here I am, trying to be your friend, and you just sit there and pout and mumble and expect me to feel sorry for you. I don't. You're acting just like your father."

That stung, but I hid it. As usual, I treated the wound the way I always do. I went home, crawled into bed, switched on my radio, turned it up, held it to my ear and tried not to think.

I stared at the ceiling and rattled to myself, "Don't think. Don't think. Don't think."

And it worked up to the point that I couldn't help but think. I thought about Mr. Bishop and Mr. Mayfield and my dad. I thought about the nights my dad stayed out late, drinking, losing at poker, and God only knows what else.

I remembered the times he seemed to go out of his way to hurt us or diminish us. For example, he and my Uncle Doyle loaded all us kids in the bed of a pickup and drove us over to Liberty City to pick purple hull peas.

Doyle, who's my dad's younger sister's husband, chewed Beech-Nut tobacco and rather than spit into a paper cup or empty beer bottle, he spit it out the window through the gap in his front teeth.

Doyle's oldest son, Mark, was sitting in the bed on the driver's side as we were headed home, and Doyle sent a stream of tobacco juice out the window, and it splattered everywhere.

At first, I thought it was an accident, but then I realized Doyle did it on purpose. I was sitting directly behind my dad, and I could see them laughing. They thought spitting tobacco juice in a kid's face was hilarious.

I'm surprised my dad didn't try to ding me with his cigarette, just to prove he could be as big a jerk as Doyle. Maybe he thought it went without spraying.

Anyway, now that I'd decided that I'd had enough, I told Lynn this story and four or five more. I let loose a string of curse words as long as her arm, including the F word, which I had never used in Lynn's presence. I used it as a noun, verb, adjective, adverb, article, conjunction, participle, and I wasn't sure what a participle was.

Guess what she said. She said, "Your father's problems don't have to be your problems."

I laughed out loud.

"Say that again," I said. "I want to make sure I heard you right."

"Your father's problems don't have to be your problems. You make them your problems, but they don't have to be."

She said it so effortlessly, like Spencer Tracy in "Judgment at Nuremberg." It was as if she'd had a month to do nothing but study my family and catalogue all the broken promises, endless carping, backhanded compliments, holes in the doors, rings around the tub, yellow stains on the toilet lid, and tobacco spit splashed in my cousin's face. It was like Lynn had studied my dad's whistling, and my mom's raging silence, and processed it, and it all boiled down to one thing: My father's problems didn't have to be my problems.

She was right, of course. If Lynn hadn't been so plain, I'd have been head-over-heels in love with her, but then, if she hadn't been plain, she wouldn't have been my best friend. She'd have been palling around with Debby Bishop, and I wouldn't have had a clue how to talk to her, so it worked best for me that she wasn't pretty or even cute. This way, I had her all to myself.

By the way, when I said, "Of course, she was right," that doesn't mean I said to her, "Of course, you are right," because I didn't. I didn't say a word.

Lynn waited for a response, and when I didn't offer one, she asked, "You understand what I'm saying, don't you? I'm saying you can't change your father any more than you can change the color of your skin or the size of your feet, so stop trying."

"That's easy for you to say, given all the insurmountable obstacles you've overcome in your life," I answered.

That was bad enough. Then, I made it much worse.

"Your biggest problem," I added, "is you have a gorgeous sister."

"What is that supposed to mean?" she asked.

"It means you don't have any problems."

"What does have to do with my sister?"

"Nothing. I'm just saying you don't have any problems."

"How can it be nothing? You brought her up."

"I don't know. It just came out. Look, forget about it."

"I'm not going to forget about it. I know what you're saying. The least you could do is admit it."

"I said something I shouldn't have said. I'll admit that, and I apologize. As for my dad, I let his problems be my problems because my dad is my problem.'"

"No," Lynn said. "You think your father is your problem. You think he's the root of all your misery, but he's not. You are. You've always been your problem. Your dad is not stopping you from being a better person, and no one would hold it against you if you tried to be every now and then."

She placed her fist on her hip and gave me a smug look, as if to say, "Are we done?"

I should have said "Yes," but, moron that I was, I said, "Well, what do you know?"

Well, she knew everything.

"I know your father has never hit you," she said. "Has he ever punched you in the face? Has your father ever broken your jaw?"

"Of course not," I said.

"Then shut up," she said. "My grandfather broke my dad's jaw. You know why? He spilled an ashtray. He accidentally tipped over an ashtray onto a living room rug, and my grandfather punched him so hard, it broke his jaw. And my dad was only 12 at the time. That's the house my father grew up in, but my father didn't pout and expect everyone to feel sorry for him. No. He grew up, and he dealt with it."

At first, I thought, "Bullshit," but her eyes suddenly glistened and turned pink, so I shut up and let her finish. When she was through, I wanted to hug her, but I didn't know how, so I lied by telling her I had dishes to do.

That night, I pictured her father's long, sunken face, his droopy, hound dog eyes, and I thought about how nice he was, how kind and fair he was, and I couldn't imagine how a father could hit his son so hard it'd shatter his jaw.

People think I'm weird because I like the movies so much. Do you want to know why I like the movies so much? It's because in the movies, anything is possible.

There's a scene in one of my favorite movies, "The Sons of Katie Elder," where John Wayne whacks a bad guy in the face with an axe handle. The bad guy never sees it coming. He walks around a corner and BOOM. Right across the bridge of his nose.

That's what I wanted to do to Lynn's grandfather. I wanted to catch him coming around a corner and lay him out cold.

—

My dad dropped out of high school after the 10th grade because he couldn't read a lick and worried he'd flunk out and get drafted into the regular army and end up getting blown to bits in France, so he joined the Merchant Marines as a 16-year-old "Ordinary" seaman. He worked the docks outside of Port Arthur, loading airplanes, jeeps, tanks, rifle ammunition, even an entire locomotive engine.

He didn't care for the work, but at least he wasn't riding atop a tank headed straight toward a bazooka, so he did what they told him to do and kept his mouth shut and hoped the war would end soon.

It didn't. The Germans surrendered in May of 1945, but the Japanese refused to give in, so shortly after my dad turned 18, he received his draft notice. For years, he'd swear he was going to join anyhow. "I was just puttin' it off for Momma's sake," he said. "She had two sons in uniform already."

The better you knew him, the more unlikely you were to believe him. At any rate, he was stationed at a Louisiana Army base and was about to be shipped off not to Europe but to the Pacific for the impending invasion of Japan.

But then, the Enola Gay dropped the A-bomb on Hiroshima, vaporizing 80,000 people, and three days later, a second, bigger bomb was dropped on Nagasaki, killing 40,000. On August 15, Japan surrendered.

And that was the end of that, which was a shame. Maybe a little hand-to-hand combat would've brought out something heroic in my dad. Maybe he might've saved the lives of 25 GIs by crawling across open ground and taking out a pillbox with a flamethrower, but he never got the chance. All he got was a couple of worthless unit citations and ribbons for meritorious valor, ostensibly in the face of brutal attacks by mosquitos and alligator gars.

I never talked to my dad about the war. It was a touchy subject because his brothers — Clarence and Ernie — saw action in Europe, and don't think they don't lord that over him. They had actual medals for bravery in battle, and my dad had unit citations. Big difference. So, my dad never had the chance to prove to himself or anyone else that he was willing to kill or be killed.

I'm not suggesting he would've been a hero. I'm saying we'll never know. Even worse, he'd never know. Once Japan went belly-up, the Army cut him loose like he was moss on a trotline. "Get a job and make your family proud," they told him, so my dad saluted and barked, "Yes. Sir!"

Then he looked for a bar and got plowed.

From there, he seemed hell-bent on confirming the suspicions everyone had about him — especially my grandfather, who was hard on him, and I mean hard. Really hard. Every little thing, my grandfather snapped at him. If a door was open, it should've been closed. If a window was up, it should've been down. If a knife or a pencil or a pair of pliers were lost, he lost them.

Once, a bunch of us were walking along the shore of a pond in the back pasture. My dad and Grandpa were ahead of me 10 yards or so because I'd stopped to skim a few flat rocks across the water, and my dad noticed a dead pine tree along the shore, so he gave it a good shove and damned if it didn't crash into the water, right onto an old rotted out rowboat that had been stuck in the mud there for years. Everyone thought it was great except Grandpa, who chewed my dad's ass out.

"Goddamn it! What if that tree had fallen on one of them boys? Did you even think of that? What if one of them boys had been in that water or in that boat? What's it going to take for you to grow up? Somebody else got to die?"

I couldn't believe what I was hearing because the pine tree was nowhere near any of us boys, but that didn't stop Grandpa.

My dad wiped his hands on his trousers, then slipped them in his pockets and stared across the pond and started whistling, but this time it was an actual song — a Hank Williams song about a wooden Indian standing by the door. Too stubborn to ever show a sign. Because his heart was made of knotty pine.

My dad stayed well ahead of us. He never looked up, never looked back to check to see if we were still around because he was embarrassed and hurt and seething, but by God, he was not going to show it, and even if he did, we were not going to see it. He swallowed his pain whole and kept it down.

I wish I could tell you I felt sorry for him, but I didn't. I thought, "Where have I heard this shit before?"

But then, I realized this wasn't the first time this ass-chewing had happened. It wasn't the 15th time or the 50th. I realized it was a deliberate act of cruelty aimed point blank at my dad. Grandpa didn't talk that way to anyone else, at least not that I noticed.

The walk to the house took forever. My dad stewed, and I noticed Grandpa's eyes were glassy, and he kept swiping at his nose. When we reached the house, the two of them cut in opposite directions, like they couldn't get away from each other fast enough. It stayed that way until we started packing up to leave.

On the way off the porch and toward the car, Mom ordered us to give Grandpa and Grandma a kiss and a hug, although I didn't see her hugging or kissing anyone. Meanwhile, Dad sulked in the car, all bunched up, drumming the fingers of his left hand on the steering wheel, fingering a Winston with his right hand.

We piled in, and Mom said, "You might want to look under the car to make sure those dogs aren't under there."

Dad scowled and jerked the transmission into drive, cutting a dusty circle on his way out of the yard and down the caliche path to the county road that took us to the state road that took us to the state highway that took us two blocks from our house.

When we arrived, Mom got everyone and everything redistributed, and then she called me into the living room, where she was laying on the couch — laying, lying, laid, whatever. I can never get that shit right. Anyway, she had a moist rag draped across her forehead.

"Sit down," she said. "I want to tell you something about what happened today. I know you've heard about your father's younger brother, Eddie — the one who drowned, the one you're named after. Here's what you haven't heard. He drowned in the Neches River, and your father was with him when it happened."

She told me Eddie fell out of a jon boat and got tangled in tree roots and panicked and drowned. That was Mom's guess, anyway, and she was a nurse, so I figured she would know.

"He was an odd boy," Mom said, and she used the word "odd" to mean "something wasn't right upstairs" — not the way I used "odd" to describe Gina.

"You can look at photographs of him and tell there was something missing, but no one wanted to admit it. He was the baby of the family, and everybody loved him. I think they saved all their affection for this one boy. He may have had a heart attack, but his parents didn't even know what an autopsy was, and, besides, they already had their minds made up as to what had happened and who was responsible."

So, I thought, "That must be what Grandpa meant when he asked, 'Somebody else got to die?'"

I didn't tell Mom about that. I just sat there, next to her, trying to make sense of it as she pulled another Salem from a table drawer and lit it. She drew in the first drag for what seemed like a minute, exhaled slowly while daintily holding the cigarette between her index and middle finger of her right hand, like she was Debbie Reynolds or Donna Reed, and then she brought it to her lips again and took a second long drag, and I could tell she had something else she wanted to say but didn't know if this was the right time or place. Apparently, it was.

"I'm sorry things between me and your father are pretty rocky right now. Some of this is my fault. I've expected too much of him. I know that, and I'll try harder. We all need to try harder, and that includes you. You're the oldest. Your brothers look up to you, whether you want to admit it or not, and I need your help."

"Yes, ma'am," I said and started to stand, but she stopped me.

"I can't and I won't excuse your father's behavior, but I know where it comes from," she said. "He's still a boy himself, a boy who occasionally pretends to be a man. I always knew he was running away from something. I wanted to believe I could help him run toward something."

She took a third drag, then added, "Does this make any sense?"

"Not really," I said.

"You little shit," Mom said. "Go to bed and get some sleep, and if you need your radio to help you, then turn it on and keep it on. No one will say a word."

She was softening me up. I could tell she and my dad were about to ship me off — most likely to spend a week or two at my aunt and uncle's dairy farm, where I'd be assigned a bed and some menial chores. I'd do them and try not to get in anyone's way, and eventually, someone would return to reclaim me, and if I was lucky, we'd swing by Six Flags on the way home.

—

The next morning, I met Lynn at her house and told her everything — the story of my uncle's drowning, and how it seems to have ruined my dad's relationship with his dad, and the pond and the pine tree and Grandpa calling my dad a dumbass. I didn't tell her about "You gotta kill somebody?"

Lynn listened, digested it, then said, "Sounds to me like they blamed your dad long before anything in that river happened."

I hadn't thought about that, but once I did, it became obvious. Hell, I didn't give my dad the benefit of the doubt, either. He didn't deserve it, at least not in my opinion. Did he try to save his brother? I don't know. Maybe he did but didn't try hard enough.

Maybe that was why he drank all the time. Maybe he drank all the time to blunt the memory of his one and only chance to save or die in the effort, which is a little like kill or be killed.

That was as much as I could deduce, Lynn took it one step farther. She said she thought my dad needed to see a shrink.

"He needs to find a way to channel his anger and let it work for him and not against him," she said.

I could tell from Lynn's voice that she felt sympathy for my dad, but I couldn't bring myself to feel sorry for him because he'd had more than a few opportunities to channel his anger and let it work for him. In short, he made his own couch and slept on it.

He could've learned to read and write. He could've risen above his circumstances. He could've landed a job that required him to wear a suit and tie and carry a briefcase. He could've been driving a new Oldsmobile every year because he wasn't stupid or lazy. He was just scared, I guess.

Even if he couldn't have pulled it off, he could've faked it. He didn't have to give up. Lynn's father didn't give up. He channeled his anger and made it work for him. Why couldn't my dad?

—

Now and then, Lynn would invite me over, and I'd sit at the table and listen as Mr. Mayfield asked his daughters questions like, "Lynn, how is that science project coming along?"

When Lynn answered, "Not bad," he'd say, "Is there a problem?"

When she said she couldn't say, he'd tell her she needed to learn how to ask for help. It wasn't a sign of weakness. It was a sign of strength, and Lynn would say, "I've never thought about it that way."

Then, he'd ask her to define "galvanize" and use it in a sentence, and she would.

"The strike at the steel mill galvanized the workers' resolve," she'd answer, then she'd spell it correctly, so Mr. Mayfield would move on to Karen.

"Karen, have you thought a little more about college? You need a plan, and it's going to be here before you know it."

Karen would say something like, "Top of my list, Dad," so he'd move on to Gina because he knew it was at the top of her list.

"Gina, my love, what did you learn today that interested you?"

And Gina would say, "Oh, nothing in particular," so, he'd reply, "Well, were you paying attention? I find it hard to believe that you could spend seven hours at school with all the fine teachers you have and not come away with at least one interesting observation."

So, she'd have to come up with an answer on the spot, or he'd have been disappointed, and disappointment was never a good thing in the Mayfield family. Disappointment in their family was what scarlet fever was in mine.

To put it another way: The Mayfields lost earrings. We lost ears.

If this scene at the Mayfield dinner table was staged for my benefit, someone deserved an Academy Award. It all seemed so well-intentioned, like it was genuine, like everyone actually cared.

It sort of made me care, too. Not long after that, I threw a rock about the size of a marble at two dogs going after each other — fighting, that is — and I missed, and the rock pinged off the Mayfield's master bathroom window.

There were no witnesses, but I decided to go over and explain to him what had happened and see if I could work out a deal to get it repaired or replaced.

I knocked on the door, and Mrs. Mayfield answered and gave me the same look she always did. I asked her if I could talk to her husband, and she said, "Wait here. I'll get him."

She didn't say "Good morning," or invite me in or offer me a slice of toast. Basically, what she said was, "Wait on the porch, and don't touch anything." Then, she shut the door and latched it.

A few minutes later, Mr. Mayfield unlatched it and stepped out and asked, "You don't happen to know anything about my broken window, do you?"

"As a matter of fact," I said. "I do."

I explained what had happened and offered my ideas for getting it replaced without costing him a dime. I would work it off. I would borrow money from a loan shark. Knock off a grocery store. Mug an old woman. Steal from my mother. Sell my younger brother into white slavery. Whatever it took, I was willing to do it.

"I appreciate your honesty, but let's cross that bridge when we get to it," he replied. "Next time, Ed, grab a water hose and spray them."

Then, he reached into his pocket and pulled out the rock.

"I guess I won't need this as evidence in your trial," he said, then smiled. "I'll talk to your father. We'll figure something out."

I thanked him and apologized and returned home, waiting on my dad to chew my ass out, but it never happened.

Mr. Mayfield never talked to my father or my mother. He talked to some fellow named Elton, who came out and replaced the glass and painted the mullions and the frame for a couple of dollars, and that was the last anyone heard of it.

A month or so later, Mr. Mayfield came home early and found me draped all over his couch. He shoved my leg off his coffee table and told me he was cleaning up his yard that weekend.

"I could use a hand," he said. "Come over Saturday about 9. Bring a pair of gloves. I'll buy your lunch."

So, I did, and we had a good time. It almost made me want to go home and clean up my own yard.

—

Like almost all of the other dads, Mr. Mayfield had been in the war. He lied about his age and enlisted at 17 because he thought it might be safer than staying home, which was ironic since he ended up in General George S. Patton's Third Army.

Toward the end of the war, he helped liberate the Nazi concentration camp at Ohrdruf, and personally saw the mass graves, the pits, and trenches. The sight and the smell knocked him to his knees. After Patton had ordered the entire local population to march through the camp and see it for themselves, he was one of the soldiers who rounded up stragglers and forced them at gunpoint to get moving. He came close to shooting one or two Hitler die-hards who insisted the Jews both deserved it and did it to themselves.

Mr. Mayfield returned home with a lot of rage, and it took him years to corral it, but once he did, he flipped a full 180. Black to White. Dark to Light.

Still, something told me he could snap, and all that volcanic rage he thought he'd put a lid on could bubble up and explode and take the side of a mountain out.

It's funny. I was never afraid of my dad because I couldn't imagine him fighting. Like with his fists. Like running the risk of having a bloody nose This was my dad's idea of a combat: Come home. Open a beer. Saunter out to the garage. Fiddle with the car. Come back in. Leave an oily handprint on the kitchen countertop.

That's how he fought.

He'd occasionally go through the motions of being a father. At dinner, he might say to me, "What's this I hear about you getting a B in math? You forgot how to count?"

So, I'd push my English peas around my plate and line them up and start counting them, "One. Two. Three. Four. Two times 3 Three times 4."

My mom would intervene.

"That's enough from you, young man," she'd snap. "Now, eat them."

My dad would shoot me a dirty look, and then he'd tramp back out to the garage, and an hour later, we'd find another oily handprint on the newly cleaned kitchen countertop.

And I thought about my dad, "Too feckless to fight. Too inept to save."

I knew that wasn't fair, but screw it. It was the best I could do. It all reminded me how much I would've enjoyed having Mr. Mayfield as a father for one day. Just one.

I would've enjoyed having a father who asked me to define a word and to use it correctly in a sentence. Maybe if I'd had a father like that for one day — just one— I would've had a fighting chance.

CHAPTER 4

Scars and nubs

The guy working the cash register at the puny service station just outside of Winnsboro sat up as best he could in his wheelchair, craned his neck and tried to focus his left eye on my dad's face.

I assumed the guy was blind in his right eye because it was all milky. He looked like he'd stepped on a landmine. Chunks of him either weren't there or were in the wrong place. He wore a long-sleeved denim shirt to hide the scars. His name was Mack.

My dad stepped around the counter, rubbed Mack's shoulder, and asked, "How you doin'? Life still a bowl of cherries?"

"Maraschinos," he replied. "We are blessed."

I thought Mack was kidding, but he wasn't. It was as if he hadn't noticed his predicament, as in wheelchair, half-blind, crooked neck, missing fingers, scars, Winnsboro.

But when Mack said, "We are blessed," he meant it. He knew guys who had it a lot worse.

Mack punched a cash register key with his right wrist, then raked out the $4.53 he needed to pay for the piddly assortment of dairy products my dad drove 16 miles out of his way to deliver. It was his smallest account by a long shot, and it cost him as much in gas as he earned by serving it, but he wouldn't give it up.

When I asked later what had happened to Mack, my dad said, "He slipped on a banana peel," which meant, "Shut up and mind your own business."

I didn't see any harm in asking, but, of course, my father did. If a complete stranger had asked him the same question, he would've told him everything. But answering my question would've violated some Stone Age clan prohibition.

In other words, he saw no harm in being asked. He saw considerable harm in my asking.

I tried not to take it personally, even though it was, so I shut up and minded my own business.

As for Mack, what can I tell you? Maybe he thought he was blessed because my dad always dropped off a box of ice cream sandwiches. No charge.

Again, if I'd asked my dad for one ice cream sandwich, he would've told me to suck tree bark, but he gave Mack a whole box of them. No charge. My dad loved doing things for people who didn't know him and never would. It made him feel blessed, I guess.

Didn't matter. His business with Mack was his business, not mine, and if he didn't want to explain it to me, fine. I brought along a book.

At the same time, my dad's business with Mack was considered "Company Business," and when one of my dad's bosses — a clipboard-carrying, flat-topped junior executive in his late-20s — mentioned something about an account near Winnsboro, my dad responded "unprofessionally," to put it lightly.

The junior exec said, "Mr. Dodson, I would remind you that the hour it takes you to service that account costs the company. It may be your time, but it is company money. Your time on company time is company money."

My dad did not need to be lectured about time and money. He knew all he wanted to know about time and money because he and the other drivers were surrounded by posters that proclaimed crap like "Time is Money" and "Every Minute Matters" and "Safety Is Like a Lock. You Are the Key."

So, my dad's clipboard-carrying, peach-fuzz boss was well within his rights to remind my dad that servicing Mack's one-pump filling station placed the entire corporation at grave risk.

"This is not about you, Mr. Dodson," the junior exec said. "It's bigger than you."

That was probably true, but all my dad heard was one more

person in his life telling him to zip it, so he asked his young exec, "Do you mind if I borrow that clipboard for a second?"

And when the young executive handed it to him, my dad cracked it in half over his right knee, then handed it back and said, "I don't know what your job is, Sonny, but it damn sure ain't telling me how to do my job."

That would have gotten anyone else fired on the spot because the junior executive carrying the clipboard was Ralph Benedict Pemberton, the grandson of Ralph Carlisle Pemberton, the company's founder and president, and the Pembertons did not appreciate nor tolerate high school dropouts showing them up in front of other snickering high school dropouts, so my dad came within a spider's fang of being fired.

He wasn't fired because he could do his job as well or better half-looped than two men could sober, and Ralph Carlisle Pemberton knew it and advised his grandson to stand down.

The fact is, my dad liked the people he worked with if not for, and — with a few exceptions — they liked him. The two or three times I accompanied him on his route, we left our house around 5 and stopped for coffee and breakfast 10 minutes later at Bo's Diner, where everyone knew him.

The second he sauntered in, a waitress would call out, "Mornin', Sketch," and some other guy with his name stitched on his shirt pocket would announce, "The party has arrived!"

People would scoot right or left to make room for him at the counter. He never ate at a table. He wanted to sit at the counter so he could watch the waitresses sashay back and forth, and he wanted to sit among burly guys with hairy arms and beer bellies and gutter-mouths and just enough education to comprehend the sports headlines.

They'd all served in the war, and not a one of them made it past corporal, and not because they were bad soldiers. It's just that they were misfits, dipshits and harelips. They were dartboards and ashtrays. Not a one of them went to college later because they couldn't spell "G.I. Bill" and thought "college" began with a "K."

They drank milk from the carton, took a leak off their front porches, poured Karo syrup on fried eggs and sopped it up with Texas toast. They were my dad's kind of people, and while I was sitting at the counter among them, one thing became abundantly clear to me — I was not.

I felt like my dad was embarrassed to be seen with me, as if I'd worn a pink poodle skirt, and it didn't take long for me to regret coming along when I could have as easily slept in, which I should have because once breakfast was over, and we hit the road, he started ragging on me.

He didn't like my book — "Exodus" by Leon Uris — especially after I told him what it was about.

"Why you want to read about Jews?"

"I didn't want to read about Jews," I told him. "I just want to read. It beats looking at stray dogs and Confederate flags."

I knew I was yanking his chain, but he started it.

"Whaddya got against dogs?" he asked.

"Nothing," I said. "What do you have against Jews?"

"You think you're something, don't you? You lazy little shit. If you weren't such a smart ass, you might just turn into something one of these days."

To which I almost replied, "Like what? A telephone pole?"

That would've been a big mistake because six or seven months earlier, my dad took a curve too fast, and his company truck skidded off an oil-top road, bounced through a ditch and clipped a telephone pole.

My dad told his boss — the junior exec, no doubt — the brakes had locked, but I heard he was looped. He'd been drinking at Oh-El's, a funky bar that was his final stop every Tuesday and Thursday.

Because the company refused to hire Black drivers, they needed one white guy who wasn't afraid to walk in the front door of Oh-El's with a crate or two of milk and ice cream sandwiches, and my dad was that guy because he loved doing things for people — even Black folks — who either didn't or just barely knew him.

The owner of the club was O. L. Green, who was 66 years old, a long-time deacon of the Living Gospel Baptist Church and the father of 13 children by three wives.

O.L. had grown up near Hawkins, Texas, the son of a tenant farmer, so he picked his share of cotton before deciding he'd had enough of that. He drove a truck in France during World War I and had the time of his life, not that he had much to compare it to. Scotch-taped to Oh-El's bar mirror was a photograph of him with a French prostitute, wearing a long string of fake white pearls, a white boa and nothing else. She was white, too.

It was ballsy to the point of being suicidal. Black men in the South had been lynched for less.

My dad loved it. It almost made him wish he'd been shipped overseas where whores were cheap and plentiful during wartime, or so he'd heard.

Anyway, the rumor was my dad knocked back six or eight beers at Oh-El's before hopping in his truck and driving it through a ditch and sideswiping the telephone pole. He got away with it because there were no cops around, and he'd sobered up by the time anyone came out to assess the damage. By then, my dad had invented a story that couldn't be proven untrue.

My dad wasn't educated, but he wasn't dumb, and I didn't smart off to him because there was nothing in it for me. I would've been stuck for an hour or two in the cab of a truck with him, and it would've been misery. Nothing I said or did would've been right or good enough, so I worked my tail off.

I hopped in and out as fast as I could. I double-counted everything. I didn't ask for anything. I wanted to get the day over with as painlessly as possible and put it behind me. I didn't want to give him a reason to do something we'd both regret.

We'd both already made that mistake. A year earlier, I smarted off, and he shoved me into a dining room chair. The caster wheels snagged on a rug, and I ended up sprawled on the floor.

He was saying something about the yard needing to be mowed or the leaves raked, and I said something like, "Go in there and sit down. These boys and I will do it."

I was mocking him to his face.

"You're just a smart ass," he said, and I shot back, "It beats being a dumbass."

That's when he shoved me. I wasn't hurt, but he was mortified Mom would find out, so he offered me a hand, and I pushed it away.

I never said a word to anybody because I started it. I knew he'd been called a dumbass by his own father, and he damn sure wasn't about to put up with that crap from me.

I guess I started it because he called "a lazy little shit." That was a cheap shot. Call me what you like, but I wasn't lazy. I did everything Mom didn't or couldn't. If she had something she needed done right, she asked me. She didn't ask my brothers, and she didn't ask my dad.

I did light years more work around the house than he did.

I never saw him make a bed, scrub a tub or fold a towel. He washed dishes once a month. For a guy who fiddle-farted around in the garage all the time, he never once thought to sweep it.

So, this "lazy little shit" stuff didn't fly. If he wanted to be a prick to me, I could handle it. I had better things to worry about than why he and I were as near and dear to each other as LBJ and Ho Chi Minh.

I later told Lynn that very same thing.

"You can be a lot like your dad," she replied.

That was not what I expected or wanted to hear, but she was right. I did little or nothing for my brothers, but I went out of my way to be nice to complete noogies like Woody Beshel, the weirdest kid at school.

For some reason, I felt obligated to make his life better, so when I passed him in the hallways or bumped into him in the cafeteria, I'd say hello and ask him how he was doing. It made his day, so why not? It was no skin off my nose.

At the same time, I rarely felt the need to help my brothers. It took an act of Congress to get me to assist either of them with their homework, and that set Mom off. She believed in taking care of your own, and that began with taking care of yourself.

She was an OB nurse, which meant she helped deliver babies. She might oodle doodle over a newborn now and then, but she saw no reason to go out of her way for a knocked-up girl who'd hopped in the backseat with some cousin's old buddy who was in town for just the weekend. If that girl nine months later was having her plumbing rearranged while trying to push out a 10-pound boy, well the best Mom had to offer was a little sage advice: think first before you wiggle out of your drawers.

She was hard because she had to be, and she believed these girls had better get hard, too, or they'd be back in 10 or 11 months, rearranging their plumbing again.

My dad, on the other hand, wasn't hard. If he'd attended school with me, he'd have been nice to Woody, too. Here's how I came to understand that: After we'd dropped off the milk and the ice cream sandwiches at Mack's in Winnsboro, he turned to me and said, "And you think you got problems."

That was as profound a conversation as we would ever have.

We left Woody's and then serviced a big supermarket on our way back to Marshall. We dropped off 15 cases of milk, along with all sorts of everything else, and he never broke a sweat, so over the course of about an hour, I saw how generous and efficient my dad could be. I saw why some people thought he was the greatest guy in the world. Those same people would slap me on the back and inform me how lucky I was to have an old man like him.

It was so painful to have to stand there and grin and listen to that crap. Ten minutes later, we'd be back on the road, and he'd be calling me worthless, and then an hour later, he'd be home, tinkering and whistling in the garage because he'd failed to do the one and only thing Mom asked him to do.

Pick up a pound of this at the store. Move this to over there. Fix that. Patch and paint that. Sweep that damn garage.

He couldn't or wouldn't do it, and that frustrated Mom to no end. Maybe it was intentional, part of his great struggle for freedom. Maybe the last thing he wanted was for me and my brothers to see them sitting on a park bench, eating ice cream, laughing, talking softly, holding hands. It would have been nice to see that. I wish they had.

Oh well, shit in one hand and wish in the other and see which fills up first.

I doubt they ever got along. I bet if you had asked any of my aunts or uncles on either side, they'd have said Mom and my dad should've never met, much less married. Given that they met and married, Mom should've dumped him an hour after the justice of the peace declared them husband and wife.

Given that she didn't, she should've dumped him before she got knocked up. Given that she got knocked up, she should've known better than to get knocked up again.

In other words, Mom, you should have followed your own advice about wiggling out of drawers.

I knew they weren't happy, but I thought that just came with the territory. Married people weren't supposed to be happy. Kids were supposed to be happy. It went without saying, so I didn't. My job was to handle my happiness, not worry about theirs.

Besides, handling my happiness was a full-time job. For every reason I had to be happy, I found a dozen reasons to be unhappy. Unlike Lynn, I never bothered to look at it from all sides. I was too blind and too selfish and too lazy and all that to appreciate how good I had it. I could've been Woody and any one of a dozen or more kids at school who had it far worse than I did.

Hell, we could have been the family that lived in an empty crude oil storage tank at the end of a cul-de-sac right off Highway 44. Their home was an empty oil tank. Welders cut doors and windows into the sides of the tank, and someone had sandblasted the insides enough to eliminate most of the fumes, and then they framed it out.

One of the kids in my grade lived in one of these tank-houses. Her name was Candy Something, and there's never been a girl more inappropriately named. If she'd have been a candy, she'd have been one of those orange circus peanuts everybody's grandparents crammed into jars.

She was fat and gooey. Her eyes were like pomegranate seeds sunk into sockets that were smothered by layers of puffy skin.

If that wasn't bad enough, she sweated like a quarter-horse. Perspiration poured down her face and pooled in the folds of her neck, so she often looked like she'd just pulled her head out of a water bucket.

Even those who felt sorry for her flinched when she walked by because she reeked of perspiration, dirty clothes and petroleum fumes. She could have made a freight train take a dirt road, and that invited ridicule and scorn.

Snot-rags like Walt McFarlin laughed at her when she tried to squeeze herself into a desk. Even teachers ridiculed her. Our P.E. teacher, Mr. Densmore, once ordered her to stay off the swings until she lost some weight.

He didn't say it nicely either. He said it right in front of everyone and thought he was scoring Brownie points for doing it, like we were supposed to be impressed. Boy, that pissed me off, and it pissed other people off, too.

I should have walked over and took her hand and told her it was OK, to go ahead and cry because it was worse to bottle it up inside. I wish I'd told her to hang on. I wish I'd told her a lie that would've made her feel better, like, "God has special plans for you, so have faith. Better days are ahead."

Of course, I didn't because I didn't believe it. Her fate was already sealed. She was poor and fat, and she was fated to be poorer and fatter. She was born to play an off-suit 2-5 hand against pocket aces forever.

No one could change that, but that didn't mean we had to make her life more miserable, and it didn't mean we couldn't make it just a little bit less miserable, so, during lunch the next day, I wedged a couple of 3-inch nails between Mr. Densmore's two back tires and the pavement.

After school, I watched him pull out, and I could hear the nails sink into his back tires, and then I watched him hop out and stare at the tires and look all around, and I heard him take the Lord's name in vain about eight times, and I thought, "That's what you get for picking on the poor fat girl who lives in an oil storage tank."

Was I wrong to do this? I don't care. I was wrong not to jam nails in all four tires. He deserved worse. I just hope Candy heard about it. I hope it made her smile, even if smiling threatened to reveal her corn-like teeth, which would have attracted snot-rags like Walt McFarlin, and it'd all start over again.

The next morning, she'd wake up just as fat, poor, sweaty, and dumb as she was when she went to bed, assuming she had a bed. But that wasn't the point. Here's the point: Justice was possible. All Candy had ever known was injustice, and I figured, if I didn't provide her this one sliver of justice and fairness, who would?

Why was this important to me? Because I'd been on Candy's end of the rope, too. I'd been reminded, over and over, that life wasn't fair, and there's was nothing anyone could do about it, so shut up and suck it.

That was why I couldn't get a new bike, or a new pair of penny loafers, or go to Six Flags, or enjoy a chocolate milk shake on a hot day.

Well, I wasn't convinced that life was unfair. Life was fair for some people all the time. They had everything while some had nothing, so this isn't a question of "Life isn't fair."

It would have been if someone had worked a little bit harder to make it fair. Maybe if they had, Mack would've had all his fingers and at least one good eye.

If life had been fair, Mom would've married a man who wanted to be married, and I would've had a father who wanted to be a father.

If life had been fair, Candy would have smelled like cinnamon or rose petals instead of petroleum. Sorry about going on about that. Shit like this still pisses me off.

—

We lived on the edge of what used to be a small town that a

bigger town swallowed whole. Our house was on the edge of our neighborhood, so if we looked out the front door, we saw the open field and a stand of pine trees in the distance.

A creek that never dried up emerged from the woods and zigzagged through the field. It was almost always full of crawdads, especially after a good rain, so we'd run across the open field with shovels and kitchen serving spoons and dam up the creek. The water would build behind it, and then we'd pretend to blow it up and watch the water pour through, like in one of those Japanese horror films where a moth mutates into a blimp-size monster that attacks a hydro-electric dam that was built upstream from the only Japanese city that wasn't bombed to bits by Jimmy Doolittle.

In these movies, an elderly Japanese professor would call a scientist and tell him, "Tell the general to emprcy the Atomic Mega-Way gun." The scientist would then tell a general to emproy it, and he would. However, the Atomic Mega-Way gun would jam because it was cheap crap made in Japan, which allowed the giant moth would destroy the dam, and a wall of water would wash the city into the Sea of Japan, and we would scream at our TV sets, "Take that, you crummy bastards."

That was because we actually hated the Germans and the Japanese, and not in some vague, abstract way. We hated each and every one of them, personally. We watched "Combat" on TV and all the World War II films starring John Wayne. We built forts and camps and treehouses, and dug tunnels and pretended it was D-Day or the Battle of the Bulge.

We ran on our tiptoes from foxhole to foxhole, zigging and zagging, dodging German hand grenades, leaping over saplings and shrubs and thorn bushes. All day long, we ran up and down the red clay paths and narrow ravines. We could run forever because our lungs were bigger than duffle bags. It was great.

The worst thing imaginable was being grounded, to be locked indoors while our and their friends ran wild outside. It was hell. And why'd we get grounded? For nothing. Maybe a broken a vase or window. Or we didn't make our beds, or we got a C+ in math, or we got a B- for discipline, or we were playing horse in the living room and someone fell and cracked the coffee table in half, so our parents grounded us.

It was so wrong. Sure. Punish us. Send us to bed without supper. Force us to eat cauliflower or eggplant or egg salad sandwiches or Chop Suey out of a can. Make us write 500 words on why we needed to learn how to follow simple instructions and stop running around like a bunch of wild Indians. Those were my parents' words. Not mine.

But still, do anything, but don't ground us. For boys, there was nothing worse. I can't speak for girls. Of course, I don't remember a girl ever being grounded. Lynn was never grounded. The worst thing she ever did was disappointing her father, but he didn't ground her. He gave her a look of disapproval. That's all.

Over and done with. And what if he had grounded her. It wouldn't have been all that bad. She'd have stayed home and read and written in her diary and found some meaning in the whole damn thing, something she'd share with me while we were sitting out on the curb.

By the time her punishment had ended, she'd know 25 new vocabulary words and how to use them, and she'd know how to make and bake an Italian cream cake.

That wasn't how it worked in my house. I'd get grounded for the weirdest reasons. When I was 14, I was chasing Dickie Askew, cut through a concrete carport, and hit a slick spot. Both feet flew out from under me, and I slid, right knee first, into a brick wall.

My mom carted me to the doctor, and he sewed me up and told me, "Young man, stay off that knee until those stitches come out."

When we got home, Mom plopped me in a chair in front of the television set and said, "You heard him. Until those stitches come out, you sit right here."

Then, she essentially said the same thing about four other ways until I said, "OK, Mom. I'm not deaf."

She gave me a dirty look, which said, "I know I'm talking just to hear the sound of my own voice, but when you disobey me and do something stupid, and I know you will, there's going to be hell to pay."

Sure enough, eight days later, I snuck out to watch the guys play baseball, and they needed someone to pitch for both the teams, so they practically begged me.

Now, did I ever to think someone might hit a line drive that would splatter my stitches? Of course not. I was thinking, "Watch this next pitch. You won't believe it."

I tried to hide the mess and avoid Mom that night, but she insisted on seeing how it was doing, so I told her what had happened.

"It's no big deal," I assured her. "You can barely tell the difference."

"Show me," she demanded.

"It's fine," I pleaded.

"Sit your ass down right now, and I mean it."

She lifted the adhesive tape and almost fainted when she saw the carnage.

She called my younger brother into the room.

"Did you know about this?" she asked him.

"Yes, ma'am," he said.

"Grounded. Two days," she said.

"He told me not to tell," my brother said, then added, "Ricky knew, too."

Mom flicked her eyes up at him and said, "I hate a tattle-tell. Three days. Now, get a bottle of alcohol from my bathroom. It's under the sink."

She looked at my knee, poked and squeezed the flaps of skin a couple of times, just to make sure it hurt, then she grabbed the bottle of alcohol and said, "You may feel some discomfort."

Did it ever. I yelled and jerked, and she smiled. Maybe next time you'll think first before you go off and do something stupid after I told you and told you and told you to stay off that knee until the stitches came out."

She finished changing the bandage and taped it so tightly I

could barely move.

"Not a peep," she said. "You reap what you sow."

She poked it one last time and added, "This is going to leave a nasty scar. Good."

She grounded me for a full week but never said a word about it to my dad. He was too busy wasting company money by giving away free ice cream sandwiches to blind cripples running pissant gas stations a mile north of nowhere.

—

One more thing: I was standing in front of Mack's counter that day, and he held his right hand out and asked me to take it, and so I did, and I could feel the nubs and the scars where his fingers and a part of his hand once had been.

He squeezed, so I squeezed, and then he squeezed harder, so I squeezed as hard as I could, and then he released my hand, and I pulled it away, rubbed it, shoved it into my pocket, and wondered what that was about.

"You have a strong grip," he told me. "I'm surprised. I have been led to believe differently. Use your strength. Do not fear it, but do not abuse it. It's not enough to be muscular. You must be strong."

He then quoted a Bible verse:

> **Wealth and honor come from you; you are the ruler of all things. In your hands are strength and power to exalt and give strength to all.**

Do you understand that passage?" he asked.

"No, Sir. I don't," I said.

"No big deal. We'll talk about it another time."

I nodded and was just about to head out to the truck when he piped up one last time.

"I hear you like those Beatles. Is that right?"

"Yes sir, I do," I said, expecting him to say something about their hair or worst song.

"My nieces are crazy about them. They scream when they're on the TV. It reminds me of Elvis Presley. You know Elvis, right?"

I said I did.

"Do you like him?"

"Not that much. I don't really know him."

"Perhaps one day you will. I have come to appreciate some of his music. Not all. I like his music more than I like him. I, myself, am more of a Frank Sinatra fan. You probably don't know Sinatra, do you."

"Of course, I do," I said. "My mom's a huge fan. Sinatra. Nat King Cole. Tony Bennett. Bobby Darin. Mills Brothers. Rosemary Clooney. All those old singers."

"Well, they're not that old. And your mother has excellent taste in music."

Before I could answer, my dad returned with a box of ice cream sandwiches. "Compliments of the company."

He turned to me and said, "Get back in the truck."

As I was walking out the door, Mack said, "Young man. I want you to know something. I kind of like those Beatles, myself."

That made my day. About an hour later, my dad and I were bouncing in the cab of the truck as we headed back toward Marshall, and I was about to doze off when I realized what I should've said to Mack when he said my mom had excellent taste in music. I should've said, "If only she had excellent taste in men."

But I suspect Mack knew that. Something tells me he wasn't nearly as blind as he let on.

CHAPTER 5
Kin folk

Two days later, we dropped everything to go to my dad's uncle's funeral. His name was Tim, and I'd never heard of him nor seen a picture of him, which made me wonder why it was so necessary for us to drive 180 miles to attend the funeral of someone no one knew when we could've just as easily driven to Six Flags or Galveston.

Of course, I didn't ask that question. My dad rarely entertained why or how questions, so I knew better than to lean over the front seat and ask "Why are we going?" so I asked, "Who died?"

"You're going to if you don't sit back and shut up," he snapped.

Mom bit her lip, then said, "He's your father's uncle. Your grandfather's brother."

"Do we know him?" I asked.

"No, but he was family," Mom said.

"Why haven't we met him?" I asked, and my dad said, "Because he had no interest in meeting you, and I can't blame him."

Mom rolled her eyes and said, "Jesus, Sketch. Can't you just answer his question?"

Then, she added, quietly, "It's not like he asked you the name of the last trailer trash waitress you screwed."

She didn't look at him, and he didn't look at her. They just sat there, staring straight ahead, until Mom said, "There was a misunderstanding, an argument, a long time ago."

"What over?"

"Over money," Mom said.

"Over money and a woman," my dad added.

"Over Grandma?" I asked.

"No," my dad snorted. "I said, 'A woman.'"

I knew better than to sniff that trail.

"It was a long time ago, and it's complicated," Mom said. "We're going to this funeral, and when it's over, you and I and your brothers are going to climb back into this car, and we are going to drive home, and there's not going to be any antics or arguments. Am I right, Sketch?"

My dad shrugged and bowed up, but that was all, so we drove on, and an hour later we pulled off a narrow county road onto a one-lane red dirt road that see-sawed for a mile or so up to my grandparents' house at the crest of the hill. We were the last of the clan to arrive. My other aunts and uncles and their kids were already there, so I suspected this Uncle Tim must have been a big shot, but I was wrong. He wasn't big. He was huge. Colossal.

Well, at least until he came down with liver cancer, and cancer doesn't care how rich you are, and you can fight it all you want to, but it'll get you if it wants you, so Tim died in his own bedroom at his River Oaks mansion, surrounded by his big-shot friends and his family by way of his third wife, Jenna, who was, of course, younger, but not inappropriately so.

His second wife had been a gold-digger, but Jenna was not. She came from money and didn't need his.

Anyway, Tim was handsome, smart, funny, and rich, and she loved him. She was right there from the day he was diagnosed to the day he died, and when it became clear he was a goner, she helped him arrange his affairs, including two funerals. The first was held on a Friday afternoon in a giant Baptist church that many of the oil and gas tycoons and heart surgeons and fancy-pants lawyers attended.

Tim knew them all. He played golf and bridge and tennis with them, and both Houston daily newspapers regularly ran photographs of him raising money for this or donating money for that. It was not a big surprise the Baptist church was crammed with Chamber of Commerce types who were truly sorry to see their friend go too soon.

Of course, we were not invited to that service. We were invited to the second service, held in a squatty, whitewashed church way out in the sticks where Tim had been baptized by a traveling preacher in exchange for a can of lard. His parents couldn't scratch together the dollar-fifty the preacher normally charged.

Tim might have grown up poor as a stable boy, but he died as rich as a sultan. He was so rich, he could've held one funeral in Houston and the other in Buckingham Palace, but he chose to hold the other in the clapboard church near Bon Weir.

His closest relations were hand-delivered personal notes from Jenna requesting their presence at a service in his honor. It was accompanied by a copy of his obituary, just in case anyone had forgotten how colossal he was.

So, relatives three deep showed up, expecting dollar bills to flutter down from the rafters. It didn't turn out that way. The service was Uncle Tim's last chance to flick his family the finger.

The church had no air conditioning, and it smelled of mold and Pine Sol and spider webs and dead doodle bugs. I suspected Tim not only knew it but made certain of it. He knew they'd squeeze and squirm and shove their big butts into those tiny pews, and it would be so hot and stuffy they'd damn near suffocate.

Tim didn't get rich by being nice or dumb or forgetful or forgiving. I'm sure he was looking down or up and watching his kin folk fan themselves furiously as the service droned on and on about how he was in heaven with Jesus, playing the back nine.

I suspected Tim knew his sister, Lydia, would wallow and wail and make a fool of herself because she always did. This time, she led a chorus of wailing that rose and fell and rose and fell as a young preacher just out of some Nazarene college in Turtleneck, Tennessee, went on and on about Jesus and salvation. At one point, he worked himself into such a lather that he screeched, "Brother Tim knew Jesus. Dew Yew?"

It was a line he'd borrowed from one of his college professors, and he literally spit it out. Dew Yew?

Mom almost laughed out loud.

She once told me, "Your dad's family would have been snake handlers if they could've afforded snakes."

Anyway, the young preacher didn't talk much about Tim, or how it was he ended up being rich while almost everyone else in his family remained poor, but there was a reason.

When Tim was 17, he ran off to join the Army, and he ended up fighting in the First World War, and he saw France and decided he'd had enough of farming, so after he was discharged, he took a job working in the oil fields with an Army buddy, and he realized there was an ocean of black gold right under his feet, so he and his Army buddy started their own oil drilling company, and they struck oil two or three times in Texas alone, which made them millionaires several times over.

Did he feel any compassion or generosity toward his poor, penniless fellow man? No. None. Not one iota. As for his poor, penniless fellow family members, he never gave, donated, loaned nor promised to leave anything to anyone because when he was down and out and needed a few bucks to get out of a jam, he went to his parents with his hat in his hand and asked for a small advance, and they turned him down, so he went to an uncle with the same request, and he turned him down, too.

And then, he went to an older brother, who said he would chip in a dollar or two but never did. They all had the same excuse. "Sorry, Tim. We don't have two nickels to rub together. We'd help if we could, but we can barely afford to feed the dogs."

So, Tim wrote them all off. Every damn one, and five years later, he was a multi-millionaire, and they were still searching for two nickels to rub together. A few later came to him with their hats in their hands, and Tim told them in no uncertain terms what they could do with their hats and their dogs.

―

As weird as my dad's family was, I loved visiting them at the old 100-acre farm about two miles outside Rogansboro, which is 10 miles outside Kirbyville, which is 50 or 60 miles north of Beaumont, which is 90 miles north of Houston.

In other words, Rogansboro was in the middle of nowhere, and my grandpa lived outside Rogansboro. It might have been a difficult place for a corn and sugar cane farmer to try to eek a living out of, but it was a boy's paradise.

My grandpa also raised hogs and sows and piglets. He kept a few milk cows and a horse, and a mess of feral cats and six or eight hounds, which he locked up most of the time because they tended to bite.

The hay barn had a loft, and there was a dense stand of pine trees, two big ponds, a railroad bridge that crossed a wide creek, and more cousins than cats, so we built forts in the woods, played hide 'n' seek, and it was great until someone gashed a knee or stepped on a nail or fell out of a tree.

I loved being there, especially in the winter. I loved the smell of the big fireplace in the front room. I loved the smell of liniment in my grandparents' bedroom. I loved the sounds the night produced, the moans and groans of Mother Nature passing gas.

As for my uncle's funeral, I didn't mind going. I stood outside with my cousins, chunking rocks at trees and squirrels, and listening to all the bizarre commotion inside. The young preacher would shout something that had nothing to do with Tim and everything to do with his wallet, and Aunt Lydia would wail.

It was all stupid and shameless. "Sounds like they're gutting hogs in there," cousin Henry said.

"A hog doesn't make that much noise," cousin Luke answered. "I think they might have smuggled in a water buffalo."

Luke was about halfway in age between me and Henry, and he was a musician, and his hair fell at least two inches over his ears. He attended a big school where boys could grow their hair to their knees if they wanted to. I went to a small school where boys got shipped home if their hair even brushed their shirt collars.

Most of my cousins lived in small towns and attended backwater schools where boys got paddled if they got caught wearing bell-bottom trousers.

Why anyone cared about hair or bell-bottoms, I'll never know. Take my grandpa. Earlier in the day, he told Luke, "You need to cut that hair, boy. You're starting to look like a Beaumont fairy."

I loved my grandpa, but he was out of line. Even my dad thought he'd gone too far.

"I don't see how that boy's hair is any of your business, old man," my dad said, just loud enough for his old man to hear.

Of course, if I'd wanted to grow my hair long, you can bet the farm he'd have made it his business. I can picture me and my dad, sitting at the counter at Bo's Diner. His burly buddies would swing by to say hi, and my dad would reply, "Good morning, boys. I want you to meet my son. He looks like a Beaumont fairy, don't he?"

Well, anyway, Luke got in the last word, and he didn't bother to whisper it. He spoke right up and said to my grandpa's face.

"How do you know what a Beaumont fairy looks like?"

Grandpa snarled, then tromped into the front room and plopped in front of the fire and looked at it and wondered when kids like Luke started smarting off to their elders. He probably blamed the Beatles.

—

Anyway, back to the funeral. It ended, and the adults staggered out, all red and puffy, and everyone loaded up and lined up and followed the hearse to the New Zion Cemetery for more hysterics.

Though my dad promised we'd head home as soon as the funeral was over, he talked Mom into swinging back by the old house so he could grab a bite and say his proper goodbyes.

Mom had already planned to pick up hamburgers in Jasper on the way home, and he knew it, so he threw a fit and accused her of always cutting corners when it came to his side of the family, so she gave in with conditions.

"One hour," she said. "In one hour, I'm getting back in the car, and I'm heading north, whether you're in it or not."

He promised he would be, but in an hour, she couldn't find him, and he had the keys. He'd snuck off behind the barn with his brothers and brothers-in-law, like a bunch of 16-year-olds, and they were passing around a bottle of Ancient Age and telling dirty jokes and trying to pop each other in the nuts.

Mom was searching for my dad when everyone heard shotguns

being fired. Uncle Ernie and Uncle Clarence had pulled matching Browning pump-action shotguns out of a car trunk and were shooting at an armadillo. My grandpa stormed out on the back porch and yelled, "Put them guns up. There are kids running around here."

"Too late. I just nicked one," Ernie shouted back, and they all giggled, then Ernie called out, "The guns are going back in the bag. Wanna join them?"

Ernie flipped the safety on and slid the shotgun back into its case, and everything would've been fine, but my grandmother bellowed in her country twang, "I done tole you boys a hunnerd times I don't allow no drinkin' in my house."

So, Clarence picked up where Ernie'd left off.

"We're not in the house."

That infuriated Grandpa.

"That's enough from you, Clarence," he said, and my dad repeated, "Yea, that's enough from you, Clarence," and Mom stepped out on the porch and said, "Sketch. Act your age for once," and my dad said, "Go read your damn book," and Grandpa called my dad and his brothers "a bunch of sorry sons of bitches," to which Ernie replied, "You married her."

Then, Grandpa slammed the screen door on his way back into the house, and my dad and his brothers stayed out there another 20 minutes, long enough to drain the Ancient Age.

To their credit, no one got into a fistfight. I mention that because, a year or two earlier, Uncle Jess, who was married to my Aunt Bridgett, took exception to Ernie making a joke about how every boy in the county could tell the difference between Aunt Bridgett's right and left boobs.

The radish-looking mole, apparently, was on the right one, about a quarter inch above the nipple.

Of course, I didn't witness this myself, but cousin Ronny did, and he told me all about it, so I was confident it was true. Ronny was more like a younger uncle than an older cousin. Every time I saw him, he offered me a cigarette and promised not to tell.

We stayed for dinner, and as much as I would have enjoyed a hamburger and a shake, I almost made myself sick on the fried chicken, green beans, mashed potatoes, collard greens, cornbread and banana pudding brought over by neighbors who seemed to vaporize out of the shadows. I'd never met any of them.

After everyone had finished eating, the womenfolk, as my grandpa called them, cleaned up. Everyone, that is, except Mom and my Aunt Shirley, who was Luke's mom. They stood outside and smoked and mocked their in-laws and bitched about their husbands and laughed at each other's spiteful take of the whole damn lot.

Aunt Shirley was the only person — man or woman — on my dad's side whom my mom liked, and the feeling was mutual. My dad's brothers and sisters thought Mom was a snob, and they thought Aunt Shirley was a fool for letting Luke to grow his hair way over his ears .

Shirley might have been a fool, but it had nothing to do with Luke. She was a fool for marrying into this family, and she knew it.

Mom was jealous of her, anyway. In addition to Luke, Shirley had two beautiful daughters who were polished and polite, and I will go to my grave believing my mom desperately wanted a daughter, but what did she get? Moron sons who seemed to delight in cracking windows and splitting coffee tables in half.

A short while later, we were on the road, and things were going better than I'd expected. Mom made fun of the screechy young preacher and mimicked his head-cold Tennessee twang.

"I need a Schlitz," she said to my dad. "Dew Yew?"

My dad laughed so hard he almost put us in a ditch. Scared us half to death and yet, we all enjoyed a good laugh. Usually, these long drives through the dense pine forests of Southeast Texas were dark and ominous. For some odd reason, this one wasn't.

CHAPTER 6

Fritters

By the time we pulled back into our driveway, and I had unpacked and jumped in and out of the bathtub, it was too late to swing by Lynn's, so I called, and she picked up immediately.

"Where've you been?" she asked.

"You would not believe it," I said.

"Try me," she said.

"A funeral. My dad's uncle."

"Was he Jewish?" she asked.

"No," I replied. "Why would you ask?"

"Jews bury their dead within 48 hours, or God sends them a plague or two," she said.

"How do you know that?"

"I know everything," she said.

True enough, I thought, but I decided to test it, anyway.

"Did you know my uncle was a Viking?" I said. "He died in an axe accident. Very unfortunate. The family wrapped him in aluminum foil, laid him in the cab of his pickup, then drove it off a cliff. After it exploded, we threw chickens at it and sang "Amazing Thor.' All 19 verses. Care to guess what kind of truck it was?"

"Easy," she said. "Fjord."

And I thought, "Damn. She does know everything."

That was about as silly as she got.

She told me she had a dental appointment the next morning.

"I'll swing by when I'm finished," she said. "I want to hear the real story of the Nordic funeral, and besides, we need to talk."

Sure, I assured her, but no sooner than I'd hung up, she called back.

"In the morning, you to stay home until I return from the dentist office. Don't go anywhere. Stay home."

"OK," I said. "Oh. Kay."

Right about then, Mom walked in. The hospital had called. They were short-staffed. Could she come in? They were willing to pay time-and-a-half. Though she hadn't slept six hours in two days, she couldn't turn it down. The money was too good.

"Don't stay up too late," she told me.

I promised I wouldn't and blew her a kiss and watched her trudge off. I returned to my bedroom and collapsed. No dreams. No midnight bowls of Raisin Bran. No 2 a.m. trips to the bathroom. I was dead to the world.

Around 7:45, I heard tires squealing and then a thud. It was Mom. She'd cut the corner too tightly and bounced off a curb. A minute later, the kitchen door slammed, so I figured I might as well roll out of bed and see if she'd brought home a box of Southern Maid donuts. Sure enough, she had.

I was about to break into them when she pulled a small white sack out of her purse,

"This," she said, "is for you."

It was an apple fritter.

"Biggest one they had. It's your reward."

"For what?"

She tried to force a smile.

"For putting up with all this," she said.

"All of what?" I asked.

"Don't play dumb with me. I know you know what's going on. I never dreamed I'd put my own child through the same…"

She hesitated and began to choke up.

"Through the same … stuff … I went through. I vowed if I ever had kids, I'd do better by them."

There had to be at least 20 acceptable responses.

Thanks. Sure. You're welcome. No problem. My pleasure. It's nothing. No worries. Forget about it. Try harder next time. Jesus still loves you. Define "better."

But I couldn't come up with one, so I sat there.

Mom reached for her Salems but then put them back.

"I'd better try to get some sleep," she said. "Take care of your brothers today, and ya'll eat every one of these donuts. Don't leave a one. You hear me?"

"No problem," I said.

"Is something bothering you?" she asked.

Again, I had several reasonable responses, the most obvious being, "Don't play dumb with me. Of course, something is bothering me. I'm bothered that the AC in your bedroom is out. I'm bothered that you worked last night because you need the money to put a down payment on a new one.

"It bugs me that my dad should've handled this but didn't. It bugs me that cabinet doors are crooked, that weeds are growing out of our gutters, that my dad is a joke, that my brothers need help, that I'm forced to have this conversation."

But I didn't say any of that. I said, "No, Mom. I'm just tired."

"Finish your fritter and go back to bed," Mom said, then patted me on my head and trudged down the hall to her room.

I sat at the kitchen table alone, tracing my fingers over the apple fritter's frosted sugar glaze before breaking off a piece. I wanted the sugar and the fried dough to melt and linger, so I forced myself to take one tiny bite at a time and let it sit in my mouth and dissolve.

It was my way of tapping the brakes on time. When you're aware of every second — you know, tick, tick, tick, tick, tick — time moves slow, and that's when you want to be doing something you want to do instead of something you have to do.

I wanted that apple fritter to last all day, but as I sat there, my mind started wandering. I thought about death, about Uncle Tim, about Uncle Eddie. I even thought about my own death. How long did I have? How would I go? Which way would I go?

Before I knew it, the apple fritter was gone, and I was talking myself out of eating one of my brother's donuts when Mom showed back up. She'd changed out of her nurse's uniform and into a pale green cotton robe that occasionally exposed a little more than I needed to see.

"Changed my mind," she said. "Let's talk. I know you know your father and I are having problems. Don't deny it. I know you do, and I suspect that's what bothering you."

I didn't deny it.

"Just so you'll know: Your father and I have to figure out what, if anything, we can do to fix these problems."

She didn't say "our marriage." She didn't mention divorce, but I knew the line in the sand had been drawn because she said, "Your father and I."

When things got rocky, it was "your father" instead of "your dad." Mom told me they needed some time alone.

"Things are going to be said. You and your brothers don't need to hear them. We need time and space to lay it all out and see if any of it is worth salvaging. Don't ask questions about it because I don't have answers. All I can do is promise you that I'm putting you and your brothers first, before anything else. Whatever decision I come to, it's because I believe it's best for you."

Then, she told me she'd arranged for me to spend a week or two, maybe three, with relatives. She didn't have to tell me which ones.

"Oh, crap," I thought.

"Are you OK with that?" Mom asked.

"Absolutely," I said.

I wasn't, of course, but I didn't dread it, either. I was being shipped to stay with her older sister, Martha, and her husband, Carl Schaper. They lived on a dairy farm about four hours away, and they had eight kids, half of whom had already grown up and moved off.

That left the farm chores to my cousins Dennis, Jeffrey, Lori and Faye. There was plenty of work to go around, so I'd be expected to do my share.

"You can make good money," Mom told me. "I told Carl you want to earn your keep. You do, don't you?"

That was her way of saying, "Sorry, kid. Done deal."

I wiped the sugar from my upper lip, shrugged and said, "Suits me. I love going up there. You know that. Always have."

Mom smiled and tried to run her fingers through my ratty hair, but I instinctively squirmed away.

"You're a funny boy," she said, then rose from the table, walked out the patio door, lit another Salem and stood there staring into the glare, her right arm crossed under her left, her left index and middle fingers cradling the Salem. She held it like it was a diamond needle. I'd seen that posture a million times.

She smoked it slowly. That was her way of tapping the brakes on time. Tick, tick, tick, tick, tick. Enjoying every puff. Damn, she loved those cigarettes.

Sure, she had better things to spend her money on, but, aside perhaps for an air conditioner, none of them brought her the same peace and pleasure as those Salems. She might have fretted over the price of a can of tomato soup or a gallon of gas, but she'd plop down four bucks for a carton of Salems without batting an eye.

That's how it was. Smoking was like everything else in our family. Something reeked. We could smell it. Sometimes, we could taste it, but no one dared talk about it. It would have confirmed the obvious, and we weren't hip to that.

So, I was still sitting at the table when Mom cracked open the patio door and said, "We're leaving Saturday."

—

Lynn showed up around 11.

"Don't you dare say a word," she warned. "Not a word."

"My God, what..."

"Not one word," she repeated, then asked, "How bad is it?"

"Compared to what," I said. "Snake bite?"

"Apparently, I'm allergic to the painkiller," she said. "I couldn't catch my breath and started to panic, so he gave me a pill to relax me. Before he was able to put me on oxygen, I fainted. When I woke up, I looked like this."

Her eyes were bloodshot, and her face was splotchy.

"Does it hurt?" I asked.

"No, but I'm woozy," she said. "I'm going to try to sleep it off, but first, I want to hear about this funeral."

I gave her the Cliff Notes version. Rich uncle. Left home. Never returned. Died. Didn't want to mix old family with new so he arranged two services. One in a fancy church in Houston. The other in a rickety church near a river. We were invited to the rickety one. After the service, my dad and his brothers got drunk. Mom got mad. I thought they were going to get into a fight but they didn't. They started laughing at each other's jokes, so it could have been worse.

"You do live a colorful life," Lynn said.

"Did I miss anything here?" I asked.

"You're kidding, right?" Lynn said.

I figured as much. Debby and Russell were off to rich-kid church camp in the Ozarks, where they hiked and swam and canoed back and forth across a crystal-clear lake. After dinner, they'd sit on the big porch of the big log cabin and watch the fireflies and listen to a bearded old geezer pick a beat-up guitar and sing a Burl Ives' song about lonely caterpillars and ugly bugs.

"Oh, and guess what?" Lynn asked. "Guess who else is going to that camp?"

"Dazzle me," I said.

"Walt McFarlin," she said. Her face might have been splotched and bloated, but her eyes flittered like fireflies.

—

After a 3-hour nap, Lynn reappeared, looking much better. I filled in the gaps about the funeral and the church and the wailing and then I mentioned, casually, "I'm pretty sure my parents are splitting up."

"That's a safe assumption," she said.

"It's that obvious?"

"The Berlin Wall is less obvious."

I told her my mom was shipping me off to work on my aunt and uncle's farm, and she listened and stared straight ahead, and I could tell this was upsetting to her, but there was nothing I could do. I didn't tell her I might be gone two weeks, maybe three.

"When do you leave?" Lynn asked.

"I don't know," I lied. "Sooner than later."

I don't know why I lied. Muscle memory, I guess.

"Are your brothers going with you?"

"I don't know."

"Looks like you've been sold to the highest bidder," Lynn said.

"I'd better get 40 acres and a mule out of it," I said, repeating a reference to sharecroppers I'd read in Mr. Hart's history class.

"I'm sorry, but I just cannot picture you milking cows and feeding chickens," Lynn said. "Don't stay any longer than you have to. You never know what might happen. Things happen."

When I arched an eyebrow, she stared at me, her face swollen and splotchy, but now in a different way. She got quiet, and I thought her pain pills might be wearing off, so I talked her into going inside and watching "Let's Make a Deal" on her family's new color TV set. She stretched out on the couch and fell asleep, and I flopped into her dad's leather rocker and dozed off, too.

I dreamed about Karen Wilkerson. We were in fifth or sixth grade, and we were out on the playground, and she was wearing a pink skirt with a white petticoat, and she kept tossing her skirt and her petticoat up and over her head, to show me her underwear. She did this over and over. I'd give anything to know what she was thinking.

Then, I dreamed Karen Wilkerson was shaking me.

Then, I woke up and realized it wasn't Karen Wilkerson or Karen Mayfield. It was Gina.

"You're snoring," she said. "I can't hear the TV."

"Where's Lynn?" I asked.

"She's in her bedroom," Gina said. "I think you need to go home."

PART TWO | CHAPTER 7
The farm

June 25, 1966

Kassel was a dusty, desolate and gritty little German-Catholic town full of people with impossible-to-spell names like Küchler and Buescher and Schlegel. It had one stop light, one drug store, one liquor store, one gas station, one automobile dealership, one drive-in, one cafe, one supermarket, one no-tell motel, and one funeral home.

There were two schools — the public school and the Catholic school. They were about the same size, and kids bounced back and forth for no particular reason other than boredom or habit or something that had do with farming because farming was big in Kassel. Everyone in Kassel farmed or sold or fixed something farmers wanted or needed.

The dairy farmers needed a place to sell their milk, so Kassel had a creamery. The ranchers needed a place to sell their steers and heifers, so Kassel had an auction barn and a slaughterhouse. Dogs and hogs and horses needed vaccinations, so they had a veterinarian. Cows needed to be impregnated so they had Jon Groehe, whose job it was to shove his arm up a cow's tush and squeeze bull semen out of a tube the size of a summer sausage.

I saw him do it three, maybe four times, and it was nasty out the kazoo. When he pulled his arm out, the cow farted, and it sounded just like a 90-year-old man slurping a milk shake. What I never understood was why the bulls weren't taking care of this themselves. Wasn't that their job?

I should have asked Jon Groehe because he'd have told me without making a sick joke of it. He had that sandy-haired, square-jawed, FFA president and varsity quarterback look you might expect from a life insurance agent.

But here he was, impregnating cows and inviting snickers from morons like me.

"Don't turn your nose up," Uncle Carl told me. "He grew up without a pillow or a sheet, and now he's richer than Guy Lombardo, and money spends the same whether it smells like shit or Chanel No. 5."

I liked the line so much I later tacked it on to a letter I wrote to Lynn.

Anyway, Kassel was full of guys like Jon Groehe. Half of them were trying to get something to grow out of the ground (corn, hay, maize, wheat) or out of a female (piglet, calf, chick, child, cash). The other half were trucking stuff in and trucking stuff out. This required a lot of trucks.

That was good news for one of the town's leading families — the Beckers — because they sold trucks. Ford trucks, to be exact, and Kassel was a Ford town. Three out of four pick-up trucks in Kassel were Fords, and three out of four of those were sold by a Becker.

The Beckers also sold auto insurance. If you bought a truck from one Becker, you probably bought the insurance on the truck from another Becker, who also sold you the insurance on your kids, car, tractor, home, barn, silo, life, and whatever else needed to be protected or replaced in the event of a tornado, ice storm, flood, fire, nuclear attack, rapture, plague of locusts, alien invasion.

The Beckers were a big deal in Kassel, and there were plenty of them. A dollar didn't change hands without a Becker skimming a dime off the top. They would have been considered the Rockefellers of Kassel if Kassel had an art gallery or an opera house. It didn't. All Kassel had was the church — Saint Paul's Catholic Church — and everyone paid for it, in one way or the other. Especially the Beckers.

The church's junior priest was Father Louis Becker. His father and his brother owned the local funeral home. One of his uncles owned the Ford dealership. Another uncle owned the bank and the Becker Insurance Agency, so, in theory, a Becker could loan you the money to buy a Ford truck and sell you a life insurance policy that wouldn't pay a dime even if you got splattered by a runaway train in broad daylight in front of half the town.

Another Becker could bury what was left of you in a fancier casket than you needed, deserved or could afford, and these Beckers would remain in good standing with the Lord because Father Louis Becker worked the confession booth.

I met Father Louis the day after I arrived in Kassel. For some reason — and, by the way, when I say, "for some reason," I mean, "for no particular reason that I can tell" — Father Louis went out of his way to welcome me to Kassel and to St. Paul's Catholic Church, even though he didn't know me from Sally's rooster.

"So, you're a Schaper," he said, grabbing and rattling my right hand.

"No sir," I said. "I'm working at the farm."

I didn't understand him because he had a horrible lisp.

"No, no. You mithunderstand me," he said. "I thaid, 'You are a Thaupper.'"

It took a second to realize he was saying, "Schaper." I thought he was saying 'shopper.'"

"Well, answer him," Uncle Carl told me.

"No, Father. I'm not a Schaper. I'm a Dodson. My mother and Mina are sisters."

"Tho, that would make your mother a...?

"A Bayer," Uncle Carl said. "His mother is Helen Bayer."

"In that kayth, your grandfather was Franz Bayer," Father Louis said. "I did not know him perthonally, but I have heard he wuhth induthtrious."

"Hmmm," I thought and glanced at Uncle Carl, hoping he might throw me a line. He didn't, so I had to decide, again, whether to respond and, if so, what to say because I'd heard my grandfather was a lazy-eyed drunk.

He made money here and there by repairing small engines,

wristwatches, clocks and so forth when he was sober enough to hold a screwdriver. If that was Father Louis' idea of industrious, well, then, OK. He was industrious.

Anyway, I was the wrong person to ask. I didn't know him. He died when I was 3 or 4, so I had only a vague memory of once eating homemade peach ice cream with him. Mom didn't have much to say about him, good or bad. She never described him as "industrious." I know that.

Maybe Father Louis knew something she didn't. All I wanted was for Father Louis to release my hand so I could take a seat on the back row.

"Well, we're happy you're joining us thith morning, Edward. Please, as my guest, I'd like for you to thit up front so I can introduce you and welcome you. What do you think of that idea, Carl?"

Uncle Carl smiled. "Louis, I think that's a dandy idea, and I know my nephew feels exactly the same, don't you, Edward?"

I don't think I'd ever seen him so self-satisfied. He was damn near gloating.

I did not correct Father Louis. I did not say, "My name is Eddie. Not Edward" because it was one thing to sass Lowell's mother and quite another to correct a priest or a nun, and I learned that the hard way. I once made the mistake of correcting a nun who, in reciting my catechism class roll, called out "Edward," to which I didn't answer because my name isn't Edward. It's Eddie.

"Edward," she again called out. "Edward, raise your hand"

And, again, I sat there.

Finally, Sister Mary Callous Hooligan, or whatever her name was, said, "I will begin again from the top. When I call your name, stand."

She strolled up one row and down the next, calling names, and she timed it perfectly. She arrived at my desk and called the final name.

"Edward Dodson."

Though she couldn't have been taller than 4-foot, 9, she

towered over me, and all I could see were layers and layers of what looked like black and white sheets and a huge golden heart pinned in the middle of her chest, where her own heart would have been if she'd had one.

"What is your name?" she asked. "Is it Edward Dodson?"

"No, ma'am," I replied, and she popped me on the forehead with a ruler.

"No, Sister," she snapped.

"No, Sister."

She shoved a clipboard in my face and pointed to my name: Eddie Dodson.

"Is this your name?" she asked, and I said, "Yes, Sister."

"Then, why didn't you raise your hand when I called your name?"

"Because you didn't call my name."

Her eyes bulged, and kids sitting around me gasped.

"Excuse me," she said. "I called your name twice. Am I wrong about that?"

She scanned the class, and every kid there agreed she had called my name, not once but twice.

"So, they heard me call your name, but you did not, which means you're either deaf or dense."

So, I said, "Well, my name is Ed-dee. Not Ed-Ward. It's on my birth certificate. You can…"

But that's as far as I got.

Sister Mary Callous whacked me again on the forehead with her Executive Office Ruler, only this time much harder.

"Humble yourself, boy," she said. "In this class, you will answer to the name I assign you. If I choose to call you Edward G. Robinson, you will answer by that name."

She leaned forward and stared at me through her rimless glasses, so I humbled myself.

"Yes, Sister," I said. "I didn't mean to…."

And that was as far as I got.

"And you will spend eternity in Hell for lying," she snapped.

That's how I learned never to sass a nun, so I figured sassing a priest had to be twice as bad, and that's why I stood there, allowing Father Louis to rattle my hand and call me "Edward," wondering if and when Uncle Carl might break in and say something like, "Father, I think it might be best if he sits with us. He's still teething."

But he didn't. He found all of this hugely entertaining, so when Father Louis said, "Are you ready, Edward?" I had no choice to but follow him to the front of the sanctuary and sit on the far-left side of the first pew, directly in front of the pulpit, where 10 minutes later Father Louis would be reading from the Book of Mark.

> **"And if your hand causes you to sin, cut it off; it is better for you to enter life maimed than with two hands to go to hell, to the unquenchable fire. And if your foot causes you to sin, cut it off; it is better for you to enter life lame than with two feet to be thrown into hell. And if your eye causes you to sin, pluck it out; it is better for you to enter the kingdom of God with one eye than with two eyes to be thrown into hell, where their worm does not die, and the fire is not quenched. For everyone will be salted with fire."**

I had no idea what that implied, but he went on and on, so I must have dozed off for a minute because I thought I heard Father Louis saying something like, "If a cow causes you to drop a bucket, kill the cow and pluck out his eyes, then pass the salt."

It was enough to jolt me awake, so I started paying closer attention to Father Louis, and something he said reminded me of something Uncle Carl had said that didn't make sense at first but did later on. Uncle Carl said to his youngest son — my cousin, Jeffrey — "I don't want to hear another word about it. We're not the goddamned Beckers."

—

Well, that was obvious. Uncle Carl was to Father Louis what Burt Lancaster was to Liberace.

Uncle Carl was tall, trim, creased, and hard. Decked out in his Sunday best, he looked like a 4-star general. Father Louis, on the other hand, looked like a cantaloupe. His head was round. His nose was speckled and swollen, as if he'd picked at it with a fishhook. He had a stubby, fat neck, which made him look like Peter Lorre trying to swallow a dachshund.

I doubt his vow of chastity broke many young girls' hearts.

In addition to all of this, there was his lisp. It sounded like this: Hail Mary, full of grayth, tha Lord ith with you. Blethed ith thyee among women, and blethed ith tha fruit of thy loin, Jeezthus.

Everything about Father Louis drove Uncle Carl up the wall, especially the way his eyes seemed to operate independently and the way he sat in his fancy red velvet chair and crossed his right leg over his left and twirled his foot and made little curly-cue circles in the air, as if he was listening to Louis Jordan sing "Choo Choo Ch'Boogie."

It took everything Uncle Carl had not to fling the collection plate at Father Louis' head.

—

Uncle Carl and Aunt Mina owned 300 acres of black soil about two miles west of town. They lived in a two-story, clapboard house they'd been given as a wedding gift.

They could've turned it down and struck out on their own, but that thought never crossed their minds. People all over the country were looking for work and a roof over their heads, so Uncle Carl and Aunt Mina stayed put, even though the old house caught the afternoon sun as well as giant grasshoppers, yellow garden spiders, hornets, wasps, dust, and whatever else was blowing in the hot southern breeze.

They both were born and raised in Kassel — Uncle Carl on a dairy farm, and Mina in a tiny, one-story gabled roof house a couple of blocks south of the church. It had two bedrooms, a kitchen, a living room, and a dining room that had originally been a front porch. The house was close enough to the church that when the bells clanged at dusk, dishes rattled. My grandmother lived in that house until she died in late 1964.

My parents would drag us to Kassel twice a year to visit

relatives, and we'd stay with my grandmother in her tiny house, and sleep on pallets in the living room. We never got used to the clanging bells. I thought God was using them to remind me that I would go to Hell unless I stopped lying and stealing and diddling with myself.

I mention the last part because Jeffrey, my cousin, told me he'd heard Father Louis say to a group of junior high boys, "For it isth a cardinal sthin to diddle with onesthelf."

When they started laughing, Father Louis got angry. "I'm trying to thave you! You boyth muth know God ith wathing, and he knowths when you're diddling with that little inthworm of yourths."

"You should've seen the look on their faces," Jeffrey said. "It was like they'd just watched their mothers run buck naked up the aisle to take communion."

But Father Louis got away with it because he was a Becker.

All of this seemed borderline comical at the time, of course, but later, I couldn't stop wondering — again — why so few had so much while so many had so little, no matter what. The wind always seemed to be at their backs. For example, Kassel hasn't always been dusty and desolate. In the 1930's, it enjoyed a small oil boom. Care to guess who pocketed most of that windfall.

In 1959, Kassel approved alcohol sales inside the city limits. Care to guess who opened the first liquor store?

Do I need to tell you? Of course not. The Beckers. And no one said or did a thing about it. It was like it was preordained, and no one dared to ask why.

It was sort of like church. No one in Kassel ever asked, "Why am I kneeling and standing and sitting and kneeling and jabbering Hail Mary this and Hail Mary that, 45 times in a row, for little more than diddling with myself while the Beckers steal everyone blind?"

No one asked because they all knew the answer, which was, "That's just how it is so sit back and shut up and don't ask questions about things that are none of your business."

—

Earlier that Sunday morning, I toddled downstairs, found an empty chair, and asked Aunt Mina for a cup of coffee.

"Coffee?" she said.

"Yes, "ma'am, please," I said. "A little milk with it, if you have some."

"Your mother lets you drink coffee?" Aunt Mina asked.

"Sure," I said. "Is that a problem?"

"No wonder you have trouble sleeping," she said, then handed me a cup of coffee and a little pitcher of cream. About that time, Lori sailed in.

"When in the world did you get here?" she asked in her machine-gun cadence.

"Last night," I said, and that's all she wanted. I later told Mina the full story. We left home around 6 p.m., which put us in Dallas around 8. We would've arrived earlier, but we stopped for a hamburger and a Coke in Canton, and then stopped to fill-up in Terrell, then we stopped in Denton so my dad could buy a fifth of courage, and then we stopped in Gainesville so Mom could pick up a carton of joy and a bottle of sanity because she had a crushing headache.

Then, we headed south down Highway 81 for 14 miles into Kassel, then turned left from downtown and drove a mile or two, and then turned left onto Schaper Road, and then drove a mile to the farm.

About that time, Lori's twin, Faye, sauntered in.

"Good morning, everyone," she said. "Good morning, Eddie. When did you get here?"

"Last night," I answered.

"And?"

So, I told her the rest of the story. Mina met us in the driveway, but my parents didn't stay long. Mom hustled me out of the car, pushed me toward Mina and told me, "You can do this. You're a big boy. I'll call you tomorrow. Brush your teeth."

Then she hugged me, and my dad handed me a suitcase along with a paper sack that contained a pair of sandals and a pair of

Sunday dress shoes and an envelope containing $25 in small bills.

He then tucked a pack of Viceroys in my shirt pocket, patted it and parroted the company's advertising slogan — "It's got the taste that's right."

He thought it was hilarious, but Mom did not.

"Give me those," she said. "And you'd better not start either."

She tried to hug me again, but I squirmed and broke her grip, and then Mina bear-hugged me from behind and said, "He'll be fine. We'll take very good care of him."

I watched their car kick up a cloud of white dust and disappear into the moonless night.

"Don't worry," Mina said. "You're in good hands."

"I know," I said, and then she led me into the kitchen and handed me a warm chocolate chip cookie and poured a glass of milk. She tried to rope me into a chat, but I was fried, so she gave up and said, "Go to bed. You know where they are."

I lumbered upstairs and through the girls' room and then into the front bedroom where Jeff, Danny and Dennis were out cold. It took a while to get used to their snoring, but once I dozed off, I was out cold, too.

I slept hard from about 1 a.m. until sunrise. I was awakened by Uncle Carl, who stood in the front yard and yelled up toward the second story of the house.

"Dennis, Jeffrey, Daniel, get up. Get your asses out of bed. Downstairs. Five minutes."

This wasn't the first summer I'd spent on the farm, so I knew the drill. Uncle Carl stood in the front yard — rain or shine, — and yelled and woke up those who weren't already awake, and everyone on the second floor scratched and farted and started or followed the procession downstairs to take a leak and then snatch a place at the oak table in the tiny kitchen where Mina served pancakes and sausage or scrambled eggs and bacon and grits, every morning.

The sausage and the lard came from the pigs they raised and slaughtered. Their chickens laid the eggs, and their cows produced the milk. They bought the flour and syrup and coffee and the grits at Schaper's Market, which had been in Uncle Carl's family since the last Comanche raid.

The kitchen was as alive as the New York Stock Exchange, and Lori ran the show. She was the talker, the doer, the pedal-to-the-metal schemer. She was short — barely 5-foot, 1. Cute as a kitten and fun. Head cheerleader every year. New boyfriend every six weeks. Got her name from one of mother's high school friends, a girl who graduated and moved away and was never heard from again.

Faye, on the other hand, was the thinker, the watcher, the planner. Class treasurer one year. Class secretary the next. No high school boyfriends, even though she could've had her pick. She wasn't interested.

In every picture I'd ever seen of her, her head was pulled slightly down, so her eyes looked straight forward. Most people tend to tilt their heads back, so you'd have to look over the hump of their mouth and nose to see the eyes. Not with Faye. She could stare a hole through a rubber boot.

Faye got her name from her father's mother. She was Hazel Faye (Reichel) Schaper. By the way, one of Hazel Faye's cousins, Major Ernst Reichel, was captured at Stalingrad and died in a Siberian prisoner of war camp, which was rarely discussed.

A lot of folks in Kassel shied away from talking about the whole Hitler and Nazi stuff. They had more immediate issues. For example, Faye accused Lori of filching one of her bras, and Jeff and Danny argued about a baseball game between the St. Louis Cardinals and the Los Angeles Dodgers.

Jeff was a Cardinal fan because St. Louis was the closest team around, and "Cardinal" sounded Catholic to him. He also disliked the Dodgers because their best player, Sandy Koufax, was a Jew.

"What?" Danny asked Jeff. "So, you're now a Nazi?"

Danny became a Dodgers fan for the best reason. He met a girl, and she was from Los Angeles, and they became pen pals. Along the way, she accidentally half-way civilized him, so he was offended by Jeff's "anti-cynicism," as Jeff dubbed it.

Even though I was groggy, I listened to their little debate and thought, "Wow. Danny can be very forward thinking," but then he blurted, "At least Sandy Koufax is white. St. Louis' best player is a …"

And Mina wheeled around, pointed a spatula in his direction and said, "Don't you say it."

And Danny said, "I was going to say, 'a catcher. Not a pitcher. Tim McCarver is a catcher."

Mina wheeled back around, flipped two eggs and said, "That's enough out of you."

I waited for a break in the conversation, then chimed in, "St. Louis' best player is Bob Gibson," thinking I might impress someone, but Danny leaned over and said very quietly so Mina wouldn't hear, "Who the fuck gave you permission to talk?"

I nodded and put my head down and didn't make a peep until Uncle Carl ordered us to finish up and get out to the milk barn.

I was leaving the kitchen when I heard Mina tell Lori, "Just because you left your bra in the back seat of some boy's car is no reason to be stealing your sister's."

Lori blew a fuse.

"Mother!" she screeched and then shot her eyes over at me.

I tried to act like I hadn't heard a thing, but I blushed because I'm not accustomed to this kind of conversation. At my house, my mother doesn't hang her underwear on the shower curtain, and she doesn't chit-chat with us about sanitary napkins and missing bras like they do here, as in, "Oh, gosh. We're out of Kotex. Have Poppa pick up a couple of boxes at the market. Make sure he gets the large ones."

Everything here seems open for inspection and discussion. No holds barred. I found it both embarrassing and titillating at the same time.

By the way, "titillating" is a real word. I learned it one day at school. One of the guys in my class, Charlie Goff, kept repeating it over and over in Mr. White's science class, and he intentionally placed the accent on the first syllable, so it sounded like this: TIT-ill-aye-ting.

Charlie had a talent for finding words that sounded dirty but weren't. His favorite was coxswain. He said it all the time. Others included asphyxiate, rebuttal, dictation, bumfiddler, and clatterfart.

Well, Mr. White heard him going on with "titillating," so Charlie got three licks — and hard ones, too, which was true to form. Mr. White loved giving licks. He'd give you one lick for wadding up a sheet of notebook paper, and two licks for tossing it in the trash can, and three licks if you tossed the wadded sheet of notebook paper at the trash can and missed.

He said wadding up paper wasted space and made unnecessary noise. I think he just enjoyed whacking teenage boys with a paddle.

Anyway, as I said, I got a good education just sitting and watching and listening because I knew next to nothing about the secret lives of females. It was certainly worth the effort. Like ol' Charlie Goff would say, it was titillating.

—

Those who were assigned to milk that morning marched over and took their stations. The cows waited outside in a holding pen, then clopped in without too much encouragement, stuck their heads in the sliding-iron gates, lapped up the feed grain with their huge tongues, munched it lazily, and surrendered their milk with little or no complaint.

My job was to watch and learn.

"When we're finished in here, you get to hose all this shit out," Uncle Carl said.

This was the first time he'd talked to me like that. Last summer, my job was to stay out of the way. Now, he was treating me like a hired hand, and I appreciated it because, otherwise, I'd have been singled out, and I didn't want that. I wanted to blend in.

I stood near the screen door leading from the stalls into the room with the cooler, and I listened to the country-western station out of Gainesville and wished someone would turn it to the rock 'n roll station out of Dallas, but I didn't say a word. That was no way to try to blend in. You blended in by doing your job, and two hours later, I got a chance to do just that.

After Uncle Carl had patted and shushed out the last cow, he told me to find a pair of rubber boots, a broom and a hose and start scrubbing. It was mindless work, but that was fine. I wanted to be busy, but I didn't want to have to think about what I was doing.

Instead, I wanted to let my mind drift and float in and out. I wondered what Lynn was doing. I thought about the Cardinals versus the Dodgers. Koufax versus Gibson. I thought about Lori leaving her bra in the backseat of some boy's car. I wondered what happened to the bra? Was it hanging from a rear-view window?

I didn't want to think about Mom or my dad. I didn't want to wonder if they were patching things or if he was packing things. Was he already gone? I tried my best not to think about them at all. The only time I thought about them was when the phone rang.

Otherwise, I relaxed and took to the work and didn't count days. I was sent here to work, and I decided I would work hard. I'd get out of bed on time. I'd work all day. I wouldn't cut corners or weasel out of something difficult.

I would finish up and clean up and watch a little TV and go to bed. I would shove cotton in my ears, so I didn't have to listen to my cousins' moans and groans and farts and assorted nightmare conversations. Whatever happened, night or day, I dealt with it.

Of course, most things were way out of my control. For example: sheer accident. I was mowing and stopped to pick up what I thought was a piece of scrap pipe that someone must have accidentally dropped.

It wasn't. It was a piece of pipe someone had clamped to the lawnmower to serve as a muffler. It had fallen off while I was mowing, so it almost red hot when I grabbed it.

I ended up with second degree burns on my thumb, index and the middle finger of my right hand. Nothing hurts worse, and I was at the house by myself, so I had to deal with it the best way I knew. I shoved my hand in a glass of ice water and kept it there until

Mina came home.

"You're going to have to take your hand out of that water eventually, so it might as well be now," she told me, so I pulled it out and almost cried.

She bandaged it, and it throbbed all night. I got a little sleep, but I don't recall Uncle Carl lightening my load. He expected me to deal with it and do my job.

That was life on the farm. Romanticize it all you want, but it's painful and sometimes brutal. We found a litter of puppies out in the field, and they didn't belong to any of their dogs. As badly as they would have liked to keep them, they couldn't. There wasn't room, and farmers can't have packs of feral dogs running around, killing calves and chickens and piglets. So, they did what they had to do. They put them down.

If this horrifies you or pops your balloon, well, that's just too bad. Deal with it.

CHAPTER 8
Useful

At home, I'd be sacked up until noon but here, I started waking up before dawn, then getting up and dressed about the time I heard Mina puttering around in the kitchen.

One morning, I pulled on a pair of jeans and an old burnt orange T-shirt and wandered downstairs into the kitchen where Mina was stirring a pot of grits and humming "Fly Me to the Moon."

"What are you doing up so early?" she asked.

I never had a chance to answer.

"I'm making grits. You like grits? Some people don't, and that's OK. What about eggs? How do you like your eggs? You still eat eggs, right? You're not allergic to them, are you? Lori is allergic to cats all of the sudden. Can you imagine? Allergic to cats? We live on a farm. What am I supposed to do about that? Chase off all the cats? Drown them? Then, she'll probably become allergic to mice because they'd be everywhere. Well, no one is going to chase off my cats while I have anything to say about it. What do you want to drink? Milk?"

She turned and handed me a plate of eggs fried over easy with smoky bacon and homemade biscuits and grits swimming in butter.

"Here. It's going to be hot out there today, and you're going to need your energy. How's that hand?"

It's getting better, I told her, then ate up and thanked her five or six times, then mopped up the last of my grits with my right index finger, not unlike my dad might have.

"Thanks, Mina," I said, then slid out of my chair and out the side door, to be greeted by four or five dogs, one of which was an old Collie named "Bets," which was short for "Betsy." I petted her face and rubbed her ears and pictured Walt McFarlin rubbing Debby

Bishop's face and ears, among other things.

I could have obsessed about that all day, but I chased it off by imagining what John Lennon was doing over in London or Liverpool or Los Angeles or wherever he was. I pictured him writing a song with Paul for their next album, and it would be amazing, perhaps their best ever, and one of my friends would buy it, and he'd invite me over, and we'd play it until our ears rang.

—

After the sun pierced the horizon, the sky turned a deep blue, and ribbons of orange, yellow and red shot out of the low-hanging clouds in the distance. At home, I was rarely if ever up that early and, even when I was, there were so many trees, I couldn't see much farther than shoulder to shoulder. Here, I could see elbow to elbow with my arms hanging at my side.

I was sitting on the porch, half asleep, petting Bets and thinking about Debby smooching Walt, and I didn't notice that Uncle Carl had slipped out the screen door and was standing right behind me.

"Nice out here, isn't it, this time of day." he said.

"Yes, sir," I answered.

"This is my favorite time of day," he said. "It's all in front of you. Right now, all things seem possible."

He walked on out into the front yard, then turned back toward me and asked, "What's your plan?"

"I'm not sure what you mean," I said.

"I mean, what do you plan to do, now that you're here?"

I hesitated just long enough for him to add, "Think about it for a second. Why are you here?"

"My parents dumped me here," I said without thinking.

"I'm sorry you feel that way," Uncle Carl said. "But that's not what I asked. I didn't ask you about them. I don't care about them. I asked you about you. What you plan to do now that you're here?"

"I plan to do what I'm told," I said.

"Sounds like a plan," he said. "We'll see if you can pull it off."

He tromped back to the front door, poked his head in and yelled, "While we're young."

Two minutes later, we were all in the milk barn. I was told to fill the bins with grain so the cows wouldn't get antsy, so I did. It wasn't complicated. It was just a little unpredictable because during milking, cows often swish and sway, so when you squeeze between two of them with a can of feed in each hand, the cow on the right might swish to the left, and the cow on the left might sway to the right, and the person in between might get squished between them.

You don't take it personally. You deal with it. Cows are big and dumb and 99.9% docile. They're not trying to bite you.

They will, however, kick the hell out of you if you give them a reason to, and so, 20 minutes into milking, two cows sandwiched me, and I dumped both cans of feed, and that set off a chain reaction of swishing and swaying and then, a black and white Jersey took a dump, so I grabbed a shovel and tried to catch some of it mid-air.

It was a terrible idea. When a cow decides to take a Number Two, you let her because if she feels the edge of a metal shovel brushing up against her haunches, she is going to kick, and the shovel will go flying, and the shit will, too, and you'd better hope your eyes and mouth are closed when it does.

Mine weren't. Everyone working in the barn cackled except Uncle Carl, who glowered at me. "Well, what do you expect me to do? Wash out your mouth and get back to work. A little cow shit never hurt anyone, and we don't have time for you to act like a schoolgirl."

Lori — who was, hands down, the best milker in the barn — didn't appreciate that comment a bit, but she was used to it. She'd been splashed and speckled, and she'd never gagged or carried on. She'd just wash her face and get back to it.

—

It takes a rare breed to be a farmer, especially a dairy farmer. I can't understand why anyone would. It's relentless. Twice a day. Every day. Doesn't matter if it's your birthday or your momma's birthday or Mickey Mantle's birthday.

Cows must be milked, and they're not going to milk themselves. Their job is to graze and chew and surrender their milk and enjoy being coddled so long as they're producing milk.

The same is true for most everything on a farm. So long as it produces, it's coddled, with one exception: Children. They are born into indentured servitude. They're expected to hustle and apply as much muscle as is needed to do the job. Then, they're expected to do it again and again until the job is finished, which it never is.

For example, picking up rocks. It's like mowing the Mekong Delta. Cut a blade of grass and another one springs up. Same's true with rocks. Toss one in the trailer and another one fights its way to the surface. We walked one field after another, picking up half-moon rocks and tossing them into a trailer. When it came close to filling up, Dennis drove to a ravine, and we tossed them out.

We did this over and over. I pretended I was spending three or four hours in the weight room, doing squats, lifts, lateral raises, and medicine ball tosses. For the better part, Jeff wouldn't shut up. He babbled the whole time about girls he claimed he'd felt up and pushy homosexuals he'd punched out.

"This guy offered to buy me as much beer as I wanted if I'd just 'Close my eyes and enjoy it,'" Jeff said. "So, I reared back, and I punched him right in the mouth, and he hit the ground, and I stood over him and spit on him."

"Where'd this happen?" I asked.

"In Gainesville," Jeff said. "At the VFW Hall."

"There are homosexuals at the VFW Hall," I said. "Lordy. Lordy. Is nothing sacred?"

"He was from Dallas. Whadda'ya expect?"

"So are the Cowboys," I said.

"Well, he didn't look much like a football player to me," Jeff said. "One thing's for damn sure: If anyone else tries to pull that shit with me again, I'll knock their teeth out, too."

I let him go on, but I knew it was a crock. He was just making it up on the fly and hoping the lie didn't loop back and trip him up.

During all of this, Dennis never said a word. Every now and then, he'd honk a horn and point to a rock we'd missed.

—

On the third or fourth day of picking up rocks, I was following the trailer, and I had a rock in my hand about the size of a golf ball, and Jeff and I saw a jackrabbit cut across our path, 40 or 50 yards away, and I launched my rock, and it looked like Don Meredith hitting Bob Hayes in stride. The rock struck the rabbit in the right shoulder, and it rolled twice, caught its balance and tore off again.

Jeff went nuts.

"You nailed that son of a bitch!" he said. "Nailed 'em!!"

He did a little jig and whoop-whoop-whooped, and then he caught his breath and shouted at the rabbit, "Take that, motherfucker. Teach you to stay out of my field."

Suddenly, it was his field. I waited for him to add, "Come back, and I'll knock your teeth out," but he didn't, so I turned to see if Dennis had seen it, and he had and was not impressed, not with me, anyway.

"Pure luck," he said. "Tough little bastard. I'll give him that."

Of course, Jeff told everyone, so I became something of a celebrity around the house for an hour or two. Lori certainly acted impressed.

"I've never heard of such a thing," she told me. "Fifty yards? Gosh."

She went on and on and then buddied up to me and whispered, "I have a big favor to ask, and you're the only one who could get away with this. I have a friend, and she needs a date for tomorrow night, so we can double, and she would just eat you up, so, are you interested? She's a little older, but not much. Two or three years. C'mon. It's time you had a little fun. You want to get naughty, don't you? I just have to make sure I get home with all my underwear."

"Is she pretty?" I asked.

"Pretty? She's gorgeous," Lori said. "And stacked. And look at you. My Lord. I'm kidding. You wouldn't know which end to bite."

About then, Faye stepped out of the bathroom, wrapped in a white towel and wearing over her hair-rollers a pair of red bikini panties. She didn't seem to think a thing about it, but I blushed and tried not to stare as she pranced through the room.

I figured she was headed upstairs to get dressed, but she returned to the TV room, sat on the arm of the couch and started flipping the TV channel. Now and again, she'd reach up and gently pat the back of her head. As hard as I tried, I couldn't look away.

Then, Lori buddied up next to me again and raised her right hand and bit down on her knuckle and asked in a breathy Ann-Margret voice, "Are you homesick yet?"

It was all a set-up, and Lori and Faye got a big laugh out of it.

Faye then pulled off the panties and tossed them at me. I didn't reach out to catch them because I wasn't sure if I was expected to.

"They're as red as your face," she said, then retrieved them and headed upstairs. Lori smiled and winked and left me sitting there, splashing around in my own baby pool of stupidity.

—

Later that day, I received a letter from Lynn. It didn't say much, but then, there wasn't much to say. She was bored. It was hot. Gina was driving her crazy. Had I heard this new song by some group I'd never heard of? What was I up to? Was I having fun? Was I working hard? Had I made any friends? Had I met any girls? When was I coming back? When was I going to write? Write soon!!!"

Then, she scrawled a big heart at the bottom and planted a lipstick smooch on top of it and signed her name in purple ink. Two days later, another letter arrived. She told me she was thinking of quitting the high school band even though she was signed up for it and had attended band camp at TCU. She said she hated everyone, especially her roommate, a flute player from Weatherford. Cindy something. Or Cyndi. Or Cyndee. Or whatever. It didn't matter. All flute players are the worst. Snotty and vapid, she claimed.

I knew "snotty," but I had to look up "vapid."

Lynn said the flute player's conversations began with an "I" and ended with a "Me," which I thought was a keen observation. Lynn also asked the flute player what kind of books she read, and the flute player said, "If I have time to read, I have time to sleep."

Lynn said she had never been so happy to get home.

That was about it. She again signed off with a big heart and a lipstick smooch and her name penned in purple ink:

Debra Lynn
Your Poor, Poor, Pitiful Friend

She wrote two or three more letters over the next week or so, and each repeated what the one before it had said, and then the letters stopped, probably because I couldn't keep up. I was working in the fields and didn't have time nor energy nor anything to say.

Every now and then, I'd pull out one of Lynn's letters and read it again and hope it would inspire me to write something to her that wasn't vapid, but I just couldn't find the words. For example, she asked if I'd met any girls.

There might have been a long way of saying "No," but I didn't bother. I'd been there going on two weeks, and I'd barely stepped off the property. We worked all day during the week. On Saturdays, I slept in and lounged out around the house, watched baseball, and threw the football if I could find someone willing to catch it.

On Sundays, church, big dinners, more naps.

There was no time to meet girls, and even if there was, I was mostly the opposite of the flute player. If I had time to meet girls, I had time to read, and I preferred to read because I was never one of those guys who could charm a crowd of strangers. I was too much like my mother for that.

So, I read a lot. I finished a book of short stories by Jack London and "All Quiet on the Western Front" by a German writer whose name I still can't remember. Eric Something.

I enjoyed being alone. One Saturday afternoon, I walked all the way to town — on my own, with nothing to do and no one to see. I just wanted to see how long it'd take.

Instead of following the roads, I walked through the fields, which was risky. The hay stubble and tall grass hid snakes and centipedes and tarantulas and scorpions and wasps, so I wore a pair of rubber boots and extra-long jeans and a long-sleeved shirt, just in case I stumbled into anything, especially spiders.

I appreciate that spiders play a special role in nature, but then, so do I. My special role is to kill spiders. Any and all. That was double confirmed a day or two after I'd nailed the rabbit. We were playing football, and I made a one-handed, over-the-shoulder catch for a touchdown, and I decided to take a victory lap, so I cut beneath the "T" of the clothesline, and it was right about dusk, and I couldn't see that a garden spider had spun a web and was just waiting.

I ran into it, face first. I still shudder just mentioning it because of all the spiders on the planet, I hate garden spiders the most. They have long, needle-like legs and fangs the size of garden shears, and I ran right into it. I could feel its legs on my face, and I screeched like a seventh-grade girl at a Beatles concert, so just like that, I went from rabbit slayer to titty baby.

Anyway, on the long walk to town and back, the only things of any interest to me were the VFW Hall and the city's swimming pool. The VFW's juke box was blaring Buck Owens and Eddy Arnold, and the swimming pool was packed with kids who looked about my age and younger. I stood next to a concrete picnic table, just looking, and I failed to notice that someone was looking at me.

After standing there for a while, I headed back toward the farm and ran into Jeff, who'd been looking in the hay barn for a set of car keys he was sure he'd left there.

"Where've you been," he asked, and I told him.

"Dang, boy. You're going to die of a heat stroke."

"You may not realize it, but there's a swimming pool in town. We ought to check it out."

"We have to get a ride," Jeff said. "I ain't walking."

We agreed it'd be a waste of breath to ask Dennis, but we didn't see a choice, so Jeff did the honors, certain he'd tell us to drop dead, but, for once, he shocked us.

"Grab your trunks and a towel," he said. "We're going swimming."

CHAPTER 9
Differences

We arrived at the pool right around 2 and needed to leave no later than 3:30 to get back in time to milk, so I got in as much horseplay and goofing around and cannonballing off the board as I could.

I wanted to get some sun on my arms and chest, so I laid face up on my towel and allowed my mind to wander. I thought about wasps and spiders and centipedes. I thought about that rabbit. I thought about Faye's flaming red panties. I thought about damn near getting killed.

Did I mention I almost got killed? I did. Here's the story: Uncle Carl was installing an automatic feeder in the milk barn, and a concrete truck came out to pour the foundation, and about the time the guy operating the truck decided to drop the chute, I decided to reach over and pick up a stick that'd fallen into the frame.

The chute weighed at least 50 pounds, and it missed my head by about an inch. Uncle Carl sputtered and stared at everyone and blurted, "Did you see that?"

Everyone did, so, I was mortified. Right after dinner, Uncle Carl collared me and said, "Don't worry about it. Next time, think first."

I laid on my towel and was thinking about how lucky I was to be alive and that's when I heard the girl. I ignored her because I couldn't imagine she was talking to me and I expected her to move along shortly.

She didn't. In fact, the voice got louder and bossy. It belonged to Judy Klement. She wanted to know who I was and where I'd come from, and so forth, so I asked her why she cared, and she told me she didn't. Her sister did.

Her sister was Kathleen Klement, though she went by "Kathy."

Judy delivered me to her and said, "Here. As promised. You owe me a quarter. Pay up, or I'll scream."

"Mom hates you," Kathy said, then dug a quarter out of a hidden pouch in her bikini bottoms, flipped it into the air and let it fall to the ground.

She then extended her right hand toward me and said, "I'm Kathleen Klement. You've met my darling younger sister. What a joy she is. Anyway, we noticed you over there, and we — my friends and I — were curious about you."

"Really?" I said.

"Yes. Really," she answered. "By the way, I think I saw you in church this morning. Am I right?"

"Well, I can't say," I said.

"You don't know if you were in church?"

"I don't know if you saw me in church."

"He got you there," one of the two friends said.

Kathy silenced her with the flick of a finger, then asked if I was staying with the Schapers, although she must have known I was.

"As a matter of fact, I am," I replied.

"Are you a Schaper?"

"As a matter of fact, I'm not," I replied.

"Do you have a name?" she said.

"As a matter of fact, I do," I replied.

"Are you inclined to share it?" she said.

"Of course," I said. "It's Richard Starkey."

"Too clever," Kathy said, sarcastically. "Are you a smart ass all the time or are you in training for the World Championships?"

"Yes," I replied. I told her my name and that I expected to be with the Schapers for another week or so. I told her my uncle needed help, and I needed the money.

"That must be awful," Kathy said.

"It's not so bad," I said. "I don't mind the work."

"I'm not talking about the work," Kathy said. "I'm talking about needing money."

The same girl giggled again. She had a long, thin face, a flat chest and freckles the size of Coke bottle tops.

"That's Helen," Kathy said. "She's my next-door neighbor. She's easily entertained."

Kathy then pointed to the other girl.

"And that young lady over there is my very best friend in the whole wide world," to which Helen spouted, "Aww. You said I was."

"To entertain you," Kathy said. "Now, be quiet. We're talking."

Kathy asked me a lot of who, what, when, and where questions, like where was I from? What grade was I in? What was my favorite subject? Did I play football? How long did I plan to be there? What did my parents do? Was I a Catholic? Was I driving yet? Did I have a car? Did I like beer? Did I have any?

I didn't offer anything that wasn't asked for, and my answers bored me, so they must have bored her, but she maintained eye contact and kept up the pretense that she was interested in everything I had to say until she looked toward the pool entrance and saw Jack, whoever Jack was.

Kathy flailed her right hand and screamed, "Jack! Jack! Over here! Where have you been? I have been worried sick."

Jack waved back, timidly, and Kathy yelled to him, "Wait right there. Don't you move a muscle."

She turned back to me and said, "So, Richard. Lovely to meet you. I look forward to enjoying your company again."

And I replied, every bit as sincerely, "Kathleen. I can hardly wait. Please, bring your darling younger sister."

She squinted and replied, "Until then," and dashed off to find out where Jack had been.

I smiled awkwardly and said of Kathleen, "Clearly a person of mercurial temperament. Well, I'd better go, too."

That's when Kathy's very best friend stepped fully out of the shadows and asked me if I liked baseball.

—

We left the pool area and dropped our gear on the same concrete picnic table I'd leaned on earlier. She sat on one side. I sat on the other. She plopped her chin in her palms and waited for me to speak without being spoken to. I waited for her to speak. Finally, she asked, "Are you OK? Are you nervous?"

"No," I said. "Why do you ask?"

"Because you act like you're about to have a stroke," she said. "Are you afraid of being seen with me? Is that it?"

"How can that be?" I replied. "I don't know you."

"Well, your lucky day," she said. "Ask me something. Anything."

"OK," I said. "What do you have against baseball?"

"Seriously? That's your question?"

I tried again.

"Where'd you buy that hat?"

"I've had more interesting chit-chats with cadavers," she said.

"You've had conversations with cadavers?"

"Regularly," she said. "I own a funeral home."

"You own a funeral home?" I asked.

"It's true. I own it. It's mine. My mother runs it, but it belongs to me. Ask anyone. They'll tell you."

I didn't say "bullshit," but I thought it. Then, I said to myself, "You dope. This is another prank." I swiveled to the right, and then to the left, but I didn't see anyone, so I asked, "Who was it? Lori or Faye or Jeff?"

"What do you mean?" she asked.

"This is a set-up, right? You expect me to believe you own a funeral home? How dumb do I look?"

"That's a subject for another day," she said. "Until then, you're going to agree to meet me at the baseball park tomorrow night. Near the concession stand. The game starts at 6. Meet me at 6:30."

"You're serious."

"This is your chance," she repeated. "I moved you to the head of the line. Don't blow it. Kathy's brother plays every Monday night, April through October. Her parents reward her if she attends his games, so Kathy rewards me if I join her, and I join her because I like rewards, so I'm inviting you to join me tomorrow night. Who knows? Maybe you'll get a reward. Now, where will you find me?"

"Concession stand?" I asked.

"Near the concession stand. Don't make me search for you. It's a self-esteem thing. I don't have time to explain."

"Just as well," I said.

She looked at her watch, then said, "My mom will be here soon. She's never late, but one more question."

"Shoot," I said.

"Mercurial? Do you use that word a lot?"

"No," I said. "In fact, I've never used it. I've never needed to."

"You're different," she said. "I like that."

"Is that different as in cool, or different as in weird?" I asked.

"It's different as in we'll see," she answered.

I should have left well enough alone, but I added, "My mom thinks I'm special."

"That's nice," she said. "I like boys who like their mothers."

I got the feeling she liked her mother, too. She liked her mother a lot. I got the feeling that talking to her was just like talking to her mother, who — thank God — was late.

"She should be here," Kathy's best friend said.

"I thought you said she's never late?"

"She isn't. She's running late," she said. "There's a difference. She's running late because she's mercurial. Very mercurial. I should know. I use that word all the time."

Just then, a black Pontiac Grand Prix pulled into the parking lot, and someone inside bumped the horn, and Kathy's very best friend was gone, and I didn't even get her name, which proves that the line between moron and mercurial is razor thin.

CHAPTER 10
Chunking rocks

Dennis said he wanted to finish his Marlboro before leaving the pool, so we stood next to his Ford pickup, which he'd bought from a Becker, and watched him take his time blowing smoke ringlets. Jeff knew better than to say anything because it'd just piss him off, and, for spite, he'd light another cigarette. We were already late as it was.

At 3:40, Dennis flicked a butt into the parking lot, climbed in the cab, turned the key, and dropped it into reverse without saying a word. We jumped in the bed, and he floor-boarded it back to the farm, where Lori was pacing and cursing.

"Goddamn it, Dennis," she said right as we pulled up.

But that's all she said. Anything else would have been redundant and wasted.

It didn't bother me that we were late, but it bothered me that it bothered Lori. Dennis didn't care, but she did, and she worried that if her father found out they'd started 15 minutes late, there'd be hell to pay.

Since she'd given up on trying to win her father's affection, Lori worked to earn his approval. She thought that if she had her father's approval, that'd lead to respect, and if she had her father's respect, that could translate eventually into affection.

So, Lori worked hard. Faye didn't care. She assumed her father loved her. You might say, she had faith her father loved her. Jeff didn't notice. Dennis wouldn't say one way or the other.

But Lori? Oh, God. It gnawed at her something horrible. It was as if Uncle Carl woke up early every day just to have an extra 15 or 20 minutes to figure out new ways to feed Lori's heart into the silage shredder without getting blood on the ceiling.

And I thought my dad and I had problems.

We may have started milking late, but we finished much faster than we would have if Uncle Carl had been there instead of attending a pot-luck dinner at the KC Hall. We switched the radio to KLIF, settled into a relaxed groove, and knocked it out. Lori even joshed with Dennis, and Dennis almost smiled. You could tell he was holding it back.

Afterwards, Jeff and I cleaned up. Normally, he would've been spouting off about something he knew nothing about, or he'd have been trying to pop me in the nuts, but that night, he was borderline contemplative.

I was hanging the brooms and buckets and hoses, and he said, "I wouldn't piss on Kathleen Klement if she caught on fire, but if you want to go to the baseball game tomorrow night, I'll get you there and back."

"How do you know about that?" I asked.

"Shit, man," he said. "Are you for real?"

"So, you know about this," I said.

Jeff laughed.

"You kill me," he said.

Up until that point, one day wasn't that much different than the one before it and the one after it. We'd been on autopilot. We got up. We ate. We milked. We worked. We ate. We worked. We milked. We ate.

Then, I read or watched TV or wrote a letter or some song lyrics, or perhaps the first paragraphs of my first novel, which would propel me into international stardom.

Around 9, we all hit the sack. The next day, we did it again.

But this Monday seemed different. The working day tried to last forever, and that was because I knew I had to decide whether to meet this girl at the baseball game or to blow her off and stay at the house and watch TV. I still suspected I was about to be the butt of a joke, and I'd almost talked myself into staying put when Jeff walked in.

"What the hell you doing? Get dressed," he said. "Dennis is driving. We'll figure out a way to get home. And put on a new shirt.

I'm sick of seeing that damn orange T-shirt."

I'd already hosed off in the barn, so all I needed to do was find some clean shorts and a T-shirt, slick back my hair, and rake a toothbrush across my teeth. I did it all in under five, so I had a few minutes to kill. I was standing in front of a fan, trying to dry my hair when Faye walked in.

"Out for the evening, I see," she said. "Meeting someone special? This evening? Out. Take me out. Ballpark?"

She smiled deviously, and I didn't need her to tell me she knew everything. I just couldn't figure out how she knew. How everybody seemed to.

Then, Dennis walked in. He'd been changing the oil and the fan belts on the tractor, so, of course, he was filthy.

"Do not sit on the couch," Faye snapped.

"No problem," Dennis replied. "I'll sit on your face instead."

"You're disgusting," Faye said. "And in front of company."

"Him? He's not company," Dennis replied. "He's a wart."

Whereas Lori might have thrown a pillow or magazine at him, Faye simply repeated. "Stay off the couch."

About that time, Mina called from the kitchen for Faye to collect the towels off the clothesline.

"Just a sec, Mom," Faye answered, then turned to me.

"I'll pick you up at 9," she said. "Don't try anything stupid."

She didn't define "stupid," and I didn't ask for examples.

———

I asked Dennis to drop me off a block from the stadium because I wanted a chance to walk around and see what I was getting myself into. He didn't say yes. He didn't say no. He just pulled into a service station parking lot and waited on me to hop out.

"I appreciate it, man," I said, trying to find some way to connect with him. "See ya' later?"

He raised one eyebrow, looked right and then left and then spotted a local cop wedged between a filling station and a storage shed across the street, so he tapped his turn signal and pulled out slowly headed in the cop's direction.

Right as he passed him, Dennis raised his left hand out the window and shot the cop the bird. The cop was a guy Dennis had gone to high school with. They once got into a fist-fight over a girl. The cop won the battle, but Dennis won the war. The cop was still married to her.

—

The baseball game should have been in the bottom of the second or top of the third inning by the time I arrived, but the two umpires driving over together from Nocona blew out a tire.

By the time I arrived, fans had pledged allegiance to the flag and were about to recite the Lord's Prayer. People in small towns love to recite the Lord's Prayer. No event is too trivial. Before picking up a ball of any kind, they take a knee and beg God to cut them some slack.

Where I was from, parents only prayed when their kids stepped into the batter's box. I asked myself "What's the harm?" but then, I asked myself, "What would Bogie do?"

Bogie, of course, was Humphrey Bogart, and his greatest film was "Casablanca," and his greatest role was "Rick Blane," so I asked myself, "What would Rick do?"

I knew this: Rick would never wait at the bar for a dame. She'd have to wait for him, and she'd be lucky if he showed up at all. If he did, they wouldn't waste time reciting the Lord's Prayer.

So, I thought, that's how I should choose to play it. Take my time. Arrive a minute or two late. Let the suspense build. Then, right as the dame is about to panic, sail in and do that thing you do so well. It'd go like this:

"How nice," she'd say. "You remembered."

And I'd say, "Not an easy thing to forget."

And she'd say, "I was afraid you might not come."

And I'd say, "I was detained."

And she'd want to know more, but I couldn't tell her more. It would put lives at risk. Besides, she'd understand that a man like me goes places where she can't follow, does things she can't be any part of.

She would understand because she knew men like Bogie and Rick Blane and me are impossible to understand, and that's what made us so desirable.

—

And so, I headed toward the concession stand. I arrived at right at 6:30 — 6:33 at the latest — and I assumed that was close enough.

In my book, I was right on time, and so I felt pretty odd standing there, looking lost. I decided to grab a Coke even though I really wanted a snow cone. I just couldn't picture Bogie munching a snow cone at a bar and waiting on a dame.

It was now going on 6:40, and I thought, "Just what I expected. Are you never going to learn," but then, I saw her. She was standing at about the fourth row of the bleachers and looking down at me.

I gave her a "what gives" look, and she twirled the index finger of her right hand, which I interpreted as, "Come up and find out for yourself," so I dropped out of the line and ambled over — trying not to replicate my John Wayne stroll — and climbed the stands and said, "We meet again."

It was the best I could do.

"You're late," she said, sounding slightly peeved.

I was no good at being noble, so I lied.

"There was an emergency at the farm," I said. "Sick cow."

"How sad," she said. "I hope you like root beer."

She handed me one and said, "I always pay for the first drink."

She picked up a denim bag and said, "Follow me." Instead of taking a right at the bottom of the bleachers, we turned left, then walked under the bleacher, then headed toward right field.

We then stopped and watched the boys run into each other because one coach yelled, "Run this way" and another coach yelled, "Run that way."

"I'd rather watch sick cows," she said. "Let's go look at graves."

Kassel's cemetery was only five or six blocks from the baseball field, but the street wasn't lighted, and it didn't take long to leave the halo of the stadium lights. Fortunately, the moon was rising, and there were a few porch lights on, so we didn't bump into anything.

"Back there at the stadium, I noticed something interesting," she said.

"What was that?" I replied.

"You were talking to yourself out there in center field."

"What do you mean?" I replied.

"You were talking to yourself," she said. "I could see your lips moving. It's not a big deal. I talk to myself all the time."

"I was probably reciting movie lines," I said.

"Well, that's original," she said. "Do tell. What movie?"

"I doubt you know it," I said. "It's an old one."

"Try me," she said.

"It's 'Casablanca,'" I said.

"Of all the gin joints in all the towns in all the world, she walks into mine," she recited.

"I'm impressed," I said.

"And you've memorized lines from it?" she said.

"No," I said. "I memorize entire scenes."

And she said, "Show me. Do you know the final scene?"

I told her I did. I knew all the characters — Rick, Ilsa, Renault, Laszlo, the soldier sent to fetch Laszlo's luggage. I knew every line.

"I want to hear them," she said.

"Do I have to do Bogart's accent?" I asked.

"Do your best," she said.

"Promise me you won't tell anyone," I said. "People think I'm weird enough as it is."

"It's not weird," she said. "It's quirky. There's a difference."

So I began, in my best Bogart voice, with, "Louie, have your men go with Mr. Laszlo and take care of his luggage."

And then, I nailed the rest of the scene.

"Eddie," she said, "I think this is the beginning of a beautiful friendship."

And I almost giggled.

We walked and talked, and every now and then, she'd pick up a rock and throw it at a stop sign, and about one out of every five times, she'd at least nick it.

"You like throwing rocks?" I said.

"Not especially," she said. "I like throwing tantrums. Rocks are easier."

"I've broken a few windows in my time," I said.

"Child's play. I got a ticket for throwing one," she said. "I was charged with disorderly conduct. Of course, my mother got it dismissed, and the poor dumb bastard who gave it to me almost lost his job"

"I can't wait to meet your mom," I said.

"You can," she said. "Trust me."

We walked another 50 yards or so in silence, and then she said, "I want to go to Casablanca one day."

"Really?" I asked.

"For the waters," she said, then paused, hoping I'd recite the next line, and I did.

"There are no waters in Casablanca," I said.

"I was misinformed," she said, and we nodded approvingly.

I made a mental note: When in doubt, mention a movie.

Then, she asked me if I liked Bob Dylan.

That was trickier. I've found that people take their music a lot more seriously than they do their movies. Personally, I don't care if someone says, "'Casablanca' is boring. 'Monster a Go-Go?' That's a great movie."

However, I do care if someone says, "The Beatles are boring. Freddie and the Dreamers? They're a great band."

As for Dylan, some people love him, and some people don't. Some people love the folksy Dylan. Some people love the rock 'n roll Dylan. Some people hate Dylan. Period.

I really don't have an opinion, but I worried that no having an opinion would reveal more about me than I wanted to reveal, so I turned my statement into a question: "What do you think of him?"

She didn't bite. "No," she said. "I want to know what you think of him."

So, I attempted a diversionary tactic.

"I prefer the Beatles," I said.

"I didn't ask you about the Beatles. I assumed you liked them. They have nothing to do with Bob Dylan. My mother prefers Peggy Lee. She has nothing to do with Bob Dylan, either."

"Oh, I guess I misunderstood the question," I said.

"Don't bullshit me," she said.

"I'm not," I said. "I just want to make sure I understand what you're asking."

She stopped. "Just answer the question. The fate of our unborn children hangs in the balance."

"That is fantastic," I said. "I've never had a conversation like this. I don't think I can keep up."

"I know you can't," she replied. "But you can tell me this: What do you think of Bob Dylan? In your own words."

I thought for a second, then said, "Not to change the conversation, but I hear your mother's a prostitute. Is that right?"

"My mother would never be a prostitute," she said. "She'd be the owner of a house of prostitution."

"I cannot wait to meet her," I said.

"Fair enough," she said. "I don't want you to think you've won because you haven't, but did OK."

Pleased with myself beyond description, I picked up a white rock about the size of a prune and hurled it at a stop sign. I missed it by a foot or more, but it drew my attention to the street sign: Walnut / Sycamore.

We had stopped right in front of my recently deceased grandmother's house.

CHAPTER 11
Mercurial

We walked up the narrow sidewalk and stepped onto the creaky wood porch, and I reached out and grabbed the doorknob and asked her, "What do you think?"

"It's not my house," she said.

"It was my grandmother's house," I replied, not realizing she knew my grandmother. She not only knew her. Her funeral home buried her.

"I don't think she'd mind," Debbie said. "Even if she did, there's not much she can do about it now. I say, 'Why not?'"

So, I twisted the knob and laid into the door like I'd been taught in football, but it wouldn't budge. For a moment, I thought I might have separated my shoulder.

"That had to hurt," she said.

I played it tough.

"Nah. I'm OK," I lied. "Let's try around back."

We should have started there because the back door not only wasn't locked. It wasn't even entirely closed. I tapped it with my right index finger, and it swung open.

"I guess the local criminals are too dumb to try both doors," I said, then swept my right hand forward and said, "After you."

She smiled and said, "Isn't there something you'd like to ask me?"

"You need to go to the restroom?"

"Yes, I do, but no. That's not it."

"Would you like a snow cone?"

"No. A little closer to home."

I told her I didn't have a clue.

"Wouldn't you like to know my name?"

"Is it Cathy with a C?"

"No. It's Deborah with a D."

"It can't be" I said.

"Why not?"

"Long story," I said. "I'll explain later."

"Well, I don't go by Deborah," she said.

"Well, then, what do you go by?"

"I go by the park on my way to school every day," she said. "It's no big deal. I'll explain later."

Though we had a lot of explaining to do, I decided to leave well enough alone, so we stepped into the tiny kitchen, which smelled of mothballs and mold and musty air and Pine Sol with a hint of my grandmother's drug store perfume and talcum powder that she received every Christmas because no one had the imagination or generosity to buy her anything else.

The aroma reminded me of happier times, but Deborah almost gagged.

"Really attacks the nostrils, doesn't it?" she said, holding a hand over her mouth and stepping gingerly across the dusty floor. Despite the odors, the house and the oddball artifacts left behind fascinated her.

"This is like stepping back in time," she said. "The wallpaper has to be 75 years old."

I'd never noticed it. Mostly, I was surprised at how small and cramped everything felt because I remembered the house as being bigger and bustling. It was where my mom and her sisters and in-laws and cousins and second cousins and neighbors and friends from church would squeeze in around a green Formica dinner table to gossip and gripe and share secrets and smoke and sip Maxwell House coffee out of the Blue Willow cups that came free in boxes of laundry detergent.

My grandmother — we called her "Gram" — kept the counters crammed with skillets of spaghetti or pans of tuna casserole or pots of white beans and ham. I hung out in there as long and often as I was allowed.

More often, I was relegated to the living room, which wasn't nearly as interesting or comfortable. It was where we slept on a pad or quilt tossed on the floor, and where relatives gathered to eat homemade ice cream and pecan pie or walnut cake. It was where the adults smoked and played cards.

My memories of Gram's house were almost all good ones, with one exception: Her bedroom. It was off limits. If we had to use her bathroom, we kept our hands off her stuff. If Mom caught us laying a finger on Gram's dresser or chest of drawers, she'd smack us with her hand or swing a fly swatter or a hair brush.

You did not mess with Gram's stuff — her bottles of White Shoulders and jars of face lotion and tubes of hand cream. When I asked Mom why Gram had all those jars and tubes, she said, "To silence the blow."

Mom was tipsy when she said it, and she said it under her breath and possibly didn't intend for me to hear it, but I did, and I knew she meant it. She wasn't the type to let something like that slip, even when she was a little looped.

So, the hairs on the back of my neck sizzled when Debbie decided to snoop around Gram's room. She found a few cardboard boxes half-filled with strays and duplicates, an end table scarred all the way around by cigarette burns, one of Gram's black work shoes, a stack of dog-eared Zane Grey and Louis L'Amour paperbacks, and a ratty braided rug rolled up and leaning against a closet door.

"I have to come back during the day," she said. "This place is a gold mine."

"Sorry, lady. We're not open during the day," I said.

"Then, I want my money back," Debbie said.

"No refunds," I said. "Read the signs."

"I don't see any signs," she said, and I shot back, "You can't see them at night. Come back during the day."

She pouted convincingly, so we returned to the living room, and I asked if we needed to get back to the ballpark.

"Not unless you're in a hurry," she said.

"In that case, I have an idea," I said. "I'll be right back."

I dragged the rug from Gram's room into the living room and rolled it out in front of the plate glass window that faced the church.

"Make yourself at home," I said, and we sat side-by-side, cross-legged, gazing out the window at the mulberry trees and waiting for the other to say or do something that wouldn't violate the "Don't try anything stupid" rule.

—

Of course, it got awkward. We'd been doing so well, walking and talking and throwing rocks, but then, suddenly, I couldn't think of a thing to do or say, so I asked myself, "How would Ernest Hemingway handle this?"

I wondered this because I'd just finished "A Farewell to Arms," which my ninth grade English teacher insisted was the greatest war novel of all time.

I liked most of it, so I drew upon those parts I liked to imagine Debbie as Catherine Barkley, and me as Frederic Henry — the book's main character. I pictured us traipsing around Europe, spending a week in Madrid to attend the bullfights, then a week in Rome to visit the ruins, and then two weeks in Paris to know what it was to be alive.

I imagined that we'd survived World War I and wanted nothing more than to get drunk and rowdy, three nights a week. Two nights a week, we'd dine alone in a corner café where no one would know us except the burly, burr-headed Algerian bouncer and the suave waiter, who'd snap his fingers, and a young busboy would deliver to our table a bottle of champagne and four glasses.

A few minutes later, the manager himself would serve us the chef's special, which was reserved for guests of honor like me and the beautiful woman at my side.

Then, the feisty café owner would notice us, and he'd throw open his arms and shout to his wife and his children — who were working in the kitchen — to come out to meet the American he'd told them so much about.

Then, he'd open a bottle of dry white he'd hidden from the Germans for an occasion like this, and I'd invite him to join us, and we'd eat and drink and trade stories about how we barely survived, and we'd toast our friends who did not. Since so many did not, the toasts would go on and on. Eventually, tears.

I decided against this scenario. It was a little too literary.

Then, I asked myself, "How would Bogart handle this?"

After all, he was the coolest man who'd ever lived. He would've known what to say in a moment like this because he always did.

He'd say, "I was running rum and Remington rifles in and out of Algeria when I met this young Dutch nurse who looked a lot like you."

Or he might say, "I woke up to the sound of my head throbbing and grown men sobbing as they watched the Germans goose-step down the Champs-Elysées."

So, that's what I was thinking while I sat there on the rug, as chatty as an earthworm. If I'd been sitting there with Lynn, I'd have been cracking jokes and doing my John Wayne and JFK imitations or even reciting entire scenes from "Mary Poppins," which, I'm now embarrassed to admit, I knew by heart.

Or I might've been making fun of Hemingway's habit of writing ridiculous crap like, "Darling, darling Elizabeth," and "Darling, darling Catherine," and "Oh, darling, you are better when you don't think so deeply."

And Lynn and I would've been in stitches. It would've been fun and easy because I wouldn't have been so jittery. Of course, the big question was: Why'd I get all jittery with girls like Debbie Gehring but not with girls like Lynn?

It was because I knew I'd never try something stupid with Lynn. I never tried something stupid with Lynn because I was afraid she'd let me, and I'd be in the same pickle as my dad.

With Debbie Gehring, I clammed up, I suspect, because I saw nothing ahead that night except for rejection and humiliation. If I tried something stupid, she'd slap me and push me away, then run home and call Kathy with a K and blab about how weird and boring, boring, boring I was.

What else could I think? She was as quiet as I was, so I assumed she kicking herself for ending up sitting on a ratty cotton rug in a dead woman's house with an idiot mute from somewhere in East Texas where they pronounce "oil" as 'ahhl."

I assumed she was kicking herself for ending up in a situation where she was forced to inhale dust and cobwebs, and I was about to call it a night when she asked, "Did your Gram beat you, too?"

"Beat me at what?" I asked.

"Beat you. Up. Slap you around. You know. Did she figure out a way to soften the blow?"

"Why would you ask that?"

"Well, I'm trying to understand why you've gone silent. I assume it has something to do with your grandmother, but it could be the moon or the church bells. Or is it the house? Does it have a root cellar? I know people who have been traumatized by root cellars. It usually has something to do with tornados but not always. Sometimes, it has something to do with roots."

"It's the roots," I told her.

"Not again," she said. "The damn roots."

"I'm sorry," I said. "Let me try again. Here goes: Hey! Look. I'm speaking. 'All good things come to those who wait. Now is the time for all good men to come to the aid of their country.'"

"Better," she said. "But enough with the typing lessons. Try something else."

"That is not a problem," I said. "The rain in Spain falls mainly on the plain. Four score and seven years ago, something happened. Yesterday, all my troubles seemed so far away. Somebody ought to belt you in the mouth. But I won't. No, I won't. To hell I won't.'"

And Debbie said, "McClintock, right?"

"Yep," I replied. "Worst Western ever."

And Debbie repeated, "Pilgrim," in her best John Wayne impersonation, which wasn't nearly as good as mine but then, I had to give her credit for trying.

And so, the ice began melting.

She asked about Gram. Did I like her? Did her jaw pop when she ate?

"Paint a picture for me," she said.

That, I couldn't do. My family — both sides — existed only in shades of gray with occasional splashes of black and white and dribbles of red, blue and green. I told her my grandmother had always been old. I didn't remember her ever being young. She was as playful as a soldier ant.

"Did you love her?" Debbie Gehring asked.

"No," I said. "I didn't know her."

"Did you like her?" Debbie said.

"She made donuts for us every time we visited," I said. "I remember watching her wring a chicken's neck. She didn't smoke or drink, but every now and then, she'd dip snuff. She loved homemade peach ice cream. She wasn't afraid of tarantulas, and she thought they had as much right to live as you or me, and once, when my dad tried to squish one with a garden hoe, Gram chewed him out. Those were her tarantulas, and he had no right to kill them. If he had time to kill her tarantulas, he had time to wash a dish or make up a bed."

I told Debbie that it wasn't the first time I'd seen and heard my dad get his ass chewed out.

"Save it for another day," she said, unfolding her arms and stretching her fingers. "We should get back."

We stood and brushed off the dust, and then she said, "Do you have a girlfriend back home?"

"I do not," I said.

"Cross your heart," she said. "Now, look at me right in the eyes. Say it, 'I do not have a girlfriend.'"

I tried to look her right in the eye, but I blinked, and she thought she'd caught me.

"You do," she said. "I knew it. I know your type."

"And what type is that?" I asked.

"The type that blinks," she said.

I should've left it at that because everything had gone so well, and she had to go, but I felt compelled to tell her about Debbie Bishop, and how I'd had a crush on her, but nothing ever came of it, perhaps because I broke her arm.

Then, I told her about Lynn, my best friend who could never be a girlfriend.

"Why not?" she asked.

"No real reason," I said.

"Must be some reason," she said.

"She's sort of plain," I said.

"Sort of plain how?" Debbie asked.

"You know. Plain looking," I said.

"And what? You're Paul Newman?"

Suddenly, she was serious.

"Lynn and I are friends," I said. "That's it. That's all."

"Because she's sort of plain," Debbie said.

"Plain has nothing to do with it," I said.

"You just said she could never be a girlfriend because she's sort of plain," she said. "Look, I know what you're saying. I have friends who'd like to be more than friends, but they're never going to be. I get that. But it's not because they're plain. It's because I don't feel anything for them."

"That's what I meant," I said. "I should have said it that way. I'm sorry."

"You don't owe me an apology," Debbie said. "You owe Lynn one."

"Good as done," I said, starting to get a little miffed.

"I hope to meet her," she said.

"That would be great," I said, thinking we'd moved on.

"I'm sure it would," Debbie said. "I'd like to tell her the next time she sees you, she should slap you."

Before I could respond, Debbie said, in a singsong, 'Follow the yellow-brick road' voice, "And now I must be leaving."

We ducked out the back door and headed toward the stadium lights. No matter how fast I walked, she walked a half-step faster. We stopped at the right field fence, and, without turning to look at me, she told me she had to work the next day.

"So, is this it?" I asked.

"We'll see," she said.

I was smart enough to know that "We'll see" generally meant "Don't count on it," so I thanked her for the root beer and figured I'd never see her again.

—

On the drive back, Jeff asked me how it went. I told him it went fine. I had a fine time. She's a fine girl. We took a nice, long walk. We had a nice chat. Thanks for asking. Turn the radio on.

"So, you didn't get any?" he said.

"No, Jeff," I said. "I didn't get any."

"Too bad," he said. "Every other guy in town has."

I glared at him, and he backed off.

"C'mon, man. I'm kidding. Lighten up."

I closed my eyes and let the hot breeze blow in my face and waited to hear dogs barking and gravel crunching.

Of course, I didn't sleep, or, if I did, I didn't sleep much. All those noises that I'd grown accustomed to now irritated me, so I was awake when Uncle Carl started calling everyone to get up and get out of bed and get downstairs. I pulled the sheet over my head and waited for Jeff and Danny and Dennis to get up and out and go down, and then I crept downstairs, hoping the kitchen was empty, but it wasn't.

"Well?" Lori asked.

"Well, what?" I said.

I didn't bother to waste her time with some cock-and-bull story, so I said, "It was good until it wasn't."

She gave me a little pout and said, "I know. She's like that."

CHAPTER 12
Lost and found

Dennis hadn't said 10 words to me in the three weeks I'd been there, so I sat catty-cornered across from him at dinner because I wasn't in the mood to chit-chat. I hadn't been since the spat or gaffe or misunderstanding or whatever you'd like to call it, two days earlier.

Debbie Gehring told me "We'll see," but she hadn't called, and I wasn't going to call her because of my chicken-shit pride, so I was confused and pitiful as I picked at my spaghetti and meatballs, and then, out of nowhere, Dennis turned to me and said, loud and clear, "Cheer the fuck up."

The roof almost flew off.

"Dennis Schaper," Mina blurted. "At the dinner table?"

Uncle Carl roared, "What in the world?"

Faye and Lori screeched.

Jeff spit tea everywhere and laughed so hard that Uncle Carl threw a napkin at him.

Dennis didn't move a muscle. He stared at his plate of spaghetti, stabbed a meatball and was twirling it around when Uncle Carl slapped the table with the palm of his hand and said, "That's enough. All of you. Jeffrey, plug it. Dennis, get up. Right now. Drop that fork and leave this table."

Dennis raised his eyes, and then he raised his fork and bit off half the meatball, then he gently placed the fork with half the meatball on his plate and said, "Sorry, Mom. Had to be done."

Fighting to suppress a grin, he sauntered out to the front porch.

Meanwhile, Uncle Carl sat in shocked exasperation. He tried to resume his meal but couldn't, so he wiped his mouth with Lori's napkin and said to Mina, "Where did you go wrong?"

If he meant it as a joke, it sailed over Mina's head.

Faye tried to act above it all, but Lori and Jeff kept giggling, so Mina started giggling, and before long, even Uncle Carl was giggling, and you know what? I cheered the fuck up. Why? Because Dennis was right. It had to be done.

The incident reminded me of an old joke by a Louisiana comedian and occasional Cajun chef named Justin Wilson.

The joke went like this: A couple had a son who never talked. The couple took him to doctors and psychologists and everything, and no one could understand why the boy wouldn't talk. Nothing was wrong with him medically. He just didn't talk, so they gave up.

One morning, at breakfast, the boy — who was now 9 years old — looked up and said to his mother, 'This toast is burned like hell.' The parents almost fainted. Once they'd collected themselves, they asked the boy, "All these years and not a word. Why did it take you so long to talk?'

And the boy replied, "Up to now, everything's been OK."

It's not the greatest joke ever, and it's a lot funnier when Justin Wilson tells it, but it makes a point. Perhaps for Dennis, up to then, everything had been OK.

I polished off my meatballs and spaghetti and bounced upstairs and began writing a letter to Lynn, casually mentioning that I'd met a girl at the swimming pool, and I saw her again the next night, and we'd walked around and talked, and "she reminds me of you," and I thought, "Boy, she's gonna love hearing that."

I didn't tell her any more than that. Nothing about my grandmother's house. Nothing about the girl. Nothing about the tiff with the girl. I expected I'd be leaving here in another day or two, so why bother? I wrote the letter because I owed Lynn a letter, so this is what she got:

Dear Lynn. How are you? Scribble, scribble. I'm OK. Busy. Working. Cousins. Oh, look! Weather. Well, that's it. See you soon. Yours truly...

I started but didn't finish it. Around 6, Lori stuck her head in the door at the bottom of the stairs and yelled up, "Eddie. Telephone. It's not your mother."

I dashed down, grabbed the phone, held the receiver a moment and wondered if I wanted to put myself through this again, and while I was making up my mind, Debbie asked, "That's it? That's all you got?"

"Who is this?"

"It's Richard Starkey," Debbie said. "You know who it is. What are you doing? I'm calling to tell you I'm meeting a friend at 7:30 tonight."

"You called me to tell me that?"

"You're the friend."

"You could use better friends," I said.

"Kathleen would not appreciate hearing that," she said. "Look, meet me at your grandmother's house. Let's straighten this out. This isn't all on you. Meet me, and let's talk about it. I'll be there at 7."

And she hung up.

It was 6:50.

Lori was draped across the couch, reading an article about the Rolling Stones in "Tiger Beat" magazine and trying to keep up with a movie starring Susan Hayward about a prostitute accused of murdering a woman who was actually murdered by Hayward's good-for-nothing husband.

Unfortunately, Hayward had a criminal record, so the judge believed the husband's story and sentenced Hayward to the gas chamber. The end.

I guess the moral of the story was, "Don't be a prostitute. You'll get screwed every which way you turn."

Anyway, Lori dropped her magazine and said, "Give me a minute to find my keys."

—

We made small talk and listened to the radio out of Sherman on the way into town. "Paperback Writer" was topping the charts, and the B side — "Rain" — was as good or better, but Lori's favorite song was Frank Sinatra's "Strangers in the Night" because she was three or four years older than me and didn't understand the Beatles.

I didn't care for Sinatra's smoking and drinking and ring-a-ding-ding Rat Pack bullshit, but I liked his music, especially old songs like "All or Nothing at All" and "The Way You Look Tonight."

I was the only kid my age who did.

I told Lori to drop me off at the baseball field, and she jerked the wheel to the right and skidded into the tractor supply store parking lot.

"First, don't play me for a fool," she said. "I know where you're going. I know who's going to meet you there. The big question is, do you know why you're going? She's giving you a second chance, so don't blow it. Don't act like a victim. Don't ask for explanations. Don't play stupid games. You have two hours or thereabouts. Make the most of them. I'll pick you up at 10."

I didn't need to ask where.

—

Debbie and I sat on the rug in the front room, staring out the big window. There were no streetlights along Evans Lane, and Debbie remembered that, so she brought a flashlight.

She also brought a quarter.

"Call it. Heads or tails," she said.

"I always call heads," I said. "So, I'm going with tails."

She flipped the coin, and it bounced twice and landed heads.

"I win," she said. "I want you to sit there and hear me out. First, was I angry at you? No. I wasn't. I was disappointed in you, which is unfair because I barely know you, so, I'm sorry about that."

Then, she added, "I know what it's like to be labeled. Plain. Dumb. Dull. Different. Damaged. It's all the same. People you don't know — who don't know you — want to put you in a box and use it for target practice."

Two years ago, she said, a boy sent her a letter. They weren't boyfriend and girlfriend, but they saw each other enough to lead the boy to believe they were.

"I didn't feel anything for him romantically, and I thought he understood that," Debbie said. "Then, I received a note from him, and he told me he loved me, and it went on and on. I should have seen it coming, but I wasn't looking because it was easier that way.

"I wrote back and told him, 'We've been friends for a long time, and I want to remain friends, but I'm not interested in a relationship.' I told him I wasn't even sure what that meant. So, I asked him if we could go back to how it was when we were just friends? Apparently it wasn't. He didn't speak to me for six months. I'd pass him in the halls, and he'd walk right past me, like I wasn't there. I knew what he was doing, but I never figured out why except that, for some reason, guys are required by 'Guy Law' to behave like jerks when they don't get what they want."

I couldn't disagree.

"We're morons," I said.

"You're not," she said. "You see, that's the problem. You think you can claim some sort of occasional mental retardation, and that'll make it go away, but you don't get off that easy."

"How about this: We're jerks," I said.

"That's closer," she said. "I can work with that. In the meantime, think first. OK?"

"No one's ever told me that," I said, then pulled my knees up and wrapped my arms around them and was all balled up, and she pushed me, and I tipped me over, and that ended one thing and started another.

—

Not that I had much to compare her to, but Debbie was a great kisser, and that's what we did. We kissed. We kissed until our lips fluttered. I didn't try anything because kissing was plenty. It was all I wanted. Anything more would've ruined it. The only thing I wanted more of was time. If this was how good it could be, I wanted it to last. I wanted that tick-tick-tick to slow down. Way, way down.

—

At 9:45, we decided we needed to reassemble ourselves and prepare to leave. Fortunately, the water in the house hadn't been turned off, so we were able to wash our faces and rinse our mouths, and all the while, we chattered like birds.

Debbie peppered me with questions about my family, especially Mom, so I told her as much as I could in the small amount of time we had left. I told her Mom was a nurse. Emergency room sometimes. OB ward at others.

"She was on duty when I was born," I said.

I considered it one of my better jokes.

I told her my mom was complicated, and some might even say snobbish for someone who didn't have enough in her checking account to fix a broken air conditioner.

I told her a little about my parents' problems but not much because I was still thinking them through. It had recently dawned on me that Mom — for as much as she appeared to despise my dad — didn't know how to get along without him.

For instance, she didn't know a thing about cars. She never thought to check the gas gauge, so we were always running on fumes and imagination. She didn't know how to turn the windshield wipers off and on. I mean, seriously. This woman helped deliver babies, and she didn't know how to operate windshield wipers?

Debbie also asked about my dad, so I told her a story. It wasn't about my dad, though. It was about an older guy who'd moved in down the street from us. He was friendly and nice. We often cut through his yard on our way to someone's house, and he never yelled at us or complained to our parents. We could see him sitting in his living room. If he saw us, he always waved.

His last name was Gilbert, but that's about all I knew about him. So, one day, I asked Mom about him.

"I never see anyone coming or going over there," I told her. "I think he could use a friend."

"I think you probably need to leave him alone," Mom replied.

"You're sounding like Dad," I thought but didn't say because she might pop me. Then, I thought, "Lynn will figure this out," and sure enough, she did.

Somehow, she learned that he'd left his wife because his wife was crazy, and he didn't love her anymore. His wife was also mean, and she knew how to get even with him. She made it impossible for him visit his own grandkids. That's why he was so sad.

As bad as I felt for him, I had to wonder what he thought was going to happen when he left his crazy wife. Unless he left her for a younger, smarter, prettier, borderline sane wife, he should have dealt with it. That's what adults tell us all the time. "Deal with it."

That's what he should have done. After all, he getting on up there. Pushing 50 for sure.

"I don't see what this has to do with your father," Debbie said.

"Mr. Gilbert never strolled over to chat with Mom or my dad, but he sometimes came out and played catch with us, and, for an old guy, he was good," I said. "I learned he had been a wide receiver at LSU, and he played in the pros until he tore up a knee. He was an All-American, and he never said a word about it."

"You've lost me," Debbie said.

"Mr. Gilbert is nothing like my dad," I said. "My dad is the exact opposite. My dad played one year of football — ninth grade, I think — but he'll swear he was greatest football player Southeast Texas ever produced. And if he thinks you're gullible enough, he'll lead you to believe he raised the flag on Iwo Jima. That's my dad."

I tried and failed to look blasé about it.

She forced a smile, and then she ran her right index finger under my right eye, and her left index finger under my left eye.

"You tell a pretty good story," she said.

And so, Debbie and I were back on track.

Of course, all this time, I was receiving letters from Lynn even though I wasn't writing her because, obviously, I had other things to do, but I knew I needed to do something, so I picked up five postcards from the market and borrowed five stamps from Mina, and every time I could remember, I scribbled a few thoughts on a card and left it in the mailbox.

Her response to a couple of my cards is on the next page. It's not what I'd hoped for, but it's kind of what I expected. Here it is:

Dearest Edward:

How thoughtful of you to send another postcard. Nothing says "I miss my best friend" like a photograph of a jackrabbit wearing a Texas Ranger's badge.

I suppose I should apologize for not writing sooner. How long has it been since you've received a letter from me? Four days? Five? Have you received letters from your other friends? Did they interrupt their summer frolic at Camp Jehovah to write you?

I apologize for the spelling and grammar errors you were forced to point out in my last letter. Karen edited this one, so it should be erorr flea.

As per your other questions: No! I have not lost my sense of humor. I've lost my patience with fart jokes.

Have I heard the new Beatles' song? No. I didn't know there was a new Beatles. What happened to the old ones? Are they coming back?

How's the weather? Let's see. It's summer. Summer is hot. Therefore, it is hot, so nothing else here is worth mentioning. Nothing at all. See you when I do. Tell the new girl I said, "Good luck." She's going to need it.

Yours,

Lynn

CHAPTER 13
Think first

The living room lights were on when I got back to the house, but no one was up. I thought about turning the TV on but decided not to because I didn't want to attract a crowd. Besides, I needed some sleep.

I tip-toed upstairs and slipped into bed and wondered why it was easy for me to doze off in a rickety chair at noon and impossible for me to fall asleep in a perfectly comfortable bed at night.

I rolled around, thinking about her, doing the whole "kiss the pillow" thing, and I probably even talked to myself because Jeff snorted, "That's enough."

I doubt he was snorting at me. He was probably dreaming about diddling with himself.

Either way, I didn't get much sleep, so the next morning, before breakfast, I stumbled out on the back porch, splashed water in my face and tried to get my hair to move in one direction. Then, Lori stuck her head in the door and asked if I was decent.

"No," I said. "But I'm dressed."

So, she came in, all smiles and giggles, until I pulled the towel from around my neck.

"Oh, my God," she said.

"What?" I asked.

"I'll be back," Lori said, then dashed out and yelled for Faye.

"In a minute," Faye yelled back.

"Now," Lori yelled. "You'll thank me later."

So, Faye stuck her head in the door, looked my way and immediately clamped a hand over her mouth.

"Oh, shit," she said.

I thought she was staring at my chin — like, maybe I'd cut it —

but she wasn't. She was staring at my neck.

Then, Lori repeated, "Oh, shit, indeed."

"Wrap the towel back around your neck and follow me," Faye said.

We crept back upstairs and headed over to their vanity table. I removed the towel and glared at the huge hickey on the right side of my neck.

"Kudos to Miss Gehring," Lori said.

"What are we going to do?" I asked Faye.

"We aren't going to do anything," she replied. "I am. I can't cover it, but maybe I can camouflage it long enough for you to get out of the house this morning. After that, you'd better be prepared to face the music."

Lori simply couldn't stop gawking.

"I'm so impressed," Lori said. "Expertly executed."

"Lori," Faye said. "This isn't funny."

Faye then found a makeup kit and started dabbing. She patted on a powder and looked at it from the right, then from the left, and then she said, "That's as good as it's going to get."

Lori agreed.

"The mark will surely fade," she said. "But the memory will last forever."

I considered changing from my burnt orange T-shirt to a button-down dress shirt, but Faye vetoed that idea.

"Nope," she said, then flopped her hand out toward the stairs, like a waiter showing a matinee idol to a corner booth. "Lori, go first. Then, try to distract Mom."

"I'll ask for French toast," Lori said. "That should work."

"No," Faye said. "Here's a better idea. Pick a fight with Jeff. Accuse him of something."

"Like what," Lori said.

"I don't know," Faye said. "Accuse him of stealing your bra."

Lori curled her lip, and we headed downstairs.

As soon as we slid into our chairs around the table, Lori blurted, "Mom, tell Jeff to stop smoking in bed. He's stinking up the whole upstairs. We can barely breathe."

Jeff looked up, confused. Mina looked at Jeff. I tried to scrunch my neck into my shoulder blade. Faye looked at Jeff and said, "Those things are going to kill you."

Jeff looked at Faye, then at Lori and then at me, trying to figure out what was going on. He then looked closer and mouthed, "All right."

Faye looked at Lori and said, "Didn't you want to say something else?"

Lori said, "Oh, yeah."

She turned back to Jeff and said, "And stop using all the hot water!"

Jeff looked at Lori and said, "I hosed off in the barn last night."

"No, you didn't," Lori said, miffed that Jeff hadn't figured out Faye's little conspiracy, even though he was staring at my neck. He leaned over and asked me, "How much blood did she get out of you?"

I waved him off.

Then, Uncle Carl saw it. I was afraid he was going to kick me out of the kitchen, but his eyes crinkled.

Finally, Mina turned around and noticed it, and though she disapproved, she returned to her grits and bacon and eggs without saying a word.

Finally, Dennis, who was sitting left of me, jabbed his thumb under my chin and pushed up, providing everyone an unobstructed view of the carnage.

"Right idea," he said. "Wrong place."

I wasn't sure what he meant, so I cut my eyes toward Lori, who said, sheepishly, "Don't ask me. I have no idea what he's talking about."

She smiled and stared at her scrambled eggs. Jeff laughed, and Uncle Carl squelched a grin and played dumb, and Mina stirred her grits.

Whether this set the tone for milking that morning is anyone's guess, but Uncle Carl didn't curse once, and he let us listen to the rock 'n roll station out of Dallas, and the DJ played "Paperback Writer" and "Rain" back-to-back, so I thought, "If I'd known, I'd have started getting these hickeys weeks ago."

These might have been the best twelve consecutive hours of my life, up to that point. I was happy, and happiness can be as addictive as chocolate-covered sleeping pills. Happiness hurls me out of bed in the morning and swept me through the day in the direction of an old rug in an old house on a dark street facing a cemetery and within ear-shot of a moaning church bell.

It pumped through my veins, and I wanted to believe it was there to stay, but I knew it wasn't. It was going to play out — and I knew it — and that's when I started to cry.

Not in public, of course. Not when someone can hear or see me. In the shower. In the tool shed. Behind the barn. In the fields. After dinner, I walked down to one of the ponds for ten or fifteen minutes and then trudged back.

If my eyes look red and swollen when I returned, I blamed the cats. If Lori could be allergic to them, I could, too.

It helped that, once all my chores were finished, Mina and Uncle Carl allowed me the freedom to do what I wanted with my free time, and I appreciated that and tried not do anything that might have tempted them to call my parents and say, "Come get him and cart him home."

So, I put on a big act. I was responsible, dependable, mature, and so big a fraud that even Father Louis bought it.

I didn't have to pretend to be cheerful. I was beyond cheerful. I was giddy. I'd meet Debbie at the pool two or three times a week. We'd stretch out in the sun next to each other and run our fingers across each other's faces and shoulders and arms and bellies. My biggest worry was allowing myself to get too excited, especially if Kathleen or Helen were snooping about.

For a guy who seemed to have it all under control, I did a lot of crying. I'd cry when it was safe and work when I had work to do, and see Debbie as often and as long as I could, knowing the clock was running. I tried to isolate each moment, to strip away context, to eliminate cause and effect because it gummed up things. I wanted to be able to pivot without feeling any hands on me except hers.

And I got pretty good at it, and any time I start to get good at something, it goes straight to my head, and it puffs up, and I get bossy and decide I know it all and deserve it all, and then I do something spectacularly stupid. It happens every time.

Here's what happened. I insisted on meeting Debbie's mom, and not just that, I insisted that Debbie tell her mother that she must invite me into their house for dinner — preferably one she prepared herself.

"I'll give it some thought," she said. "Mom's not the hostess type."

"I'm serious," I said. "I think it's time. I want to meet her."

"Be careful what you wish for," she said.

What she didn't tell me was that she'd already had several conversations with her mom about me. Her mother had already warned her to slow it down.

"He makes me laugh," Debbie said.

"And he's a good kisser, right?" her mom replied.

"Mother!"

"Look, I'm not a prude. I'm not unreasonable. Have your fun. But I pray you keep it respectable."

Debbie snorted. "You pray. Oh, Mom. You pray? Is that with an 'a' or an 'e'?"

"P R A Y," Debbie's mother shot back. "I pray you keep it neck and above so that you won't fall prey — P R E Y — to some new and improved curiosity with a 5-inch bottle rocket and a two-second fuse."

"You're horrible," Debbie said.

"Call it what you like," her mother said. "I know, and you know I know what I'm talking about, so no surprises. Neck and above."

Debbie's mom paused for a half second, then tacked on, "Young lady."

"Young lady" meant, "Conversation over."

Of course, I didn't know any of this at the time, and all Debbie ever said was, "I'll mention it."

"I promise to bring a bottle of our best milk," I said and leaned back on my towel and asked her, "Any chance your dad will be there?"

The pool almost iced over. Debbie stiffened and she bit her lip and looked like she'd just lost the homecoming queen crown to a fat girl who lived in an oil storage tank.

"I need to run," she said, then began collecting her towel and lotion and hat and sandals.

"What?" I asked.

"I have to go," she said. "I forgot something, uh, I need to do… (deep breath) for Mom. This afternoon. We'll talk later."

And like that, she was gone. I looked at Kathy, and she seemed as shocked as I was, not that Debbie packed up and scooted off, but that I was that big an idiot.

"You asked about her dad?" she said. "You must be kidding."

Then, she held her hands in front her face like she was about to cough, then she raised them, palms up, and mouthed, "Poof."

We did talk later. She called at 6 — on the dot.

"I know there's something I need to apologize for," I said. "What is it?"

"Hold on," she said. "You didn't know about my father?"

"How would I know about your father?"

And, she said, "Because you would have asked someone, one of your 85 cousins, and they would've told you. Why? Because you wanted to know a little about the person you've been seeing every night. That would seem normal to me. Of course, I'm not from East Texas. Maybe that's not how you do it there."

"Do we have to discuss this on the phone?" I asked.

"Why not?" she said.

"I kept waiting for you to say something, and when you didn't, I respected your privacy. I told you about my dad. I figured when you were ready, you'd say something about your father."

"I don't have a father," she said.

"Lucky you," I said.

And she hung up.

This time, I didn't hear from her for two days, but I didn't mope or carry on this time. I was still running on the vapors of my own bossiness, so I told myself I didn't need her bullshit, and I worked hard to convince myself of that. In fact, when Mom called, I told her I was ready to come home.

"It's been great," I said. "But I think I'm done here. How are the boys?"

"We saw them last weekend," Mom said. "They're having a blast. They've been to Six Flags twice. They're not going to want to come home."

"Well, I do," I said.

"That's not going to happen this week," Mom said. "Your father and I are not where we need to be, yet."

I didn't ask what "yet" meant. I just said, "Whatever you need."

Of course, I was thinking: "Oh, sure. No problem. Take care of yourself first. My brothers and I can handle this, being shipped off, so you two take all the time you need. Besides, I'm having a blast — me and my goddamn splattered heart."

So, drat, I thought. Another week or more, stuck here — and when I said "stuck," I meant it literally, because I couldn't go to the pool or The Fritz, knowing I might run into her. I assumed she'd moved on and was talking shit about me to her very best friend in the whole wide world, who never liked me, anyway.

So, I clammed up. I finished my chores and lost myself in a book I found on a table in Mina's room about the murder of a farmer's family in Kansas. I was hurt and angry. I couldn't imagine why no one bothered to tell me about Debbie's father. They knew. They had to know, but no one said a word.

I asked Lori about it, and she said, "It's complicated, and people have funny ideas, and I decided it was none of my business."

That blew me away. Suddenly, it was none of her business. Up until then, everything had been her business. Faye, too. She knew.

Everyone knew, and no one warned me, so look who ended up playing Major Strasser.

—

For lunch, Mina served Swiss pork chops and German potato salad and a big fat dollop of humble pie.

"I bumped into your special friend at Schaper's Market this morning, and she asked me to ask you if you'd be willing to meet her tonight," Mina said.

"How was it?" I asked.

"If by 'it,' you mean 'Miss Gehring,' then I'd say Miss Gehring is a mess," Mina said. "I want you to fix this."

It was the first and only time she ever asked me to do something that didn't involve soap and water.

That night, I met Debbie on the steps outside the Palace Café where my grandmother had once waited tables, and Debbie told me she was embarrassed by her behavior and wanted to know if I could forgive her.

"I'm not always so histrionic," she said.

I didn't know what "histrionic" meant, but I figured it out.

Debbie told me about her father. She spoke in a flat voice that sounded like a sixth grader reading a research paper to her class.

Abe Ra'Ham Linkin.
Our Six-Teenth Pres-ah-dent.
Was'born in'a log cabin.
In tha'woods.

I listened carefully and let her finish, then said, "I don't know what's worse — a bad father or no father."

"It doesn't matter," she said. "This isn't about your father, my father, anyone's father. It's about me. Kathy was so mad at me. She kept telling me, 'Call him. You're making a big mistake.'"

"Maybe this whole thing was a mistake," I said, acting more pathetic than I actually was. "I'm just here for the summer. I could be gone by this time tomorrow, so what did we expect?"

"I didn't expect anything," she said. "I met a boy I liked, and we had fun, and everything was going really well, and I ruined it."

"It's ruined?" I asked. "I think you're being histrionic. I don't think it's ruined. I don't think we're ruined. I feel OK."

She leaned over and rested her forehead on my shoulder, and I took that for "Apology accepted, and thank you."

Two hours later, I met Faye in the kitchen and asked her the same question I'd asked Lori. Why hadn't anyone said anything about her father?

"I like Debbie as much as anyone can," Faye said.

"Care to explain that?" I asked.

"She's complicated, but I don't judge her because she has her reasons," Faye said. "Look, she's been hurt. Hurt in about several different ways."

"Sorry," I said. "Still lost."

"That's right," Faye said. "That's your problem. You're lost because you're not paying attention. Let me ask you a question: Have you seen her wear her hair up in a ponytail? I bet you haven't. Ever wondered why? I bet you haven't.

"You're always wondering how I know everything. The fact is, I don't know everything. Most of the time, I'm guessing. But I pay attention, and I try to figure out why people do what they do. Spend a little time doing that, and then, maybe we'll talk. ༃

CHAPTER 14
Father Gus

For as long as I can remember, I've woken up with a song bobbing around in my head. On good days, it's the Beatles or the Beach Boys or Hank Williams or Nat King Cole or Ray Charles or the Supremes.

On not so good ones, it might be "Big John" by Jimmy Dean, or "G.T.O." by Ronny & the Dakotas or "My Boy Lollipop" by Millie Small.

One morning, I woke up to "Dominique" by the Singing Nun. No kidding. That was the name on the record, and the singer was an actual nun. She came from Belgium, and she had a "before becoming a nun" name, which was Jeanne-Paule Marie Deckers.

She also had an official nun name, which was Sister Luc Gabriel. I suppose it was easier to go by "The Singing Nun" than either of those other names. At any rate, "Dominique" reached No. 1 on the Billboard Top 100 charts and was nominated for Grammy Record of the Year in 1963.

That explains as well as anything why it was so easy for the Beatles and the Stones and the other British Invasion bands to sweep in and conquer America in 1964. Anyway, I woke up with "Dominique" barnacled to my brain, and it would have taken a blowtorch to gouge it out, so I decided to have a little fun with it by re-writing the lyrics.

This is what ended up with:

> **Father Louis stole the undies,**
> **Of a nun and even more.**
> **He sold them to his whore.**
> **She said, "I can't wear these rags,**
> **Send them back to those old hags.**
> **Now, lay back for the encore."**

I thought it was hilarious. Jeff did, too, so we memorized the lyrics and were singing them after Mass, and Sister Geraldine, who was 92 years old and 93 percent deaf, somehow heard us and made out just enough of the melody to waddle over and ask us to sing the song again.

"I like that tune," she said in her spry voice. "It's catchy."

We exchanged glances and snickered because we thought we'd hoodwinked the old gal, but then, out of nowhere, Father Gus parachuted in.

"Yes, Jeffrey. You and your friend here, please sing these lyrics so Sister Geraldine can hear you clearly. You know, she is hard of hearing, so, speak up, or she will be unable to hear. And sing them exactly as you did just now. Would you enjoy that, Sister?"

Sister Geraldine thought about it and replied, "I live here, Father. I work in the nursery."

Father Gus patted her papery hand, shook his head, and said, "Of course, Sister Geraldine, and how fortunate we are for that. Your job is to serve our Lord and Savior, and you are one of our most valued servants."

She understood that and beamed.

Then, Father Gus turned back to us and said, "Well, what are you waiting on? Sing! Raise your voices. Sing so even the angels in heaven, the ones who may determine your fate one day, can hear every word."

"Every word?" Jeff asked.

"Are you deaf, too?" Father Gus said. "Every word. Do not skip a syllable."

So, we sang, and after we'd finished, Sister Geraldine turned to Father Gus with a baffled look on her face and said, "Tomorrow, I would like an apple jelly donut."

And Father said, "Of course, Sister. I pray that you and I will each have a jelly donut. Tomorrow. Now, Sister Geraldine, I want you to return to your tasks. I know you have important work to do, as do I."

Again, her face glowed, and she tottered toward the nursery.

Father Gus, then, turned his attention back to us.

"Jeffrey, I will deal with you later. Go somewhere," he said, then thumped me in the chest with his right index finger and said, "You. Young man. Follow me."

I trailed him through the sanctuary, down a narrow corridor connecting the church to the high school, then up a flight of stairs and into his office. It reeked of cigarette smoke and burnt coffee and dusty books and moldy magazines because that was how he wanted it. No one was allowed to move so much as a paperclip.

Father Gus took his seat behind an oak desk that had served the church's past three or four pastors, and brushed aside a stack of folders, an issue of the Catholic Digest, and several thick books on the War Between the States.

Father Gus also taught a senior history class, although he was not required to do so. He taught it because he wanted to. Military history fascinated him. He'd earned a master's degree in history from Tarleton State, and his sermons were often punctuated with quotes from Julius Caesar, George Washington, Robert E. Lee, George Patton, Napoleon Bonaparte, even Erwin Rommel.

On the wall beside his desk, he had framed a quote from Hannibal: I will either find a way or make one.

"Find a way, or make one," was one of Father Gus' favorite lines. His other favorite line was, "So, it's come to this," and that's what he said to me after I'd taken the seat directly in front of him.

"So, it's come to this," he said, and I had no reply.

"Sit up," he ordered. "You'll not slump in my chair."

I thought I was sitting up, but I stiffened my back and shifted my shoulders and raised my chin.

"Jeffrey is a follower, and he's followed every idiot this town has produced during the short time he's graced this planet. We have plenty of idiots here, so we don't need to ship in more from wherever you come from. By the way, where do you come from?"

"Marshall, sir."

"Marshall, Texas?"

"Yes, sir."

"Is there a Catholic church in Marshall, Texas?"
"Yes, sir."
"And do you attend mass regularly?"
"Well, as regularly as we can. Mom works, and my dad is…"
"Did I request a speech?" he said. "I asked a simple question: Yes or no. Do you attend mass regularly?"
"No, Father. I don't."
"Imagine my shock. You are not a member of this church, so I have no stake in you, no jurisdiction over you. I could banish you, but that would embarrass your aunt, and she would feel shame although no one would blame her for your shameful behavior. That's just how she is. I assume you understand the word 'shame?' The length and width of it. What it means. What it suggests. Shame. Do you know what it means?"
"Well, I guess it…"
"Yes. Or. No," he said.
"Yes, Father."
My stomach churned. My head spun. My mouth dried to powder.
"About these lyrics. You wrote them. Jeffrey is lucky to write his own name. I'm curious how it is you chose to mock Father Louis. Do you know something about him that I don't? Does steal women's undergarments? Does he give them to his consorts? Does Father Louis have consorts?"
"Well, Father, this was just a … you know, a…"
"No," he said. "I don't know. Tell me. I'm desperate to hear."
"It's just a joke," I said.
"A joke?" he said. "This is your idea of a joke?"
"Well, not actually a joke. I woke up with the tune in my head. I couldn't shake it, so I re-wrote the lyrics, and, well, you know."
"Again, I don't. I would appreciate it if you'd stop suggesting that I do. How long did it take you to compose this masterpiece?"
"An hour or so."
"So, if I understand you correctly, you devoted an hour of your life writing this puerile doggerel," he said. "You devoted an hour or

so of your life writing crude lyrics that accuse an important person, a special man, a dear friend of mine of theft and of consorting with loose women when he has taken a vow of chastity and, as a Catholic, you would know that, even if you attended Mass only once a year, and yet, still, you wrote these words. Why in God's name would you choose to do such a thing?"

"I was just having fun," I said.

Father Gus had memorized the lines, verbatim, and he recited them, and it was agony hearing them come out of his mouth.

> **Father Louis stole the undies,**
> **Of a nun and even more.**
> **He sold them to his whore.**
> **She said, "I can't wear these rags,**
> **Send them back to those old hags.**
> **Now, lay back for the encore."**

"You think this is funny?" he said. "Father Louis stole a nun's undergarments and sold them to a prostitute, who in turn performed sexual acts upon him. This is your idea of humor? Should I invite Father Louis to see if he appreciates your humor? Should I invite your aunt and uncle for a special performance? Perhaps they'll recognize your genius. It certainly escapes me."

I stared at the floor and chewed my lower lip and tried to keep from fainting, but then, Father Gus told me to stand up and stiffen my back and accept the consequences.

"You'll leave here soon enough, and this will remain a joke to you, something you can brag about to your friends back in Marshall where you can't be bothered to attend Mass regularly, but we will have to live with it, especially if Father Louis hears of it. And if he does, it will hurt him because he treated you with great kindness and generosity, and you've belittled him. You've mocked him, and why? Because he's different. This has been the story of his life. He's different, so he's mocked, but I will assure you, his heart is pure, and he tries his best, despite the endless carping he receives from some members of this church."

He didn't name names, but I knew who he was talking about,

and it wasn't Mina.

"You are the perpetrator of a senseless, despicable act, conceived out of boredom because you could not find anything useful to do with an hour of your life," Father Gus continued. "There will be repercussions. Jeffrey will soon sit where you are seated now, and he will feel more than the sting of my words. After all, he is a member of this church, and he does fall under my purview.

"But you? I don't know you. For all I know, you might be snickering under your breath right now. You might be thinking you've pulled the wool over my eyes. But you're wrong. I see you for what you are, and your punishment will be worse than Jeffrey's."

He paused and took a sip from a coffee cup.

"How many letters are in the word 'repercussion?'" he asked.

I told him I wasn't sure. Ten or 11.

"No," Father Gus said. "There are 12. I hope Jeffrey thinks of you with each of the 12 swats he will receive on the 12 consecutive Saturdays he will clean this building's toilets. That will be his punishment. But it will start and end. Your punishment will accompany you for a long time. You will be forever remembered as the ungrateful guest who came from far away only to invent and spread scurrilous lies about Father Louis, my dear friend, my trusted colleague, who believes in the essential goodness of his fellow man and in the mercy of the Lord, even though he has been bullied and mocked and used and abused.

"Now, you have arrived to belittle him further. And why? You don't know. You can't say. It was just a joke. Well, is it still just a joke to you? I don't see the humor, and I have a keen sense of humor. Unfortunately for you, I have a keen sense of propriety, and a tendency to seek retaliation even though the Lord commands me to forgive, but I am a sinner, too, and I'm not in the forgiving mood."

Father Gus leaned forward, then lifted himself with both hands. He bowed his back and said, "Now, I want you to leave this building. I suggest you find a quiet place to think about who and what you are. In the meantime, I will pray for the wisdom and grace I need to understand why I am forced to waste my time on wastrels like you."

He turned and left through a private door behind his desk.

He didn't excuse me, so I waited a moment, then sprinted out of his office, down the hall, down a stairway, and out the double doors. I barely made it to a flower bed before throwing up on the rose bushes.

Once I'd finished, I walked over to the cemetery, found a concrete bench in the shade of a willow, and was thinking about who I was when I gazed up and noticed a statute of St. Francis of Assisi. He held two doves, wore a black robe and hippie sandals, and leaned slightly to the left.

Despite his beard and mustache, he looked young, maybe 30 or 35. I studied his wide-set eyes and his slight pout. I wondered what someone like him would make of someone like me. A wastrel like me was likely the reason saints like him preferred animals.

Father Gus returned to his office, walked over to a bookshelf, and pulled a bottle of Johnny Walker out from behind a biography of Franklin Delano Roosevelt. He poured two fingers into two stained coffee cups, then handed one of the cups to Father Louis, who had eavesdropped on every word.

"Guth, you'fth thscarred that boy for life," Father Louis said.

"I hope so," Father Gus replied. "Let's grab lunch."

The two priests polished off their Johnnie Walker and headed toward the parking lot. On the way, Father Louis softly whistled "Dominique."

For the record: Father Gus never punished Jeff. As he told Father Louis, "What would be the point?"

He then recited from memory Matthew, Chapter 6, Verse 14: "For if you forgive other people when they sin against you, your heavenly Father will also forgive you."

CHAPTER 15
On assignment

I thought about Debbie constantly. I couldn't shake her out of my mind. I wondered what she was doing, who she was talking to, what was she saying, what was she feeling, what she was wearing, what she was wearing under that. I wondered if she was wondering about me.

I became super conscious of little things I thought she might enjoy or appreciate, like a new song by a group she'd never heard of. "Bus Stop" by the Hollies, perhaps.

I tried to recreate in my head the sound of her voice, which wasn't easy because her voice didn't bounce up and down like a lot of girls' voices. Instead, it shifted up and down smoothly and effortlessly.

I also tried to conjure the smell of her hair — that is, I guess, the smell of her shampoo. I never thought to ask what brand it was, but it had a fruity, medicinal scent. I couldn't inhale it deeply enough.

I wanted to walk through her house to see if it looked and felt like her. Were there were dirty dishes in the sink? Was her bed made up? If not, was it a mess? Did she have pictures of an old boyfriend still taped to a mirror or tacked to a door? Did she have dirty clothes stacked in a corner?

I still wanted to meet her mom, even if she didn't care one way or the other. I wanted to know what they talked about at the dinner table. In truth, I needed to, but Debbie ignored my subtle hints, so I decided to give it a rest. It didn't take long to realize she was an only child, and I was glad she was. I didn't want to waste time being nice to a nosy younger sister or suspicious older brother.

I didn't want anything to interrupt our walks and talks, and I wanted our walks and talks to lead us more quickly to the corner of Walnut and Sycamore and into my grandmother's house and onto a ragged cotton rug on the living room floor, where we almost suffocated ourselves making out.

We'd begin sitting on the floor and facing the front window. She'd rotate to face me, then place her hands on my shoulders, and I'd raise my arms and wrap them around her waist, and she'd pull me toward her until our lips were almost but not quite touching, and she'd say something ridiculous like, "Don't cry for me after you're gone. Cry for me now," which was a line she'd picked up from a movie starring Marlene Dietrich.

We'd laugh, and that would be our cue to make out until it was time to go or we collapsed from heat exhaustion.

I remember reading an article in a Catholic Digest that said married people engaged in sexual intercourse because they love each other so much that they want to become one person. It sounded ridiculous then, but during our more furious moments, it seemed as if we were trying to swallow each other whole.

It was glorious.

—

Ten minutes after I arrived back at the farm, Debbie would call, and we'd talk until someone on the party line had an emergency or until Lori threw a shoe at me, which was her way of reminding me she had a love-life, too.

At first, I worried someone might ask me why it was that I needed to talk to Debbie on the phone, given that we'd just spent a couple of hours together, but then, I thought, "These people aren't stupid. They know."

They knew what we'd been doing, and they knew the clock was ticking, so they let us talk as long as we wanted, and so, we did. I told her about a friend's mom who seemed to cry all the time, and why? I couldn't figure it out. It wasn't money. She'd married a lawyer, and they had a swimming pool and a Buick Continental and a Ford Mustang convertible, and she had nothing better to do than sit out by her pool and sip tropical drinks and read trashy novels and bake all over and cry.

It seemed strange and ridiculous. My mom almost never cried. When she did, it wasn't in broad daylight, and she wasn't sitting out by her pool with a tropical drink in one hand and "Peyton Place" in the other.

If Mom cried, it wasn't because she was sad. It was because she was mad. Once, the Burger Barn offered free milkshakes with each hamburger, and so, we drove over to get hamburgers, and when my dad returned to the car with the burgers, he didn't bother to pick up the free milkshakes because he didn't want one, and he didn't care that we did.

Mom lost it. She chewed his ass out, and he had to return to the window with the receipt and say he'd forgotten to ask for the free milkshakes. The girl working the window said, "I thought you didn't…"

And my dad said, "Give me the damn milkshakes," so she did.

Mom fumed about that for two days, and I knew it had to do with more than free milkshakes.

—

I told Debbie that story and other stories, too. I told her about Mom's infatuation with cemeteries. My dad thought she was nuts. If we were driving out in the country, and she spotted a cemetery, she'd start pointing and slapping the dashboard, but he'd ignore her, hoping she'd let it go, but she rarely did.

"Pull over," she'd command. "Pull. Over. I want to look at that."

"Look at what? You've seen one. You've seen 'em all."

"It's beyond you," she once said. "You'd understand if you'd learned to read."

Of course, I sided with Mom, so I kept an eye out for tiny churches or family plots.

"Mom! Mom! Look! Cemetery!"

"Where?"

"3 o'clock."

Mom ordered him to whip back around, and my dad would say, "Goddamn, not again," but he'd do it and pull up to the cemetery gate or chain-link fence or whatever, and Mom would hop out, and he'd give me the evil eye and say, "Get your ass out. You ain't sitting in here with me. And take these other two with you."

So, no wonder the bastard hated me, but he asked for it.

—

I also told Debbie about a kid at my school who had something called "Tourette's Syndrome." I asked her if she knew what that was, which was like asking Chuck Berry if he knew what a guitar was. Anyway, this kid's name was Peter, and most of the time, he was normal, but then, out of the blue, he'd squawk like a parrot or bark like a dog. Now and then, he'd spit out a string of curse words, and everyone assumed he did it on purpose because they didn't know any better.

Teachers didn't either. One teacher slapped Peter so hard she almost knocked him out. I saw her do it. Peter fell to the floor and wailed and couldn't stop, so the teacher called the office, and a principal came and hauled him off.

Those same teachers ignored the endless times when Peter was pushed and shoved and tripped and ordered to get the fuck out of the way. Eventually, Peter's dad intervened, not by trying to appeal to a teacher's sense of fair play, but by teaching Peter a few martial arts moves he'd learned while serving in Korea. One day, a jerk thumped Peter's ear, and Peter snapped his left thumb.

No one bullied Peter after that. Of course, being bullied was the least of his problems. He still had Tourette's. He told me he just wanted to be able to sit and finish his homework in peace.

"That's all I want," he said. "If I had just that and nothing else, I'd be the happiest kid in the world."

I told Debbie this story as a way of saying, "And you think we have problems."

Oh well, things we often talked about:

- "Gone With the Wind" (the movie)
- "The Diary of Anne Frank" (the book)
- Hemingway. LBJ. MLK
- Snobs. Jerks. Brown-Noses
- Kissing above the neck

Things we didn't talk about:
- Funeral homes. Milk routes
- Crooked front teeth. Overbites
- Baseball. Football. Lucille Ball
- The Warren Report. Vietnam
- Kissing below the neck

Things I thought about while we were talking:
- Don't think about kissing her below the neck. She's not that kind of girl.
- But what if she is that kind of girl?

Things she thought about while we were talking:
- I'm not that kind of girl. Yet.

One night, we were wandering through the Kassel cemetery and noticed a lightning storm moving in from the north. It seemed a long way off, but then, a bolt crackled across the sky — left to right — along the front of the storm, and the lightning was so bright, it was as if someone had flashed headlights on and off.

In that brief sliver of light, I caught a glimpse of the biggest owl I'd ever seen, perched at the top of an obelisk headstone.

"It's amazing how much you can see even at night," I said.

She replied, "It helps if you're looking. And you sure better be."

I thought it was an odd response, but I let it go because I knew she could turn on a dime, flipping from breezy and sweet to suspicious and sullen as a baby's funeral.

For example, I told her that Aunt Mina kept copies of old Catholic Digests stacked in an upstairs cubby-hole, and I'd been thumbing through them, and they were pretty much all the same.

They went on and on about who goes to Heaven, and who goes to Hell, and why the Pope is infallible, and why Catholics must recite the rosary every day, and why nuns can never be priests, and why Catholics eat fish on Friday, and why priests like Father Louis wear funny-looking slippers and Marti Gras hats.

It was generally the same nonsense, issue after issue, until I noticed this cover headline: "The Rape of Berlin."

It was about the Russian assault on the German capital, where Hitler was holed up at the end of the war, and it made it sound as if the Russians had invaded Germany for no reason at all, and that the poor German people were victims of Stalin's bloodlust.

I was no expert on World War II, but I knew enough to know the German people weren't innocent bystanders, but that's not what the author of this piece in the Catholic Digest claimed. He suggested the Germans were minding their own business when the Mongolian horde arrived at their doorsteps, killing all the old men and raping all the females and then building a wall to keep the females from escaping so they could rape them some more.

The article never mentioned Leningrad or Stalingrad or the concentration camps or Warsaw, which I'd read about in Leon Uris' "Mila 18." It just made it sound as if the Soviets had nothing better to do than to obliterate Berlin.

I told Debbie about the article and how it tried to portray the Germans as victims and the Soviets as Mongoloid beasts. I told her the Pope never said a word about the Holocaust, and that the Vatican helped Nazi war criminals like Adolph Eichmann and Josef Mengele escape to South America, and I insisted the Germans got what they deserved. I laid it on thick because I was showing off.

Maybe she was impressed, and maybe she wasn't, but she rubbed her lower lip, right about where the little scar was and said, "I don't care if men want to slaughter each other, but they ought to leave the women alone. Even if they're wearing Hitler poodle skirts, no woman, and certainly no girl, should be touched."

Then, she retreated into herself. It was the first and last time I discussed military history with her.

—

The Fritz was owned and operated by a pudgy, balding man named Arnold "Cupcake" Zimmerman. He got the nickname from his former wife, who'd died of a heart attack three years earlier. She dropped dead about a month before turning 40. They found her body in a bathroom. She was wearing blue rubber gloves because she'd just finished scrubbing the tub.

She called Arnold "Cupcake" because he was so sweet. Every now and then, she'd kiss his forehead and say, "Sweet as strawberry icing."

It was no accident he called her, "Sunshine," though her real name was Edith.

I liked Cupcake the minute I met him, and I think he liked me.

"Are you here on business or pleasure?" he asked me when I popped in one morning.

"Actually, I'm here for coffee," I said. "But I hope to be joined by my new friend at any moment."

"Well, then, I'll jot that down as 'on assignment,'" he said. "Other than the coffee and the company, want anything else?"

I told him I'd already eaten but wouldn't mind a glazed donut if he had one. Then, I slipped into the booth in the back facing the kitchen because I wanted some privacy when Debbie arrived and because I wanted to be able to duck out of sight if anyone else strolled in.

Sure enough, the front door swung open, and Kathy Klement strolled in and headed my way.

The café was half full, and everyone knew her, so she stopped by all the tables and booths to say good morning and how are you and, gosh, aren't you looking wonderful, and then she arrived at my booth and slid in without asking and said, "Just the person I need to talk to. I have a problem. My best friend is missing. She just up and disappeared."

About that time, Cupcake dropped off my coffee and a donut, and Kathy said, "Good morning, Mr. Arnold," flirtatiously, and he almost blushed.

"Good morning, Miss Klement," he replied. "Anything?"

"Just water, for now, Mr. Z," she said, then continued. "This girl. My friend who's missing. I can't imagine what has happened to her. I've not seen hide nor hair of her, and we used to be so close."

"I wish I could help you," I said.

"You haven't seen her? Long blond hair. Blue eyes. Kind of pale.

A little pouty. Slightly crooked front tooth, right there, but in a cute way. Ding-a-ling. Ring any bells?"

"Can't say it does. Have you talked to Jack? Maybe he knows."

"Possible, but unlikely. I hear she's been seeing someone else."

"I do wish I could help, Miss K," I said. "Tell you what, if I hear or see anything, I'll notify the authorities."

"The authorities?" Kathy huffed. "The authorities couldn't find black hair in China."

Though I was generally terrified of her, I laughed. I didn't realize she was serious, and not about the authorities, so I asked, "Are you jerking my chain, or is there a real problem?"

"It could be a problem, eventually."

"Is it a girl thing?"

"No, it's not a girl thing. It's a 'you' thing."

"Do you mean 'you' as in 'me?'"

"I mean 'you,' as in 'you worry me,'" she said.

"You're worried about me?"

"No. I'm worried about her. You're the reason I'm worried about her. I'm worried about her because she seems to be happy."

"She's happy, and that worries you?"

"If you knew what I know, you'd be worried, too," she said.

"What do you know?" I asked.

"I know everything," she said. "I know she likes you. A lot. And that's an understatement, and I'm happy for her, but I'm worried about what will happen to her after you're gone. I worry it'll be very hard for her, and I worry you don't fully appreciate that."

"I do appreciate it," I said. "It's going to be hard for me, too."

Kathy shook her head in a "Good, Lord. You don't know pinwheels from petticoats" sort of way.

"I'm going to tell you something you need to know," she said. "I'm surprised you haven't heard anything about it already. Or perhaps you have. Do you an inkling about what I'm talking about?"

"I have no idea what you're talking about," I said.

"OK," she said. "Here it is: She's taken a big risk with you, and

I pushed her to take that risk because I thought you'd be nothing more than a fling, good for a few laughs, some serious making out, and whatever else came naturally. God knows she needs it, and, as I'm sure you've heard, I have no moral high ground. I've never claimed I did. In fact, a moral high ground is the last thing in the world I want."

I nursed my coffee and waited, but she never got around to telling me whatever it was she thought I should've known because she glanced up just in time to notice Debbie about to enter the front door.

"Oh, Heavens," Kathy gasped.

I swung around and saw her, too. I then gave Kathy a look that sort of begged the ridiculous question, "She's not going to think we're …?"

And Kathy almost threw up in her mouth.

"Good Lord, don't flatter yourself," she said, then raised her hand and beamed and waited just a moment, then said, "Girl, I love what you're doing with your hair."

PART 3 | CHAPTER 16

Otto Becker

April 1949
As told by the author

There's a difference between an oath and an affirmation. An oath is a solemn promise. If you break it, you answer to a deity like Jesus or Agni, the Hindi minor deity in charge of fire. If you were a member of the Ostyak tribe of Northern Siberia many years ago, you answered to a dead bear.

Here's how it worked: Witnesses in legal disputes involving Ostyaks would be seated next to the severed head of a bear and told that if they lied, the bear would spring to life, maul and eat them.

If only justice were administered this efficiently.

As for an affirmation, it's just a declaration. God is not involved. If someone affirms that a horse is only two years old, but it turns out the horse is eight years old, the witness loses personal credibility and perhaps status in the community, but he's not condemned to spend eternity in Hell or end up as bear chow.

Knowing this is inconsequential until it isn't.

—

Jennifer Mae Gehring was born and raised in Kassel, hated it, and left as fast as she could, despite her parents' strenuous objections.

She enrolled in a Fort Worth secretarial school that her mother feared was more in the business of sexual antics than in stenography or shorthand.

"I fear she'll be among women who, when times get rough, are quick to maximize the earning potential of their nether regions," her mother wrote in her diary.

Jennifer Mae — Jenny — was never one to worry about what other people knew or thought they knew, not even her stern mother, whom she loved dearly. Jenny knew that most people's opinions were about as reliable as a string of last year's Christmas lights, so, she enrolled in the secretarial school because she couldn't afford to go to college and because she wasn't ready to compete directly against men in the field of her choice, which was accounting. Attending secretarial school was as close to accounting as she could get at the moment.

Fortunately, she had the right disposition and bearing. Tall. Teutonic. Golden. She looked a little like Rosemary Clooney in "White Christmas."

Though she had no formal training in accounting, she was wicked smart and sensible, so she figured she could handle herself and, for the better part, she could. She was hit on shamelessly, but she bobbed and weaved and blocked the jabs, not because she was a prude but because she wasn't a rube.

She liked to mingle and sip champagne and dance with men she thought to be her equal or better. She had a couple of spirited romances, but they left her wanting more, even though she wasn't sure what "more" involved or required.

In late April 1949, she and three girlfriends from secretarial school attended a party at a ranch outside Weatherford, thrown by a man named Harry Tuttle. Mr. Tuttle owned a pair of successful Fort Worth funeral homes, and most of the guests at the party were connected to the death care industry. They'd been in Dallas, attending a trade show.

Jenny and her friends were invited to the party because they were young and attractive, and they decided to go because they were hungry and thirsty, literally and figuratively.

Harry Tuttle had one son. His name was Darrell, and he was everything his father dreamed of being. Darrell had been a member of the 2nd Ranger Battalion that fought in the Battle of Hürtgren Forest. It was a senseless waste. Military historians now say it should never have been fought, given that it had no impact on the outcome of the war.

The American generals responsible for the debacle underestimated the dense, rugged landscape just east of the Belgian-German border, as well as the fanaticism of the SS and Panzer Divisions dug in there, so more than 33,000 Americans were killed or wounded in that battle.

Darrell fought gallantly and earned a fistful of medals and ribbons to prove it, not that he had anything to prove. He was a hero, even though he scoffed whenever someone said so. He wouldn't argue. He'd either tune out or walk out because the last thing he wanted to do was re-live the war.

Most of the those who went on and on about the war never saw what Darrell saw. Darrell saw heads blown off. He saw men impaled by the jagged wood fragments that rained down on them after German mortar shells blew the tops off pine trees. He personally shot at close range anything even marginally resembling a German, and that included prepubescent Hitler Jugend who had the audacity to raise a rifle or toss a grenade in his direction.

When Darrell arrived home, he was 21 going on 41, and he had no interest in the family's funeral business. He told his father he'd drive a garbage truck before dabbing makeup on a dead woman's liver spots.

So, Harry made him an offer: Run the ranch. It had been a losing venture, anyway. Maybe he could make something of it.

"Pay the bills, and then every dollar you turn is yours," Harry told him. "You want to be a cowboy? This is your chance."

A year later, the ranch turned a $75,000 profit. Darrell chased off the riffraff and replaced them with real ranch hands even though most of them were neither U.S. citizens nor speakers of the English language. Darrell did not care. Cows didn't speak English, either. They answered to clicks and whistles and hoots and eventually, Darrell came to understand all the yips and clicks and whistles, and he got to know the cows and the Mexican cowhands who spoke Bovine with a Spanish inflection.

He rode a stout Morgan horse named Penny because she was the same color as an American penny. Darrell was generally in the saddle before dawn and only out of it to eat, take a leak, or sign something. He was wide-shouldered, tight around the waist and taut in the seat.

His ears cupped out slightly, and his jaw jutted out a little too far. Work or play, he wore standard khakis, long-sleeved cotton shirts and black roper boots. He didn't own a bolo tie, a fancy belt buckle or a pair of pointy-toed, lizard-skin boots.

His smile was slightly off-kilter because he had a habit of grinding his teeth, not that anyone — especially young women — noticed. They flocked to him — a few because of his money, but most because they could tell he knew how to sit in the saddle, and you can read that any way you like.

Jenny might have been one of those young women if he hadn't already been roped and tied by Babette, a tawny brunette who once had ambitions of being an Olympic swimmer. She wore skin-tight blue jeans and a crimson-and-white cowboy shirt, and she clutched his arm like it was the Titanic's last life preserver.

If she sensed Darrell might be gazing a bit too long at another woman, she just unsnapped another button on her cowboy shirt, and that put an end to that.

Darrell and Babette were followed around by one of his father's associates — an odd fellow Darrell's father had met at the funeral director's tradeshow in Dallas. He invited him to the party as a professional courtesy. Harry didn't expect him to show up, so when he did, Harry asked Darrell to give him the grand tour.

That didn't exactly coincide with Darrell's plans for the evening, but he did as he was asked to do. He showed the fellow the ranch house, pointing out this piece of Western art and that piece of taxidermy and trying to palm him off at each station along the way.

Eventually, Darrell made his way to a billiards table where Jenny's three friends from secretarial school were standing and sipping a sugary drink they'd never heard of. It was called a "margarita."

Darrell introduced himself, then introduced Babette, then said, "Thanks for coming all this way for our little get-together."

He started to introduce the odd fellow but couldn't remember his name, so he did a work-around.

"And this gentleman is more than capable of introducing himself, so I'll leave him in your company, and ya'll make yourself at home and don't steal anything too expensive."

He winked, knocked on the side of the pool table twice, and headed toward the patio, with Babette clutching his arm.

"What a prince," the odd fellow said. "Ladies, my name is Otto Becker. At your service."

He was ridiculous.

"Are you rich?" one of Jenny's friends asked.

Otto Becker laughed.

"No, ma'am. I'm not in the oil business, if that's your question," he said.

"Are you a rancher?" another asked.

"No. I'm not a rancher," he replied.

"Are you from Fort Worth or Dallas?" the third friend asked.

"No. I'm not from Fort Worth or Dallas. I'm from a little town I doubt any of you have heard of. A little town just east of Wichita Falls called Kassel."

"I've heard of it," the first friend said.

"Is that so?" Otto said.

"We have a friend from Kassel," she said. "In fact, she's here, somewhere. I think she went to the ladies room. She should be back in a jiff."

Jenny wasn't back in a jiff. She'd been cut off at the pass by a real cowboy, a scrub oak of a fellow named Larry Dickson. He was a former rodeo star who'd broken almost every major bone in his body once, yet he could still ride and rope at full gallop.

He was 5-foot 6 and bow-legged, and Jenny thought he was charming until she noticed chewing tobacco stuck between his teeth, so she told him she needed to check in with her friends.

"Perhaps a little boot-scootin' later?" Mr. Dickson asked.

"Perhaps," Jenny said. "I'll be around."

Meanwhile, Otto Becker wanted to know more about this friend from Kassel.

"What's her name," he asked.

"I'm sorry, but you'll just have to wait," the second friend said.

About then, the third friend spotted Jenny and trotted across the room to intercept her.

"We've just met someone you might know," the third friend said. "He says he's from Kassel."

"Really?" Jenny asked. "What's his name?"

"Pecker. Double decker. Something like that. Do you know him?"

"Becker?" Jenny asked, walking toward the billiards table. "If it's Becker, I know him. I know a whole kit and caboodle of them."

When Otto recognized her, he placed his Chevis Regal on a coffee table and said, "Jenny Gehring. As I live and breathe. You're all grown up."

"I am," Jenny said. "And your daddy still owns the funeral home, I'll bet."

"He does. I'm working for him full-time now. Let me think. The last time I saw you — let's see — it was your aunt's service. And her name was…?"

"Ruth."

"Tip of my tongue. Ruth Hertel. Ruth Eileen Vogt Hertel, 94 years young. Born in Elwood, Nebraska. Moved to Kassel as an infant. Her husband was a butcher. His name was Earl. Am I right?"

"You are," Jenny said. "Uncle Earl."

"I think I was 17 or 18, and you were 14 or 15 when your aunt died," he added.

"I'd just turned 15," Jenny said.

"That means your aunt died in August of 1942," Otto said. "Nothing worse than an August funeral. Thank God the dead don't sweat. Mortuary makeup runs like a scalded ape."

No one needed to hear that.

—

Otto was 26. During the war, he was a radio operator in the Philippines and had earned a Purple Heart after a piece of shrapnel about the size of a Brazil nut ripped into his right hip. He almost bled to death.

He spent six weeks in a Manila hospital before being shipped to Honolulu, where he spent the remainder of the war on crutches that kept him from performing any physical labor but rarely interfered with his social life. Between the whorehouses in Manila and those that had sprung up near Schofield Barracks, he acquired an appetite for exotic hedonism.

All it took was money, and he had plenty of that, so he could indulge his fantasies and proclivities. He preferred the younger ones — as young as 11. Some nights, he'd entertain two or three. His appetite was insatiable.

After the Japanese surrendered, he was shipped from Hawaii to San Francisco, where prostitutes were older, harder, smarter, and far more mercenary. They didn't appeal to him in the least, so he plotted to return to Hawaii and then, perhaps, to Manila if he could cobble together the cash.

He thought his father might give or at least loan him a couple grand, but it didn't happen. "Get a job and earn it yourself," the old man told his son. "I'll co-sign the loan on a car because you'll need one, but that's it."

He handed Otto a slip of paper with a name and a phone number.

"Call him Monday morning," he said. "He arrives at 7."

By Wednesday noon, Otto was working at a downtown Lawton, Oklahoma, furniture store, selling sofas and coffee tables and lamps out the front door and bootleg whiskey out the back.

Though he'd just turned 22, he didn't look much older than the high school boys he sold booze to, so they invited him to parties after football games and such, and he'd show up with a couple of bottles that were enough to keep the guys busy while he sweet-talked high school girls into strolling upstairs or out back with him.

Then, he'd go a little farther than they were comfortable going, but they did anyway.

When he'd finished, he'd wash up, comb his hair, disappear into the night, drive home, hit the sack, show up to work the next morning, and try to convince young wives and their husbands that they fought and whipped the Germans and the Japs to protect their God-given right to own a new sleeper-sofa.

Everything was working fine until he charmed the wrong girl into hopping into the backseat of his 1939 Mercury. It was after a big football game between Lawton High and the newly opened Eisenhower High, and he wrangled his right hand into the Sears & Roebuck panties of a 16-year-old girl who happened to be the daughter of a prominent Baptist preacher.

The next night, Otto stepped out of a juke joint for a breath of fresh air, and two granite-faced off-duty police officers in matching navy-blue suits grabbed him by the collar, jerked him into a headlock, wrestled him into an alley, and clubbed him with leather batons.

At first, Otto thought he was being robbed, but the taller of the two officers put him into a chokehold and squeezed, harder and harder, then turned loose and shoved Otto to the ground.

"Jesus may forgive, but the preacher don't. Get out of town tonight. If we find you tomorrow, and we will be, we won't be so delicate."

Otto was lucky to escape with an inch-long gash about above his left eye, a busted lip, and a few bruises. It helped that he'd learned enough Judo in the Philippines to block the more potentially disfiguring blows.

He staggered back to his studio apartment, raked his things into a suitcase, tossed it in the backseat of his Mercury, and headed south.

Around 3:30 a.m., Otto jimmied open his parent's front door, squeezed inside the living room, tip-toed into the guest bathroom, drew a hot bath, bandaged his eye and lip as best as he could, then threw a bath towel and a pillow on the floor of his old bedroom because he knew he'd catch hell if he bled on the mattress.

Three hours later, his mother found him curled up on the floor, oozing like a pink meatloaf. She called to her husband, who woke Otto by clanging a fork in a sauce pan. While his suspicious father hovered over him, his bleeding-heart mother blotted the gash and his lip with a damp dish towel.

"What trouble have you gotten yourself into this time?" his father asked.

Otto told him he'd been sucker-punched at a county fair by a stranger — some local hayseed.

"For no reason I assume," his father said. "A local boy just came up and slugged you for no reason. How many is this? The third time?"

"He's hurt," Otto's mother snapped. "Can't you see that? He needs a doctor. Call Robert and get him here."

Otto's father scoffed and headed toward his library.

Otto's mother continued to dab at his wounds until his father was out of ear shot. Then, she poked at his busted lip until he yelped.

"You're a better liar than that," she said. "I suggest you keep a low profile until whatever mess you've created blows over."

And that, he did.

He also abandoned his fantasy of returning to San Francisco or Honolulu or Manila. It wasn't in the cards, he figured, so he joined the family business. He hated the idea of being under his old man's thumb, but he quickly warmed to the idea of strolling in on Day One as the crown prince.

—

Otto was a natural. The funeral business had always attracted shysters, liars, and cheats like him. All he had to do was play to his talents. Of course, the long-time employees he leap-frogged and lorded over despised him. The Becker Funeral Home had always had a reputation for honesty and sincerity, but changed soon after Otto arrived.

Unctuous, officious, and patronizing, he squeezed an extra dime out of the living and the dead by skimping on embalming chemicals and jacking up the prices of caskets — like the ones he'd inspected the day he accepted an invitation to attend a party at a ranch near Weatherford, where he bumped into none other than Jenny Gehring, who was all grown up now.

—

"I'm working for my father," Otto told Jenny. "I'm attending a trade show in Dallas. We want to upgrade our product line."

"By 'product line,' you mean caskets," Jenny said.

"Heavens, no," Otto replied. "There are other essentials. There's embalming…"

But Jenny cut him off. "That's OK. I get the point. How is the funeral business in Kassel these days?"

"No complaints," he said. "Death never takes a holiday."

Jenny's friends rolled their eyes, but she found his off-putting ways to be oddly cute. He wasn't handsome, but he was educated and artificially sophisticated, which suggested some effort. At least, he didn't have chewing tobacco stuck between his teeth.

Even if Otto wasn't Mr. Right, so what? The night was young, and she was sipping a syrupy Mexican drink and having fun, so what could be the harm?

She wasn't attracted to him, and he wasn't to her. Remove the fact that they'd both grown up in the same small town, they might not have even shared a glance, much less a dance.

But on this night, for whatever reason, she was curious and careless, and he was lonely and desperate, so he courted her. When her friends chose to leave around 10, he begged her to stay and dance. Against her better judgment, she did.

Around 1 a.m., he drove her home, walked her to her door, kissed her hand, told her he'd like to see her again, bowed awkwardly and pranced away. The perfect gentleman.

The next morning, Otto sent her a dozen yellow roses and a personal card inviting her to dinner. She declined. That afternoon, he sent her another note and a box of Russell Stover chocolates and invited her to a happy hour. Again, she declined.

Around 5, he called her.

"I'm leaving tomorrow, and I would curse myself if I didn't try one last time to convince you to join me for dinner," he said.

This time, she asked, "What time should I expect you?"

The second she hung up, the hairs on the back of her neck bristled. She knew she'd made a mistake, but she told herself, "It's just dinner. Order a ribeye and rice pilaf if they have it, and get home."

Otto reserved a table at one of the better steakhouses near the Fort Worth Stockyards and allowed her to order lobster once she saw it was on the menu, even though the waiter discouraged it.

"We're known coast-to-coast for our steaks," he told her.

"In that case," she replied, "I'd like a shrimp cocktail, too."

Otto's high pitch laugh pinged off every wall.

After dinner and a bottle of Cabernet Sauvignon, he convinced her to swing by a small but swanky nightclub where he'd recently met the owner and the piano player, who allowed him to sing Hoagy Carmichael's "Old Buttermilk Sky."

For that, he received a standing ovation, and Jenny was beginning to feel warm and woozy. That's because Otto had been pouring her a little Jack and Coke, and then a little more Jack and not so much Coke, and then, mostly Jack. Around 2:30 a.m., he suggested they grab some fresh air.

"Good idea," Jenny said, thinking it would do her good.

They walked around the block and returned to his car, which he'd parked just beyond the reach of the streetlights. As he opened her door, he pressed against her, and she didn't object. He then closed the front door and opened the back door and said, "After you."

She joined him under the condition he behave himself.

He did, but not for long. He insisted. She resisted. He persisted. She resisted. He persisted more. She relented just a little, thinking it would stop with some heavy petting, but it didn't.

He took no precautions because he didn't believe in them. Besides, he had convinced himself that he'd mastered the whole "pull the rabbit out of the hat" routine. This time, the bunny hopped out sooner than he expected, much to his embarrassment.

"Must be the long days," he complained. "Normally, I'm a…"

Suddenly sober, Jenny wiped herself with his handkerchief, pulled up and tucked in everything that needed to be put back in place, then she ordered Otto to call her a taxi.

"If you were anyone else, I'd be calling the police," she added.

Three months later, Jenny called the funeral home in Kassel, and Otto answered. After reciting the funeral home's somber greeting — "Good evening. This is the Becker Funeral Home. You're speaking to Otto Becker, associate director. How might I be of service?"

"Take a wild guess," she said.

Otto jerked his head around to make sure no one was listening, then snapped, "Why are you calling me? I don't even know you."

"Must be the long days, again," Jenny said. "You know very well why I'm calling."

"Please call back during regular business hours," Otto said curtly, then hung up.

Jenny then called her father, who still lived in Kassel.

"Dad, I need a favor," she said. "Can you check tomorrow's funeral schedule and call me back? I'll explain later."

She wanted to make sure Otto would be there when she showed up.

Two nights later, she slid through a side door and waited in the shadows for him to wrap up the visitation for 79-year-old Joyce Seestadt, a vivacious old gal who finally lost her battle to uterine cancer. The funeral home was packed, so Jenny had to be careful not to be spotted by a former classmate or neighbor.

After the last guests had paid their respects, Jenny stepped out from behind a partition, directly in Otto's path, startling him so much, he almost squealed.

"What is the meaning of this?" he snapped, in a voice that

made him sound like a New York City maître d.

"Don't ever hang up on me again," Jenny said.

She then handed him a sheet of paper, listing the names of all those willing to corroborate her story.

"Rip it up, if you like," she said. "I have several, and they're all notarized."

Otto began to speak, but then, a door opened, and Otto Becker's father walked in.

"What's this commotion?" Otto Becker's father bellowed. "And who are you?"

Jenny told him who she was and why she was there.

"This is all a misunderstanding," Otto stammered. "I hardly… that is, I barely…"

"I have witnesses," Jenny said, then grabbed the sheet from Otto and handed it to the old man.

"All right," Otto said. He looked at Jenny again and realized he knew her and her parents. He didn't ask how they were doing.

Otto conceded that he'd met Jenny, and yes, he had taken her to dinner out of courtesy, but that was all. Nothing more.

"If that was all, why is she here?" the old man asked.

Otto waited one second too long to answer.

"I'm here because I am pregnant, and he is responsible," Jenny said.

"That's outrageous," Otto screeched, his voice bouncing up and down with each syllable, as in, "THAT's out-RAY-jus!"

So, Jenny pulled from her purse a note, a letter, and a packet containing what was left of a yellow rose. The old man examined each carefully. He checked typewriter strokes, signatures, watermarks, any sign of a conspiracy. For once, he wanted to believe his son, but he found no evidence of a shakedown.

Then, Jenny handed him Otto Becker's calling card, which actually contained the line, "Death never takes a holiday."

He flipped it over and recognized his son's prissy handwriting.

"You should keep this," the old man said, handing the card back to Jenny. "You might need it later."

He was impressed with her confidence and candor, the way she stood — tall and erect — and the way her eyes followed his.

Otto, on the other hand, reeked of unctuous mendacity, but then, that was his natural state. Jenny told the old man how his son had courted her and taken her to dinner and then dancing, and that he'd forced himself upon her in the back seat of his car. She told him she had not fought fiercely enough, so she accepted her share of the responsibility.

"I drank too much," she said. "I was stupid and careless, so I am not without fault."

"Not without FAULT?" Otto blared. "Yew WANTED it. Yew used ME. If anyone was RAPED, it was ME!"

Otto grew more hysterical with each word.

The old man was familiar with this performance. He'd seen it several times. Since Otto was old enough to construct a sentence, he'd blamed someone else for his screw-ups. Big or small, they were always someone else's fault. Never his. He was always the victim. Every time.

This time, though, the lie was so blatant that Otto's father took one step toward his older son and slapped him, full palm, across the face.

Otto staggered backwards, then yelled, "You, you…"

But he couldn't spit out the rest of whatever it was he wanted but wasn't brave enough to say.

"Silence," the old man said in a suddenly thick, German accent. "You have embarrassed me and your mother more times than I care to remember, but I will not allow you to bring further shame upon this family. You will handle this."

Of course, by "handle this," he meant marriage, which was the last thing Jenny wanted, but it was 1949, and options were limited but not impossible. Jenny's mother advised her to return to Fort Worth and have it fixed.

"Surely, you know someone who knows someone," she told her.

After all, Jenny had worked, off and on, in a doctor's office while attending secretarial school. How hard could it be to find a physician who'd fix it?

But Jenny couldn't bring herself to do it. She didn't care so much that it was illegal. Or that it was considered a sin. She simply could not bring herself to have it "fixed." She would have Otto's child, and she would keep it. She would marry Otto Becker so the child would have a legitimate surname, and then, she'd take it from there.

So, Deborah Becker was born January 3, 1950 — long and lean, just like her mother. She weighed 7 pounds, 6 ounces and was as bald as a cue ball. Jenny named her after Deborah Kerr, her favorite actress.

Otto was present at the time of the delivery, but he didn't participate. He didn't even inform his parents. They found out from a friend who volunteered at the hospital.

By then, Otto was already searching for ways to leave Jenny. She was too tall, too demanding, too headstrong. He wanted a more pliable woman — a woman who wouldn't ask questions about when and where and why, and he found one.

Unfortunately, she was unavailable because he was married and a new father, and she was a good Catholic girl who would not carry on with a married man nor marry a divorced man. So, Otto was stuck until he could conjure up a legitimate excuse — a doozy, a whopper.

—

"I can't live like this," Otto yelled. "You're driving me insane. If I stay here, I'll kill myself."

"In that case, please stay," Jenny replied. "I'll fluff your pillow."

"That's it," Otto yelled. "I'll not be mocked by a trollop like you," and then he grabbed his fedora and his manufactured outrage and stormed out.

He moved that night into a guest apartment behind a house owned by Kassel High School principal Harvey Lange, who, like just about everybody else, owed the Becker family a favor.

Otto Becker's father had given Lange the job as high school principal, even though he was disliked and disrespected by students and teachers. He'd been an ineffective math teacher, a gutless assistant principal, and a clueless assistant football coach.

He got the job because Otto Becker's father — despite all his airs of nobility and honor — was an unvarnished racist. Old man Becker threw a fit when Lange's predecessor had the audacity to suggest he would be forced to obey the law and enroll a Negro student in the public schools should one ever move to Kassel, which was not merely unlikely. It was impossible.

Filipino leprechauns would be welcomed in Kassel before Negroes would. So, Lange's predecessor was fired, and Lange was hired, knowing he could be fired just as capriciously, so he was reluctant to refuse the rather strange request that Otto be allowed to move into the empty mother-in-law apartment around back.

Otto lived there for six months, long enough to file for divorce on the grounds of irreconcilable differences. Though his lawyer urged him to remain quiet and invisible, Otto couldn't do it.

He told everyone Jenny had thrown herself at him, and he had been too kind and too compassionate to toss her back into the gutters where she belonged. To gild the lily, Otto said he offered to help her financially, but she rejected him — even threatened him with bodily harm, thus proving she was mentally unstable.

If that wasn't shameless enough, he claimed he felt nothing but pity for her, not to mention a sense of selfless commitment to the child. By the way, he never said "his" child. It was always "the" child.

Finally, he insinuated that Jenny drank all day, most days, and when she wasn't too tipsy to drive, she'd meet her old boss at a ratty motel near Decatur. "I begged her to stop," Otto claimed, but he couldn't stop her. The best he could do was watch the child until her mother returned the next morning.

No one believed him.

The doctor for whom she had worked was a 69-year-old family doctor named Walter Hudspeth. A diabetic, he was as studly as Mickey Rooney.

Jenny not only denied the accusations, she laughed at them.

So did a Cook County judge, who told her he didn't believe a word coming out of Otto Becker's mouth. He granted the divorce, awarded her full custody of "her child," and ordered him to pay $25 a month in child support, which he never did.

Jenny didn't care, and Otto should have left well enough alone, but he couldn't help himself. He became a regular at the VFW Hall, where he told anyone who'd listen how he'd stared down the legal system and proved his innocence and protected his good name against a strumpet and inveterate liar.

One night, he was wallowing in self-pity and searching for a little brotherly support from a wide-shouldered, square-jawed Fort Worth cowboy wearing a pair of standard khakis, a long-sleeved cotton shirt and black roper boots.

"You look familiar," Otto slurred. "Do I know you? What's your name?"

"My name is irrelevant," Darrell Tuttle said. "But your name is Becker. Right?"

"That's right," Otto replied. "Otto Becker. At your service."

"You met a girl at a party at our ranch near Weatherford," Darrell said.

"That's right," Otto screeched. "That woman is a whore. I'm telling you. A whore."

"I would prefer you keep your voice down," Darrell said.

"Or what?" Otto said.

And Darrell grabbed him by the throat and squeezed.

"Or you might end up sooner than you expected in one of those caskets of yours," Darrell said, then released his grip.

Otto fell to the floor, clamored to his feet and slammed his hand on the bar and bellowed, "You'll regret that. My lawyer…"

Darrell cocked his head and took a step toward him, so Otto grabbed a dirty beer glass.

"Put it down, or I'll make you eat it," Darrell said, so Otto threw it at a dartboard, wagged a finger at Darrell and then noticed that everyone in the joint except Darrell was grinning, happy to be watching his humiliation.

Otto staggered out, climbed in his new Ford Fairlane, floorboarded it, and sailed through three red lights, knowing no cop dared to pull him over. After arriving at his apartment, he caught his right foot on a garden hose and tumbled into an azalea shrub.

"Goddamn it," he screamed, and Mr. Lange had to rush out and ask him to hold it down because it was a school night, and the little children needed their rest or else tomorrow would be a long day for everyone.

"Fuck you, Harvey," Otto screamed. "Fuck all of you. Especially the little children."

He rose to his feet, slicked back his hair, walked over to Mr. Lange, thumped him in the chest, and said, "Next year, you're back to coaching junior high track. I'll see to it."

—

Though Otto obtained his divorce, he continued his campaign to smear Jenny's name and reputation. No one in Kassel cared, and Jenny was by then long gone. She'd returned to Fort Worth to take a job at General Electric as an administrative assistant to the head of accounting.

She didn't lift a finger to force Otto to pay child support, so he should have been happy, but he wasn't. Why?

Because of Harriet Gail Baird.

Otto had fallen in love with her, but she would not marry him because she was a good Catholic girl, and Otto was a divorced man, and the church back then would never sanction their marriage.

There was a loophole, of course.

Catholic Canon 1097, Section 2 states, "You or your spouse intended to marry someone who either possessed or did not possess a certain quality, e.g., social status, marital status, education, religious conviction, freedom from disease, or arrest record. That quality must have been directly and principally intended."

To marry Harriet Gail, Otto would have had to prove that —

unbeknownst to him at the time of his marriage — Jenny Gehring was the daughter of Satan himself.

The Church also had to be convinced that "something essential was missing at the moment of consent."

Easy enough, Otto thought, wrongly. In his first petition for annulment, Otto failed to adequately define "something essential," so the Dallas Diocese denied his petition.

A few months later, Otto's second petition was granted, mostly on the basis of a letter corroborating the "something essential" accusations made against Jenny. That letter was written by Father Louis Becker, Otto's younger brother.

Otto had bullied his brother his entire life. He'd made fun of his lisp. He'd snuck up behind him on cold days and thumped his ear. He'd shoved him into the girl's bathroom and held the door shut.

Father Louis never fought back. He assumed the Becker family primogeniture granted the oldest male offspring the right to torment the younger offspring, and since there were only two of them, he caught it all.

Father Louis wept when he learned Otto was moving back to Kassel to work at the funeral home. He knew the bullying would continue, even though he was a priest, and, of course, he was right.

Otto bullied Louis into writing a letter stating unequivocally that Jenny was a harlot, the mother of all abominations, and so forth and so on — a lot of Catholic gibberish — and Father Louis obeyed. He didn't toss in the seven heads and 10 horns, or Gog and Magog, or the lakes of fire, or the Whore of Babylon, but Father Louis wrote what his brother ordered him to write — that Jenny Gehring was the beast, and Otto was the lamb made drunk and led astray with the wine of her fornication.

Somehow, Father Louis convinced himself he was doing Jenny a favor, too. He knew how despicably his brother had treated her. Now, she would be born anew. The lie would serve a higher purpose.

So, not more than a month later, the Bishop of the Diocese of Amarillo, The Right Reverend Joseph Ambrose Hockley, personally signed the annulment papers, and Otto was free to marry Harriet Gail, a nice and simple girl.

Also, Bishop Hockley was free to drive the new gold-and-white Ford Fairlane 500 that appeared in his parking space early one Sunday morning. The keys and title were in the glove compartment. The Lord works in mysterious ways for the Beckers.

—

Otto married Harriet Gail in the St. Benezet Catholic Church. She was 20, pleasant and mostly pliant, not pushy and generally bullheaded like Jenny.

What Otto either failed to notice or deliberately overlooked was that Harriet Gail was also more than a little conniving. She married him for his money, something she'd never had. She wanted to live in a new house with a proper dining room table, a complete set of dining room chairs, a cushy couch, and a new TV set. She often said, "My goal in life is to have a house with a veranda and a porch swing and a glider."

She later tacked on, "and an upright piano."

She wanted a piano because she'd taught herself to play in junior high, and she had a gift for it. If she had a piano, she might be invited to play at school functions or Christmas parties. Of course, if she played publicly, she'd need $20 for a new dress and a new pair of shoes that didn't squeak when she pushed the pedals.

If Otto would buy her a new house with a proper dining room table, and all the other things she'd never had, she'd be the happiest girl on Earth, even though she didn't love him and never would. She loved a boy named Steve Conrad, whom she dated briefly in high school.

He dumped her for a girl named Jeanette Harris, but she convinced herself that he'd eventually come to his senses and return to her.

She was a little dingy.

Two years later, Otto came along, driving a fancy car and wearing a fedora and trying to look and act like Clark Gable. By then, she had abandoned any hope of marrying for love. If Otto could obtain an annulment, she'd marry him.

For a simple and pliant young woman, Harriet Gail was brazenly mercenary. The day of her wedding, she recited her lines with precision and conviction, and blushed on cue at the reception when her tipsy girlfriends toasted her with their own little secrets and tricks related to the art of erotic fulfillment.

That night, as she changed from the lavender gown she wore to the reception into the peek-a-boo bridal lingerie Otto had bought for her, she wept, and not because she didn't love the man who was about to take her virginity. She wept because she was happy. Her scheme had worked, and she would live in a nice house, with a man she didn't fear or hate, and she had most of the creature comforts she craved.

All she had to do was keep up her end of the bargain. "A deal's a deal," she told herself, so she conceded to all of his urges and fantasies. She would close her eyes. Bite her lip. Manufacture the appropriate noises. Wait for him to finish. Mop up. The next day, she would drive to Gainesville to buy something shiny.

Ten months after the wedding, she gave birth to a jar of joy she named Christine Diane. Christine Diane was delightful in every way. Craggy old men would cross the street just to say hello to her and listen to her sing-song voice and tussle her golden ringlets and hear her sweet giggle.

Christine Diane even melted her daddy's heart, and he loved her more than anything he'd ever loved in his life except himself, so he stopped attending mortuary trade shows in Fort Worth and Dallas and Oklahoma City, and he gave up poker and Jack Daniels and Macallan 12, and he started back attending Mass regularly and reading the Bible.

He read Matthew and Mark and Luke the first thing in the morning and during lunch. After regular work hours, he'd read Paul's and John's letters. Before bed, he'd read Revelations. For a short while, he appeared to be developing what might be described as a conscience, possibly even a soul.

He began chronicling his countless shortcomings and sins —

some feckless, some fatal — and vowed to repent every one. Some, he knew, would take longer to explain to the proper authorities than others, but he thought he could pull it off.

It was oddly noble but horribly ill-timed. Christine Diane — the tiny twinkle of light barely visible through the cosmic gas clouds of his heart — died two weeks before her fourth birthday. Normally a happy child, she'd begun crying and acting out, and her tantrums grew worse and worse.

Harriett Gail thought her daughter was just late in experiencing the Terrible Twos, but she took her to see her doctor in Gainesville, and it went downhill from there. Her doctor noticed the child's "raccoon eyes" and ordered an ambulance to rush her to see a pediatric oncologist in Dallas. He found a malignant neuroblastoma wrapped around the left eye's optic nerve.

"We have a protocol," the doctor told Otto and Harriet Gail. "We'll see how well she responds. Don't ask me for numbers. They don't mean a thing. We're just going to deal with your daughter."

The doctors tried everything. Pills and shots and radiotherapy. They even tried something called "chemotherapy," but it didn't work either. Nothing worked.

So, Christine Diane joined the angels around midnight in Room 431 of the Fort Sill Veterans Clinic in Lawton, where she'd been returned by the doctors in Dallas, who told Otto and Harriet, "There's nothing more we can do for her. Make her comfortable. Anything she wants, give it to her. Anything."

Her last meal was just a pinch of a Reese's Peanut Butter Cup.

Otto was a funeral director, and funeral directors rarely if ever touch bodies, but Otto didn't care. He was not going to let anyone touch his precious daughter. Everyone in a position to know thought it macabre, but Otto had his reasons.

He remembered how he had touched little girls back in Manila while he was supposed to be recuperating from a shrapnel wound. He surrendered to his worst instincts and took advantage of families that were so desperate, they surrendered their daughters to grown men to do with as they pleased in exchange for a carton of cigarettes.

Knowing what he'd done when presented the chance, he couldn't trust anyone else to do better. To settle his conscience, he convinced himself that everyone was as putrid as he was.

After the funeral service, Otto returned to the bottle, lashing out until he passed out. In his dreams, he'd see his baby girl, her face grotesquely deformed. He'd hear her endless crying and pleading. "Make it stop, Daddy. Make it stop."

Then, he'd wake, take a swig and start all over again.

He blamed the doctors. He blamed himself. He blamed Harriet Gail. He blamed God.

Every Friday right after lunch, he'd find a liquor store and walk out with a cardboard box of whatever whiskey, vodka and/or gin that was on sale, then, start drinking after his duties at the funeral home were dispensed. Fortunately, there weren't that many since he was no longer trusted to be around customers.

Eventually, he'd empty what he'd bought, then visit the VFW Hall, pick a fight, get kicked out, go to the cemetery, throw his empty bottles at the monument of Jesus on the Cross, which wasn't more than 20 yards from where Christine Diane's body lay in a tiny blue casket with pink lining, her arms folded around her favorite doll, "Sally Anne."

Otto would sit and cry and curse and wail, and people living nearby thought he might be possessed. This was tolerated under the condition Harriet pick up the shards Saturday morning.

She kept them in an empty trash can. She'd planned to use them to create a stained-glass window showing her daughter ascending into the arms of Christ, but she never got around to it. She was killed two years later in an automobile accident near Wichita Falls. Her new Chevrolet Impala hydroplaned, skidding sideways into a concrete barrier, and she was crushed on impact.

It was surreal. Nothing like it ever, old-timers said. First the child. Now the mother. Even those who disliked Otto felt a tinge of sympathy for him. "No one deserved this," they said to each other. The only person, it seemed, who didn't feel sorry for Otto Becker was Otto Becker's father.

Near death himself, he offered his son no compassion, no condolences, no solace, no words of wisdom, not even 30 seconds of funeral home boilerplate. All the old man ever said about it was, "The wrong ones died."

Meanwhile, Father Louis was forced to watch his older brother wallow in booze and bile and self-pity, and the more he watched, the more disgusted he became. He couldn't stop thinking about the letter he'd been bullied into writing, and he remembered in tiny detail the afternoon when he stepped out of a confessional booth, and Otto had verbally assaulted him — and in front a gape-mouthed 13-year-old choir boy, no less.

"I'm not asking you — you worm — I'm telling you. I want that goddamn letter on my desk in the morning. When I get up, that letter better be on my desk, or I'm going to drag your ass out of this church and…"

Well, it was something singularly crude involving the Virgin Mary and her virginity.

Even though Father Louis knew he might be condemning his soul to Hell, he wrote the letter and typed it himself and signed it. Every keystroke and every space oozed with lies.

"And now, look what happened," Father Louis told himself. "Two dead and buried, and my older brother gone mad and soon to be in Hell no doubt — and God forgive me for saying it."

The real pity was that Otto would have obtained the annulment, anyway. He didn't need his brother's letter. All it took was a set of car keys. Otto knew that. He bullied his brother into writing the letter so he'd have a partner in crime. If he were accused of anything later, he could say, "My brother is a priest. He wrote the letter. He signed the letter. He mailed the letter. Do you think a priest would go that far if it were in the service of a lie?"

The answer to that was, "Damn right, he would."

Father Louis lied, and he knew it, and he could not forgive himself. If he had not written that letter, Harriet Gail would never have married his brother. She would be alive, happily married to another man, a good and decent man, a loving father. Maybe he and Harriet Gail would have had one or two or maybe even three children, each as beautiful and delightful as Christine Diane.

But look what happened.

Christine Diane had inherited the cancer — the poison — from her father. It was all he had to offer. She certainly didn't get her ringlets or her sweet laugh from him.

Despite his brief religious dalliance, Otto remained as toxic as spent tractor oil. The cancer killed Christine Diane, and Christine Diane's death killed Harriet Gail. It wasn't the bald tires or the wet pavement or the concrete barrier. It wasn't the fact that her car was traveling at 55, maybe even 60 miles per hour, when it struck the pillar. It wasn't the fact that she was a lousy driver. It was Otto.

But Father Louis blamed himself. If he hadn't written the letter, they would all be alive. He was certain of that, and the guilt was strangling him.

As for Jenny, she'd made a single, stupid mistake, but she owned it and she moved on. She had asked for nothing, and Otto gave her nothing but trouble.

Father Louis blamed himself for that, too.

"Oh, how she must hate me," he told God. "How could she not? How could her friends and family not blame me? How could they not hate me?"

Whether real or imagined, he felt their anger, their disgust as he walked up and down the aisles, and administered The Communion Rite, and dared to preach to them about temptation and weakness and salvation.

The shame weighed him down so much he began to stoop, as if he were lugging a load of bricks up a steep hill. He couldn't sleep, so he had difficulty shaving and often came to breakfast with pieces of tissue clinging to bloody razor cuts. He had trouble remembering morning prayers he'd been saying for 50 years.

Of course, he stopped hearing confessions. He kept to himself and refused to ask for God's mercy. He told Father Gus he didn't deserve God's mercy, and he would not seek it in any way.

So, Father Gus prayed for him, in earnest. For the first time in years, Father Gus begged God for help. "I can't do this alone," he prayed, and God replied, "Yes. You can." So, Father Gus dragged Father Louis away from the ledge. He counseled Father Louis, prayed for him, talked him into praying with him, cajoled him, challenged him, lifted him, and ultimately saved him.

"Louis, you are not your brother," Father Gus told him. "You are my brother, and you will not abandon me or this church or the members of this church. I forbid it. God forbids it. Listen to God. He is speaking to you now. I can hear Him. My faith is renewed, Louis. Listen! Surely you can hear Him, too. What is He saying, Father Louis? What is He saying? Louis! He is saying, 'Rise to your feet. Do the work I have prepared for you and you alone. There are many more like your brother out there, and I need your help.' God needs you, Louis. I do, too."

In time, Father Louis found the strength to forgive himself and to seek God's forgiveness and to begin the process of repairing the damage done.

—

Otto, on the other hand, slid deeper into the muck, and he exhausted whatever patience and sympathy the people of Kassel offered him.

One night, he showed up at the Knights of Columbus Hall, drunk, making a fool of himself, and Father Louis happened to be there, standing behind a pillar, just out of Otto's line of sight. He did nothing when his brother began cursing at the jukebox, laughing and singing wildly, sloshing a Jack and Coke on himself, directing lecherous remarks at a young waitress who was too inexperienced to tell him to fuck off.

But when Otto grabbed her and squeezed her breast, Father Louis bolted. He barreled into his brother, slamming him against the lip of the bar. Before Otto could respond, Father Louis whacked him in the jaw with an empty beer bottle, and that was all it took.

Otto spit out a sliver of his tongue, wiped blood on his sleeve, tried to say something, then collapsed to his knees. He looked up and saw his pansy, pissant brother, standing over him.

"Get up," Father Louis ordered. "Get to your feet. I'm not finished. You have lied to me and to our parents and to everyone in this town and everyone in my church and even worse, to your wife and your daughter, God bless their souls and rest in peace."

Father Louis took a deep breath, bent down, grabbed Otto's shirt collar and pulled him closer.

"God sees you. He knows you. He knows your heart, and it is black as tar and stained by the lies you've told and the lives you've ruined. Now, get up. And get out. If I find you here again, I will beat the living shit out of you."

Dazed, Otto clamored to his feet and shoved away two regulars who tried to help him.

"Get'chure hands off me," he slurred.

When a guy offered to drive him home, Otto swatted at him.

"I don't need no fucking driver. I can drive myself."

He grabbed his Stetson, smeared his mouth with a bar towel and staggered out into the warm, dark night.

—

On Sunday morning, Father Louis first thought he heard rain, but there wasn't a cloud in the sky, so he slowed and listened more carefully to the smattering of applause that grew into a rousing ovation by the time he ascended the steps to the pulpit.

Father Gus did nothing to discourage it.

"Thank you tho much," Father Louis said. He then extended his arms, then brought his hands together to pray and said. "God be with thew."

And the congregants replied, "And also with you."

CHAPTER 17

Whatever works

Everyone assumed it was just a matter of time before Otto did something delusional enough to cost him his life. Those who were paying attention figured he'd stumble and fall and impale himself on a piece of rebar or crack his skull, or spout off to the wrong guy in the wrong bar and get knifed or shot or smacked with the thick end of a pool stick.

No one expected Otto to kill himself. He'd always been too much of a narcissist, the kind of person who couldn't imagine the Earth spinning on its axis without his personal magnetism.

Besides, he was a dandy. His fingernails were always meticulously trimmed, his mustache perfectly clipped, his hair oiled and parted just so. It was not like him to leave a mess.

For a short while, he seemed to want to pull himself together. He didn't stop drinking, but he stopped throwing beer bottles at headstones and cursing Jesus in supermarket parking lots and sucker-punching strangers. People thought he was healing, but he wasn't.

He was seething. He wadded up his anger and crammed it down and prayed for it would turn black and express itself as a raging tumor. That's what he wanted. He wanted to die knowing the agony his daughter had suffered. He thought his suffering would redeem him, make everything right with God.

When no tumor emerged, Otto took matters into his own hands. He shot himself. He planned it all out. He wanted to watch the 1962 Cotton Bowl because he'd bet Harry Bauer, the bartender at the VFW Hall, $50 Texas would play in it, and sure enough, the Longhorns did. They beat Ole Miss, 12-7, and after the game, Otto hunted down Harry and demanded his winnings.

"Shit, I was going to bring it to you," Harry said. "You didn't need to come looking for me."

"Just give me my money," Otto said. "I want it in cash."

Harry reached into his wallet and pulled out three tens and four fives, and Otto counted it carefully, then slipped the money in his wallet and said, "It's been nice knowing you," which Harry interpreted as something along the lines of "See you around."

"I could tell he wasn't in his right mind, but I had no idea he was that far gone," Harry told a police officer, who had handed him an envelope containing three tens and four fives — the same bills Otto had demanded from him. Harry's name was written on the front in Otto's hand. "For Harry Bauer."

And, on the back, Otto wrote across the flap — again, in perfect penmanship — "None of your business."

Otto had been renting a farmhouse two miles north of town. The previous occupant died at the age of 96, and the heirs were scattered to the wind, so a real estate agent in Gainesville rented it to Otto with strict instructions not to change a thing.

That suited Otto fine.

On the bitterly cold afternoon of January 5, 1962, Otto emptied his bowels and cleaned them with an enema filled with salty water and white vinegar. He trimmed his nails. He groomed his mustache and evened off his Elvis sideburns.

He put on a white dress shirt and the beige tie with blue stripes Harriett Gail had given him for his 31st birthday. He put on his favorite black suit, the one he wore to weddings, not to funerals. He went barefoot.

Otto then pulled a dining room chair into the bathroom and draped a black bath towel across it. He fiddled with it for a moment, making sure it hung at the precise height and angle.

He then crawled into the tub and turned on the hot water and waited for it to fill. When water was almost lapping over the sides, Otto turned it off, reached and picked up a Colt M1911 — better known as a .45 — and raised it to his right temple.

He held it there for a moment, pushed the barrel into his skull gently, waggled it, recalculated the angle, then lowered the pistol for a second to allow his mind a last chance to contemplate the finality of what he was about to do. After a moment, he shushed the voices in his head who were beseeching him. "Otto, don't. Don't do this, Otto. Take your bath. Get out. Go to bed."

"Too late," he told them.

He returned the pistol to the side of his head and, without wincing, pulled the trigger.

Otto Becker's body was found four days later. Since he was soaking in water, and because he had taken other precautions, and because it was freezing outside, there was no mess. Not only that, the stringy hair on the top of his head remained perfectly parted and combed. The bullet did exactly what it was designed to do.

Otto left no will, so, under Texas law, his estate — primarily the funeral home — passed to his next of kin. Otto's wife and child were dead. His father was still alive, but just barely. He'd suffered for years with colitis and recently was diagnosed with colon cancer. He wouldn't live another two months.

Otto had a several cousins, but no one he was close to. Fortunately, he had a brother.

—

"Are you sure you've looked everywhere," Father Louis asked. "I just can't believe he didn't prepare a will."

"I advised him many times to write one and send a copy to me," said Thomas B. Tollefson, a top-drawer Dallas lawyer who'd represented Otto's father for years. "It is possible that one exists, but if it does, I don't have a copy of it. So, Father Louis, prepare yourself to take ownership of the family business."

"I am a priest," Father Louis told him. "I minister to the living, not the dead."

"Well, you're about to be the richest priest in town," said Mr. Tollefson, who was 6-foot, 5 and thin as a rake. His hairline was in full retreat, and his nose looked like a bicycle horn. He wasn't hired for his movie star looks or his sense of humor or his put-on Southern drawl. He was hired because he took no prisoners.

"You should be grateful it's this simple," Mr. Tollefson added. "Most estate and trust cases are highly contentious. I've not dealt with one this cut and dried."

The idiom "cut and dried" struck Father Louis as entirely inappropriate and possibly intentional.

"Thank you for your wise counsel," he told Mr. Tollefson. "I will consider your suggestions and get back in touch with you as soon as possible."

"I would appreciate it," Mr. Tollefson said. "It's best to move quickly on these things before the deceased changes his mind."

Father Louis just stared at him.

"A little gallows humor," Mr. Tollefson said, then shoved papers into his black leather briefcase and said, perhaps to himself, "I've handled a lot of weird cases, but I never dreamed I'd be handling a case quite like this. At least, not for the Beckers."

Father Louis heard him and bristled.

"For the record, Mr. Tollefson, neither my family nor my church thankshuned thith," he said, his lisp — for some reason — suddenly more pronounced. "On the whole, we dithapprove of thuicide."

—

"If there's one thing I've learned, it's the difference between a problem and a hassle," Father Gus said, handing Father Louis two fingers of Lagavulin, his favorite Scotch, which he reserved for special occasions.

"The Lagavulin 16?" Father Louis said.

"Why not?" Father Gus replied. "This situation is not a problem. It's a hassle."

"I know it is," Father Louis answered. "I could sell it, but what would I do with the money? I don't need it. I don't want it. I will inherit my parent's home when my father dies, and I don't want that either. I know this all happened for a reason. I know there's a purpose in all this. God has a plan. I just can't figure out what it is."

"Well, I've found that good Scotch leads us to the keyhole where we can peek in and watch the Big Guy shuffle papers,"

Father Gus said.

He then raised his cup and toasted the Big Guy. It was unlike Father Gus to say such a thing, even though he had his doubts about God. He believed in the Catholic Church. It was real. The building was real. The pews were real. The robes and the cross and the Holy water were real.

But God was an ephemeral idea, as malleable as moist clay. If you want to think of God as a slender, blue-eyed, beak-nosed Swede, fine. Do it. Whatever works for you. And that's why Father Gus could take God or leave him.

That was anathema to Father Louis. He now possessed an almost evangelical relationship with the Almighty, and that zest had increased twofold since he'd conquered his doubt. He began to see God's hand in all things. Buttermilk biscuits. Baseball scores. Older brothers who blew their own brains out.

A single grain of sand blowing in the wind was an act of God worth examining for meaning, so, of course, the question of what to do with the funeral home weighed on Father Louis' mind so heavily he couldn't sleep.

Instead, he wandered the halls and the grounds early in the morning, carrying on long conversations with himself about where he was in his life, what he was doing, what God wanted him to do, and why God hadn't revealed to him a plan.

Early one morning, Father Louis wandered through the cemetery and came upon the graves of Harriett Gail and Christine Diane. He stood there and thought, "If only they were here, this would not be my problem. His wife. His child…"

And he stopped, and his face froze, and his eyes filled with tears, and he looked skyward and said aloud, "His child!"

He fell to his knees and said, "Thank you. How did I not thee thith thooner?"

The next morning, he wrote a letter to Jenny. Rather than mailing it, he asked Father Gus if he would deliver it. It read:

> As Otto Becker's brother, I have inherited his estate. At this moment, it includes one valuable piece of property. I do not want it. I do not need it. I shall not possess it. It will go to his next of kin. His next of kin is his daughter. That is, your daughter. I am meeting with a lawyer soon. His card is enclosed. Through him, I will transfer ownership of this property to your daughter.
>
> I know what you must think of me. For a long time, I thought the same. I was a dupe and a coward, and you bore the burden of my complicity with the despicable fraud that was my brother. It harms me to speak unkindly of the dead, but I will no longer lie or apologize for him.
>
> I deeply regret causing you such grief, and I do not presume that the decision I am making now shall assuage your anger. Nor do I seek your forgiveness. I do not deserve it. One day, the Lord will judge me. All I want is for your daughter to receive what is rightfully hers.
>
> Respectfully yours,

By then, Jenny was office manager for a trio of family physicians who had purchased a two-story building in a small community far out on the prairie west of Fort Worth, aptly named White Junction.

The three physicians catered to those high-tailing it to the suburbs and small towns to avoid public school integration. Even though the Fort Worth school board had bent over backwards to find exotic ways to postpone the inevitable, integration came, and whites got out while the getting was good. White Junction seemed — and sounded — like as good a place as any to escape.

Jenny's decision to move there was purely financial. She enjoyed her job. It paid her well enough. She was valued and treated with respect, even though she was a single mother, and so they settled in. Jenny even enrolled in a real estate class, hoping to get a license in a year or so and cash in on the boom. She was no dummy, and the prospects looked almost too good to be true.

The receptionist at the clinic where Jenny worked was a ruddy, flat-faced 21-year-old named Audrey Kelso. Her senior year in high school, she served as president of the Future Homemakers of America until she got pregnant, and then she was advised to drop out and get married, which she did. The marriage lasted two years, then she was a single mother who needed a job.

Audrey was typing an invoice when she looked up and saw a tall, stern man wearing a black suit and a black raincoat, and she almost fell out of her chair because he seemed to appear out of the walnut paneling.

"Excuse me," he said. "I didn't mean to startle you."

"I didn't hear you come in," Audrey said.

"Again, my apologies. Tell you what. Let's begin anew. Good morning, young lady," the tall man said. "I'm here to see Jenny Gehring. Is she available?"

"OK. Uh, yeah. Good morning," Audrey said, then tapped her forehead with her right index finger. "I mean, good morning, Father. Uhmm. Do you have an appointment?"

"I do not, Audrey," Father Gus replied. "I was hoping to get lucky."

"You and everyone else," Audrey joked, then realized her faux pas and almost hyperventilated.

"I didn't mean it that way," she said.

"Nor did I," Father Gus replied. "Nor did I, but I do need to speak with Miss Gehring. Or is it Mrs. Gehring?"

"Oh, no, Father," Audrey said, shaking her head. "Miss Gehring is married to her job."

"Well, if I could speak to her for just a moment, I can dispense with an important matter and be on my way, and she can return to her job, and you to yours."

Audrey thought about it for a second, then scurried back to Miss Gehring's office, tapped softly, stuck her head in the door, and said, "There's a Catholic priest at the front desk who says he needs to talk to you about an urgent matter. I think you should come up to the front. OK?"

Jenny looked up. "Audrey, 'Catholic priest' is redundant. All priests are Catholic or fallen Catholics. You probably know them as Episcopalians."

"No," Audrey said. "I don't. I don't think we know any Episcopalians. Anyway, he's waiting. He's wearing one of those funny little collars."

"A clerical collar," Jenny said.

"Of course. Well, he said he needs to speak to you right away."

"How old is he?"

"I don't know. I can't tell. Pretty old. Do you want me to go back and ask?" Audrey said.

"No," Jenny said. "That won't be necessary. Is he tall or short?"

"Tall," Audrey said, then raised and cupped her hand above her head and added, "Taller than this."

Jenny closed a payroll tablet, stood, ran her hands down the front of her black dress and led Audrey back to the reception area.

Father Gus recognized her immediately.

"Miss Gehring," he said. "Thank you for seeing me on such short notice."

"Am I being dragged back to Kassel for the Inquisition?" Jenny asked, deliberately provocative.

"This year's Inquisition has been postponed until further notice," Father Gus replied. "The girls are in the regional basketball finals, so that's chewing up a lot of time and attention. If we make it to State, we might postpone it altogether."

Jenny lowered her guard and smiled.

"I don't remember your having a sense of humor," she said. "How can I help you?"

"Well," Father Gus said, then drew a long breath. "I would prefer to discuss this rather sensitive matter in private."

So, Jenny told Audrey to hold her calls, and she walked Father Gus back to her office, closed the door, crossed her arms, and asked bluntly, "What is this about? Please tell me it has nothing to do with Otto Becker."

"I can't do that. I've been asked to deliver this letter to you, to hand it to you, personally," he said. "I have not read it, although I am familiar with the subject matter, and it does involve Otto Becker. That is, the late Otto Becker. I am happy to wait for you to read it and respond. I will attempt to answer any questions you might have that, uhm…I am prepared to…"

He paused, slightly flustered with his inexplicable inability to complete a coherent sentence. He stopped and started over.

"I'll answer any questions I can," he said.

He pulled Father Louis' original letter and a duplicate from his suit pocket and offered them to her.

Jenny hesitated, then accepted them. She read the original quickly, scanned the duplicate, folded the original, slipped it into an envelope, sealed it, signed her name across the seal and handed it back to Father Gus, then stuck her head out the door and called Audrey.

"Place this in my cubicle," she said to Audrey, then turned to Father Gus and said, "Is there anything else?"

Father Gus said, "Would you care to buy a raffle ticket? It goes to a good cause — the girls basketball team."

"If they make it to State, call me," Jenny said, then added. Curtly, "I will be in touch."

She then opened her door and called out, "Phyllis, please escort our guest to the front."

Without offering a hand or a kind word, she said to Father Gus, "Phyllis will show you out."

"I appreciate your time," Father Gus said. "My regards to your daughter."

He expected a response but when it didn't come, he followed Phyllis for two steps, hesitated, smiled devilishly, and craned his head to the left.

"And Miss Gehring. Consider a little bell on the front door. Your girl up there seems a bit jumpy."

"I'll put Phyllis on it, right away," Jenny replied, then nodded to Phyllis, who smiled and said, "This way."

Phyllis walked him out, and Jenny returned to her desk,

her payroll tablet, and her life as an office manager for a trio of family physicians who'd purchased a two-story building in a small community out on the prairie west of Fort Worth, aptly named White Junction.

That night, Jenny called her father and read him the letter.

"I'm not surprised," he told her. "Father Louis has been behaving very oddly lately, and for him, that's saying something."

"What are we talking about here?" Jenny asked.

"Well, the funeral home is worth a pretty penny, I would imagine," he said. "Let me snoop around and get back to you on that. There's no emergency. In the long run, you should do what's best for you. And Debbie, of course. Think about that and nothing else. I'll get back to you as soon as I can."

A week later, he called.

"Well, this appears to be a sincere effort by Father Louis to make amends," he told her. "He's turning ownership over to you — that is, to Debbie. You will need to decide what to do with it. If you keep it, you'll have to run it. I have no doubt you can, but do you want to? Do you want to return here? Do you want your daughter to grow up here? Think about it carefully before you decide. What's the effect now? What's the effect in five years? In 10 years? Talk to someone you trust."

Jenny said, "I trust you. Off the top of your head, what do you think I should do?"

He admitted he'd love to have her closer to home.

"I know your mother would love that, too," he said. "But you have your own life to live. Don't sacrifice yours for ours. Again, talk to Debbie. She should have a say."

"It'll be her call, Dad," Jenny said. "Not mine."

—

Of course, Debbie hated the idea.

What? Leave her friends? Her school? No way. They were doing fine out on the prairie. Why would they want to move back? No. Let's stay here.

That was Debbie's initial reaction, but once she thought about it, she told her mother, "I don't want to, but I will if you think it's the right thing."

Debbie knew her grandparents were getting older and needed help, and White Junction was more than an hour away.

So, Jenny was forced to make the call. Was this opportunity too good to pass up? The funeral home had always made money. Everyone vital to its success had promised to remain on the job. It would take some getting used to, but it was doable.

She made a list of the pros and cons, then made a list of pros about the cons, and another list of cons about the pros. As hard as she tried, she couldn't find the tipping point until her mother called.

After 10 minutes of chit-chat, Jenny asked, "How's Dad?"

"He's OK," her mother said. "He's come down with another sore throat."

That did it.

—

Jenny didn't know a thing about the funeral home business, but she had the business acumen and personal smarts for it. She was a good communicator, a good listener, a good counselor. She was composed and empathetic but strong. She knew how to keep books and turn a payroll. She was organized and punctual and flexible and loyal, something Otto Becker had never been.

She was also sensitive to her employees' needs and sought them out instead of waiting for them to come to her because she was confident in her abilities and judgment. When two employees got into a spat, Jenny stepped in and offered innovative yet reasonable solutions.

Emotional outbursts were forbidden. That was as true for the staff as it was for the customers.

She knew how to deal with people during the worst moments of their lives. Funerals are hard. There's a lot of grief, a lot of conflicting agendas, a lot of family in-fighting.

There are also all kinds of macabre requests like wanting to crawl in the casket and snuggle with the deceased, or wanting to toss in a favorite pet right before the lid was closed.

She would have to entertain these oddball requests and others with a straight face, then politely refuse them and explain why.

"Unfortunately, state law prohibits us from granting double occupancy requests," she'd tell them, although it doesn't. Common sense does.

That was as dishonest as she got, so the few people who mattered in Kassel came to respect her, even if they did not embrace her. In return, she tried her best to let bygones be bygones.

She wasn't shunned, but she wasn't courted. She was kept at arm's length. She was invited to Christmas parties, but she was never encouraged to host one. That was fine with her. She was single, occasionally lonely, but all-in-all, content because she believed her daughter could be happy and safe growing up in this dinky, desolate little German town.

PART FOUR | CHAPTER 18

Damaged goods

August 1966

I still hadn't met Debbie's mother, so I didn't know why I was expected to know her story. I barely knew my own mother's story. I just wanted things to be easy because I'd been having such a great time, and I knew it wasn't going to last, so I wanted to squeeze as much fun as I could out of whatever time I had left.

By that, I mean the time I had left with Debbie, but also the time I had left working on the farm, which I'd come to enjoy. I never dreamed that would happen, but it did because I did what I said I was going to do.

I paid attention and learned my way around the milk barn, the hay barn, the silo, the fields, even the tool shed. If Uncle Carl was repairing a gate and asked for a pair of pliers, I knew whether he needed slip joint or lineman's pliers.

So, I didn't feel like a fraud when I pulled on rubber boots and grabbed a claw hammer. I could be trusted to do my share and more, and I looked for little things that needed attention. For example, lights that needed to be replaced. Bolts that needed tightening. Weeds that needed to be pulled.

If I could do it, I did it, and people noticed. Uncle Carl thanked me for organizing the screws and nails in the tool shed. Mina thanked me for scrubbing milk glasses.

I was noticed for all the right reasons, and it felt great being appreciated. It was almost as cool as scoring a touchdown. Best of all, I didn't have to stomp anyone to get attention, and by the way, let me clear the air about that — Debby Bishop was right. I did stomp Lowell.

I stomped him on purpose, and I didn't have to. I could've pulled loose, but I stomped him instead. Something inside of me — something ugly and mean — told me to bully the skinny kid.

And how'd that turn out? Well, if my goal was to prove I could be as big a jerk as anyone, then mission accomplished, and forget all that crap about being nice to the weak and the downtrodden.

It wasn't easy admitting this to myself, but once I did, I vowed to make amends. When I got home, I would apologize to Lowell and to his mother and ask if they would forgive me and promise I'd do better.

All Lowell ever wanted from me was to be his friend. All Lowell's mother ever wanted from me was to be nice to her boy. She never expected special favors, and if he fails, he fails. But give him a shot.

In return, Lowell's mom gave me the benefit of the doubt, and what'd I do? I abused her generosity and patience. So, I decided that when I got home, Lowell and his mom would be the first bolts I tightened.

—

At lunch one day, Mina asked me if I was still seeing my "special friend."

"No, Mom," Lori said, butting in. "He's seeing the hickey lady now."

Mina popped her with a rolled-up newspaper. "No one asked you a thing, young lady," and waited for my response.

"Yes, ma'am," I said. "I'm still seeing my special friend."

"Good," Mina said. "I like her. I wish she'd go to church, but I understand. She has her reasons."

I later asked Lori to explain.

"People say one thing and do another," she said.

"What does that have to do with Debbie and her mother?" I asked.

"I'm not saying it does," she said.

"You're not saying anything," I said. "I asked what Mina meant by 'She has her reasons.' What are her reasons?"

"I'll make you a list," she said. "But don't worry about it."

"I don't know what 'it' is," I replied.

"It's nothing," Lori said. "You like her. Hickey Lady likes you. Go make some baby hickeys."

—

Debbie called the next day. She asked if we were going to meet that night, although I couldn't imagine why she'd think we wouldn't.

I thought for just a moment that I'd work in a little Bogart, just to lighten the mood, but something in her voice warned me not to."

"Are you OK?" I asked.

"Meet me at The Fritz at 7," she replied.

I strolled into The Fritz at 7:05 and found her slouched in a booth in the back corner near the kitchen, as far away from the jukebox and the front door as possible, as was our habit.

"You're late," she said.

"Detailed briefly," I said. "Major Strasser."

"The letters of transit?"

"I don't know what you're talking about," I said.

"Good. I don't either," she said, so I let her talk.

"I know you've heard stories about me," she said.

"Actually, I haven't," I replied, in my non-Bogart voice. "I've heard rumors of stories, but no stories."

"No one has talked to you about my father?"

"You told me you didn't have a father."

"Of course, I have a father," she said. "A biological father. I assume you know about the birds and the bees."

"Was your father a bird or a bee?"

"Please. For once, give it a rest," she said. "My father is decaying in one of the nicest caskets on the market, and he has a perfectly round hole in his skull that he put there himself. You don't know about this?"

"News to me," I said.

"Well, then, let's start with this: He was never a father. He married my mom because he was forced to, and then he divorced her because he wanted to marry someone else."

"Where I'm from, Catholics aren't allowed to divorce and remarry," I said.

"You're right. Generally, they're not," Debbie said.

"Was your father a general?"

"He was not."

"But he was a Catholic?"

"Yes."

"And he was allowed to divorce and remarry, right?" I said. "When he remarried, he married a Catholic girl? They married in the Catholic church? Right?"

"Yes. Yes. Yes."

"How did he swing that?"

"He got the marriage to my mother annulled."

"Annulled. How's that possible?"

"It's possible if you live here and your last name is Becker."

It took me a second to crunch the numbers.

Otto Becker.

Louis Becker.

Are.

Brothers.

"Father Becker?" I asked. "He's your father?"

"Is Father Becker in a casket?" she said. "Rev. Louis Becker is my uncle. My father was Otto Becker. Look, I'm going to tell you everything, but first, place your hands on the table, palms up. Like this."

She placed her hands atop of mine, and our fingers dovetailed, and she squeezed as hard as she could for about 30 seconds.

"That's better," she said and exhaled. "Here it is."

Just as she began to tell her story, a perky high school freshman working our booth swung by with two large root beers and a basket of French fries.

"Heear-ya-go," she said. "If I was slow, tell me so."

Debbie answered with a "safe-at-home" sign, then replied,

"Toot-a-loo, Cindy Lou," and Cindy Lou toot-a-looed.

"I love that girl to death, but yikes," Debbie said.

She paused, then added, "She reminds me of me at that age."

She then smiled sadly, and said, "Before it happened."

And I said, "Ah, 'it' again."

In an instant, Cindy Lou's rainbow and lollipop vapor trail dissolved. Debbie dumped her fries on a napkin, pushed it off to the side, crossed her arms, and looked at the ceiling.

"I was 14," she said, still looking up. "I was her age when it happened. When I was raped."

She reached for her drink and waited for me to respond.

So, how did I respond?

I have no idea.

I know I was holding a French fry. I know I slowly returned it to the basket, raised my elbows off the table and slid my hands into the pockets of my jeans.

I knew I needed to raise my eyes to meet hers, to take her hands into mine, to try to understand even though I knew I couldn't. I didn't have the math skills, and I hadn't read enough Hemingway.

In a similar situation, I might have relied on a Beatles tune except that I'd never been in a similar situation. This was a first, so summoned Bogart to help me out. I pictured being on that tarmac at the airport in Casablanca with Ilsa and Captain Renault and Victor Laszlo, except I wouldn't say to Ilsa, "You're getting on that plane with Victor where you belong." I'd say, "We're getting on that plane with me, and we're going to Lisbon, and then we're going to catch another one and another one and another one until we find a place where none of this matters. And Victor can finish off these French fries, and Major Strasser can go straight to hell."

—

Of course, it was easy for me to say, "None of this matters" because none of this happened to me.

It happened at a party on Lewisville Lake. Debbie told her mother she was spending the night with Kathleen, then they hitched a ride with a couple of friends, one of whom had commandeered her father's station wagon. She assumed they'd drive out to the lake, hang out for an hour or so, and head home before midnight, at the latest.

But the party wasn't mostly high school kids. It was college students. One of the older guys had brought along a hi-fi receiver and record player (he called it a 'turntable') and a pair of speakers made by a Japanese outfit no one had ever heard of.

Sunny or Sony or something like that.

Debbie didn't expect that by the time she and her friends arrived, around 9, half these guys would be stoned and/or stumbling drunk. They certainly didn't expect to see a couple of college girls dancing topless around the bonfire to raucous music by groups she'd never heard of. Them. Cream. The Mothers of Invention.

Debbie and Kathy mingled, chatted with some college boys, sipped something fizzy and liked it, then sipped one more and got a little tipsy. Debbie needed to pee, so she walked behind a couple of trucks, pulled down her bikini bottom and squatted.

She was almost through when someone came at her from behind, clamping his right arm around her neck.

Her immediate reaction was, "This isn't funny," but then, she realized it wasn't meant to be, so she kicked, and he jerked her back and forth, then pushed her face into the mushy ground and kept it there by grabbing the base of her ponytail. She couldn't see his face or his hands, and, in some surreal way, she still couldn't believe it was happening.

Using his left hand and right foot, he pushed her bikini bottom the rest of the way off, pried her legs apart, jabbed until he found the right spot. She began to gag and thought she might choke on her own vomit, and she thought, "I'm going to die. Oh my God, my mother will kill me."

And so, in her delirious panic, the last thing she thought before passing out was, "Look. I made a joke."

—

"When I came to," Debbie said, "it was over, and he was gone, and Jeff was washing my face and neck and talking to me. Of all the people in the world, Jeff. He wrapped me in a towel and carried me to his brother's truck and drove me to the emergency room in Denton."

She said she was taken into a little room and told to wait. The doctors would see her shortly. Her lip was bleeding, so nurses brought her ice wrapped in a washcloth. One stayed with her until two cops came in and told her to take a hike.

It was almost comical, Debbie said. Good cop. Bad cop. One old. One young.

The old cop was tall and gangling, droopy ears, nicotine eyes, short, bushy hair plastered straight up, rumpled black suit, black tie, scuffed up brown wingtips.

The young cop had a baby face and looked like he should have been starting on a junior college basketball team. He wore a crisp blue shirt and a light beige sports coat. Maroon and white striped tie. Cordovan Ropers as buffed as he was.

"The old one told me they needed to interview me right then," Debbie said. "I told them I wanted to wait, but he insisted it had to be done immediately. He asked me if I wanted them to catch whoever did this, and I said of course I did. So, he said I had to answer a few questions, right then."

The interrogation went like this:

Young cop: "We need to ask a few questions. It's standard procedure. We'll file a formal report later."

Old cop: "Why don't you give us your version of the story."

D: "There's only one version."

Old cop: "Tell us your version."

D: "It was dark, and I didn't see a face, but I could tell he was big. Like a football player. He grabbed me around the neck from behind and fell on top of me."

Old cop: "While you were urinating?"

D: "I'd just finished."

Young cop: "You'd been drinking. Right? How many drinks

would you say you'd had?"

D: "A couple."

Old cop: "How many is a couple? Two? Three? Four?"

D: "Two, probably. Possibly three."

Young cop: "Try to remember. It's important."

D: "I'm not sure."

Old cop: "We'll go with three."

D: Blank stare.

Old cop: "How old are you?"

D: "Almost 15."

Old cop: "You're aware that the legal drinking age in Texas is no longer almost 15."

D: No answer.

Old cop: "What were you wearing at the time the assault took place?"

D: "How does that matter?"

Old cop: "It matters. Just answer the question."

D: "I was wearing a tuxedo."

Young cop: "Don't go down that road, Little Sister. You won't be doing yourself any favors."

D: "I was wearing a swimsuit."

Old cop: "Describe it."

D: Angry glare.

Young cop: "One piece or two?"

D: "Two."

Old cop: "That's all you were wearing?"

Debbie: "I was at the lake. I wasn't singing in church."

Old cop: "Do you go to church?"

Debbie: Angry glare.

Young cop: "Look, we're trying to help you. Work with us. Can you tell us anything material that might help us identify a suspect in this case?"

D: "No. I don't remember anything else right now."

Old cop: "OK, then. Let's size this up. You're 14. Almost 15. You were at a party with older boys — some of whom may have been college boys. The party was at a lake. You drank so much you needed to urinate outdoors. You chose to urinate in the dark next to a truck, at which time a large male allegedly attacked you from behind and then sexually assaulted you. You did not see his face or any distinguishing features other than his hands, which you have described as 'large.' Is there anything I've missed? Anything you want me to correct?"

D: Furious glare. "I want you to go…" And she stopped with that. They interpretedit as "I want you to leave." What she really meant was, "I want you to go fuck yourselves."

—

Debbie said she have answered a few yes/no questions, but mostly she just sat there on the hospital bed, waiting for her Mom, and when she finally arrived and found out about the interview, she hit the roof.

"Completely off-the-charts, and not at me," Debbie said. "At the hospital. At the cops. But not at me. I was still in shock, and she hugged me and told me I was safe, and that was all that mattered.

"I had lied," she continued. "I had snuck out, and I blamed myself. I was glad it happened to me. I kept thinking, 'What if this had happened to Kathleen?'

Finally, a doctor came in to examine her and stitch up her lip, and the nurse returned, and then a woman she didn't know came in and asked her if she wanted to talk to a priest or a nun.

"I never told my mom about that. She would've gone ballistic. I spent the night in the hospital, and they sent me home the next morning. I heard a doctor telling my mom I was lucky I'd escaped without any serious 'vaginal lacerations.' He actually used the words 'lucky' and 'escaped' and 'vaginal lacerations' in the same sentence.

"I cried for two days. I'd sit in the bathtub and stare at the bruises and try to pull myself together, but I needed someone to talk to who wasn't my mom or a priest or a nun. I needed to talk to someone who'd gone through what I had, but I didn't know anyone. I needed someone to assure me the bruises and lacerations would go away and I would heal and be as good as new.

"For the next couple of weeks, Mom kept calling the Denton County Sheriff's Department, asking if they'd found anything. You know, car keys, or a ring, or a pair of socks. They never did. They just gave her the same run-around each time. The cops said they talked to some guys who were in charge, but they said they didn't know anything. They said they weren't aware we were there, and if they had been, why, they'd have sent us home.

"They lied, and the cops didn't care. If I'd told them I thought the hand that grabbed me might have been black, they'd have filled the jail," Debbie said.

At about that point in the conversation — if you want to call it that — Cindy Lou reappeared.

"You good?" she asked.

"I could use a cup of coffee," I told her.

"Cream and sugar?" she asked.

"Nope."

"Coffee, black," she said. "Be right back."

"Is she like this all the time?" I asked Debbie.

"Pretty much," she replied. "If only she could stay this way."

Word of the party and what had happened got around. It even made the Denton newspaper. The story said police were searching for a suspect in connection with an alleged sexual assault during a party at Lewisville Lake where teens as young as 14 were "known to have been consuming alcohol."

"My name was never mentioned in the papers, but, of course, you're not going to keep a secret like this for long, not in a small town, anyway," she said. "That was the worst. People gawking and talking, saying all kinds of horrible things behind my back. No one ever said a word to my face, but behind my back, some people said I got what I deserved."

Debbie said the investigation dragged on, and so did the gossip.

"I had no right to complain. I shouldn't have been there, and I admit that. I punished myself by bobbing my hair and dying it brick red, but Kathy nagged me into growing it back. The color and length of my hair doesn't matter. I'm tarnished. You can't see it because you don't understand how it works. It's subtle. I'm not a member of any clubs or teams at school. I might have gone out for basketball or volleyball — even track — but I can't deal with the idea of people looking at me. That's why I don't go to church. All those people judging me, pretending to be better than me. I don't need it."

She paused to take a breath, and I asked, "Are you done?"

"No," she said. "One more thing. About a month after it happened, Mom drove me to Dallas and took me to this exclusive dress shop in Highland Park and bought me a cocktail dress made with a gold and black brocade, and we got dressed up, and we went to Ports O'Call, the fancy downtown restaurant on top of the Sheraton Hotel in Dallas. Have you been there? It's incredible. On a clear night, you can see 50 miles in any direction.

"I wore a string of my mother's pearls, and every man there watched me walk in and sit down, and mom ordered two glasses of champagne and two Caesar salads and two shrimp cocktails, and when they arrived, she picked up her glass and she said to me, 'Raise your chin, Sweetheart. You have nothing to apologize for. Look around. What do you see? There's not a woman here who wouldn't trade places with you for at least this moment.'

"I got choked up. Then, Mom said, 'All they see is a beautiful young woman, and they'd trade their silver and gold to look as stunning in that dress as you do. So, perk up and bottoms up. Let's get sloshed.'"

I thought that was the end of the story, but it wasn't over.

"You know about periods, don't you?" Debbie continued. "Girls' periods? The little friend who visits once a month?"

"I know enough," I lied.

"I know enough Chinese to order an egg roll," she said. "I missed two periods. Mom took me to her doctor, and he told me I was pregnant. The chances were one in a zillion. Mom was crying. I was crying. I didn't know what to do, but I was afraid I didn't have a choice. I mean, what were my options? Go to Mexico?

"But Mom pulled herself together, and she handled it. She said she knew what to do and who could and would do it, and I knew she was talking about an abortion, so I told her I wasn't sure I could do that. I didn't believe in God, but I believed in Hell. Funny how that works, isn't it?

"Anyway, Mom said, 'I don't give a shit if the both of us burn in Hell forever, we are going to take care of this. You and me. That's how it's always been. You and me. Us. Together. We are going to take care of this, and we are going to move on, and I will crush anything or anyone who steps in our path.' And that's what she did."

Debbie's mom contacted Dr. Donald Hudspeth, the son of Dr. Walter Hudspeth, the Fort Worth physician she'd worked for. The old man had died in 1961, and "little Donnie" — as he was called — took over the practice. He remembered Jenny fondly and agreed to do what needed to be done.

When it was over, Dr. Donnie hugged Jenny and kissed her on the cheek and said, "My father adored you. You were the daughter he never had. Don't let the bastards get you down."

Then, he kissed his right index finger and placed it gently on the scar on Debbie's lip, and he told her to take care of her mother.

"This is as hard on her — if not harder — than it is on you," he said. "That might be impossible for you to believe, but it's true. If she starts crying again, just let her cry. It's very therapeutic. You might even try some more of it yourself."

—

It was getting late. I glanced at my watch and couldn't believe Lori or Jeff hadn't picked me up already.

"I know you need to go," Debbie said. "I want to finish: Did I bring this on myself? No. Am I sorry I had an abortion? No. Do I feel like I committed a sin? No. Do I feel guilty that I had an abortion? Yes. I do."

"You shouldn't," I said.

"I appreciate that, but you don't know. You can't know. You never will," she said. "My mother was forced to make the same choice, and here I am. I'm going to have to live with my decision every day for the rest of my life. So, if you wonder why I'm not as chirpy and cheerful and sweet as Cindy Lou, well, now you know."

Minutes later, Dennis stuck his head in the front door of The Fritz and thrust a thumb in the air, which meant, "Move it."

That was his idea of chit-chat.

"Bye," Debbie said. "Thank you."

I wanted to hug her or even kiss her on the forehead or cheek, but I couldn't. Not in public. Especially not in front of Dennis. I wasn't that evolved yet.

That night, I laid in bed and tuned out the clatter and tried to make sense of everything. Mostly, I tried to figure out when and how I screwed up. I couldn't believe I told her she shouldn't feel guilty. How would I know that? How could I know what she'd been through, what she was still going through?

I wished I'd kissed her. I wished I'd at least kissed my right index finger and tapped on the forehead or on the lips or on the scar on her lip.

The more I thought about Debbie, the madder I got at Kassel, the whole damn lot of them. How could they be so nice one-on-one and such jerks collectively?

I guess that's true for all small towns. Individually, they're kind and helpful and generous and brave, but collectively, they're petty and mean and cruel and small and scared of their shadows.

The world changes, and they don't or won't or can't. They feel isolated and threatened and picked on and made fun of. They think the world's out to get them, and it is. Sam Cooke warned them, "A Change Is Gonna Come," and Bob Dylan told them, "The Time's They Are a Changin.'"

Well, it was 1966, and change had finally arrived, even in dinky hamlets like Kassel. Hair got longer. The war in Vietnam got bloodier. The anti-war protesters and the civil rights protesters and the women's rights protesters and the anti-protest protesters got crazier. The music got louder.

Even the Beatles cranked it up. Kids like me who grew up on

"She Loves You" and "Yesterday" couldn't make heads or tails out of sitars or "She Said She Said" or "Tomorrow Never Knows."

Of course, everybody got angrier. They turned on their TV sets and glared at the pock-marked face of Richard Speck, a nobody who raped and tortured and murdered eight student nurses in Chicago.

I was still at the farm when Charles Whitman, a former Marine, lugged a small arsenal of rifles to the observation deck of the Main Tower at the University of Texas at Austin and shot 17 college kids and innocent bystanders and an unborn baby. The day before, he stabbed his wife and her mother to death.

No wonder everybody was so confused and frightened. After World War II, Americans were accustomed to a world where things were clear and distinct: Yes or no; up or down; us or them; first or last. It was also black vs. white; best vs. worst; and right vs. wrong.

Somewhere in the late 1950's it began to blur. Harvard psychology professors might have been able to make sense of it, but North Texas dairy farmers could not. They were still trying to figure out color TV sets and seatbelt regulations.

And so, it was difficult for people living in small towns to keep up with the change, much less than to make sense of it, and that threatens the very fabric of small-town life. In small towns, a person is more than a name and a face. In a small-town, a person is expected to reflect all the virtues and high principles the community claims to possess, and that person is judged on how successfully he or she helps sustain the fraud.

This is hard, so people create lines. Small-town people need lines. They need traditions and directions and paint-by-number instructions. They need dogmas and protocols and rules, spoken and unspoken.

People who buckle, who try to cut their own path are often ostracized and, in worst case scenarios, disenfranchised or even excommunicated, and it's not because they broke a rule. It's because they disobeyed God.

Small town people need God involved in everything because

they don't trust themselves. Without God, they'd lie, lust, cheat, steal and kill without abandon. With God, they'd still lie, lust, cheat, steal and kill, but only when necessary.

Of course, it's tough to decide when something's necessary, so there's all kinds or wiggle room, especially when it comes to God.

For instance, is it a sin to get hammered and fall asleep at the wheel and slam into an oncoming station wagon, killing a mother and father and two children?

No. It's tragic, but it's not technically a sin.

Is it a sin for a 17-year-old girl to have sex before she marries her 18-year-old boyfriend? Yes.

Is it a sin for a 14-year-old girl to go to a party where alcohol is being served? No.

Is it a sin for a 14-year-old girl to go to a party where alcohol is being served and drink too much? No.

Is it a sin for a 14-year-old girl to go to a party where alcohol is being served, drink too much and be raped? No.

Is it a sin to rape a 14-year-old girl who attends a party where alcohol is being served? No.

Nothing in the Ten Commandments says anything about raping anyone except if it involves two people of the same gender. Then, it's a sin.

Finally, if you're 14 years old girl, and you drink too much at a party, and you're raped and impregnated, is it a sin to end the pregnancy?

Of course, it is. no matter what, ending a pregnancy is murder. At least it is among Catholics living dusty, dinky little towns 14 miles south of nowhere.

Always has been. Always will be.

—

Jeff was never a deep-thinker, but he had a big heart, and he knew when to call bullshit bullshit. One night, he'd pulled over to gab with a guy who was selling a two-stroke Honda motorcycle when a Kassel High junior named Larry Muntz decided it was his duty to tell Jeff that he should warn me to cool my jets vis-à-vis

Debbie Gehring.

"Before your lover-boy cousin gets too head over heels, you might want to warn him that she's damaged goods," Muntz said.

"Say again?" Jeff answered.

"She's been around," Muntz said. "You know what I mean."

"I'm not sure I do," Jeff said.

"Shit, man," Muntz said. "Do you need me to draw you a picture?"

Jeff pulled a cigarette out of his shirt pocket, lit it, took a long draw from it, licked his index finger, put it out, and repeated Muntz's remark.

"Draw me a picture," Jeff said. "Do you need me to draw you a picture?"

"You gotta problem, man?" Muntz asked.

Normally, Jeff would have weaseled his way out of a situation like this because he saw no reason to lose two front teeth over some piddly comment made by some dipshit junior, but calling Debbie Gehring "damaged goods" and suggesting she "got around" tripped his wire. After all, Jeff had found her, cleaned her face, and calmed her down, and got her dressed and drove her to the hospital.

And he'd never felt more important in his life.

So, before Muntz could say anything else about "damaged goods," Jeff punched him. The left jab split his lip and knocked him backwards but not off his feet. Muntz stumbled, got his balance, and then lurched at Jeff, trying to bull-wrestle him. If he had, it would have been bad news for Jeff because Muntz outweighed him by 50 pounds, at least.

But Jeff ducked and knee-whipped Muntz. He screeched and collapsed to the ground. Shocked that he was getting his ass handed to him by Jeff, Muntz swiped his right hand across his busted lip, checked to make sure his tongue was still attached, smeared his nose, and screamed, "Schaper, I'm going to rip your fucking head off."

And he might have if he hadn't made two more big mistakes

First, he tried to lift himself by grabbing a Chevy Bel Air's passenger side rear-view mirror.

Second, he left a bloody handprint on the Chevy Bel Air.

The owner of the Chevy Bel Air was a 20-year-old high school dropout named Gary Inzer. He was leaning on the hood when the fight broke out, and when Muntz grabbed his rear-view mirror, Inzer walked around and hovered over him.

"Gimme a hand, Inzer," Muntz said. "I'm gonna..."

"You ain't gonna do shit," Inzer said, slapping the hand away.

"That's for getting your blood on my car," Inzer said.

When Muntz tried to get to his feet, Inzer shoved him back to the ground again.

"That's for being an asshole," Inzer said. "Now, get up and get in your car and get the fuck out of here before I decide to hurt you, and if the cops hear about this, you'll hear from my older brother."

Of the Inzer boys, Gary Inzer's older brother — Brady — was considered the true bad ass. Rumors were he was a member of the Bandidos motorcycle gang, so the cops never heard a peep from Muntz.

Even if they had, they probably would've brought in the Inzer boys and shook their hands.

CHAPTER 19

Common ground

I was enjoying a cheeseburger and a Dr Pepper at The Fritz by myself while Dennis deposited a couple of checks and picked up something at the meat market and talked to someone at the Co-Op about grain or girls or something else. Who knows?

He rarely briefed me on his agenda, so I was reading a story in The Dallas Morning News about Don Meredith and the high expectations everyone had for the Cowboys when the barometric pressure in the room plummeted. I looked up, and there standing in front of me was Jenny Gehring — tall, striking, and terrifying.

She wore a charcoal-gray dress that on any other woman in town might've looked sensible, but on Jenny Gehring, it looked like a million bucks. Her toffee-colored hair was twirled into a bun, and she wore raspberry lipstick and no jewelry that I noticed.

She carried a look of disdainful curiosity as well as a smooth, black leather purse. I'd seen the look before, but I'd never seen a purse like that. It must have cost a fortune. The zipper and rivets were brushed gold, and when she dropped it on the table, it landed with a thud. I still can't imagine what she had in it. Petrified scrotums, perhaps.

"Care if I join you?" she said, sliding into the booth before I had a chance to respond. "How's the burger? Does it measure up to your East Texas standards?"

I shrugged. "It's fine."

"What a ringing endorsement," she said, then raised her left arm, which summoned a short, plump waitress named Doris.

Jenny picked up and perused the paper menu, then said to Doris, "This young man tells me he thinks your hamburgers are fine. I think I'll have one."

"The regular, Miss Gehring?" Doris asked.

"Doris, I believe I'll have it with a dab of mustard on one side only and extra pepper on the tomato."

"So, the regular," Doris said.

"That's correct," Jenny said. "And thank you for remembering."

"Yes, ma'am," Doris said and waddled over to the window between the counter and the kitchen. "Gehring. Double P."

That meant, "Plus Pepper," which meant, "It's for the mother. Not the daughter."

Jenny watched Doris and then turned her gaze back toward me, and I at first averted her stare. It was like looking down the barrel of a 12-gauge shotgun.

"Doris," she said. "What a character. I like her quite a bit. Not personally, of course. I don't know her personally, but I do know her story. She's 50-something and looks 60-something, at least. What do you think? Fifty or 60? I'm not sure. She definitely looks older than she is.

Of course, there's a reason for that. Would you care to guess what it is?"

"I think I'll pass," I said.

"Why am I not surprised?" she said. "Her husband left her about 15 years ago and took almost everything except the coffee cups with him. Shocking, isn't it? That a man would do such a thing. A Christian man at that.

"It almost destroyed her, but she pulled herself together, and she's made the best of it, and I admire her for that. I like people who pull themselves together, don't you?"

"I guess so," I said.

I assumed she wasn't truly interested in who or what I liked or disliked — except her daughter — so I sat there, holding my cheeseburger and my breath.

"Your burger is getting cold," Jenny told me. "Eat. Please. I insist. There's nothing worse than a cold cheeseburger."

I nibbled carefully and tried to keep my mouth shut so I wouldn't make any noises, and she wouldn't notice if a piece of lettuce got jammed in between two teeth.

Jenny smiled, then added, "I meant to say, nothing worse than a no-good husband."

"No argument here," I said, and she gave me a funny look, as if she thought I was being fresh with her.

"I happen to know that Doris attended college for a while," Jenny continued. "She wanted to be an elementary school teacher. It had been her dream since kindergarten, but then her father died unexpectedly. Heart attack. He smoked like a fucking fiend...Oops. My apologies. Creature of habit. Like a fiend, but then, she didn't have a choice. She had to make a living, and when her father died, she had to take care of her grieving mother, and her mother grieved for 20 years until her death not long ago. It was either right before or right after Kennedy was shot.

"Regardless, Doris has spent almost her entire life in this town. Can you imagine?" Jenny said. "She's been waiting tables here for at least eight or nine years. The pay's OK, and she gets to polish off the leftover fries and onion rings, and that probably explains why she's as thick as de Gaulle's accent. You wouldn't believe it, but Doris was a handsome young woman. I saw a photo of her in an old yearbook. She was a homecoming queen candidate. And look at her now. I bet she would've been a fantastic teacher, too, if she'd had a chance. But life isn't fair. Have you noticed?"

"Yes, ma'am," I said. "I have."

"At such a tender age, oh my," Jenny said. "Well, what are you going to do?"

"Muddle along, I guess," I said.

"That's one option," Jenny said. "Doris has muddled along. To be brutally honest, Doris could've become a teacher if she really wanted to, but she didn't. It's been easier for her to muddle along, waiting tables. Don't misunderstand me. There's nothing wrong with waiting tables, and I still like her, but I don't feel the least bit sorry for her. She's made her own little basket of fries, so to speak, but we can chat about that at another time. What I really want to talk about is my daughter."

"Yes, ma'am," I said and waited.

Jenny took her time without once lifting her eyes off me.

"Deborah is a very special girl," Jenny said, then called to Doris, "Doris, bring me an iced tea right away, please," and an iced tea appeared immediately. Jenny took a sip and continued.

"Well, she's special to me, anyway. Oh, who am I kidding, she's just a special girl, period. Don't you think so?"

"Yes, ma'am," I said. "I do."

"Please. Don't call me ma'am. Call me Jenny."

"I can't do that," I said.

"Why on Earth not?"

"I just can't," I said. "I don't feel comfortable."

"In that case, call me Miss Gehring," she said.

"OK. I can do that," I said.

"Well, lovely. Look! We've found common ground, and so quickly Let's see if we can stake out some more. I have no objections to this little romance," Miss Gehring said. "I think it's sweet. Every teenage girl needs one or two per summer. And you will hear no objections from me as long as it continues to be short and sweet and innocent. I just want to make sure we understand each other. You do understand, don't you?"

"Yes, ma'am," I said.

"Did I hear you correctly?" she said.

"Yes, Miss Gehring," I said slowly.

"Thank you. Little things matter," she said. "Now, where was I? Oh, I was making a point regarding this sweet and innocent fling, I do not want my very special daughter to end up spending the rest of her life in a little town like Kassel, Texas, or wherever it is you're from. I'm fairly confident it's neither New York nor London, and if it's Paris, it's Paris, Texas. The only reason she and I are here is because it offers me the best opportunity to help her escape. I don't expect you to understand. It's complicated, but trust me, I know what I'm doing. I did not move here because of the mountains and the beaches. I moved here for her, and now, my job is to make sure she ends up somewhere else, preferably with someone who seems to be going somewhere. Are you still with me?"

"Yes, ma'am."

She slapped her hand on the table and snapped, "Instructions?"

"Yes, Mrs. Gehring."

"Your teachers must adore you," she said. "It's Miss Gehring. M.I.S.S. Not Mrs. I am not married. If you are to believe the Catholic Church, which I strongly discourage, I never have been married, if that helps you to remember. Miss Gehring. Got it?"

With anyone else, I might have had a smart-ass response, but I thought the better of it.

"Yes, Jenny," I said. "I understand."

The last thing she wanted was the one thing she asked for. She smiled suspiciously and said, "I'm glad we've had this chance to chat and get to know one another. The horrible things you've heard about me are true. I've heard good and bad about you, and I'll be honest — you're not quite what I expected, although I can't say exactly what I did expect. Perhaps a little more of this and a little less of that. Not so much pepper on the tomato, so to speak. It doesn't matter. Right now, she's happy, so I'm happy. She was a happy child once. She wore pink a lot. She hasn't worn pink in quite some time. Oh well, c'est la vie. If you hurt her, I will be quite unhappy. In that event, I will feed your lips and hips and finger tips to a kettle of buzzards. Did you know that a group of buzzards is called a 'kettle'?"

If I flinched, it wasn't because I thought she could or would do it. It was because she had the nerve to say it. I thought, "Best line I've heard since 'Dinosaur dick.'"

Then, she backed off. Maybe she worried she might've legally threatened me with bodily harm. I'm not sure.

"Forgive me," she said. "Sometimes, I forget myself. One day, I suspect, you'll understand. Until then, just know this: Life comes at you like an angry bull, so get a sword and learn how to use it. I've been gored. She's been gored, too. We won't be gored again."

I stared at the salt shaker, then looked up and said, "You don't have to worry. At least, not about me. I don't plan to do anything stupid. I'm not that stupid."

She smiled, in as patronizing a way as possible.

"Out of the mouths of infants and sucklings," she said. "That should comfort me, but it doesn't because I know it's not true. There's always something to worry about because boys like you are not in the least bit aware of their intentions or plans. They just muddle along until opportunity presents itself, and then they do what they want to do, or try to. My job is to make sure they don't."

She paused for effect, then continued.

"All that's important is that you understand me because I'll do whatever I have to do to look out for her best interests, which — by the way — I control, and don't fool yourself thinking otherwise."

She paused one last time, expecting me to faint or at least have a panic attack, apparently.

"Well, I must go," she said. "Busy. Busy. Death doesn't take a holiday."

She stood and told me to stand and shake her hand like I meant it, so I did.

"Let's have lunch again soon, and next time, I promise, we won't have to work so hard to find common ground," she said. "And won't that be nice?"

"Yes, Miss Gehring," I said. "It will."

She smiled half-heartedly, then recited a line from Hamlet: "I must be cruel only to be kind."

She didn't recite the next line: "Thus bad begins, and worse remains behind."

Just as I began to think it was safe to exhale, Miss Gehring said, "I loved Shakespeare, but when I was in grade school, I hated English. I hated English because my English teacher would smack my hand when I failed to properly punctuate a compound sentence. You know what a compound sentence is, don't you?"

"I do," I said, "because my mother taught me."

"Well, touché. Good for you. Did she have to smack your hand you every time you failed to punctuate one correctly? That's how my English teacher taught me. She just smacked my hand. In an odd way, you remind of my mother," she said. "Now, it's your turn to ask me the obvious question"

"I'm not sure if I know what the obvious question is," I said.

"Oh, sure you do. That's why it's called 'the obvious question.' Don't over-think it. Your obvious question is this: 'How do I remind you of your English teacher?' Well, here's the answer. My mother was my English teacher, and I loved her and still do, and having met you, I think I understand her a little better. I think I understand she was so afraid of my growing up and going out into the world alone before I knew what was out there. I think smacking my hand had nothing to do with commas and compound sentences. I believe the intent was to remind me to think first before putting my hand where it didn't belong. Now, hold out your hand."

I expected her to smack it. Instead, in broad daylight, she reached into her black purse and pulled out a little black, square package containing one condom.

"Bows and arrows. I expect to get that back, unopened," she said. "Actually, I insist."

Then, Miss Gehring snapped her fingers, and Doris came tottering over with a white sack that contained a hamburger with one slice of tomato and extra pepper.

"Put his burger on my tab and add a 25 percent tip for yourself, Doris, and bring this fine young gentleman another Dr Pepper."

"Yes, Miss Gehring," Doris said. "Thank you and come again."

Jenny brushed salt grains off her charcoal gray dress and waltzed out the front door of The Fritz, and every man in there including Cupcake could not help but gape at her and hope she didn't wheel around and catch them in the act.

CHAPTER 20

Hands and eyes

As told by Jenny Gehring

Afterwards, I slid into the driver's seat of my Grand Prix, shut the door, dropped my purse in the passenger's seat, grabbed the steering wheel and tried to make sense of the little tête-à-tête I'd just had with Mr. East Texas Lady-killer.

This boy — this Eddie character — was more challenging than I'd anticipated. To be honest, I'd hoped to scare him half to death, but I had trouble reading his hands and eyes.

Maybe I was just off my game. After all, this was all new to me, too. Eventually, it dawned on me why Debbie was so ... oh, I don't know. What's the word? Infatuated? Is that it? If it's not, it'll do. Why she was so infatuated with him.

It certainly wasn't love. It was far too soon, but it was something similar to love. There must be a word for that, too. Oh well, regardless, it was real, and that worried me. Debbie played tough, but she wasn't.

I never wanted her to date in high school, and I almost got my wish. One last year to go, and, just my luck, in walks this boy, this Eddie Something from Somewhere. The day she met him, she came home as high as a kite. I asked her, "What are you so giddy about?" but she just gave me that look — You've seen it. That face. — and darted upstairs and put on the goddamn Beatles.

She didn't have to tell me. I knew she'd met a boy. I tried not to overreact, not to be too positive or too negative. I didn't think it'd last 24 hours, so I just asked the obvious questions. "Who is this boy? Where is he from? What is he doing here? Does he have a full set of teeth?"

She didn't know the answers to most of them. I told her I was happy for her, then warned her to be careful, not to think that this boy is the last boy on Earth. I told her she'd burn through a boatload of boys before she found the right one. I told her to take her time.

But she was 16, and when a 16-year-old girl decides it's time, then it's time, and there's not a thing God or Elvis or LBJ or anyone else can do about it.

So, here we are.

I don't often allow myself the pleasure of crying. I don't have that liberty. My job does not permit it, so I gave myself five minutes to get it out of my system. Boo-hoo, then brace up because a half an hour later, I would be sitting next to the young widow of an oilfield hand who'd been electrocuted on the job because some idiot making five times the money than he made failed to flip a switch.

His children — a third-grade boy and a first-grade girl — and his widow were, of course, devastated. The little boy, he was inconsolable, so I had to be strong, professional. I do not agree with those in the business who grieve with the survivors. My job is not to grieve. It is to help them find a way to survive the horror, and don't you kid yourself. That's what it is.

In my opinion, that's why they're called "survivors." They don't survive the deceased. They survive the horror.

So, I offer a sympathetic smile and perhaps a gentle pat or hug, but anything beyond that, in my opinion, is unbecoming and ultimately counterproductive.

I hope you don't interpret this as my being cold or calculated. I am not. I know their pain. I understand it. But they don't need my tears. They need my strength and poise. They need to be reminded that life goes on, and it can be beautiful. It should be.

That's why I wear pearls. Hanadama Akoya pearls. Considered the finest in the world. Light just dances off their surface. At times, it creates a kind of rainbow effect that reminds me of Japanese cherry blossoms.

You would faint if I told you what I paid for them, but they serve a purpose. They infuse beauty into what is typically a ghastly mess. Details regarding "what now" and "what next" and "who gets what" have to be ironed out by those who are either screaming in sorrow or scheming for an easy buck.

It never takes me long to figure out who is actually grieving, and who is actually grifting.

Brothers and sisters can live next door to each other for 25 years, golf and bowl and barbecue together, raise children together, live in perfect harmony for decades, but when the final parent dies, the talons come out, and there is blood.

By the way, this happens in every family, in the best of the best, where no one needs anything, and in the worst of the worst, where no one has anything. That's why I've learned it's best to lay it all out at the beginning. At my first consultation with the family, I make a point of reminding everyone that it'll get very messy if we don't play well with others.

Of course, this triggers a chorus of denials.

"Maybe in some families, but no in this one."

"You can't think we'd stoop to such behavior."

"I don't expect to inherit a dime."

And other ridiculous lies. That's the fun part. I can pretty much figure who's who just by paying attention to their hands and their eyes, and that's what makes me so good at my job.

And that's why this Eddie character worried me. I couldn't read his hands or eyes.

PART FIVE | CHAPTER 21
The phone call

August 1966

I wasn't the least bit surprised when I woke up with a mouth ulcer. I tend to get them when I'm stressed to the gills. Fortunately, it was a small one — no bigger than the tip of a kitchen match — and it wasn't on my lip, which is torture and would have been doubly so given my adventures with Miss Gehring.

I'd just started my seventh week at the farm. Football two-a-days would start soon, and I should've been there, running laps and catching balls and lifting weights with the other guys during the voluntary workouts the coaches forced us to attend. They kept records of who showed up and for how often, so I knew I had some explaining to do when I got back.

I hoped the fact I'd been working outdoors, all day, every day and was in the best shape of my life would suffice, but coaches love to carry clipboards and keep stats and hold everyone accountable because the school's football program would not be entrusted to the timid or the weak, or so they claimed.

—

The call came 30 minutes before lunch. Mina took it and dispatched Lori to find me. It took her a while because I was in the silo with Jeff, spreading silage, which is essentially shredded grass and weeds that's fed to cows.

This is worth explaining. A big machine chops up the grass and weeds and blows it into a wagon that's pulled by a tractor. When the wagon's full, the tractor pulls it up next to a conveyor belt, and the chopped-up grass and weeds are shoveled onto the conveyor belt, which carries it into to a big fan that blows it up a tube to the top of the silo so it can drizzle back down. At this point, it's no longer considered grass and weeds. It's considered "silage."

It's important to spread it evenly because if you don't, it'll form a tall cone, and it won't pack. If it doesn't pack, it won't ferment. If it doesn't ferment, it rots. If it rots, the cows will have nothing to eat that winter, and they'll starve. If the cows starve, Uncle Carl will be forced to go to the bank and beg for a loan from a Becker.

He'd rather eat silage, but no one else in the family would, so he ordered me and Jeff climb into the silo and spread the silage as it flutters down. It's horrible work. We wore long-sleeved shirts buttoned all the way up, and hats and gloves and thick goggles to protect us from the needles, centipedes, splinters, spiders, ground hornets, and God-only knows what else.

That's not the worst of it. Silage produces a gas that smells like laundry bleach and can — in the right conditions — suck oxygen out of the air, thus suffocating expendables like me and Jeff.

Then, there's the possibility of a fire or an explosion caused by dust accumulation. Or, we could fall off a ladder and land on a pitch fork, or we could suffer heat exhaustion, or we could simply be buried in the silage.

Of course, the chances of that happening were about the same as getting killed by a cement truck, so I didn't complain when I was assigned to climb in the silo. After all, I promised I was there to do what I was told to do, and I did not intend to welch on that promise so close to the end.

I was soaked in sweat and caked in dust when Lori clanged on the side of the silo and yelled up, "There's a phone call for Eddie, and he needs to take it now."

"The spiders got him," Jeff yelled back.

"Mom's orders, dipshit," Lori yelled back. "Two One Four."

That told me all I needed to know. It was our telephone area code. Though Lori shouted, "Your mom is waiting," I took my time. I lumbered up to the barn, undressed, hosed off, pulled on a pair of jeans, and walked barefoot across white rocks to the house.

Somehow, I thought Mom might hang up and try again later,

but when I trudged into the kitchen, she was still on the line, chit-chatting with Faye.

"Here he is," Faye said and handed me the receiver. Right as I took it, she mouthed, "Butthole."

I held it for a second, then said, "Hello," in as fake a voice as I could manufacture.

"Well, hello," Mom said. "Sounds like you're thrilled to hear from me."

"Of course, I am," I said. "I was working. What's up?"

"Your brothers are dead," Mom said.

"What?" I asked, incredulously.

"Both of them. Killed and carted away by wild dogs," she said. "We found their shoes. And one ear. Can't make it out who it belonged to. Never found their bodies."

"Are you drunk?" I asked.

"No," she said. "Are you crippled? It took you 15 minutes to walk from the silo to the house. I could crawl that far in 15 minutes. I don't know what took you so long, but when I call, I expect you to answer, promptly."

"Well, I had to wash off," I said.

She didn't buy it.

"Look, I know you're angry, but we didn't intend for you to spend all summer there," she said, "I know it messed up your plans, and I don't blame you for being mad."

I stifled a laugh and thought, "Shit, Mom. You have no idea. This has been the best summer of my life. I haven't thought about you or him or them, and if it were left up to me, I'd stay here forever. I'd die a dairy farmer."

But I said, "It's not a problem."

And Mom said, "I know better, but we'll be there Friday or Saturday to pick you up, so start putting your things together. Are you ready to come home?"

What could I say?

"Sure."

I guess she believed what she wanted to believe, so she perked up and went on and on about how my brothers missed me so much and were looking forward to seeing me, and how she and my dad seemed to be making progress with their troubles.

I responded with a series of one-syllable words: Yeah. Great. Right. OK. Sure. Yep. No. Yes. Maybe. They allowed her to believe I was listening, but I was not. I was running the numbers.

"Tonight. Tomorrow night. The night after that. The night after that. Saturday. That's four nights, and then, it's over. Four nights. One. Two. Three. Four."

My eyes began to glaze, and I asked, "What time?"

"What time what?" Mom said.

"What time do you think you'll be here?"

"I don't know. It depends," she said. "We might come Friday, but probably, Saturday morning. Does it matter?"

"No," I said. "Just curious."

"I'll let you know more when I know more." Mom said.

"Great," I said.

"I love you," Mom said.

"Yeah. Sure. Me, too," I replied and hung up.

I didn't mean to confuse her or hurt her feelings, but I had to get off the phone. I turned, and Mina was standing there.

"You knew this day was coming," she said, and she wrapped her arms around me and hugged me, and I held it in, but it was hard. A lot harder than hearing my brothers had been eaten by wild dogs.

I washed my face and tried to splash the red out of my eyes before everyone rolled in. Lori came from the henhouse. Faye came from upstairs where she was sewing together patches for a quilt. Jeff and Dennis came from the silo. Danny was sitting at the table. He'd just returned from an auto parts store in Gainesville.

"Are you OK?" Danny asked me. "You look hung over."

"Dust," I said.

"Well, you look like you've been crying."

"Silo," I said.

"You're not supposed to smoke it," he added. "You smoke the

other kind of weed."

About then, Uncle Carl strolled in. He'd been in a good mood that morning. He washed up and wiped off with a dish towel.

"If we keep up this pace, you boys will be sipping those beers you got hidden in the pump house by 3:30."

That was his idea of a joke, and he waited for a response, but Mina plopped a plate of fried pork chops in front of him and announced, "Well, it's official. Eddie is heading home soon."

Lori and Faye pouted and pretended to pet me.

Jeff gawked at me and said, "I was about to get used to you."

Dennis looked up at Jeff, then looked back down at his plate.

Uncle Carl's expression flipped from sort of cheery to sort of grim just like that. Everyone noticed it, especially Lori, and it infuriated her. She later told me, "If Mom had announced, 'Lori's taking off for Tanzania tomorrow,' Papa wouldn't have said a word except 'You're still milking in the morning.'"

So, she brooded until it was time to return to her chores, which she completed without complaining except to the chickens, cows, and Betsy, who always knew when Lori needed a nuzzle.

That afternoon was a disaster. Uncle Carl bitched about every little thing and blamed Dennis when the conveyor belt slipped and tore, then ordered him to get in his goddamn truck and go into town and get another one, and it was coming out of his pocket, which wasn't fair because it wasn't Dennis' fault. It wasn't anybody's fault. The conveyor belt had to have been 10 years old, at least, so that threw us behind by an hour. We didn't open a Schlitz until a quarter 'til 6.

Debbie called at 5:30, and Mina told her I was still in the silo.

"Good," she said. "Tell him I need to work tonight. Betty Fricke is sick, so I'm filling in. See if he can postpone until tomorrow."

"Sweetheart," Mina said. "He's leaving Saturday."

There was a pause, then she said, "I'll call back in an hour."

She called at 6:30, and I was there, waiting for it.

"So, I don't have to tell you," I said.

"I heard," she said. "Look, there's a visitation tonight. I have to work. It starts at 5 and should be over by 8. You never know. These things can drag on forever. I'll be there as soon as I can."

"OK," I said. "I'll be there."

Neither of us wanted to hang up or, at least, to be the first to hang up, so, I said, "Hang up. Just hang up. I'll see you soon."

So, she hung up, and I hung up and we both said, "Shit."

I walked outside and over to the chicken coop, and then I closed the doors and yelled at the chickens for a while. Then I walked to the swing set and sat down and listened to the male doves' sad cooing.

Coo. Coo. Oo. Oooooo.

Coo. Coo. Oo. Oooooo.

It sounded like they were asking God, "Give us this day. Give us this day. Please God, gives us, just one more day."

Then, I approached Lori about taking me to town, but she'd already planned that far ahead. She'd told Mina a little fib about needing to visit one of a girlfriend.

"She has the cramps and wants me to come over," she said. "They're bad."

"What does she expect you to do about them?" Mina said.

"She just needs a friend," Lori said.

"Well, you're milking in the morning, so don't stay out late, and try to get home with all your undergarments."

"That's not fair," Lori snapped.

"It's fair because I know why you're going to town, and you could have been honest with me," Mina said. "I would've driven him myself."

Lori shrugged and remembered Rule One: Don't bullshit Mom.

"OK. You're right," she said. "It's been a hard day. It won't happen again."

"Of course, it will," Mina said. "In the meantime, be careful in that car and be back here by 10:30 — the both of you."

I arrived around 7:30, stretched out on the rug, squirmed around to scratch my back, and waited to hear the kitchen door creak open. Around 8:15, Debbie tip-toed in, kicked her shoes off, and slid across the kitchen floor in her black pantyhose.

"Knock, knock," she said. "Anyone here?"

"Sorry," I said. "We're closed."

"Oh, dang," she said. "I had hoped to meet a young man here and make out with him for an hour or so. What a shame. and I'm so ready. How about you? Are you busy?"

"Young lady," I said. "I'm on duty. I don't have time for shenanigans."

"Yes, you do," she said, then took two big steps and jumped on me, bowling me over. It was her way of saying, "Look, we both knew this day was coming, and so it has. Let's wrestle and make the best of it."

And so, we wrestled, and we laughed and pretended to pin each other down, and then we took a breather, and I saw that her eyes were redder than mine, and her cheeks were flushed, and she kept wiping her nose with the top of her wrist.

She moved behind me, locked her arms around my neck and kissed my cheek.

"No hickeys, I promise," she said. "What would your girlfriends back home say?"

"They'd say, 'When did I become your girlfriend?'"

I thought that was clever enough given that I was working really hard to my emotions in check. Before I knew it, I heard Lori bump her horn, and Debbie said, "You need to go. I'll call you tomorrow."

I took her face in my hands, drew her close, and said, "I love you." About 14 times.

It was the first time I'd said it to anyone except my mother.

I didn't wait for her to answer because I wasn't sure she would, or if she did, I wasn't sure what she'd say, so I pushed her toward the kitchen door, followed her out, pulled the door shut and walked around the north side of the house toward Lori.

I knocked on the passenger's side window, and Lori unlocked the door. I jumped in, and she handed me a Schlitz.

CHAPTER 22

The full story

When you think you're going to have trouble sleeping, you find plenty of reasons to make sure you have trouble sleeping. It'll be too hot or too humid. The pillow will be too hard or too soft. The sheets will be too coarse or too slick. Someone somewhere will be shuffling a deck of playing cards, over and over and over, and that'll keep the spiders awake, so they'll be munching on grasshoppers, who'll scream bloody murder, and the thought of their dead eyes and empty green husks will keep you from sleeping for nights on end.

Love also keeps you from sleeping.

It did me, anyway. I laid in bed and stared into the darkness or out an open window and wondered if Debbie was sleeping and, if not, what she was thinking and hearing and watching?

Was she thinking about that night at the lake? I sure as hell was. I wondered what it must have been like to be grabbed, lifted up, thrown down, jerked around, shoved, choked and raped. What was it like to believe you were going to die?

I wondered how in the world do you put that behind you and move on, to be light and gay, friendly and socially graceful, to trust and be positive. How do you stop your lip from bleeding?

I still can't imagine, and it still fills me with rage. I want to hunt that son of a bitch down and catch him coming around a corner, and catch him with an ax handle, right in the face in front of his wife and kids, and then tell them why I did it.

That's what I felt that night, and it's why I had so much trouble sleeping that I finally got up and slipped on a pair of jeans and a T-shirt and crept barefoot through the girls' room, down the stairs and out of the house.

I stood on the front porch for a moment and tried not to stir the dogs. When I saw Bets coming my way, I high-stepped it over to the milk barn, flipped on a light and tried and failed to find anything worth listening to on the radio.

I sat on a milking stool and put my hands over my ears and screamed under my breath, "Let it go. Let it go. Let it go. Let it go," which, of course, I could not, so I tortured myself for a while.

Was she really damaged goods? Was that why she fell for me? Probably so. She had to be. There's no other explanation.

Then, I heard the screen door creak, and Uncle Carl stepped in.

"What are you doing out here at this time of the night, talking to yourself?" he asked.

"Nothing," I said. "I just couldn't sleep."

"Sounds like you're rehearsing a speech," he said.

"I'm sorry," I said. "I was just about to head back to bed."

"Don't," he said. "Stay there. I want to talk to you."

We sat opposite each other in the middle of the milk barn, and he said, "Milk turns sour eventually. Remember that."

Of all the inexplicable things I'd heard lately, that topped the bill. He twirled his right hand, as in, and so forth and so on. That's the way of the world. One day, this. The next day, that.

He said all that just by twirling his hand.

"I know," I replied.

"Knowing and understanding aren't the same," he said. "Understanding and accepting aren't the same, either. You have to do all three. You don't have to do them all at once, but to survive you have to do all three. It also helps you get to and stay asleep."

He waited a second, then asked, "What's that song? The one on the radio right now."

"Wild Thing," I said.

"It's terrible," he said. "Good Lord."

"You sound like my dad"

"For once, I agree with him."

He waited a second, yawned and said, "Martha and I lost our

first child to the croup. She was 17 months old. Her name was Emily. Emily Joyce. I didn't know if I was going to survive her death. I certainly didn't think I could ever love anything as much as I loved her, and maybe I haven't, which is on me. Not on her.

"After her death," he continued, "I was angry, and I took it out on everyone around me. Martha and I had eight more children, but I couldn't bring myself to love them as much as I did Emily, so I've held back. And then, I..."

And Uncle Carl started to choke up.

"And then I forgot how. How to love," he said. "I'm not sure I would if I could because I'm still afraid to. I'm afraid if I give in, and something happened to Lori or Faye, I don't think I could handle it. Especially Lori. I don't know what I'd do. She's as close to Emily as there ever will be. There are times when it takes everything I have not to grab her and hold her, hug her, but I'm afraid to because I might not ever let her go, and then who'd do the milking? Jeff?"

He laughed, and then he wiped his nose with a barn rag.

"Let me tell you something," he said. "It ain't worth it. The fear of fear. Don't give in to it. Just don't. If you love that girl, tell her. Nothing that's happened before, and nothing that's going to happen later matters. The only thing that matters is the here and now. So, that's my advice. Take it or leave it."

He stood and touched me on the shoulder.

"Stay as long as you like, but I suggest you go back to bed and get some sleep. We milk in a little over two hours, and you're still on the clock."

"Yes, sir," I said. "Thank you. Thank you for everything."

"Turn that noise off before you go in," he added.

I switched off the radio and pulled the stool back to the corner and headed toward the house. I thought Uncle Carl was following me, but when I turned around, I saw his silhouette out in the south pasture.

I got maybe an hour and a half of sleep, but I got enough to have two or three bizarre dreams. One of them was a sex dream.

Debbie and I were making out, and I worked up the nerve to touch her breasts, and she didn't refuse, and I got all excited and tried to force myself on her, and she started screaming because she thought I was the guy, and that woke me up.

I didn't think I'd fall back to sleep after that, but I did.

The second dream was even worse. Debbie had been elected Homecoming Queen, and she was riding on a float, and there was a banner, "Miss Damaged Goods 1966."

I was on the float, too. I was sitting on a bale of hay and waving like an idiot at people I didn't know, people who talked behind my back, snickered at me, and shunned her, and I didn't notice or hear the snickers or the laughs. And they were thinking, "Is this guy for real?" And I looked back at Debbie, and her lip was bleeding.

And then, I heard Uncle Carl. "Get up. Downstairs."

—

At breakfast, I must've looked like death warmed over because everyone kept asking me if I was OK, and I told them I didn't sleep very well. I didn't tell 'em the rest of it.

After milking, Dennis volunteered to clean up, and then he volunteered me to help him. Normally, I wouldn't have objected, but I was in a black mood, and nothing was going to change that. Of course, Dennis didn't try. He bossed me around, using as few words as possible. He'd point here. He'd point there.

Wipe that. Sweep that. Sweep that again. Hurry up.

Finally, I dropped my broom and said, "Hey, cheer the fuck up."

He dropped the hose and walked over to me and said, "Or what?"

I couldn't think of a thing, so I said, "That's for you to figure out."

He laughed it off and said, "Fair enough."

Then, he paused and said, "I hear you're outta here."

"Looks that way."

"Lucky you," he said. "Looks like I'm about to be outta here, too. Draft notice arrived last week."

"Oh, shit," I said. "Have you told anyone?"

"You," he said. "I'm trying to orchestrate my exit plan. If I stay here, I'd just end up killing myself. I might as well die for my country."

"Not exactly a positive attitude you've got going there," I said. "You sure you'll end up in Vietnam?"

"They ain't sending rich kids, and I don't plan to go to divinity school, so it's me, or the Commies will be at our doorstep," he said. "You can thank me later."

"Have you told anyone?" I asked.

"Nope. I'll send 'em all postcards from Saigon."

I shook my head in disbelief.

"What?" he asked. "You have an opinion about this?"

"No, but you can't just hop on a bus and disappear."

"Who died and made you president?" he said. "I can do whatever the hell I want, and I want to get out of here, and if I have to go to Vietnam to get out of here, so be it. I'll be fine."

"That's what they all say," I said.

"You know," he said. "I'm going to really miss these heart-to-hearts."

Dennis then crouched and, without lifting a finger or an eye, said, "You're still wondering why she didn't tell you her story sooner, aren't you? Like she was supposed to bring it up, first rattle out of the box. As if, you had the right to know. Am I right?"

"I don't know how to answer that," I said.

"That's because you're a shit-head," he said. "If she cared about me the way she apparently cares about you, I'd chop off two toes to stay out of Vietnam, and I'd grab her, and we'd drive until the tires melted, and then we'd hitchhike, and we'd find a place where she'd never, ever have to think about any of that again."

I sat there, almost in shock. So many words...

"Let me tell you something else," he said. "You've come a long way since you got here. I wouldn't have traded one Jeff for five of you when you arrived six weeks ago…"

"Seven weeks," I said.

"Shut up," he snapped. "Seven weeks ago. And Jeff's as worthless as a used rubber. But you've grown up. Before, you assumed you couldn't, so you didn't, and that's why I wouldn't have trusted you with a water hose, and that's why I didn't give you the time of day. Why would I want to waste my time talking to someone who couldn't figure out that his problem isn't there."

And he tapped my shoulder blade.

"It's here."

And he tapped my forehead.

"And it's here."

And he tapped my heart.

"So, bravo," he said. "You won me over. But know this. You never get too old to turn back into a chickenshit."

—

That night — it was a Wednesday— Debbie and I met at the same place at the same time. We were both wrung out. I told her about Uncle Carl and the milk barn. I told her about Dennis. I asked her if there was anything I could do.

"I don't think so," she said. "I've tried to forget. I've tried to pretend it never happened, but it's like a scar. There's not enough make-up to hide it.

"I knew you'd find out eventually," she continued. "I wasn't sure who from. I was so afraid if you heard it from the wrong person, that would be it. I wouldn't see you again."

I wanted to assure her that that was impossible, but I couldn't because, even though I'd come this far, it was never too late to turn back into a chickenshit. So, I told her another lie.

"I don't want to know," I said. "I don't need to know. I don't care. If you think we're good where we are, then I'm good where we are. I just want to be here. That's all I want. To be right here, with you."

Debbie closed her eyes, rubbed her face, scratched the top of her head with both hands and said, "You know what? I'm going to tell you what happened because if I don't, you're going to play it all out in your mind, and I don't trust your imagination, so I'm going tell you things I haven't even told Kathleen. The only person I've told is my mother. She's the only person who knows. Do you want to hear this? You can stop me at any time."

So, she told me everything. Her words came out in a steady, even stream, like she was reading a cake recipe to a deaf aunt over the phone during a hailstorm.

"Cream your butter. Break three eggs and scream. Add flour and baking powder and baking soda. Pour salt on the wound. Scrape sides and insides. Throw up and lay in it, face down. Bake at 350. Slice and serve warm. Chill after each use."

I had never been — nor will I ever be — as humiliated as I was listening to her recite in detail what happened. A word — crestfallen — kept bopping around in my head. I came across it in eighth grade English and liked the way it sounded.

Crest. A peak, summit, crown, apex.

Fallen. Dropped. Plunged. Plummeted.

"Adjective. Having a drooping head or hanging head. Feeling shame or humiliation."

I tried it in an essay, but it sounded trite, so I filed it away, thinking it might come in handy a few months and 250 miles down the road.

—

We scissored into each other in the dark. We didn't make out. We tried, but it seemed forced and clunky. Making out had always been fun. There was nothing fun about that evening.

Around 8:30, we walked back to the baseball park, and that's where I left her. She headed toward the concession stand to meet Kathleen, and I headed toward The Fritz, to meet Jeff, but he wasn't there, so I walked to the VFW Hall and looked for his truck, but it wasn't there either.

I wasn't in the mood to beg anyone for a ride, so I decided to walk. At first, I figured someone would come along and offer me a ride, but then, I decided I didn't want a ride. I wanted to cut straight through the fields. I'd done it once. I could do it again, if I could find a place to cross Coons Creek, which was full and pooling in spots.

I followed the creek downstream and found a bottleneck in a ravine. I hopped from the muddy bank to a large, white rock, then from the rock to the other bank. My biggest fear wasn't falling. I assumed I would, given that the rocks were caked in algae.

My biggest fear was slipping and breaking a thumb or dislocating an elbow.

Anyway, I climbed up the side of the ravine to try to get my bearings, but damned if I could figure out where I was. I walked on up a hill, through an open field, and, about five minutes later, I saw the yellow light on top of the silo, so I headed directly toward it, tromping through the stubble. I carried a stick I'd found along the creek bed, just in case I needed to whack a snake or scare off an Apache warrior out looking for scalps

Every now and then, a dog would howl, and a kitchen light would flip on, and I worried someone might take me for a thief and take a shot at me, but nothing happened except that I ripped my jeans climbing over a barbed wire fence.

The barking dogs made me think of our yappy little dachshund-chihuahua mix named Chester and how much Mom hated him. I remembered the afternoon I stepped off the school bus and saw my mom in nothing except a beige nightgown, bending over and rustling the flowerbeds along the narrow corridor between our house and our next-door neighbors, the Thompsons.

I stood in the street and waited for the other kids to head home, and I hoped they weren't seeing what I was seeing, but they were. Mom was swinging a flyswatter and cursing poor Chester.

"Get out of here," she snapped. "Get out of this yard."

I approached her cautiously because I'd been on the fly end of that swatter more than a few times. I tried to make just enough noise that she'd hear me and recognize me before she turned and took a swipe at me.

"Mom," I said. "What are you doing?"

"That damn dog that damn dog that damn dog," she said. "That damn dog peed on my bed, and I am not going to have a damn dog peeing on my bed."

I dropped my textbooks and inched closer.

"I'll take care of it," I said. "Go inside. Go sleep in my bed, and I'll take care of Chester."

That seemed to snap her out of her moment. Her eyes were blank, and her mouth was slightly oval, like she was about to start singing the national anthem, and she let out a deep breath and wobbled toward the carport door.

I heard it creak open and bang shut, so I rustled in the grass to see if I could find Chester, and that's when Steve Thompson leaned out his bedroom window and said, "Damn, Eddie. Your mother's crazy as a loon."

"Screw you," I said.

"I mean it," he said. "No wonder you're so messed up."

If I'd had something in my hands —a pair of bent nose pliers or a ball peen hammer —I'd have flung it at him.

—

I gave up looking for Chester, so I grabbed my books and walked inside, and there, sitting on the couch, was Chester. I picked him up and held him, to see if he was hurt or injured. He seemed fine.

I then went into her bedroom to inspect the sheets, and they were fine. So, I searched for Mom to see if she was OK, and I found her, sprawled across my little brother's bunk bed, smelling like an ashtray, dead to the world.

Why that memory bubbled up, I can't imagine. It just did.

—

I got back to the house around 10. Mina was up.

"Where's Jeff?" she asked, assuming I'd ridden back with him.

"I don't know," I said. "He's not here?"

"No, he's not," she said. "Who brought you home?"

"No one," I said. "I walked."

"You walked?" she said. "All that way?"

"Yeah, I cut through the fields," I said.

"You didn't," she said.

"I did. I've done it before. It's not a big deal."

"Good Lord," she said. "Go brush your teeth and come back in here. I have something to tell you."

My dad had called. He said he planned to drive to Gainesville Friday night and stay at a hotel. I was to be packed and ready to go Saturday morning.

"How early?" I asked.

"If he's staying in Gainesville by himself Friday night, I'd say no sooner than noon," Mina said.

Jeff showed up shortly after midnight, dangerously drunk. He'd left his truck at a friend's and hitched a ride with Melvin Gaddis, another dairy farmer who lived a mile or so down Schaper Road. Uncle Carl found Jeff on the couch in the front room the next morning.

Milking hungover is bad enough.

Milking drunk is the worst.

CHAPTER 23

Cookie breath

We finished filling the silo around 3:30 that afternoon, and Uncle Carl gave Jeff and me the rest of the day off, so we drove down to the big pond. I was itching like mad, and Jeff's head was about to explode. Though he'd sweated out the beer and bourbon, he wanted to cool off and wash the weeds and bugs out of his hair. I was all in for that.

Jeff showed me how to smear the gooey, black mud on my arms and face — even in my hair — and let it sit there for a minute, then wash it off.

"It pulls out the splinters," he said. I wondered why he waited until the last day to tell me this, but then, I thought, "It's Jeff."

Mystery solved.

Around 4:40, I double-timed it back up to the house, hosed off the moss and silt and dressed and waited for Debbie's call, which I expected to come around 5. I stood in the kitchen, chewing a thumbnail and guarding the phone. It didn't ring at 5, or 5:05, or 5:15, and I began to panic.

"A watched pot never boils," Mina said. "Go somewhere. Do something. Read a book. You're getting on my nerves."

I looked at her, not sure if she was being serious until she said, "Scram," so I walked into the TV room and thumbed through a Newsweek and started on another fingernail.

It was the first time I'd chewed my nails since I got there.

Around 6, the phone rang. Faye was also waiting for a call, so she grabbed it first.

"Faye, hand him the phone," Mina said. "His is more important, and you know it."

She pouted and handed me the phone.

"Hey," I said.

"Is Faye there?"

It was some guy who sounded like a dork.

"Sure," I said. "Just a second."

I turned to Faye and said, "Barney Fife."

Faye smirked and took the phone.

Mina didn't bother to turn around.

"Faye, tell Barney you'll call him back."

Faye huffed, then said to the guy on the phone, "I'll call you back in 10."

She handed me the receiver and said, "Ten."

Two minutes later, the phone rang again, and I answered it.

"Don't talk. Just listen. I'm on a pay phone. We lost a fan belt this side of Henrietta. It's taken forever to find someone to fix it, but we did. He just started, so I have no idea when we'll be back. Probably be too late to see you tonight."

I let her say everything she needed to say, and then I said, "I'm leaving tomorrow. Maybe early."

"What?"

"My dad called."

"Hold on," she said, then dropped another quarter into the slot.

"He's picking me up, so I may not get a chance to see you again before I leave. I just want to tell you these past couple of weeks have been the best of my life. And all that other stuff, I don't care, not one bit. I want you to know that. If I don't see you again, I will …"

"You'll see me tonight," she said. "I don't know what time, but I will see you tonight. I'm out of quarters, and I have to go, but you be there when I arrive."

We both hung up right as Lori walked in.

"What was that about?"

"Nothing," I told her.

Big mistake. Lori was every bit as smart as Mina.

I could've asked her or Faye or Dennis or Jeff to drive me to town, but asking for a ride to town would've required arranging a ride back from town, and I had no intention of returning to the farm until it was absolutely necessary.

Around 7, Uncle Carl announced he was going to bed, and he said to me, "I understand this is your last night with us. I figured you'd be in town already to see that pretty girlfriend of yours."

I told him my pretty girlfriend was stranded somewhere between here and Wichita Falls with her mom in a car that had lost a fan belt.

"It could have been worse," he said. "It could have been an oil leak. That's a problem. It doesn't take much to replace a fan belt. I'll see you in the morning."

Then, Mina cornered me. "What's this I hear about a fan belt?"

"They're somewhere near Henrietta. They're having car problems. They're not sure when they'll get back. It's OK. I'll see her tomorrow."

"Bullshit. Do you really expect me to believe you're going to just go upstairs and climb in bed and go to sleep?" she said. "What are you planning?"

It was the first time I'd heard her curse.

"Don't look so shocked," she said. "I only curse when I need to, and this is bullshit. I'm not talking about the fan belt. I'm talking about you. Look me in the eye and tell me what's going on."

So, I told her she was right. I had planned to sneak out around 9 and walk to town and wait for Debbie.

"Walk? Again?"

"What are my options?" I asked.

She shook her head. "Meet me in front of the house at 9. I'll drive you. Don't say a word about this to anyone. Slip out the side door and close it gently."

"Are you serious?" I asked.

"What are my options?," she replied.

I ran upstairs and tossed a few essentials together, then sauntered back downstairs and watched TV while everyone came and went. At 9 on the dot, I slipped out through the kitchen door and worked my way around the house to the driveway, where Mina sat behind the wheel of their black 1962 Chevrolet Impala station wagon. She was barely tall enough to see over the dashboard.

I delicately opened the backseat passenger's side door and climbed in. In the seat next to me was a cotton blanket, two pillows, a Tupperware jug of iced tea and a cigar box. I leaned over the seat and placed my hand on her right shoulder.

"Thank you," I said.

She patted my hand, then said, "Let's see if I can drive this thing without killing us both."

In no time, we pulled up in front of Gram's house, and I hopped out. Mina rolled down her window and said, "This is a night you will never forget. Don't make it a night you wished you could forget and don't act you don't know what I'm talking about."

"I know," I said.

"I'll pick you up at 6," she said. "Don't make me honk the horn."

"Yes, ma'am."

I grabbed the blanket, the pillows, and the cigar box, which I had opened because I couldn't help myself. It contained two stubby white candles, a box of matches and four still-warm pecan chocolate chip cookies.

"There's nothing like kissing with cookie breath," she said.

I laugh every time I think about Mina and Uncle Carl making out with cookie breath. No wonder they have so many kids.

I also thought, "If Jenny Gehring had packed this box, it'd have contained another condom that she'd have demanded returned, unopened."

The grass smooshed under my feet because of the off-and-on afternoon showers we'd had the past week. It was as humid as the Amazon, so I raised two side windows in the living room and left the kitchen door wide open. I didn't dare open the front door because it might've caught the eye of a curious Kassel cop.

I placed the candles by the front door, away from the windows and grabbed two plastic glasses from the kitchen and spread the blanket on the rug. I tossed the pillows on top of the blanket and laid back with my hands folded under my head, closed my eyes, and realized the Beatles were playing a double concert in Memphis, at that very moment.

And I wouldn't trade places for the world.

That was my last thought until I woke to find Debbie sitting next to me, her legs tucked up under her chin, her arms wrapped around her shins. After taking a shower at home, she threw on the first thing she grabbed: a white cotton T-shirt and pair of blue jean cut-off shorts. She washed her hair quickly, but she didn't comb it, so when I saw her, she looked like Medusa.

"When did you get here?" I asked.

"Maybe 20 minutes ago."

"Why didn't you wake me?"

"You looked like you needed the sleep, and I wanted to watch."

"Watch what?"

"Watch you sleep. You sing in your sleep."

"I don't."

"You do. Haven't we talked about that?" she said, then smiled, leaned over, and we bumped foreheads.

Then, we kissed. And kissed again. Then, we kissed a lot. We wore ourselves out kissing, and we fell asleep around 3:30, maybe 4. The church bells woke us at 5:30.

"That was fast," Debbie said.

"Way too fast," I answered. She picked up her wallet and rifled through it and pulled out a small color photograph of a 2 or 3-year-old girl with chipmunk cheeks and blonde hair pulled back into a short ponytail that was held in place by three inches of pink yarn.

"That's me," she said. "I was noisy and bossy and sure of everything. Wouldn't it be nice to be that age again, to be that sure of everything, to not care that you're chubby, or that you're not invited to sleepovers, or that you may never see the boy you've fallen in love with again?"

It wasn't a real question, so I didn't answer. Besides, we were both too physically and emotionally drained to contemplate what if and why not. Instead, I decided to channel Bogart.

"Well," I said. "Here's looking..."

And Debbie cut me off, "Don't say it."

"Why not?" I said.

"Save it for next time," she said.

"Next time," I said. "I promise."

We kissed one last time. It was more of a smooch, and then I marched out the back door, rounded the corner, trudged across the wet lawn, climbed into the back seat of the station wagon, threw the blanket over my head, and kept it there until we pulled into the driveway at the farm.

"We're here," Mina said to me. "Time to go."

I peeled the blanket off and peeked out and saw my dad standing on the porch, holding a Winston in one hand and a coffee cup in the other. He saw me, too. Neither of us smiled nor waved. I wiped my nose with the back of my left hand, caught Mina's eye in the rear-view mirror and blurted, "Oh, shit."

CHAPTER 24

Words of love

Saturday, August 20

My dad stubbed out his Winston on a wood railing and moved in my direction, but Uncle Carl cut him off. He pinched the sleeve of my T-shirt and pulled me over his way and said, "Go in the house and take a shower and find something to eat."

I looked at my dad for a sign of some kind — I'm not sure what — and he said, "I ain't in no hurry, but hurry up."

My dad then eyeballed Uncle Carl like he was trying to figure out if this was a throw-down or some such, then decided it wasn't worth it, one way or the other. He lit another Winston, sipped his coffee, and jangled the car keys in his pocket.

Once I'd gone inside, he turned back to Uncle Carl.

"Carl, I just want to say thank you for looking after the boy," my dad said. "He sure does seem to like you."

Uncle Carl looked at him for a moment, then said. "It helps if you like him."

It was a great line, and my dad had no trouble noticing that the guy who'd just put him in his place was wearing patched overalls that were sopping and speckled with mud and shit while he was looking almost dapper in his khakis and boots.

The disparity wasn't lost on either of them. Uncle Carl didn't care how he looked because he was comfortable in his own skin. My dad cared because he wasn't, so he jingled his car keys and smoked one cigarette after another.

"Those cancer sticks are going to get you," Uncle Carl said.

"Maybe so," my dad said. "Looks like I'll still be standing here when it happens. What the hell's taking so long?"

Uncle Carl waited a second, then said, "I'll go check on him. He's a good boy. He just needs adult supervision now and then."

"Don't we all, Carl? Don't we all?" my dad said. "If you're heading that way, tell him the train leaves in five minutes. We got places to go and things to do."

That was it for the throw-down. Uncle Carl won, mostly on sincerity. My dad pretended he didn't have a care in the world when, in fact, Mom had just kicked him out. She'd finally found proof he'd been having an affair with a woman he worked with.

Her name was Hildegard, and she was a war bride, brought to the U.S. from Germany by a New Orleans native named James Michele "Boots" Breaux. Before the war, Boots was in and out of jail regularly, mostly for bootlegging, money laundering and trafficking stolen merchandise.

Run out of Louisiana, he landed in East Texas to work for a professional wrestling promoter, who caught him stealing from him, alerted his mafia pals in Shreveport, and they chased him over toward Waskom, where he jumped out of his car and hid under a 9-ton bulldozer that had stopped in thick brush.

Boots was drunk asleep when the bulldozer cranked back up the next morning, and that was the end of that.

Not that Hildegard cared. She and my dad had been sleeping together for three years at least. Together, they had a 3-year-old son, Butch, who looked way more like my dad than I did. Mom bumped into them at a 7-11 once, and it almost made her sick to her stomach.

Uncle Carl didn't know and didn't care about any of this, so it had no effect on his relationship with my dad because Uncle Carl had no relationship with my dad. He never liked him. He couldn't understand why Mom married him.

Anyway, the house was empty. Mina had gone out to feed the chickens, and Lori and Faye were finishing up in the barn. Jeff and Dennis were dropping hay in the south pasture, so I had the bathroom to myself.

I wanted to cry, but I didn't have time, and I didn't want to have to explain the bloodshot eyes and snot to my dad, so I just stood there, feeling sorry for myself and mad at the world. Who knows how long I would have stayed there if I hadn't heard a soft tapping on the door.

"Are you OK in there?" Mina asked.

"I'm combing my hair," I said. "Be out in a minute."

"Your dad's waiting," she said. "And we're tired of him already."

I slapped my face, hard, then scooted upstairs and found a new plaid shirt, a new pair of Wrangler jeans, a new pair of white socks and a new pair of white Fruit of the Loom briefs, folded and laid on top of my suitcase.

I dressed, shoved my dirty clothes into a paper sack, grabbed the suitcase and started down, but a gust of cool breeze hit me, so I stopped and returned to the front window.

I thought about that first morning — Uncle Carl yelling for everyone to get up and get going. It seemed like seven years instead of seven weeks ago. Again, I allowed Bogey the last words.

Bogey: "It doesn't take much to see that the problems of two little people don't amount to a hill of beans in this crazy woyld."

Me: "Easy for you to say. You just spent the night with Ingrid Bergman."

—

I lugged the suitcase downstairs and bumped into Mina.

"You ready?" she asked, and I said, "Nope, but I'm going, anyway."

She folded a dishtowel and walked around the table and pulled me into her arms, yet again. She barely came up to my chin.

She didn't ask anything about what had happened that night, whether I'd done anything I'd regret. She just gave me a beefy hug and then handed me one more paper sack. It contained a ham and cheese sandwich, a bag of Fritos, a sliced-up apple, and a chocolate chip pecan brownie.

I didn't try to say anything because I knew I couldn't get the words out, so I just looked at her and held on tight, and she understood.

"It's going to all turn out fine," she said. "Cheer up."

For a second, I thought she was going to say, "Cheer the fuck up." That would have almost made it all worthwhile.

While I was taking my time wondering and hugging and being hugged, my dad pulled the car around and popped the trunk, and Jeff and Lori and Faye showed up, waiting for me so they could say their goodbyes.

Of course, they all knew where I'd been all night and, I guess, they thought they knew what I'd been doing, so there were a few winks and smirks, but everyone seemed sad to see me go. Lori and Faye were misty-eyed, and I thought Jeff might even get a little choked up, but, to his credit, he remained true to himself.

He reached for my hand and said, "Shake," and when I offered it, he jerked his hand away and faked like he was going to pop me in the nuts.

"Gotcha last," he said.

Lori and Faye then cozied up and wrapped themselves around me.

"It went so fast," Faye said. "Are you sure you wouldn't just like to stay? We have room."

"I think it's a little late for that," I said.

"It's never too late," she added. "By the way, I know I don't have to tell you this, but write her often."

"I will."

Faye walked over to my dad and said, almost defiantly, "You should be very proud of your son. He's a gentleman."

"Which one?" my dad replied, then laughed.

Mina grabbed me one last time. "Good luck on the drive. Give your mother my love. Help her. She's going to need a lot of it. If you need help, you call me. Night or day. You have the number. If you feel you're getting in over your head, you call me."

"I will."

Then, she looked toward the milk barn where Uncle Carl was standing, and she said, "Carl, would you like to say something to your nephew before he leaves?"

"As a matter of fact, I would. Step over here for a minute," he said, summoning me with the hook of his right index finger.

This time, I didn't seek permission.

"First, I want to apologize about the lawnmower," he said. "I know how much that hurt. And the cement truck, too. If it had hit you, I'd have had a lot of explaining to do."

I laughed.

He then handed me an envelope and told me to open it. It contained 11 $10 bills.

"I tossed in the extra 10 to cover pain and suffering."

"Where do I sign?" I said.

He held out his hand and said, "Make your mark right here. I didn't prepare a speech, but I want you to know that you did good. Next summer, I expect you to be driving that tractor."

It was great to be reminded there would be a "next summer."

He shook my hand and then he walked toward the house and up to my dad and said, "By the way, Sketch, I already damn near got him killed, so try not to succeed where I failed."

He then disappeared into the house.

"Well," my dad said. "Before I get all emotional, I guess we'd better hit the road."

But then I looked toward the milk barn and saw Dennis looking out a window.

"Just one second," I said. "I need to go, one more time."

"Well, go do it," my dad said. "There are trees everywhere."

"I'll use the one in the milk barn," I told him. "Be right back."

I double-timed it over and walked in.

"Hell, I was afraid I was going to have to come out there and drag you in," he said. "I have something for you."

He handed me another paper bag, and it contained two cans of Schlitz, one can of Miller High Life and a bag of potato chips.

"This ought to make the drive more bearable," he said.

Then he handed me an empty milk bottle with a paper lid. "You'll need this, too."

I put the bottle in the bag and tucked it under my arm like it was a football and said, "I gotta go."

And Dennis said, "Two things: One, your old man is an asshole, and everybody knows it, so you might as well admit it too and stop feeling guilty for thinking it.

"Two, if I end up in Vietnam, and if I don't get my ass shot to pieces, and if I make it back here, then you and I will sit down and have a long talk about a lot of things."

"How about this," I replied. "Don't get your ass shot to pieces."

"Novel idea," he said. "I'll consider it."

I asked him to write so I'd know he was alive.

"I'll send you a postcard."

"Good enough," I said.

"Get out of here," he said.

I made a move toward embracing him somehow, but I knew that wasn't going to happen. He was not the embraceable type. He might've been long ago, but now, he was as bottled up as the beer he'd just handed me.

"We're done," he said. "See you later."

So, I walked out first, and he walked out right behind me. I jumped in the front seat of the car, and he slowed for just a second, licked a finger and drew a long line down the side of the hood. Then, he headed back to the milk barn, making a point of slamming the screen door behind him.

PART SIX | CHAPTER 25
The long drive

Saturday, August 20

My dad lit another cigarette and blew his nose and told me to get comfortable. "It's a long drive, and I don't plan to stop any time soon, and I don't want to hear any bitchin' about it."

"I'm good," I told him, then felt the car lurch as he pulled the transmission into drive and punched the accelerator to whip up a cloud of white dust through which we could ceremoniously exit.

Right out of the driveway, we had a choice. Take a left onto the county road, then take a right toward town. Or, take a right and drive through the country and then take another right onto the state highway north of town.

My dad hesitated. "If it weren't so damn early, I might crack open one of them beers you got in that bag," he said. "Might help with my headache."

"Be my guest," I said.

"Not yet," he said. "I'll wait 'till lunch."

He looked right, then left, then asked, "You care?"

"Let's go through town," I said.

"Any particular reason?" he asked.

"You'll have to cross a low-water creek this direction," I said, pointing right. "You want to get your car all muddy?"

"Nope," he said. "I do not."

I pointed to the left, and he headed that way.

"Check the glove compartment," my dad said. "There's a pair of sunglasses in there."

I found and put them on and rolled the window down and hoped the hot air would dry my puffy eyes.

The radio was set to a station out of Sherman, a country station, of course. David Houston was singing "Almost Persuaded," a big hit on the Nashville scene. It was one of those drinking and cheating songs where everyone is dying, crying, or going somewhere.

"You want to change it, go ahead," my dad said.

"No," I replied. "I like this song."

"Well, whenever," he said. "You're in charge of the radio," and I thought, "What's gotten into him? The sunglasses. Now the radio."

Though it was only a mile or so to town, Dad floor-boarded it, and we were flying, and yet, I somehow noticed how scabbed the fields looked, now that the grasses had been cut to make the silage. I noticed the ridges on both sides of the road, and how old harvesters and combines had been left to rust in the fields. I noticed that half the shutters on the Fedderman's house were hanging by a single nail.

How'd I miss all that before?

Right before we crossed Coons Creek, I saw three brown hawks perched atop three telephone poles, which is rare because hawks are territorial. They mate for life and fight trespassers to the death.

Once we crossed the bridge, I noticed the VFW Hall, and it struck me how small it was. Not much larger than the baseball field's concession stand. Several cars were still parked outside, which meant someone was too drunk to drive and had hitched a ride or passed out in the bathroom or in a back seat.

I wondered what it would be like to go in there and hang out with all these old men who needed each other's company. I realized how much in common they had with my dad, who looked down on dairy farmers even though he sold milk. I wondered if my dad saw the irony in that. I doubted that my dad knew what irony was.

I assumed there was a VFW Hall in Marshall, though I'd never seen it. I wondered if my dad ever went in there, and if he did, who'd he saddle up next to? Was it the guys who saw action in North Africa or France or on Guadalcanal or Inchon? Or did he hang out with guys like himself — guys who served but never fought?

For whatever reason, I figured the guys at the Kassel VFW would've embraced my dad, and that was why I suspected they'd never embrace me. I was sure the jukebox at the VFW Hall didn't play the Hollies or the Supremes. It played a lot of David Houston.

Oh, well. It was quiet, and the road was ours as we sped past the Ford dealership and Handy Dan's Package Store and the Tex-Sun Motor Courts where the hookers banged the long-haul truck drivers.

And then, I saw The Fritz coming up on the left, and it looked like it was hopping. It usually drew a decent breakfast crowd, especially on Saturdays in the late summer and early fall. Old guys had their designated tables and chairs, and they talked high school football or farm subsidies or the worthless government or whatever it was that was going on in Southeast Asia that required their sons to fly halfway around the globe just to tromp around a rice paddy.

In addition to the normal hubbub, I saw something else. Someone was standing in the bed of a pickup, apparently waving a sign, like one of those "Going-out-of-business" signs.

My dad saw it, too, and slowed to look, and then I realized who it was. It was Debbie Gehring. She held a long piece of butcher paper that she'd glued to several sheets of poster board, and she'd written in thin, black letters, each at least 24 inches high.

HERE'S LOOKING AT YOU

Lori had called her and told her we were headed that way.

Though we'd slowed down, we were still going 25 or 30 miles an hour, so it couldn't have taken us more than 15 or 20 seconds from the time I saw her to the moment we crested a hill leaving town, but in those 15 or 20 seconds, I stared at that sign for what seemed to be 15 or 20 minutes.

I couldn't believe it. How in the world did she come up with that? I read the sign, then I saw her face, and I read her eyes, and I hoped she was reading mine, and I wish now that I could say that we enjoyed a final perfect moment, but I can't because I was wearing those damn sunglasses.

I didn't realize I had them on until we were half a mile over the hill, and I actually bit my hand to keep myself from screaming my favorite four-letter word about 40 times. It begins with an "F."

I could see her eyes, but she couldn't see mine, and our eyes said everything we didn't have the time or the words to say. Her eyes said, "I have given myself to you because I trust you, and I believe you when you told me you loved me, and I have no regrets. I know I'll write you more often than you write me, and I understand and accept that. You've changed, and in changing, you've changed me."

At that point, whatever was left from my moment in the shower started bubbling, but I choked it all back. Eventually, I'd let it splatter everywhere, but until then, I swallowed hard. I'd save it for Mom because she'd understand. She'd been choking back crap like this forever, with the help of Salems and Johnny Mathis.

For now, I just needed some time alone, but my dad didn't know that. All he knew was that something had happened between me and a girl, and he thought we could kill some time talking. He was trying to be friendly, but his timing could not have been worse.

"Tell me about it," Dad said.

About what?

"About being up here all summer. How was it?"

It was OK.

"What does that mean? What was so OK about it?"

I don't know.

"Hell, you must know," he said. "You just said it was OK."

It was just that. It was OK. Some of it was great.

"Nothing stands out?"

I always looked forward to lunch.

"Where were you last night?"

Stayed with a friend.

"Is that so? All night?" he said. "What was it, a sleepover? You boys had a sleepover? Did you take your jammies?"

Yep. It was a sleepover.

"You haven't joined the other team, have you?"

I didn't bother to answer.

"So, if was a sleepover, how come I didn't see no sleeping bag."

I turned away from him and said, "Someone lent me one. He had two. Shit, I don't know."

Dad hit the brakes, and I almost slammed into the dashboard.

"What'd you just say?"

I told him the house provided both sleeping bags.

"Watch your mouth, boy. I don't know when you learned to cuss like that, but I'm not going to put up with it."

"I learned how to cuss like that from you."

Dad again hit the brakes.

"Goddamn it. I'm trying to have a civil conversation."

But it's OK for you to curse, but I can't?

"I pay the damn bills," he said. "And I'm the adult."

I almost laughed at that.

"Look, Dad. I didn't get a lot of sleep last night," I said. "I'm really not in the mood to chat. Can this wait?"

"That sounds like a personal problem to me," he said. "Tell me about this girl. What's her name?"

Her name is Debbie Gehring.

"You're shitting me. Another Debbie? What are you up to now? Three? What is she? Debbie Number Three?"

If you say so.

I thought he might shut up for a while, but he kept going. He asked how I met her, and when I told him I didn't want to talk about her, he asked about the cement truck incident.

Not a big deal.

"Well, that's not what Carl told me. He said the chute missed you by about an inch."

I don't know.

"Carl said he almost got you killed."

He paused, then added, "He's a piece of work, isn't he? I don't know how he does it."

Does what?

"I don't know how he gets out of bed every morning. Well, I know how. I can't imagine why. He gets up every morning. To milk. Then, he busts his ass all day so he can get up the next day to milk and bust his ass all day again so he can go to church and fiddle with his rosary. He's something."

"He's the best man I've ever met," I said.

"That so?" my dad said. "The best man you've ever met?"

"He's up there," I said. "I haven't met John Lennon."

"That's not where I'd start," he said.

I asked him, again, if he could please change the subject.

"Sure," he said. "Hell, I'm just killing time, and we got a lot of it. By the way, I like Carl. He has no use for me, but that's understandable. Half the time, I got no use for me, either."

I thought that was a curious comment, coming from him.

He turned the radio up, and then, turned the radio down, and then he turned to me and said, "I'm not as stupid as I look. I know what you're saying. You don't have to write words on a big sheet of butcher paper and wave it from the bed of a pickup truck. I know what you think of me, and I don't blame you. I ain't been a much of a father, and I'm surprised it's taken you this long to say it to my face."

"I wasn't talking about you," I said. "I was just saying…"

"No. No. Don't walk it back," he said. "It might've been badly timed, given that we're stuck here together for the next five hours, but you said it because you meant it, so don't try to weasel out of it. I understand. A boy ought to look up to his father, respect him, and I've given you little or no reason to do that."

I sat there in shock, and he turned the volume back up. It was Jack Green singing, "There Goes My Everything," and I thought, "Enough with the goddamn irony, already."

CHAPTER 26

Dark shadows

Even though I was right, I immediately regretted saying what I'd said. I didn't respect him. I didn't like him, even though I guess I loved him because he was my father. Humans are wired to love their parents, and they do until the wires get snarled.

That's pretty much where we were. He was the cause of all the chaos and misery in our family. Sure, Mom could be impossible, but she was working four jobs a day on 45 minutes of sleep, and he was about as helpful as a didgeridoo in a violin quartet.

If he hadn't been out to all hours of the night, maybe the family wouldn't have been such a mess. Of course, if the family hadn't been such a mess, I wouldn't have spent seven weeks in Kassel, and I wouldn't have met Debbie Gehring.

Somehow, that thought cheered me up, and I even decided to cut my dad some slack. I thought, "If my dad had been Mr. Bishop, I'd have spent the summer at rich-kid or Jesus camp, and I probably would've done something stupid and gotten kicked out, so gosh, thanks, Dad, for being a rotten husband and father," and I started laughing.

"What's so funny?" he asked.

"Nothing," I said. "I was just thinking."

Apparently, he wasn't interested in whatever it was I'd been thinking, so I rested my head against the window and dozed off.

I dreamed about running up and down the red dirt paths leading into the woods back home. In my dreams, I was running up one side and down the other. Everyone else rode their bikes, but I ran. Up and down, and I never ran out of breath. It was magnificent.

And then, the car hit a hole the size of a wash tub, and my

head bounced off the window.

"Son of a bitch," I said.

"Sorry about that," my dad said. "You talk in your sleep."

"I've been told I sing," I said.

"That's a story I'd like to hear," he said. "You hungry?"

"I am," I said. "I have something in a bag, somewhere."

"Forget about it," my dad said. "Let's grab a burger."

"That works."

The drive from Kassel to Marshall is a straight shot, west to east, but when we reached Dallas, we turned southeast toward Houston. I didn't say anything. I thought he might be taking a shortcut. An hour later, we were still headed east by southeast.

"We going to Houston?" I asked?

'No," he said. "We're going to Rogansboro."

"Why?"

"I'll tell you later," he said. "Until then, look around. This is beautiful country. Ugly ass people, but beautiful country."

He was right. Endless rolling hills and thick stands of native pines, but the roads were full of potholes, and the ratty little towns were full of desperate, down-and-out people trying to scrape out a living by selling second-hand crap and scrap and menial services to their just-as-desperate, bottom-feeding neighbors.

Here's some of the crap they tried to sell to people like us: local honey, haircuts, birdhouses, barbecue pits, barbecue sandwiches, Gulf shrimp, firewood, watermelons, wigs, lawnmowers, trailers, tractor tires, peaches, porch swings, puppies, parakeets, used refrigerators, confederate flags, and Elvis on black velvet.

One little town looked the same as the next unless a pocket of oil or gas had been struck nearby, in which case the local high school had a fancy gym, a fancy football stadium, and/or a new auditorium named after an ex-coach, or a popular superintendent, or former student who got killed in a war.

We mostly saw the schools for the white kids. They may not have been brand new, but they were well maintained. The schools for the Black kids tended to be hidden out in the sticks. A lot of times, if two mostly white communities consolidated, they'd build a new school between them and buy new books and microscopes and all that and leave the leftovers for the Black kids.

No matter how rich a town or county was, it never seemed to have enough money to spend on the Black schools, so their broken windows and rusty pipes had to do for now — just like their textbooks, which might or might not mention Hiroshima.

The farther east and south we drove, the worse the poverty and the roads got. There were highway shutdowns for bridge repairs, jack-knifed 18-wheelers, creaky farm vehicles, and worst of all, old folks poking along on their way home from church or the donut shop or lunch at the all-you-can-eat catfish buffet.

Dad would honk and scream at 'em and wave his left arm like he was conducting a performance of "The Stars & Stripes Forever."

"The light ain't getting any greener," he'd scream if some 85-year-old widow didn't zip through fast enough to suit him. I could tell he was about to melt-down.

I would have changed the radio station, but we were driving through the middle of nowhere, so the DJs were local cranks.

Every now and then, we might pick up a station that played a song I recognized, like the Mamas and the Papas, but the signal would flicker and disappear as soon as we drove under a canopy of oaks or through a canal of pines.

"The radio giveth, and the radio taketh away," my dad said, and I said, "He taketh more than giveth.".

"Kind of reminds me of Mom," I said.

"How's that?" he asked.

"The glass is always half empty."

And my dad said, "Your mom's glass is always half empty of something she wanted until she got it, and then she didn't."

I wanted to defend her, but he was right. I'd seen her bully him into buying something and then, the next day, bitch at him for buying something she never wanted and we couldn't afford.

So, we shared a laugh at her expense.

Just north of Fairfield, my dad asked me if I'd like to drive.

"You trust me?" I asked.

"You want to drive or not?" he said. "Besides, how are you going to get them pretty girls to the drive-in theater if you don't know how to drive? This looks like as good a place to learn as any."

"Well, pull over," I said.

"Tell you what. Let's stop and get some gas, and you can buy yourself an ice cream cone with one of them 10-dollar bills in your wallet, and then I'll let you drive for an hour or so."

"Deal," I said.

So, we stopped at a gas station whose owner pointed us toward a burger stand with a drive-thru window, and we ordered two cheeseburgers and two fries and one Coke and one root beer and one vanilla ice cream cone, and after gulping it all down, my dad switched places with me, and suddenly, I was driving, and he was driving me nuts.

- **Keep both hands on the wheel.**
- **Let the wheel slide through your fingers.**
- **Stay off the brake.**
- **Keep a two-car distance.**
- **Look two cars ahead of you.**
- **Check your rearview and side mirrors.**
- **Relax and enjoy the ride.**

Then, he asked me if I was sure about this, and I told him I was, and he said, "I'm going to close my eyes for a moment. Keep it moving in one direction and watch your speed. This thing will take off if you let it."

"I can do this," I told him, and he must have believed me because he popped his seat back, and a minute later, he was out.

I wasn't sure which was worse — him awake or asleep.

There I was, driving a 1961 Dodge Polara — a ton and half of steel — cruising at 65 miles per hour down a state highway while searching for a decent radio station that carried a song written in the past two years by someone who's first name wasn't Lefty or Sonny or Patsy or Buck or Red.

Meanwhile, my dad slept on. If he'd been awake, he'd have pointed out 200 things I was doing wrong. So, I figured he must have enjoyed as long a night as I had. I suspect he also did some of the same things I did, except I got mine for free.

Anyway, I came across a country station out of College Station that wasn't too bad, but I turned the sound down low enough that while he might be able to hear it, it wouldn't bug him.

I tried to focus on the road, but my mind bounced around. Again, I wondered what Debbie Gehring was doing at that moment.

Was she crying? Taking a nap? Feeling as empty as I did?

Was she having second thoughts? Regrets?

Was she re-living that first day at the pool, or the first night at the ballpark, or the first night in Gram's living room?

Was she thinking about walking the cemetery, and sitting on the concrete picnic tables, or was she thinking about kissing my ear, or rubbing my neck, or listening to me sing in my sleep?

I wondered if she'd already moved on. Was I really just a summer fling? You know. Out of sight. Out of mind. Then, I wondered why the car in front of me had slammed on its brakes and whether I should too, and then I slammed on my brakes and yelled, "You fucking asshole."

My dad jolted awake, but before he could say anything, I blurted, "Not my fault. He just slammed on his brakes."

"What'd I say about distance?"

"It happened so fast," I said.

"Well, yeah. That's how it happens. You gotta keep the distance. Two cars. Now, try not to get us killed."

He shut his eyes and mumbled "give me 15 minutes" and then he dozed off. About an hour and a half later, he woke up.

"Where are we?" he asked.

"Almost to Lufkin," I said.

"Lufkin?" he said. "You've been driving for two hours? Damn, boy."

He rubbed his eyes and said, "Pull over up there. I gotta pee."

He'd spotted a Dairy Queen, and I whipped in, and we both ordered a chocolate-dipped ice cream cone and then another one, and we peed and stretched, and it was almost like the two of us were good buddies on a road trip.

The nap did him good, and when we climbed back into the car, he was humming "Kaw Liga," which I took as a good sign because my dad whistled when he was down and hummed when he was up. Marcel Marceau had a better poker face.

Anyway, he took the wheel, and an hour or so later, we were picking up decent radio stations out of Beaumont and Port Arthur, so my dad twisted the dial, and I'll be damned if the first song that popped up wasn't "Wouldn't It Be Nice," but it didn't hit me as hard as I thought it would.

I mean, I thought about her, but I didn't choke up. I thought about how she hiccupped when she cried, and how she liked to rub my left wrist and trace her right index finger back and forth across the full length of my palm. I thought, "Wouldn't it be nice to be doing that right now?"

For just a short while there, the long drive wasn't all that bad, but then, Dad pulled out the pint and took a swig, and it started going downhill from there. As the shadows of the great East Texas piney woods fell upon us, my dad grew more and more agitated.

The humming stopped, and the bitching started, and then the yelling, though not at me. He yelled at other drivers and anyone or anything he thought was impeding his efforts to get from here to there.

When he rolled up at a light behind a young couple out for a leisurely drive, or some cute young parents with a carload of kids, he'd pound on the dashboard and honk if they didn't stomp their accelerator the second a light changed.

I knew it was just a matter of time before he began accusing me of impeding something — like a song that didn't bother him an hour earlier suddenly chewed holes in the roof of his mouth.

"Change the goddamn station," he carped. "Put on some fucking music."

Everything became goddamn this, and fucking that, and he was fidgeting and craning his neck and rubbing his legs, trying to get comfortable.

"Dig around in that glove compartment," he said. "There's a church key in there. Open one of them beers for me."

I knew it was a bad idea, but I decided that wasn't for me to say, so opened him a lukewarm Schlitz, and he drained it.

"How 'bout the other'n?" he said, so I popped the top again and handed it to him.

"That last one's for you, if you want it."

I told him I didn't.

"Suit yourself," he said. "Hand it here."

Then, he told me to find the bottle in the paper bag under my seat, so I did. It was a pint of Jim Beam.

"Hand it here," he said, wiggling his fingers.

He broke the pint's seal with his teeth, then poured about a quarter of the bottle into what was left of a paper cup of watered-down Coca-Cola, and then he offered a toast, "To heart attacks and hospitals and early graves and worm-eaten pine trees."

He raised the cup to his lips and sipped slowly and allowed the whiskey to linger in his mouth. Then, he started talking.

"I remember the first time my old man caught me drinking. I guess I was about 13. He cornered me and told me drinking was a sin. It was like he'd caught me screwing the neighbor's mule or something, so he took his belt off and went after me, but I dodged him, and he swung and lost his balance and fell on his ass, and that embarrassed him, so he quit trying to whip me and took up cussing me nonstop instead."

He raised an eyebrow as a way of saying either, "And you think I'm a bad father" or "I guess you see where I get it."

I sat up straight and looked ahead and tried to be as invisible as possible.

"He and I never did see things eye-to-eye, and that was even before all that," he said.

I didn't know what "all that" meant, so I said, "I don't know this story."

"Well, it's high time you heard it," he said, then took a sip. "My mother and my father blamed me. Both of them. It was the only thing they ever agreed on. That I was to blame."

I let him believe I knew what he was talking about.

"If I was guilty of anything, it was allowing my brother to step foot in the boat in the first place," he said. "I only did that because my old man forced me to let him tag along while I checked some trot lines, even though the river was up and running to beat the devil."

He took another sip.

"That river's dangerous enough when it's dead still, but when it's running, the water swirls. It's cold and black. And the under current and the tree roots under there, and wire that's been washed downstream. Shit. I knew if he fell in that river, he'd go down and never come up. And I told my old man that."

Another sip.

"You know what he said? He said, 'You ain't leaving him here.' I could've left him on the shore, but who knows what he'd have done, so I didn't have a choice. I got him in the boat and told to sit down and don't stand up unless he sees a 20-foot water moccasin carrying a double-barrel shotgun coming right at us. Well, we got hung up on some limbs. I was trying to untangle us, and what does he do? He stands up. I told him to sit his ass down. Right then, we floated into a log, and he spilled right over the side, just like I said he would."

Another sip.

"He went straight under. I jumped in and tried to find him, but I couldn't. I was getting caught in the current, too. Then, there he was. I grabbed ahold of him, and we floated for a minute or two, and he fought me the whole time. I told him to relax and just go with it because there was a sandbar just ahead, but something brushed against him, I guess. He panicked and started flailing, and I couldn't keep a grip on him, so he went under again."

Another sip.

"He had no business being out there. No business at all, and I told them that."

My dad turned and looked at me, and his eyes were so bloodshot they looked like calf liver. Then, he lowered his voice and said, very softly, "I told them that, but I didn't need to. They knew it. Hell, I should've just driven him home. Those trot lines weren't going anywhere, and so what if they did?"

Another sip.

He stared straight ahead.

"Take him with you. You know what my old man told me? He said, 'Get him out of my hair.' Those are his exact words. So, I did, and sure enough."

Another sip.

He tilted his head back slightly and asked, "How old are you?"

I told him I was 15.

"That's what I thought," he said. "Sixteen in November."

I hesitated before answering.

"That's right," I said.

"Almost exactly my age when it happened," he said. "Now, ain't that a coincidence?"

—

We pulled into the hospital parking lot around 5 p.m.

I was a wreck. I hadn't slept in almost three days. My dad was drunk and belligerent and looking for someone to head-butt, so I agreed with everything he said, did or didn't do.

"I don't know why in the hell we drove all this way," he slurred. "That old man don't give a shit if I show up or not. Well, partner, you and me are going to walk in and piss on the bed, and then we're going to walk right back out, and it shouldn't take longer than five minutes. Then, I'm going to find me a bottle of slightly better sipping whiskey than what you've been serving here, bartender, and if you want some, you can damn sure have it. That sound good to you?"

"Sure," I said.

—

We entered through the emergency room and found a pretty young nurse who agreed to walk us to my grandfather's room because, as she explained, "It's easy to get lost."

I'm sure she was thinking, "Especially if you're drunk."

My grandfather was asleep when we slipped into his room. He appeared frail and pale and doped-up. He woke a couple of times and looked right past us. Around 6:30, he woke again and saw someone standing in the doorway and asked, "Is that you, Cecil?"

"It is," my dad said. "You're alive, it would seem."

"And you're drunk," Grandpa said.

"Well, I couldn't let the boy drink by himself," my dad said.

Grandpa snarled something and then ordered the other four or five people in the room to clear out.

I stood there for a second too long, and Grandpa said, "That means you too, Wayne."

"Classic," I said, then followed everyone to the visitor's room, where we watched "The Red Skelton Hour."

A half hour later, Dad found me on the floor in front of the TV. "Get up. Let's go."

I popped to my feet and followed him to the car.

"You need to pee, there's a tree over there," he said. I nodded, then flopped in the front seat and pulled a dirty shirt over my head. The tires squealed, and we took off toward the county line where the liquor stores were lined up like rows of corn. Dad pulled into one called "Sad Hank's Liquor & Live Bait" and came out with a big bottle of Wild Turkey 101 and a Dr Pepper for me.

Then, we headed toward my grandparents' place way out in the woods. It was packed with kinfolk who seemed to be in an oddly festive mood given the circumstances. Mom wasn't there, but I didn't expect that she would be.

There was a lot of commotion when we stumbled in. So good to see you. How've you been? Where 'yer brothers? I got passed around a couple of times, then wiggled free and joined a couple of cousins in a bedroom right off the kitchen.

Dad tossed me a pillow and a light blanket, and I wrapped

up and fell asleep, despite all the ruckus of slamming dominoes and whiskey and retelling stories that'd been told countless times about working on the railroad tracks, and getting drunk and falling asleep in a corn bin and waking up eyeball-to-eyeball with a hog or a rat or a rat snake.

I slept through it but the hounds didn't, so they barked and howled. Didn't bother me a bit. I would have slept to noon if it hadn't been for a sliver of sunlight that hit me right in the face around 9, so I got up and threw my clothes on and started looking.

The house was dead silent. The first breakfast had already been served, so I scavenged and found a biscuit and some butter and some Karo dark syrup along with a thick slice of bacon and a recent copy of the "Rogansboro County Register."

I kept expecting someone else to show up, but no one did, so I kept nosing around, peeking in cabinets and closets. I found a cubbyhole where I spotted my grandfather's squirrel bag. He'd probably had it since he was 6, and I figured his hunting days were pretty much over, so I snatched it and hid it in a bath towel and shoved it in my suitcase.

I knew I'd never use it, but, damn, I wanted it.

A little before 10, my dad's Polara roared up the dirt road and screeched to a stop. I heard the car door slam, and then the front screen door slam, and then I heard my dad clomping around the house, looking for my grandmother.

He found her on the back-porch, shelling purple hull peas. She looked up and asked, "Good Lord, Cecil. What happened this time?"

"Same old shit," my dad said. "Good luck with him. Hope it all works out. Call me when he's dead. I'll come to the funeral, but I'll be damned if I'll carry his coffin."

He was serious.

My grandmother dropped the colander of peas. "Don't leave, Cecil. We don't know what's going to happen. He could go at any moment."

There was a pause, then my dad said, "Stay in touch."

Then, I heard him tromping around some more, so I threw my things back into my suitcase and plopped myself on the couch and was pretending to be reading a "TV Guide" when he found me.

"Let's hit it," he said.

—

By then, others were descending on the house, and they all wanted to know what the big hurry was, although I suspect they knew because nobody tried very hard to talk him out of leaving.

I hopped in the front seat and buried my head in a book I'd found on a shelf behind a bedroom door, so I doubted anyone would miss it. It was written by a guy named Cornelius Ryan, and some of it dealt with the fall of Berlin. I was particularly interested to see if Mr. Ryan agreed with the Catholic Digest.

This is neither here nor there, but I didn't hug or kiss anyone on the way out, and no one tried to hug or kiss me. I got patted on the head and shoulder, but that was it. Compared to leaving Uncle Carl and Mina's, it was like I was checking out of a motel in a strange town where people wake up hung-over and pissed off that the TV didn't work and the water never got hot.

—

And then, we were back on the road. It was Sunday morning, so there was no reason to turn on the radio. It would have been nothing but a gaggle of screaming preachers promising me that God would cure my gout if I'd send 10 dollars to his post office box in Tulsa.

So, we sat in silence and watched the trees whiz by. Around noon, my dad tried the radio again and found a country station out of Carthage that played Marty Robbins and Glen Campbell and Merle Haggard, so we listened to that.

Every now and then, I'd also hear him flipping open the top of his fancy Zippo cigarette lighter, then popping it shut. Clink. Pop. Clink. Pop. Clink. Pop. Over and over.

He also talked to himself, and I tried to follow what he was saying but couldn't put it together. I imagined him surrounded by forest demons who were whispering in his ears, stroking his neck, telling him he'd been done wrong by everyone he ever knew, and none of it was his fault.

I didn't look at him because I didn't want the demons to notice me. In short, I asked for nothing. He offered nothing. Somehow, that added up to something. I read about the fall of Berlin, and he found a radio station that played the honky-tonk music he wanted to hear, and we got along fine.

Somewhere between Diboll and Jacksonville, I fell asleep and didn't wake up until we were driving into Tatum, which meant we were close to home.

"You need to go?" my dad asked.

"I can make it," I said.

"Want an ice cream cone or anything?" he asked.

"No, sir," I said. "I'm good."

It was like he was trying to drag it out, and I felt sorry for him. He was about 15 minutes away from being one lonely son of a bitch. He was going to dump me, and he had no idea if or when he'd see his oldest son again.

He was pretty sure he'd never see his father alive again, and he was right. His father — my grandfather — died the next morning, and I didn't find out about it for two weeks. Mom knew but didn't say a word.

My dad went to the funeral alone. One of my cousins later told me he bawled like a baby.

Dad pulled into our driveway and let the car coast to a stop. "Your mother's waiting."

The way he said it — very flat and cold — lifted the veil, and I realized this was it. He and Mom were done, which meant he and I were done. He sat in his Polara, listening to the 8-cylinder engine hum and drumming his fingers on the steering wheel.

He didn't even bother to pat me on the shoulder. He just sat and drummed his fingers on the wheel and waited for me to get out.

I walked toward the front door and then stopped and turned around and walked back toward his side of the car and did the whole little "roll the window down" gesture with my right finger, and he did, and I said, "See ya'."

He lifted his right index finger off the steering wheel, which meant, "same here," and then he popped it into reverse, lurched backwards, jerked it into drive and split for good.

As soon as Mom heard the tires squealing, she opened the front door and stretched out her arms. I dropped my suitcase, ran, and collapsed into them.

I only saw my dad once or twice after that. He died in 1984 of throat cancer. At the visitation, Hildegarde pulled me aside. She said she had something she thought I might want to hear.

This is what she told me.

> Your father, he said he did not have the courage to tell anyone else before the truth. He said he was telling me because I had told him the truth about what happened to me at end of the war in Berlin when I was still just a girl. It's not a good story. I am not proud of it, but I had to tell him because if I don't, then I go crazy.
>
> I told to him that I loved Hitler. I thought Hitler was sent by God to save civilization from the Jews and the Communists. What did I know of Jews and Communists? Nothing. I was young and stupid. I was told over and over, "To serve Hitler is to serve Germany. To serve Germany is to serve God," and I believed it. I had no reason to doubt it. I was 16 years old when the Russians arrived, and, like all the women and girls trapped there, I was attacked many times. More than you can believe.
>
> To save myself, my sanity, I became the property of a Russian officer, a man from Moscow. He was not a big man, but he was violent, and he would beat me if I gave him a reason to, so I had to choose, but there was really no choice, so for maybe nine months, I was this Russian officer's — for lack of a better word — whore. I did whatever he asked without question or hesitation. He did not even have to ask. I knew what he wanted before he knew, and so I did it, and I pretended I enjoyed it, and sometimes, I did.
>
> Anyway, about this, I can only say that I did what I had to do to survive, and that is what matters.
>
> My country is no more, and it will never come back, but I

am here, and now, I am living a good life as a good wife with a good boy. And I have no secrets and no shame.

So, I say to your father, "Something you are not telling me is killing you. Whatever it takes, you must tell me your secret. You must tell me or tell someone because it is eating you to death."

I can see that he is not dying of the cancer. He is dying of the guilt. I can tell, so, he tells me about his brother and the boat and the river, about which I know you are familiar. But this part, I am certain, you do not know.

He told me the brother sank in the river. He tried to find him, but he could not. The water was black and cold. Then, the brother grabs his foot and pulls, but he is caught in the roots and the current, and he is sinking. Your father fought to pull him to the surface. The surface of the water. But he could not. The current. The roots. So, your father kicked his brother's hand away. Like me, he did what he had to do to survive.

That was his secret. That is what killed him. Not the cancer.

He kicked his brother's hand and fought to the surface. His brother sank, and his body washed away. Your father told me he doesn't know if he could have saved his brother, but he thinks he should have died trying.

That was the secret your father carried with him for all those years, and secrets are like ulcers. If you have one, and it's a bad one, no one else will see it. All anyone will see is your face, and it will look like you are trying to swallow acid. I am sorry to tell you this. I am also sorry for your loss. And mine, and my son's. Just so you know, he tried to be a good father to my son.

—

As if that was supposed to make me feel better.

By the way, for a Kraut, I couldn't believe how good her English was. 🕯️

CHAPTER 27
Broken hearts

Sunday, August 21

Mom and I had a ton of catching up to do. I told her about milking, the cement truck, filling the silo, picking up rocks, beaning jackrabbits, draft notices, and Debbie Gehring. I told her how we broke into Gram's house, and how eerie and fun that was. I didn't tell her how much fun.

I didn't tell her about Father Gus and Dominique or how I'd written those lewd lyrics about Father Louis.

I didn't tell her about Uncle Carl's admission — about why he was afraid to show any more affection for Lori or Faye than he was for Bets, although I later figured out that she probably already knew that.

I told her about the long trip to Grandpa's and how I drove for two hours while he slept it off.

I told her about how he seemed to get madder the closer we got to Rogansboro, and I told her about the trip to the hospital and sleeping on the floor and the long ride home.

I told her everything he told me about the day his brother drowned. I told her he almost started crying, which was awkward because I thought I'd be the one crying all the way home, not him. I told her I wanted to feel sorry for him, but I couldn't, and I felt guilty about it.

I asked her "why?"

Why'd she marry him? Why'd he become a father when he had no desire to be one?

"He didn't become a father. In fact, he never grew up. He didn't know how. There were days when he tried, and I'll give him credit for that. It just wasn't in him."

Mom said she didn't recognize how damaged he was until it was too late.

She said she couldn't imagine how petty and mean his mother could be, and how miserable his father was.

"If love were dust, they had the cleanest house in Texas," Mom said. "Cecil never heard a kind word from his mother, and after Eddie drowned, he never heard one from his father. I'm not making excuses for him. He made his own bed, but they broke his heart a thousand times, and he tried to dull the pain with whiskey and one-night stands."

It was one of the few times I heard Mom call my dad by his Christian name.

She told me he'd wanted to play high school football, but his father made him quit school to work on the farm because his older brothers were off to the war, and there was no one else except Eddie, and Eddie didn't know a rake from a rainbow. So, my dad dropped out of school to plow and plant corn and slop hogs when he should have been playing football and having fun and maybe even learning how to read and write.

"Then, Eddie drowned, and they blamed him," she said. "Well, your father put up with as much as he could, and when he couldn't put up with any more, he hit the road. He joined the Coast Guard and then got drafted into the Army and was about to ship off when they dropped the bomb, so the Army handed him an envelope with some money and some ribbons and thanked him for his service. He ended up taking a job in Fort Worth, and that's where we met."

I told her I'd seen photographs of him in his Army uniform and that he looked snappy.

"He was," she said. "Snappy and happy. It might've been the only time in his life he was genuinely happy. I know I never made him happy."

She told me they started dating, and she got pregnant, so they got married, and then I came along. She told me he was a sweet father at first.

"He'd hold you and sing to you," she said. "He'd try to put you down, and you'd just wail. For a while, it looked like he might make it. But your father came with an expiration date."

In other words, he wanted to fool around. It satisfied a need she could never understand.

"When I told him I wouldn't put up with it, he recoiled," Mom said. "I married a damaged boy, thinking I could repair him, but I couldn't. Whatever part of him that might've evolved into an adult washed up a mile down from that trotline strung across the Neches River."

I asked her if he was coming back, and she said, "The short answer is no."

"What's the long answer?" I asked.

"The long answer is, 'It doesn't matter. He was never here in the first place.'"

I asked her if my brothers knew any of this, and she said, "No, but they haven't asked. I called them the other night. They said they're ready to come home. They miss their father. I didn't say anything. It's going to break my heart to tell them. You want to?"

She was kidding.

As we talked, she kept stirring a spoon in her coffee. Round and round. She was drinking a lot of coffee, too. With cream and two teaspoons of sugar.

"Speaking of broken hearts, how are you holding up?" Mom asked.

"How much do you know?" I asked.

"Just what you've told me so far," she said.

"How much more do you want to know?" I asked.

"I don't expect you to tell me everything, so just tell me what you want me to know," Mom said. "I'm not going to be a grandmother in nine months, am I?"

I played it cool.

"Good Lord, Mom," I said. "That's ridiculous."

Well, as far as she needed to know, it was ridiculous. The truth was, I'd left home seven weeks ago more of a boy than a young man, and she wanted that boy to return, but that boy was history.

It didn't happen all at one time, but it culminated that last night at Gram's.

Here's the rest of that story.

I'd dozed off at Gram's when something startled me. I wasn't sure if it was something I'd heard or something I'd dreamed. Either way, I jolted awake.

Debbie was lying on her side next to me, her head propped in her hand.

"You sing in your sleep," she said.

"When did you get here?"

"Oh, not that long ago."

"Why didn't you wake me up?"

"I wanted to watch."

"Watch what?"

"Watch you sleep."

"What was I singing?"

"I think I'll save that for later," she said, then she leaned forward and kissed me, and she held her lips on mine for a little longer than usual, then broke off the kiss, and then she kissed me again right away, and this time, her tongue flittered across my lower lip, and I shuddered.

"You like that, don't you?"

And I said, "No. I love it."

"Well, then," she said, "This next thing is going to drive you insane."

She kissed my face, starting with my right cheek, then moving across my jaw, down my chin and down my neck, then back up to my right ear. I had no idea what actual sex — that is, intercourse — felt like because I hadn't yet had actual sex except with myself, but, at that moment, I had a difficult time believing it could feel any better than this.

"Where did you learn to do that?" I asked.

"Kathleen. Of course," she said.

"God bless her," I said.

"Well, I'm hoping you were paying attention," she said. "You might be asked to return the favor."

"I have it all down, right up here," I said, tapping my temple.

She rolled onto her back and said, "Prove it."

—

For a long, long time, we made out. We kissed until our lips turned to jelly. Each time we came up for air, I repeated her name, first and last. I loved the way it sounded, the perfectly balanced cadence. Debbie Gehring.

She would never, ever be Deborah Gehring because it didn't sound right. Deb. Oh. Ruh. Gare. Ing.

Nope. Never.

Eventually, the candles melted, so it was dark except for the moonlight peeking through the clouds. It was hot and steamy, and the breeze had died down, so my shirt was soaked.

"I'm taking my shirt off," I told her. "Is that OK?"

I needed her permission. I didn't want to do anything stupid.

She smiled, and I took that for a "yes," and then I said, "You can take yours off too if you think it'd be more comfortable."

She said, "Do you want me to?"

Well, I wasn't ready for that. Of course, I wanted her to, but I expected her to say, "No thanks," or "I'm OK," or "What kind of girl do you take me for?" I wanted her to say, "Great!"

But she didn't. She said, "Do you want me to?"

My immediate impulse was to pretend to be a gentleman, to rise above my primitive desires and reply, "I'm more concerned with your comfort and well-being. I don't want you chafing or coming down with a summer cold."

Or something regretfully stupid. Fortunately, I didn't. I said, "Yes. I do. But don't do it if you don't want to."

"I want to," she said. "But I need to tell you something first. I'm as nervous as you are because this is my first time, too. I didn't tell you everything about that night because I was afraid to. I didn't know how you might react. I didn't trust you. I don't trust anybody except my mother. But now, I trust you. I can trust you, right?"

"I think so," I said.

"I think so, too," she said. "I held back because I was afraid you would call your parents and tell them to come and get you. I was afraid you'd realize Lynn isn't all that plain after all. I was afraid you'd leave."

"Why would you believe that?" I asked.

"Eddie. Be real. You've abandoned plenty of girls," she said.

Before I could respond, she said, "It's one thing to be rejected. No thank you. You're not my type. I'm not ready. So forth. You deal with it. Being abandoned means you had a chance and failed. When you're rejected, you have to ask yourself why."

When I flinched, she said, "I've been called a slut. I've been called a whore. I've been shunned, and there's always been an excuse. Something popped up. Maybe next time. Except, something always pops up. There never is a next time. And you know why? It's because I had an abortion. I've only told one person — Kathleen — and I know she'd never betray me. So, I can't stop people from believing what they believe, and I'm not going to try."

She wiped her face, brushed her hair back and continued.

"I don't date. I've never had a boyfriend. I don't want one. The guys who hang out at The Fritz are terrified of my mother, and the nice boys, well, their mothers would never allow their sweet young darlings to date someone as damaged as I am because they assume they know something. They assume they know I've had an abortion, and they're right. I have. I've committed the ultimate sin, and that's why I don't get invited to tea.

"I'm Hester Prynne, the untouchable, even though there are girls here who have sex every other night, often with different boys. Kathy Klement, my best friend, is one of those girls, so I'm not judging anyone. I just wish they'd stop judging me.

"The truth is, I am a virgin," she said. "What happened to me has no bearing on that. It can't be taken by force. You have to give it away for it to matter.

"Until I met you, I had no intention of giving anything to anybody. I thought I had everything I wanted. Who knew? Now, I want to. I do. I'm not embarrassed to admit it. I vowed a long time ago to wait for the right person and the right time, and I have, and here we are."

And she took her shirt off.

I rolled over on my back, and she rolled on top of me. I could feel her breasts flattened against my chest, and then, she sat up, and I could see them in the moonlight. For a moment, I waited for permission, but then I reached forward and cupped them in my hands, and they felt perfect. They were pear-shaped, not the gigantic melons I'd gaped at in Playboy and Montgomery Ward catalogues.

What can I compare them to? Nothing. Nothing else was, is, are, will be or can be as wondrous.

I inhaled the mist of her breath and tried not to giggle even though I was almost delirious. Her hair fell across my face. It was like nothing I'd ever smelled before, some exotic fragrance from Istanbul or Cairo, full of saffron or jasmine. Every sensory nerve in my body at that moment was pinched, pulled, dinged, pinged, elbowed in the ribs, and ordered to focus solely on the feel, smell, taste, sound, and glory of her hair.

If it had suffocated me, if I'd sucked it into my lungs and choked to death, well, what better way to go?

—

Around 2, maybe 2:30, we took a break, drank some tea, and ate the last two cookies.

"I should have brought a toothbrush," she said.

"Not me," I said. "I'm never brushing my teeth again."

She faked a gag, then said, "I have one more confession. That day at the pool. I orchestrated that. Not Kathleen."

"What about Judy? You arranged that, too?"

"Pretty brilliant, huh? Judy is a tramp," Debbie said. "She will do anything for money. She's going to be very popular with the boys in high school. Oh, and by the way, do you want to know where Lori and Faye get their information?"

"Let me guess," I said. "Judy?"

I asked her about Jack, the guy Kathleen called over.

"Jack Schulte?" she asked. "He's as dumb as dirt. He didn't have a clue what was going on, but he's wrapped around her finger, so when she said, 'Stay right there,' he wasn't budging an inch."

"You know, you should be ashamed," I said.

"I am. Maybe I'll start going back to church," she said. "I'll confess my sins to Father Louis."

"Today's Sunday," I said. "You can go today. Just as you are."

That is, wrapped in a blanket.

"I think I'll wait," she said. "I want to embrace my shame for a week or so. I got what I wanted, and that's what matters."

Debbie also admitted that she'd started crying as well. Nights in the shower. Mornings getting ready. She'd be reading a book and just burst out, but her mom never asked why or said a word about her puffy eyes or runny nose. She knew why.

"I kept telling myself, 'You know it's going to end. Stop crying.' But I couldn't. It was going to end, and it would be like a dream. I'd be back to my real life. You'd be back in East Texas, and sooner than later, you'd meet someone, and she'd be pretty and nice and fun, and you'd stop writing, and that would be the end of it.

"So, I've tried to convince myself this has been a summer romance, and nothing more, but I couldn't because I love you," she said. "I think I started falling in love with you the second I saw you at the pool, standing over by the fence, with your hands in your pockets. And then when you were doing those stupid backflips off the diving board. I didn't have the courage to walk over myself. That's why I told Kathleen to send Judy."

"Blind hog finds an acorn," I said.

"What?"

"It's an old East Texas saying," I said. "It means, sometimes, you get lucky."

Again, I didn't tell Mom all of this. I didn't tell her half of it, and yet, she still shook her head and said, "You're just a boy."

"Not nearly as much as I was," I said.

"I don't want to hear it," she said. "I don't want to hear another word. Everything is changing. I can't stand the idea of you changing, too. I thought it would take longer. I never dreamed it would end this soon."

"What do you mean?" I asked.

"I mean, I don't want you to be in such a big hurry to grow up," she said. "It's not all it's made out to be. Whatever little bit of boy you still have in you, hold on to it. OK?"

She blinked away tears then turned back into Mom. She shot me a mean eye and said, "With my luck, it'll be twins.

—

For breakfast, Mom and I each ate an apple fritter. I drank a Nehi grape soda, and she had two cups of coffee with cream and two teaspoons of sugar. She'd worked nine nights in a row, and a couple of those involved difficult deliveries. Her hands trembled, and she had to clasp them around her coffee cup to keep it from spilling.

"Have you noticed anything different?" she asked.

"Other than your husband leaving," I thought but didn't say. "New robe?"

Mom raised the index and middle fingers of her right hand to her mouth, as if she were taking a drag, then she pretended to stub it out.

"I've quit," she announced. "Cold turkey."

And I thought, "Jeez, how did I miss that?" It was so obvious. Normally, she'd have one in her mouth and one in an ashtray and one floating in between.

"When did this happen?" I asked.

"A month ago," she said. "And, right now, I would kill you for a Salem, but there's not a one in the house, so I'm on suicide-watch."

"I'll see if I can borrow a straitjacket from the Bishops," I said. "I'm sure they have one."

Mom offered a toast.

"To apple fritters and straitjackets," she said. I raised my bottle of Nehi, and we clinked. Then, I said, "Honey, don't worry about these dishes. Me and the boys will take care of them."

And Mom said, "Thanks, darling. That's real thoughtful of you."

And I replied, "Anything for you, Sugar Booger."

Then, I took her plate and mine, ran them under the faucet and placed them in the dish-rack.

Mom swept the powdered sugar from her lap and took a long drag off the Salem she didn't have and said she needed to get some sleep because she was working tonight, again.

"One more thing," I said. "Have you seen Lynn lately?"

And Mom said, "Well, I was hoping that could wait."

"Wait for what?" I asked.

"Lynn's not here," she said.

"How do you know?" I asked.

"Because they moved to Houston," Mom said.

"What?" I asked. "You're kidding. She didn't…"

"She didn't because you didn't," she said. "Her father was offered a promotion right before you left. He turned it down at first, but they came back with a second offer, one he couldn't refuse. Lynn told me. She told me she knew about it in April, but she kept hoping something would happen that would allow them to stay here, but her father took the job, and they drove down to Houston, and they found a new house with a pool, and they came back and packed up and drove away."

Mom told me Lynn literally prayed she'd hear from me, and when she didn't, she knew something was up, and she didn't want to butt in.

"She made me promise I wouldn't say anything to you unless you asked," Mom said. "And you never asked, and I wasn't going to break a promise I made to her."

I asked her if Lynn had left a phone number or an address.

"She left this," Mom said, then handed me a brown manila envelope. There was no address, no name on the front, not even mine. I found a paring knife and carefully sliced open the top of the envelope and found her letter, typed on a single sheet of white paper that had been folded in half. I opened it, read it, and then handed it back to Mom. It went like this:

Dear Eddie:

I knew before you left that we were moving. Well, I was 99 percent sure. I thought I'd wait and tell you when you got back. I didn't realize you'd be gone all summer, and then I couldn't imagine that you'd stop writing or calling, but once you did, I knew you had met someone. You've always been an easy read.

I've spent a lot of time trying to picture what she must look like and be like. I am sure she is pretty, but please, tell me she is not another Debby Bishop. You can do better. Maybe this new girl and I will meet one day. Who knows? I would like that, but if she's anything less than incredible, I'll be very disappointed. My dad will be, too.

I'm not going to tell you everything I would've told you if we'd continued our correspondence, and I'm not saying this to make you feel more guilty than you do. I know you do. In fact, I know you're already chewing a nail. I know you better than you know yourself. I know you a lot better than this new girl does, and it's painful knowing that eventually, she'll end up knowing you in ways I never will, if she doesn't already. That's how it is for plain girls like me.

I've included a poem I wrote. It sums up everything. I hope you like it. I hope it hurts.

My phone number and address are below. Write or call. Despite it all, I love you, as a friend and, unfortunately, in other ways. I love your mom, too. Give her a hug for me. Be nice.

By the way, I'm back to my first name. I never liked my middle name. It's too plain for a magnificent human being like myself. One day, you'll read about me in the newspapers. Until then, yours most fondly,

Debra Mayfield
3121 Banning Drive
Houston, Texas 77024

The Plain Truth

By DEBRA MAYFIELD

Will we be friends in the days ahead?
Of course, we won't. We'll write instead.
How's the weather? How's school?
Are you happy? Is everything cool?
Have you heard the new song?
The words are fab,
but it goes on too long.

That's it for now. Hello to all.
I've been waiting for your call.
But enough of that. It's getting late.
I have so much left still on my plate.
By the way, that's a plain lie.
Not that it matters.
So go ahead. Cry.

So, will we be friends in the years to come?
You must be kidding. You can't be that dumb.
You'll write me one,
I'll write you four.
I'll grow sick of keeping score.

You'll move on, just disappear.
I'll do nothing to interfere.
I'll bob and curtsy, then step back
Read the signs of my zodiac.
I am Air. You are Fire
I am forced to douse my desire.
But first, a favor. Tell me straight:
What have I done to deserve such a fate?

What has she done to deserve such a fate?

For starters, she made the mistake of being my friend. My best friend, and I loved her, so, of course, I had to fail her to prove that I didn't deserve her. That was my fate. Her mom was right. She could've done so much better, and I knew that. Everyone did.

You know, at those funerals, when the preacher talks about spending eternity in heaven, playing poker or fishing with Jesus, I always think, "What a horrible idea. Fishing forever? Playing poker forever? No thanks."

Well, if it were true, if I died and somehow landed in heaven forever, I'd want Lynn there with me. I'd want Debbie Gehring there, too, of course, but I'd imagine she and I would get on each other nerves after a few hundred thousand years, whereas Lynn and I would've talked and talked forever.

I couldn't explain falling in love with Debbie Gehring because I had no control over that. You fall in love with the person you fall in love with. It's out of your hands. But being a jerk is a choice. You decide to put yourself first, and that's what I did with Lynn. I chose the selfish, cowardly path, knowing I would break her heart. She waited every day for a letter from me, and it never came.

Sure, I had excuses. I was working. I was tired. I met a girl. I fell in love. The clock was ticking. I needed sleep. My old man. Maybe tomorrow. Maybe the day after that.

It was bullshit. I was lazy and cruel. That was my excuse. Lynn didn't pluck the closing line of her poem out of thin air.

"What have I done to deserve such a fate?"

She knew she'd found the perfect way to say to me, "I'm not the loser. You are. You're not what you appear to be."

And she was right.

I slid Lynn's letter and poem back into the envelope and placed it in the drawer of my bed stand, and I walked into the bathroom and closed and locked the door and turned off the lights. Then, I crawled into the tub and turned the water on as hot as I could stand it, and I soaked there until the water turned cold.

—

Mom didn't interrupt me or try to console me when she heard me crying because she knew I had it coming, and, boy, did it ever. The sobs came like waves of nausea from food poisoning.

Eventually, I emptied the tank. No more tears. No more retching. No more anything. I literally threw up until I passed out.

The next morning, I woke around 8 and looked for Mom and couldn't find her. Her car was in the driveway, but she wasn't in her bedroom or the kitchen or garage. Finally, I found her outside, digging in a flowerbed, trying to work off her nicotine cravings. I offered to help, but she waved me off.

"There's a bag of donuts on the table, if you're hungry," she said. "I'm going to finish this, and then we'll talk."

I decided I needed to get some air myself, so I changed into a pair of khaki shorts and a Western Auto T-shirt my dad had given me for Christmas because he got it free with a set of new tires. I slipped on an old pair of sneakers and left Mom a note telling her I was going to wander around and see what if anything was up.

Well, nothing was up. Families were returning from their summer travels, but no one was awake. I saw a basketball in the Bishops' driveway, but there was no one out shooting free throws.

I walked over to see if Jeep was around, but their car was gone, and the house seemed empty. I saw Mr. Gilbert picking up his newspaper, and I waved. He waved, too, then went back into his house. I noticed in his driveway a red Pontiac Bonneville. It belonged to a new lady friend of his. Good for him.

I knew I wouldn't see Lynn, but I walked to her house anyway. It looked the same as always until I got close enough to see that it was empty and locked and latched. There was nothing left, and my eyes began to drizzle again, and I looked around to make sure no one was coming my way.

I circled the house, half expecting Lynn to tap on a window and point to an unlocked door, but no such luck. They were gone. Every room was empty. The carport was empty. The shed was empty. The patio was empty. It was like they'd never lived there.

I rattled the front door, anyway, then stopped and walked down the stairs to the curb where Lynn and I used to sit and talk, and then I bopped back up the sidewalk and took one last peek through the keyhole and again saw nothing, but I refused to believe that they'd vanished, so I rang the doorbell 15 or 20 times. I thought I could find a re-set button, like something out of an episode of "The Twilight Zone."

I thought, "If I push the doorbell one more time, just one more time, just one more time, things will return to the way they were."

That is, Lynn would open the door and say, "Where ya' been? C'mon in. Grab a Coke. Let's watch 'The Price is Right.'"

And her dad would be there, and he'd say, "Well, look what the cat drug in. Good to see you. Come in. Join us."

Everyone would be thrilled to see me.

Well, everyone except Lynn's mom.

So, I rang the bell four or five more times and finally gave up. Screw it, I thought. Out of sight. Out of mind. As far as I cared, they could bulldoze the place and burn the rubble. The place meant nothing to me.

The last thing I wanted was to see someone else move in. That would be hard — so hard I'd probably throw rocks through their windows, steal stuff off their clothesline, poison their trees and paint the curb in front of their house some color so obnoxious, people would be too embarrassed to sit out there.

This is what you mutter to yourself when you have no one to say it to. You curse. "Goddamn son of a bitch," and when you realize you're cursing, you order yourself to stop cursing and muttering because you sound like the imbecile you are.

—

Jeep and Duane saw me circling the Mayfield's house and came out to say hi. They'd just returned from breakfast downtown.

"We weren't here when they left," Jeep said. "We got back, and the house was empty. Doesn't seem real, does it?"

I wished Lynn could have heard that. She wouldn't have believed it, and I was thinking something along the lines of "Isn't this a sweet moment," but then Jeep turned to Duane and said,

"Show 'em."

So, Duane pulled out of his pocket the clothesline wire on which Karen's underwear used to hang.

"What is that?" I asked.

"Clothesline wire," Jeep said, then turned to Duane and said, "Show him the other thing."

Duane pulled out of his other pocket what looked to be a white handkerchief but was, in fact, a pair of Karen's white, cotton panties he'd stolen off their clothesline. I should've grabbed them and growled something like, "You're certifiably sick."

But what good would it have done? Karen didn't miss them, and if they gave Duane something to do with his hands at night, well, what was the harm?

The three of us stood there a while longer, and no one bothered to ask where I'd been or what I'd been doing. They mostly wanted to talk about 10th grade, what they thought it'd be like and so forth. They talked about the senior girls, about how loose and easy they were supposed to be. For a moment, I thought I was back at the farm with Jeff.

Jeep and Duane and I strolled back toward my house and stopped in the middle of the vacant lot where, among other things, I'd stomped Lowell Hardwick, and Jeep was still yammering about how many senior girls he expected to nail on the first day of class, and I decided I'd heard enough.

"Boys? I gotta go," I said. "Lots to do."

"Really?" Duane said. "Hell, you just got here."

"Yeah, I know. Sorry. Gotta go," I repeated, then turned and walked and then sprinted toward my house. A few seconds later, I heard Jeep shouting out to me, "Hey! Are we playing football tomorrow or not?"

I stopped, wheeled around, then yelled, "It's your goddamn ball, Jeep. Figure it out. I'm not in charge."

CHAPTER 28

On our own

A few days later

The sun had dipped below the tops of the pine trees, and I'd already crawled in bed when Mom tapped on my door and said, "Someone's asking for you."

"Who?" I asked.

"Put a shirt on and answer the door," Mom said in a prickly voice that reminded me that we weren't equal partners and wouldn't be any time soon.

I raked my hair with my hand and slipped on a pair of blue jeans and a black T-shirt and hurried to the front door, where Mom was waiting.

I gave her a "What the hell?" look, and then cracked open the door and peeked out, and there stood Debby Bishop. It was the one and only time she'd ever stood on my doorstep and waited for me to come out to talk to her.

"Who died?" I joked.

"No one," she answered, timidly. "I wanted to say 'Welcome back. Seems like forever.' Everything's fine. No one died. It's been a long time, it seems. Did I say that already? I did, didn't I. I'm sorry. How are you?"

At first, I couldn't tell what she was fishing for.

"I'm OK," I said, and then she jumped back in.

"I mean, it seems like forever since you and Debra. That is, Lynn. It seems like forever since I've seen you and her, sitting out on the curb. I wonder how she's doing. Have you heard from her?"

I thought, "Since when did you start caring about Lynn?"

But I stepped out and pulled the door shut, and Debby Bishop's lower lip began to quiver, and I asked, "Are you OK?"

When I realized she clearly was not, I reached out to kind of offer her a hug because that's what Faye would have expected me to do, but when I did, Debby Bishop leaned into me and wrapped her arms around my waist. We stood there like that on the front porch for a minute, then I said to God, "No way."

I'd spent so many nights fantasizing about a moment exactly like that, with Debby Bishop's arms wrapped around my waist, and my arms wrapped around her waist, and her face pressed against my chest, and my chin resting on the top of her head, and every time I fantasized about this, I could hear the Beach Boys singing, "Wouldn't It Be Nice."

Now that it had finally happened, it was too much. I had to fight the impulse to break her grip, and I can't say why. She was as pretty as ever, and she was being sincere, which was doubly puzzling since I thought she hated Lynn.

We stood there for another minute or so, and then I reached over and tapped softly on the door, and Mom answered, and I asked her to bring Debby a glass of water.

Mom reappeared immediately with the water and a bucket of ice, and she handed them to me, and I handed the water to Debby, who had dropped her arms and wiped her eyes and nose and stepped back and said, "I'm a mess."

"Sweetheart, we all are upset," Mom said.

"I know," Debby said. "Well, it's late. I just wanted to say hi."

"Take all the time you want," Mom said. "I'm going to call your parents and tell them where you are. If you need anything, tap."

"Thank you, Mrs. Dodson," Debby said. "I appreciate it."

Mom looked at me with a look that said, "I'm watching you."

Debby and I walked down the driveway and sat on the curb and gazed across the vacant lot that led to the red clay trail that snaked its way into the woods and up the hill that I loved to run down and occasionally dreamed about.

The last rays of sun shot over the tall pines, and the sky turned deep, deep blue, and I knew it was time for her to go, so I said, "If Lynn knew I was sitting out here with you, she would throw a fit."

"If Lynn knew I was sitting out here with you, she'd throw a knife," Debby replied.

Then she added, "She really hated me."

"Oh, I don't know about that," I said.

"C'mon, Eddie," she said. "She did."

"She was my best friend," I said. "It doesn't mean she hated you. You two are just so different."

"No, we're not. At least, we weren't. Before you moved into this neighborhood, we were friends," Debby said. "And even after, I tried to remain her friend. I really did. I tried to be nice to her. I invited her over. I tried to get her to come over and watch TV together, but she turned on me, and so I quit trying. It took a while to figure out it wasn't about me. It was about you."

"Lynn and I are just friends," I said. "Really good friends, but nothing more. You've got it all wrong."

"I don't," she said, then rubbed her eyes.

"You want me to walk you home?"

"Not yet," she replied. "Five more minutes. Just five more."

"OK," I said. "Enough about that. OK? Let's change the subject. What should be talk about, other than Lynn?"

"I don't know," she said. "What would you and Lynn be talking about? I always wondered what you two were talking about when you were sitting out here late at night. I was afraid you were talking about me. Maybe that's just me being weird."

"Nah, we didn't talk about you, and if we did, it was probably something nice," I lied. "If Lynn were here now, I'd probably ask her about band camp. Like, was it fun? Boring? Horrible? What was the best thing about it? The worst? The weirdest? That kind of thing."

Debby said, "I didn't know she went to band camp," and I replied, "She did. She was there while you were at rich-kid camp."

"I wasn't in rich-kid camp," she said. "I was at church camp."

"So, how was church camp?" I asked.

"Well, I'll tell you something. If you ever want to be fully corrupted, go to church camp," she said. "Kids were sneaking in beer. Some girls were sneaking out after curfew. Some were smoking cigarettes. Maybe I'm just too small-town. I wanted it to be nice and friendly, and it wasn't."

Then, I asked, "How was Walt McFarlin?"

"Why would you ask me about him?"

"Well, it must've been convenient," I said.

"Convenient how?" she replied.

"I mean, he is your boyfriend," I said.

"He is not my boyfriend," she said. "Walt McFarlin is a pig. Don't mention his name to me again."

I bonked my forehead with my fist and thought, "Let me get this straight. Debby and Lynn are friends. Walt McFarlin is a pig."

"Debby, I saw you two together," I said. "He was all over you."

"When?"

"At the library, earlier this summer," I said.

"That was a mistake," she said. "Walt McFarlin is…"

And she tried to think of another word for "a pig," and she couldn't bring herself to say "asshole," so she settled on "scum."

I don't know what happened at rich-kid camp, but I suspected he tried to do more than shoot her squirrel.

—

It was late, so I stood, and she stood, and then she said, "I'm glad you're home."

I curled my right arm around her shoulder, buddy-style, and she then rolled into me and pulled tightly, and if I'd have looked down, she would've been there, looking up, waiting for me to look down, but I couldn't do it, so I gently pulled away and said, "I'll walk you home."

I'm sure that confused her. She'd known all along how I felt about her, and now, I was walking her home?

"You don't need to," she replied. "I can get home myself. I'm glad you're back, Eddie. I really am."

Then, she smiled and said, "See you," and then she ran home, leaving me standing there, at the curb, under the streetlamp, wondering what the hell had just happened. Was this just a friend thing? Was it a romantic thing? Was I hallucinating?

I didn't know. I did know this — for the past two years at least, I'd had a crush on Debby Bishop, but I knew she was out of my league. My dad didn't wear a suit and tie and carry a briefcase. Her dad did. My mom didn't slice the crust off our sandwiches. Her mom's maid did.

And yet, there she was, at my doorstep, sitting on the curb in front of my house and talking and hugging and almost begging me to kiss her, and it made me wonder: Had I moved up, or had she moved down?

The next morning, I tried to write Lynn, but I couldn't find the words. I tried to write a poem, but the best I could do was rip off Lennon and Dylan lyrics. I thought about calling her, but I didn't have the courage to face the possibility that her mother would answer and hang up on me.

So, I spent most of the morning lolling around, listening to the radio, and thumbing through old copies of Life and Time and Newsweek magazines I'd found in a basket in Mom's bathroom. They all dealt with the war in Vietnam. The February 11, 1966, issue of Life ran two pages of tiny mug shots of American soldiers who'd just completed their one-year tour "in country."

Most of them were no more than three years older than me. They looked 10 years older. They looked like they'd just watched their younger sisters napalmed. Many of them had that World War II thousand-yard stare.

Their original rah-rah, gung-ho "kill 'em all and let Jesus sort out the details" bullshit had been supplanted by "I'm tired and scared, and I want to go home and hug my mother."

I thought about Dennis and wondered if he was going to end up in the middle of this mess. I wondered if it'd have the same effect on him. There was a time when I thought, "Those Viet Cong have no idea what's about to hit them."

Now, I thought, "Dennis has no idea what's about to hit him."

I knew I'd never receive a postcard from him, so I had to hope he'd make it back in one piece so we could sit in silence and enjoy a beer and a basket of fries together.

—

Football two-a-days were scheduled to begin the next week, so I had time to rest up. I stopped playing outdoors because I feared I might jam a finger or roll an ankle or splatter a knee while running across wet cement.

Besides, it was August. The pool had closed, and the creek was dry, so everyone was cooped indoors, watching TV, or talking on the phone, or sleeping.

My brothers returned, too, so I tried to hang out with them, but they had their own friends and didn't need me. I spent a lot of time with a guy named Jerry McClanahan, who'd just moved into the neighborhood. He was one year older and two decades years cooler than me.

He had record player — except, he called it a "turntable" — and a fancy Marantz receiver and pair of JBL L100 speakers that his older brother had picked up in Japan after he left Vietnam.

The Beatles had just released "Revolver," which I'd read about but hadn't heard until I got home and dropped by his place.

"You gotta listen to this album," Jerry told me. "It's fucking amazing. Wait here, I'm going to grab a beer."

For the first time, I said, "Grab me one, too."

He bopped into the kitchen, then back out with two cans of Miller High Life, and then he put on "Revolver," and we tried to turn off our minds and relax and flow downstream. I would've surrendered to the void if I had known what the void looked like and where I might have found it.

I spent a lot of time thinking about Debbie Gehring and moping and wondering what she was doing. I must've listened to "Here, There and Everywhere" 50 times. It said everything I was feeling.

I loved the song because it made the pain even more acutely painful. I began to understand the expression, "It hurts so good."

Meanwhile, Mom told me and my brothers what little she knew about our dad. He had left us for another woman, and she did not know when we would see him again. Since we were now living on a single paycheck, she said we had to tighten our belts.

"The luxuries you've come to expect will be suspended until such time when we have achieved a stable financial situation."

Those were her words, verbatim. She laughed after saying them. Oddly enough, she seemed happy.

We gawked at her, and she said, "I'm kidding. Look, we're going to be stretched, but we'll be fine, so long as I don't have to replace a coffee table every week."

Suddenly, everything was a joke. To top it off, she pointed to me and said to my brothers, "He's in charge."

Then, she looked at me and said, "You're in charge."

Then I said, "I'll be in the garage, working on the car."

Then, I started whistling.

—

I received my first letter from Debbie Gehring before I started my first letter to her, so I forced myself to sit down and write some of the things I'd been feeling. I decided I was going to lay it all on the line, and if she decided I'd gone too far, well, she could let me know, and she could move on, and I could hang myself with a belt.

I told her I loved her. I told her about Lynn and about Debby Bishop. I told her my dad had left and wasn't coming back.

Then, I told her how much I missed her. I saw no reason to hold back. All of my coy crap had never worked for me anyway. My stupid pride chased or scared off more girls than it ever attracted, so, I spilled my guts. As I stood in front of the mail slip at the downtown post office, I went through the whole "Do I mail it or dump it" inner conversation.

Even though I worried this letter might freak her out, I sealed the envelope and dropped it in the big, blue box.

Meanwhile, Mom seemed to be talking to Mina several times a day. Normally, I couldn't have cared less, but this time, I sensed something was up.

I heard Mom say, "Martha, school starts here in a week."

Another time, I heard, "What am I going to do for a job?"

Another time, she said, "I will have to talk to the boys about this. I can't decide this alone."

But she did. The day before football two-a-days were to start, she woke us all up and told us to come to breakfast because she needed to talk to us about something crucial.

We dragged ourselves out of bed and tromped down the hall to the dining room. She opened a box of donuts and poured my brothers each a glass of milk, and she poured me a cup of coffee.

Then, she sat and announced, "I quit my job tonight. I have one month of vacation coming to me, and I'm going to take it, and we're going to make some big changes."

My brothers and I looked at each other, trying to make sense of what she was saying.

"You quit your job?" Andy asked. "Why?"

"Because it's time," Mom said.

"Do you have another job?" Ricky asked.

"No. I don't," she said. "Not yet."

"Is Dad coming back?" Andy asked.

"No. He's not," Mom said. "We're on our own."

"Are we going on welfare?" Ricky asked.

"No, sweetie. We're not going on welfare. We're moving."

She turned to me and smiled and said it again. "We're moving."

"Where are we going?" Ricky asked.

And Mom replied, "We're going home."

PART SEVEN | CHAPTER 29
The rest of it

Monday, September 6

Because I knew I could screw up a one-car funeral, I was 15 minutes early to my first class — sophomore English. I assumed I'd get lost or turned around or misdirected or ambushed and skinned alive by Barbary pirates masquerading as vampire nuns. Shit like that happened to me all the time. Still does.

That could go double on the first day at my new school, so I arrived to an empty classroom early and stood around and waited for someone to show up. It almost made me pine for Bo's Diner.

Finally, two girls meandered in and eyeballed me, the way they might've examined a new pimple on their nose the morning of the prom.

It was "hi" and "hi" and "how are you?" And "nice to meet you" and then they grabbed two seats on the next to the last row and resumed their discourse on Kipling or Defoe or Orwell or red fingernail polish.

Then, a lanky guy shuffled in and super-slinked himself into a desk on the row behind the two girls and dropped his head down into the cradle of his folded arms and fell dead asleep. I would come to learn he did this in every class, every day.

His name was Robert Allen Schulle, and he was the smartest kid in his class when he wanted to be, which was about half the time. The other half, he'd smart off and pick fights with teachers who were just trying to help him reach his potential, so, he'd wind up in Father Gus' office, getting chewed out, suspended, or expelled.

I never understood why Robert had to play the "too cool for school" game, but he and I would later become close friends. Not best friends, but good friends. When I told him my "Dominque" story, he told me he'd sat in that same chair in Father Gus' office and listened to a version of that same speech, not once but twice.

Soon enough, the other kids in the class trickled in, and they all appeared to be related to one another. I'd already met several of them this summer, either at the store or church or perhaps at the pool. I didn't know them by name, but one by one, they introduced themselves to me.

"Hi. My name is…"

Clifford Ermler
Luke Runkle
L. C. Rheinhardt
Elsie Groen
Drew Groen
Alice Maaland
Charlotte Barin
Ramona Stahl
Beverly Hinkle
Clyde Eberhardt

Over the next two years, Clyde and I would become best friends. He was also tall and raw-boned and long-armed but not lanky like Robert.

Clyde had a big head covered with kinky brown hair and a ka-boom laugh. Every other year, he was elected class president, and in the years when he wasn't, he was elected class favorite. Everyone assumed that if Kassel were to ever produce a governor or a U.S. senator, it'd be Clyde.

Given that he was so popular, I wondered how I hadn't met him already. Turns out, he spent most of his summers with his grandparents in Hannibal, Missouri. That didn't stop him from greeting me on my first day as if he'd known me since diapers.

"Well, look who's here," Clyde said. "Eddie Spaghetti. Tell me something. I hear you play football. You're coming out, right? Don't tell me you're not. It's too early to get on the shit list. Wanna know who keeps the shit list? You're looking at him. You're coming out. Don't argue with me. I'll have you buried alive."

"I'm coming out," I said.

"Fan-tastic," he said. "By the way, we're not worth a shit."

And he said "shit" right as Sister Mary Agnes walked in.

"Clyde," she said. "On the first day? Really?"

"Sorry, Sister," Clyde said. "I didn't see you there."

"God sees you, Clyde," Sister Mary Agnes said. "He hears you. That's what matters."

"Yes, Sister," Clyde said. "I will try to remember that."

Sister Mary Agnes rolled her eyes and turned to me and said, "Never let anything come out of your mouth that you wouldn't hold in your hands."

"Yes, Sister," I replied.

Then, Sister Mary Agnes inspected me a bit closer and said, "I've seen you in church. Tell me your name."

"My name is Eddie Dodson," I said.

"Dodson," she repeated. "Oh, yes. I remember."

She picked up her clipboard and ran a finger down the class roster and said, "I don't see your name on this list."

I said, "Sister, my first name is Eddie. It's not Edward."

She looked up and then down at her clipboard and said, "Eddie. That is your christened name?"

"It is, Sister," I said.

"Not Edward?" she asked, almost in disbelief.

"No, Sister," I said. "It's Eddie."

"That's the name on your birth certificate?"

"Yes, Sister. My name is Eddie. I was named after...."

And she interrupted me.

"OK. OK," she said. "I'm sure it's a lovely story, but we don't have time. Welcome to our class, and it is 'our' class, so you will be expected to participate fully, which means you must keep up. Are you a reader?"

"I guess so, Sister," I said, although I wasn't sure how much reading qualified me as "a reader" in her estimation.

"Can you write?"

"Of course," I said.

"The correct answer would be 'Yes, Sister' or 'No, Sister.'"

"Yes, Sister," I said.

"Do you enjoy writing?"

"Well, yes and no," I said. "It depends…Sister!"

"Close enough," Sister Mary Agnes said. "You're on the literary magazine staff. We will meet at 7:30 tomorrow morning. This room. Bring a writing sample."

Then, she turned to Clyde and said, "Watch your mouth. We're watching."

When she turned her back, Clyde looked at me and mouthed, "Fffffuck."

That's how it went the rest of my first day at St. Paul's Catholic High School. I liked my classes. I liked the kids in my classes. I ran into freckle-face Helen, the girl who thought she was Kathy with a K's best friend, and she didn't look as bony. In fact, she looked pretty in her blue and beige plaid skirt and white blouse.

I asked her what she was doing there, and she yelled back, "What are YOU doing here?"

I told her my story. She told me hers.

"My mom wants me to go here this year," she said. "She says I'm at a vulnerable age. She'll let me switch back if I behave myself.

"LIKE THAT'S GOING TO HAPPEN!"

I sat with her at lunch, and she introduced me to her friends as "our football team's only hope." I liked her friends. They seemed light years more genuine than Kathy with a K.

I also liked my teachers, especially Sister Mary Agnes.

I bumped into Father Gus and Father Louis, and they each welcomed me with neither suspicion nor regret.

My algebra teacher coached the varsity football team, and he excused me from practice "today only," so I could settle in and help my mother unpack. After my last class, I hung around in the hall for a few minutes to talk to two of my soon-to-be sophomore teammates. I promised I'd join them the next day.

Then, I headed out, toward what used to be my grandmother's house and what was now our home. The front door was locked, so I walked around back and found Mom in the kitchen, emptying boxes and organizing spices alphabetically. My younger brothers had already put their things away and were now exploring the dusty garage.

I dumped my squirrel bag on the kitchen table, picked up an apple and rolled it around in my hand.

"How was it?" Mom asked. "Tell me it was super. It was. Right?"

"Couldn't have been better," I said.

She blotted her forehead with a dish towel and exhaled.

"Thank God," she said. "I've been worried sick. It's all happened so fast. I was afraid it all happened too fast. If I'd had a carton of cigarettes in the house today, I would've smoked every damn one of them."

Mom again dabbed the sweat from her nose and draped the towel over the oven handle and said, "I'm almost finished in here. Get out. Go put your feet up."

She wasn't finished and wouldn't quit until she was. After all, she ran a tight ship.

I opened the fridge and found a pitcher of lemonade.

"Is this community property?" I asked.

It was, so I poured a glass and then flopped into a huge leather chair that faced the front window in the living room. Uncle Carl and Mina gave it to Mom because they were desperate to get rid of it. It had come out of Grandpa Schaper's study and had collected dust since his death five or six years ago.

I loved it the moment I saw it and claimed it as my own. I sipped my lemonade and pulled out of my notebook a letter I'd written to Lynn during homeroom that day. It began with "You probably don't remember me but…" and then went on to explain and grovel and apologize and promise.

I signed it with a heart and a lipstick smooch and my name in red ink because I couldn't find purple — Eddie 'Spaghetti' Dodson.

I figured that alone would guarantee she'd write me back, and she would find something interesting to say about it, something that I'd never, ever thought of, and that was why I decided to write her every other day until I received a letter from her.

I realized how much I missed her, and how much I wanted to remain friends. I wasn't sure if our friendship could survive distance and time, but I was determined to find out. If it didn't survive, it wouldn't be for my lack of trying.

Most importantly, I needed Lynn to forgive me. I also needed Debbie Gehring to know that Lynn had forgiven me.

By the way, that first day at school, I was thumbing through a Time magazine and read an article that claimed the Beatles were kaput. After "Revolver" and Lennon's remark about the Beatles being greater than Jesus, they had nowhere to go but down — or so said some blowhard big-shot New York City music critic.

I didn't believe it. Not a word of it. Everyone else was jumping ship, going with the Monkees or Dylan or the Kinks or the Rolling Stones, but not me.

"Wait and see," I said. "Just wait and see."

I thought I might write about that for the literary magazine, if Sister Agnes would allow it. If I wrote it, and it was published, I'd send it to Lynn, and she'd be impressed.

Two rabbits with one rock, I figured.

Of course, thinking about Lynn made me miss the old neighborhood, which surprised me. I wondered if anyone had walked over to our empty house and peered into the windows to confirm that we were gone and probably for good. I wondered if anyone jimmied a door lock open and snooped around to see if we'd left anything worth taking.

I thought it'd say a lot if no one bothered to ransack our house. I mean, not exactly high praise.

I also thought about all those football games we played in the open field. I wondered whether Russell or Duane or Jeep or any of the guys missed me. I assumed Russell had moved in at quarterback.

I wondered how long it'd take before that open field would be sub-divided into quarter-acre lots containing cookie-cutter brick homes, each one nestled inside its own 7-foot privacy fence. People were building storm or tall cedar fences around the houses that already existed. Soon, if you wanted to run to Russell's house, you'd have to go to the end of the block and back around to get there.

The same was true for the red clay trails that ran along the creek. I remembered running and riding my bike up and down those trails. I wondered how long it'd take before the pine trees were bulldozed, and the big hill was flattened so some rich guy from Dallas could build more brick houses and 7-foot privacy fences.

If I hadn't moved to Kassel, all of this would have happened right in front of my eyes, and I probably never would have noticed it.

I recalled Robert Frost's poem "Nothing Gold Can Stay," especially the last three lines.

> **So Eden sank to grief,**
> **So dawn goes down to day.**
> **Nothing gold can stay.**

Every now and then, I thought about my dad. How was he doing? What was he doing? Did he ever think about us? Did he miss us even a little? I doubted it. Even if he did, I couldn't imagine him admitting it because that's not how he rolled.

I wanted to share these thoughts with Lynn — or Debra, now. That would have been something worth the time it took to write it, and I vowed that I would as soon as I was able to wrap my head around it.

I sank into the leather chair and tried to relax, but my mind wanted to conjure images of Debbie Gehring in her floppy straw hat, walking into The Fritz, and hovering over me in the dark. Then, I saw her. She was walking up the street, and then she turned into the yard and breezed up the sidewalk and knocked on the front door.

"Door's jammed," I shouted, but it wasn't really. I was kidding. So, I opened the door, and there she was, wearing a white long-sleeve dress shirt and cut-off blue jean shorts.

Then, Mom rushed in, and she and Debbie hugged, and Mom made it official. "She's pretty to the bone."

Finally, my brothers scrambled in, and they liked her, too, and she liked them, and we all sang "Dominique."

Then, I woke up. This is what really happened.

Debbie gazed into the front window and saw me in the chair, but she walked around back because she assumed I'd nodded off, and the front door was still as jammed as ever.

She knocked lightly on the kitchen door, although she didn't need to knock because she wasn't a stranger. She'd met my mom the day we arrived, and they seemed to click.

"I think he's napping," Debbie told my mom. "I'm just going to sit in there and do a little homework, if that's OK."

"I'm afraid you're going to have to get used to it," Mom said. "He's about six years behind on his sleep."

I wasn't napping. I was resting my eyes and letting my mind run naked through the woods. I didn't hear Debbie come in, but I heard her rustling papers she'd brought home for her mom to sign. Debbie attended public school, of course. Her mother would have turned her over to Chairman Mao before enrolling her in a Catholic school.

By the way, Jenny Gehring had gotten herself a boyfriend, too. A real cowboy named Darrell. Darrell Tuttle. He worked on a ranch somewhere around Fort Worth.

"She's a giddy as a girl scout," Debbie told me. "You think she was insufferable before? Wait to you see her now."

No hurry, I thought. Take your time.

Debbie returned to her papers, and I watched as she organized everything into neat piles. Every move seemed calculated for efficiency and speed. She was her mother's daughter.

When Debbie noticed me staring at her, she folded her arms,

and asked, "Where's the rug?"

"In my room," I said.

"Clever boy," she said. "Oh, by the way, you can say it now."

"Say what?" I asked.

"You know," she said. "That line I told you not to say. Remember? Go ahead. Say it."

I remembered, and so I said it in my best Humphrey Bogart voice: "Of all the gin joints in all the towns in all the woyrld, she walks into mine."

"That's the one," Debbie Number Three said, then smiled softly, and chewed her pencil, and opened her English textbook, and twirled her long blonde ponytail.

So, all things considered, not a bad day.

THE END

SHOUTOUTS

As I've told several friends, I whipped this thing out in just over 10 years. I wrote the first chapter in 2010, then shopped it around, wrote some more, showed it around, wrote some more and then stopped because I had other projects that paid rather than cost money. These projects were followed by other projects and opportunities and distractions, which I fashioned into excuses whenever someone asked me, "How's that book coming along?"

"Great," I'd say. "Almost done."

That went on forever. I'd start and stop. Start over. Change tense. Change it back. Change names and names of places. Change them back. Rewrite dialogue.

My greatest fear during all of this was that I wouldn't be able to re-capture the main character's voice or figure out a way to get him and others from here to there.

But I was lucky. I had friends —Jack Getman and David Knight in particular — who nagged me to "get off your dead ass and finish the damn thing," so I decided to give it another shot. I'd just turned 65. I was overweight and out-of-sorts, and I thought, "They're right. Finish it or flush it."

So, I started over, and soon enough, Eddie's voice returned. Then, Debbie #1 and Debbie #2 joined him, so I began building scenes and writing dialogue. I took long walks and conjured the conversations I thought these kids would be having. I was never sure where the story was headed, so I had to have faith that one thing would lead to the next and that I wouldn't be forced to rely on clichés or impossible coincidences.

It helps to have friends like Joe Stafford. I was explaining to him how I needed to find a way for a main character to do what she'd vowed never to do, and he told me a story. Without it, D#3 marries a local boy, and Eddie ends up driving a bread truck.

Fortunately, I found a groove and wrote non-stop.

A few months before the pandemic, I taught a writing workshop at Michigan State. I'd wake up and write, lecture, grab lunch, and write, lecture, coach, grab dinner, grade, and write. By the end of the workshop, I'd finished 99 percent of the first draft. It sucked, but that didn't stop me from forcing it upon more friends, all of whom provided polite suggestions, ruthless assessments, concrete tips and/or enough rah-rah to keep me going.

Among the more enthusiastic of my early readers were Tom Herod, Thom Prentice, Terry Nelson, and Michael Zagst.

About 70 percent of writing a book is re-writing it, so I spent an ungodly amount of time proofing and editing, which was a waste. I'm completely inept at editing my own copy, so I leaned on other friends such as Lori Herbst, Rhonda Moore, and Lori Oglesbee-Petter.

Thanks also to Terri LeClercq, Andy Salmon, Larry White, Betsy Rau, and Sandy Hall-Chiles and Andy Chiles, who hosted me in their home outside Brenham, Texas.

Thanks to Dick Holland and Cynthia Bryant, Rick and Donna Hill, Linda Bayless, Bruce McCandless, John Moore, Cary White, Kyla Mora, Chris Barton, Kem Kemp, McKenzie Rankin, Malina Dragu, and Mona Olaru. Thanks to Tom Eberhart.

Thanks to Mary Keller for putting up with me during the highs and lows of this wacky, seemingly never-ending venture. I'm talking about the book project here. Not our marriage.

Thanks to Sarah Cain for reading it without gagging.

Thanks to my youngest brother, Ken Hawthorne.

Better than anyone, he knows where this story comes from, how much of it is real, and how much of it is fiction. His approval means more to me than all the other kudos combined.

Special thanks to Howard Spanogle, Brad Bailey, Thom Prentice and Suzanne Bardwell. I promise to bring copies of the book next time I'm up your way.

THE **AUTHOR**

Bobby Hawthorne is a writer and a popular instructor at scholastic journalism workshops, state and national student media conventions, and publishing company seminars.

He has taught in almost every U.S. state as well as in Hungary, Romania, the Netherlands, and the Czech Republic.

He is the author of "The Radical Write," widely considered the go-to textbook on reporting and writing for student publications.

1971

In 2022, he finished a companion book, "Copy That: A Beginner's Guide to Yearbook Copy."

Hawthorne also wrote and curated photographs for "Longhorn Football: An Illustrated History," and he provided text for "Home Field: Texas High School Football Stadiums from Alice to Zephyr." Both were published by the University of Texas Press.

Hawthorne also writes opinion pieces, feature stories and personality portraits for magazines you've never heard of, and he's received a slew of big fish/small pond awards from associations you'll have a hard time believing exist.

He currently plays second and third base in an Austin-based senior (55+) softball league. He loves the Beatles as much today as ever.

Actually, more.

www.utbobby@gmail.com
bobbyhawthorne.blogspot.com
Facebook:bobbyhawthorne81/

FEED**BACK**

"**I recently finished** a novel by my friend Bobby Hawthorne titled Debbie Number Three. I knew I would probably like it because he is a talented writer. I didn't know that I would love it. That I would feel such strong emotions for the narrator/protagonist. That this novel would stick with me every day for the past two weeks. That this boy growing up in East Texas with a difficult childhood could resonate so much with me, a girl who grew up on the rainy coast of Washington in a "normal" family. This coming-of-age novel is perfect for teens and anyone who ever was a teen."
— Kathy Daly, Denver, Colorado

"**Yes, it's a great** coming of age story that's full of wit. And, it is impeccably written by a person who has spent his life teaching writers to "just say what they mean" in a no-nonsense way. That said, it's more than a sweet journey of a high school boy's infatuation with "girls." Bobby Hawthorne takes you on a stream of consciousness awakening of a teenage boy growing up in East Texas in the late 1960s. At one moment, he will bring to life wonderful a character, then jump off into a story about why he should hate or love that character because of some conflict that he then details that happened years before. Then, in the next moment he brings you back to his present dilemma without skipping a beat. You "experience" the witty meandering of his Eddie Dodson character's mind, and get to grow up with him. The story is not so much about Eddie's navigation of relationships with his family and potential girlfriends; the story is how Eddie grows up by interacting with these other well drawn characters. Bobby's book will put a smile on your face and in your heart." — Tom Herod, Austin, Texas

"First time novelist Bobby Hawthorne waited until he was in his 60s to get around to writing his initial book of fiction. It's a damn shame because this is one to be treasured. Narrator Eddie is a pretty normal 15-year-old in small town east Texas in the mid-60s. He loves football, the Beatles and is obsessed with an unattainable girl named Debbie. He spends most of his time with his best friend, improbably also named Debbie, although she goes by Lynn. When Eddie's parents' marriage starts to fall apart, he's sent to spend the summer at his Aunt and Uncle's farm. There he starts to learn life lessons and, of course, meets the titular Debbie number three. What starts as a somewhat tentative, if likeable, coming-of- age tale blossoms into a novel of remarkable depth; a touching meditation on family, first love and those awkward early steps toward becoming an adult. It's not shocking that Hawthorne, a long-admired guru for high school journalists, writes this well but it's still a rush to find that his first foray into fiction hits the bullseye. Let's hope he has more in him."
—C.E. Sikkenga, Grand Haven, Michigan

"A beautiful coming-of-age novel the combines the regionalism and story-telling of Larry McMurtry with the nostalgia of 'A Christmas Story.' Hawthorne doesn't hide the issues rampant in life in the US during the 60s. Those issues are interwoven through this story of small-town Texas and Eddie, the main character, who navigates all the hardships and heartaches and of a young man finding his way through a life that is both familiar and realistic. And even though the book is set during the 60s, readers will be able to relate. Coming-of-age stories can be tough, but Hawthorne gives his readers a heartfelt page-turner about a time of great change in the country. If you enjoyed 'The Last Picture Show,' you will enjoy Debbie Number Three."
— Mary Beth Lee, Fort Worth, Texas

"**Texas: Football is King**. Boys are fairly clueless about girls--forever. Bobby Hawthorne takes readers back where they never were—to awareness of their adolescent selves. This book is a fun romp through the trials and failures and brief successes of a contemporary Tom Sawyer. I had forgotten how, as teenagers, we picked on the skinny guys, how girls flirted just because. Hawthorne reminds us, and, though sly humor, helps us laugh at, and be embarrassed by, our own young selves. Honest book. Honest writing. A pleasure to read.
 — Dr. Terri LeClercq, Austin, Texas

"**I wonder how many** readers will glimpse their own coming-of-age stories in Debbie Number Three? I know I did, though I grew up in a different time and place than Eddie Dodson in 1960s East Texas. Do you remember those endlessly hot summer days and weeks running into one another until, one summer, everything changed in the blink of an eye? Whether it was a first love, a first job, a dismantling family unit, or starting to see your folks for the people they are when they're not mom and dad. For Eddie, all of these things happen in one summer. All at once, this book is as languid as those July days of your youth and as urgent as trying to slow time down before summer ends.
 "I might be a little partial to Bobby Hawthorne's writing — after all, it was during a doggedly hot week in August when 15-year-old me took his class and learned to love language. As anyone who knows Bobby probably expected, this novel is a master class in character development. I found myself, like Eddie, wishing I could slow the tick-tick-ticking of time and keep reading." — Jayna Rumble, Chicago, Illinois

Hawthorne is a clever master of detail whose descriptions and vibrant dialogue make reading this classic coming of age journey so effortless to get lost in. It's an easy read, not because it lacks any complexity, but because its humor and the absolute magnetism of his characters make it so compelling.
— Sandy Hall-Chiles, Brenham, TX

I'm a sucker for coming-of-age stories, and I rank this one as one of the best I've read. I enjoyed getting to know Eddie and the three Debbies and watching them navigate their way through adolescence. The characters ring so true and are incredibly relatable. Among the supporting cast, Eddie's mother particularly stands out, as does Debbie Number Three's mother. The author does an excellent job getting into the minds of all the characters, and especially the females.

"Reading "Debbie Number Three" was like being transported in time to the East Texas of Eddie's youth. The scenes were so well-drawn that I could almost see, smell, and touch my surroundings. The story is wonderfully told, a joyous and poignant look at the pain and wonder of growing up. There aren't many books I'm willing to read twice, but this was definitely one of them. I highly recommend it.
— Lori Herbst, author of the Callie Cassidy series

It's going to take a village of East Texas homespun characters to help 15-year-old Eddie survive the summer of 1966. Author Bobby Hawthorne takes his readers back to the times of high school football and poolside flirtations, dysfunctional families and warm apple fritters; to when reputation, kindness and integrity meant a damn. A fun but important read that helps us remember who we are, and why we should care.
— Terry Nelson, Muncie, Indiana

"The book was beautifully done. The state of vulnerability that most or all of the characters came to, the sign Debbie held as her love rode out of town and his realization that he had his sunglasses on and she couldn't see his eyes, the details of the era from cars to soda pop and smoking, football, Texas, farming, the perils of being female, the connections to four wars.

"It was a good read with a lot of surprises, filled with colorful and rich characters. The right mix of humor and pathos and suspense. It made me long for another time and also remember the dread of being that age and of that era."
— Robert Salas, Austin, Texas

"I could not put down this novel! What a terrific read! There'd better be a sequel. And a movie."
— Lisa Schwartz, Houston, Texas

"For Eddie, growing up in mid 1960's Texas, small town Texas, everything interesting and exciting seemed to be outside of Texas, out of reach. Every family, even in Texas, struck him as more worldly and sophisticated than his own. ("I often wondered what separated us from them, why our yard looked like Omaha Beach two days after D-Day, and their yard looked like the White House lawn at sunrise on Easter morning.") When Eddie is sent away to live and work with relatives as his mother and father try connecting with each other once again, what should have been the rug being pulled out from under him is the fresh perspective he needed. He might even have found true love. At 16? Why not? "Debbie Number Three" is a good story, a drive on a hot summer day with your head out the window, the scenery rushing by."
— Michael Zagst, Houston, Texas

"**Nobody can turn a phrase** like Bobby Hawthorne. In his debut novel, Hawthorne turns his critical eye and extraordinary wit and insight to the 1960s, to the life of Eddie Dodson, his 15-year-old narrator from a small town in East Texas.

"Eddie is a typical teenage boy in his love of the Beatles, football, and Debbie #1 — the town "it" girl. As summer approaches and his parent's marriage begins to self-destruct, Eddie's life takes a turn that carries him away from home and his best friend, Debbie #2 (who goes by the name "Lynn"), to his uncle's farm and family. As Eddie becomes determined to use this opportunity to sharpen his work ethic and become a man of his word, he meets the third Debby, who will open his heart and eyes to the cruelties of small minds and the injustices leveraged by the powerful to maintain status quo.

"Through Eddie's coming of age, we hear Hawthorne's searing observations and are reminded of that awesome time of life when, as teenagers, we first realized the hypocrisy that surrounded us and resolved to do better than previous generations. In one key scene, Eddie's internal monologue speaks miles to the wisdom of youth:

> "Perhaps the big cities can tolerate a few shades of gray, but small towns can't, not that they want to. If one line gets blurred, they'll paint another one. The only question is, "When and where and why and how and with what?" Small town people need lines. They need fences and stalls and borders. They need directions and paint-by-number instructions. They need rules that carry consequences. Otherwise, people are forced to think for themselves, and that's a recipe for chaos because it eliminates the need for God. Small town people need God to remind them not to lie to, steal from, cheat on, or kill each other. They need God to define for them the nature and wages of sin."

"And man, Hawthorne can crack you up with the simple turn of a phrase, with his almost perfect dialogue. At times,

he chooses to slip away from Eddie to explore the past through another character's experiences, at which point the tone of the novel shifts and feels a bit removed from Eddie's story. Still, "Debbie Number Three" delivered extraordinary characters and a perfect teenage plot that would make for a prime John Hughes '80s movie."
— Ava Butzu, Ann Arbor, Michigan

"Just finished Bobby Hawthorne's wonderful book. What a surprise! It's everything a book should be — poignant, sad and happy at the same time, well-written and thoroughly charming. Got my attention from the get-go and stayed there until the end. I would highly recommend it to anyone looking for a good read."
— Sandra Cook Crother, Tustin, California

"It's a hell of an accomplishment. It's clever and well written, and I really loved the romance with Debbie Gehring.
— Cary White, Galveston, Texas

"I thoroughly enjoyed "Debbie Number Three." It was sweet, charming, sad, anger-invoking, and heartwarming all rolled into one. I would love for author Bobby Hawthorn to do an audiobook because he has such a way of telling stories and his voice is so smooth and enchanting. I'm reccmmending it to my librarian sister who is a huge Beatles fan. Fabulous job!
— Theresa Proctor, Austin, Texas

Made in the USA
Columbia, SC
18 June 2024